Green Fairy

by Kyell Gold

GREEN FAIRY

Copyright 2012 by Kyell Gold

Published by Sofawolf Press
St. Paul, Minnesota
http://www.sofawolf.com

ISBN 978-1-936689-16-3
Printed in the United States of America
First trade paperback edition: March 2012
Third printing: June 2019

Cover and interior art by Rukis

For foozzzball, who brings Montmartre to me.
Even without the absinthe.

Contents

Chapter 1

Sol was only reading a news story about a college student who'd killed himself, but the student had been gay, so when the young wolf's fur prickled with the feeling of someone staring at him, he hid the story behind the picture of a car on a local auto dealer's website. The quick keystroke had become as reflexive as twitching his tail or ears, even though his parents had never caught him looking at gay pictures or reading gay stories.

The feeling of being watched usually went along with either that or texting his boyfriend—his four-hour-away different-species secret boyfriend—and he was certainly waiting for Carcy to reply to his last text. But this was stronger, this was a presence behind him. Even after he'd turned and made sure nobody had climbed up the side of his house to stare in his second-story bedroom window, even after he'd sniffed every corner of the room and caught nothing but the constant background of his own scent, his parents, and the seven-month old scent of his brother, the feeling persisted. He couldn't get through more than a paragraph of the story before sniffing over his shoulder again, so he gave up.

If his parents did catch him reading the story, he could've told them it was because of his cousin, and that would not have been a complete lie. It was just close enough to the truth that it might raise awkward questions. They might send him to a priest or a counselor to "answer his questions about homosexuality," or, God forbid, try to have a talk with him themselves.

His phone buzzed, jolting him back to reality. There was nobody in the room, nobody watching him through the window, but his fur still prickled with the feeling. He tried to ignore it as he picked up the phone to see what Carcy had said.

What does it matter? School's over in three months anyway.

Which was true. And then…Sol drank in the picture of the car, staring at it until he could see himself behind the wheel, driving four hours up to Millenport. *And then I'll get to see you,* he typed.

Yep. :) And what your dad thinks doesn't matter here.

It would still matter that Sol was gay. But his dad wouldn't have to know that, even then, maybe ever. What mattered right now was what his dad would think about Sol losing his starting spot on the high school baseball team, which was the reason he was holed up in his room avoiding his parents to begin with.

Sol had barely had time to process it himself, even though he'd known this was coming for three months. It had been almost that long since any of his teammates had mentioned the December shower incident (now, there was a time it would have been useful to have the feeling of being watched). Only Taric, the muscular coyote who until that afternoon had been Sol's backup at second base, made snide comments when he thought the others couldn't hear. But the guys, especially the other wolves, had been more distant from him, hadn't taken as much time to talk before or after practice. Sol, grateful just to be left alone after the horrible last week of December, had wrapped himself in a warm cloak of dreams about the future.

Then Mr. Zerling had called Taric up after practice that afternoon, had praised his progress, had told him he'd be starting at second base "indefinitely." He hadn't mentioned Sol at all. Sol could still feel the isolation, the whole team looking away from him. And Mr. Zerling was a wolf, too; he was supposed to look out for other wolves.

Sol had thought about calling Natty, but his brother was busy in college these days, between classes, football, and girls. Sol hadn't told him about being gay, and if he told him about getting demoted, Natty would just say something like "work hard and get your spot back."

Which was about what his dad would say. Only not as nice. And if it had stung Sol this much, with his months to prepare for it, he could only imagine how his father would react. Natty wasn't starting, but he was already getting highly complimentary reports on his play. There was talk that he could get into a real game, rare for a college freshman. But he wasn't eating at home every night where the family could bask in his glow. There was only Sol's flickering light, now even dimmer. It wasn't, Sol thought, like when the sun sets and you can finally see the moon. It was like when the sun sets and you can finally see how much the moon sucks.

He picked up his phone and typed, *I won't have to care what my dad thinks ever again.* Then he stared at the words, erased the "ever again," and added, "when I'm with you." That looked better. He sent that.

And then he had to look behind himself again. There was his small bookshelf, a wall of movie posters and one small "Phantom of the Opera" poster, the disheveled bed and pile of dirty laundry: no parents, no shadow at the window. But the feeling was strong enough that Sol imagined two of his teammates hiding just outside the window, looking in when he turned. Or the Hendersons across the street, looking in his window with a telescope. Maybe all of that was happening right now, the whole neighborhood of Prospect Hill and the population of Richfield High staring through walls to see Sol tell his most intimate secrets to a man he'd never met in person in a city four hours away.

Or maybe it was a ghost watching him. He didn't know many people who'd died: his grandfather and his cousin, and his grandfather had died when he was five. So maybe it was his cousin's ghost watching him. That led to Sol imagining if Percy would appear like a ghost in a horror movie with wrists dripping blood and eyes glazed with death, or if he would be like a ghost in a family movie, still the cheerful fifteen-year-old that Sol remembered from three years ago at the shore house.

The image made his fur prickle when he opened the news story again. So he hid it back under the picture of the car, and opened his phone's web browser to a site where his study partner had set up a list of books for him to read for a school project. Might as well do homework, which as far as he was concerned the whole town could watch him do.

He'd looked at the list of book titles three times that afternoon. The problem was that the titles all looked boring, or at least, less interesting than figuring out how he was going to tell his father that he was a failure at baseball.

He read the same titles again, only—not. One new one had appeared in the list.

At least, Sol thought it was new. The title "The Confession of Jean de…" stood out to him—specifically the word "Confession," which might as well be blinking in bold block font—so much that he was sure he would have noticed it before. He clicked on the book to find out more about it.

Under "Tags," people had written, "Montmartre," and "Art," which explained why it was on the list for their project. Other tags read "Moulin Rouge" and "Dance." And the last tag read, "Gay."

Sol's fingers didn't seem to work, and the phone nearly slipped through them. He stared at the tag "Gay" and was preparing to scroll down to see the book sample when the list was obscured with a message from Carcy saying, *So when are you going to tell him?*

"Aah!" Sol jumped and the phone clattered to the floor. How the hell did he get recommended a book about a gay confession when he was talking to Carcy about how to break bad news to his dad? It was too weird. He stared at the phone, lying face down, and forced himself to reach down and pick it up. Both the message and the book were still there. Don't be an idiot, he told himself. It's only coincidence. So he responded to the message (*Soon, I guess.*), took a breath, and opened a sample of the book.

The introduction to the translation told him that the book had been originally written in French. The translator called it "a rare and important record of politics and gay relationships in the artistic community that had become so famous, the Montmartre quarter of Lutèce at the turn of the century." *Confession* had enjoyed a brief period of popularity in the mid-twenties for its "salacious" content, and that was enough for Sol to flick his ears back, look over his shoulder, and click "Buy."

He paged forward and read the first paragraph of the actual story.

Dear *père*, I know that this is not what you meant when you said you wanted all of Lutèce to speak my name. From the prison window, I hear the scurrilous rumors and whispers, and it pains my heart to think that you may be hearing and believing them. They make me out to be devoid of morals, the exemplar of the *bourgeoisie* and their contempt for the peasants. They call for the return of the guillotine, for my head to be mounted at Les Halles as assurance to the lower classes that the government has their interests at heart, that it is not an attempt to re-create the monarchy. As if my head could bear all of those meanings! Dearest father, my story is a love story, a story that could be told between farmer and flower-girl, between landowner and minister. That it was told between a senator's son and a common dancer is incidental to the heart of it, and to the tragic turn it took.

His mother called him down to dinner, and he closed the book just as he got one more message from Carcy: *just get it over with.* And the gratitude Sol felt for the ram's support was enough to convince him to do something else he'd been thinking about for a long time. Carcy, of course, was vegetarian. He'd told Sol it wasn't a problem that Sol ate meat, but the wolf wanted to make the sacrifice. If Carcy ate only vegetables and remained healthy, then so would he—especially if they were going to be living together that summer. Sol wanted to be used to it before he moved to Millenport.

So Sol decided he was going to get it all over with, and if his father was going to kill him for losing his baseball spot, he might as well start giving up meat tonight, too. It might take some of the heat off of the baseball news. He went down to dinner, and though he glanced behind himself once, the feeling of being watched did not follow him down into the warmth of the dining room, the rich smell of steak, the light air of classical music his mother liked to put on over dinner.

His tail stayed curled around his hip as he took his seat, but if either parent noticed, they didn't say. He scooped a big pile of peas and carrots onto his plate, grabbed a dinner roll, and chewed the bread. He stared at the third steak, sitting alone on the serving plate in the center of the table, and waited.

His mother said something first. "Sol, take your steak before it gets cold."

He swallowed. It would be easy here to just eat the steak, to put off becoming vegetarian until tomorrow. Only Carcy had been so helpful, and Sol had wanted to do this for weeks. Courage was easier to find when he knew his father was going to end the meal angry anyway. So he stared down at the round green peas and square orange carrots, and moved them around with his fork. "I'm—not having any."

"What do you mean?" His father laughed. "Never seen you not hungry for steak."

"I mean—I'm not having any, anymore. Ever."

The room grew cold and still. His father set down his silverware. "No steak?"

"No meat."

His mother said, softly, "Are you not feeling well?"

"I'm fine, I just—I'm not interested in eating it anymore."

"Not interested? Not interested?" His father leaned forward, glowering. "You're an athlete. You need your protein. Your brother recorded the second-most tackles in Richfield High history, and you know how he did it? Eating steak. How are you going to turn double plays without steak?"

Then he had to blurt it out, to deliver the other half of the bad news. The hope that his father's rage at the combined news would be more bearable than going through this twice was fading fast. "I'm not starting anymore!"

In the silence that followed, Sol felt Natty's absence as acutely as if his brother had only just left the previous day. The fraternal scent, the low voice and infectious laugh, those belonged in the silence that stretched on and on. Alone, Sol could not come up with anything to say that would make the news he'd just delivered go down any more smoothly. He tried to relax the tight curl of his tail against his hip, to lift his ears, to unlace his fingers from each other, anything to not look like a little cub. But the best he could manage was to pull his paws apart, shedding black fur onto the white napkin on his lap.

The faint classical music from the living room seemed to grow louder, reverberating off the stone walls. His heartbeat throbbed harder, the smell of steak pushed its way into his nose. His mouth watered, but he forced his eyes to remain on the vegetables heaped on his plate. He didn't have to add more words, not yet. He had said all he needed to, all he could right now.

"Do *you care?*"

Sol's father conceded the battle of silence, which meant that perhaps it had not been a battle after all. "How," the large grey wolf growled with velvet, disarming softness, "after three years, do you get *demoted* to backup second baseman?"

Sol knew the iron that lay beneath those words. "Taric's just better than me," he said. His father stayed quiet. "He hits better, he fields better, he…he's better."

"If you were trying your best, he wouldn't be better." His father's condescension made Sol grit his teeth. Over the smell of steak, his father's scent had acquired the acrid tang of anger, though the older wolf's voice remained calm. "Didn't you work with him a lot last year?"

"Yeah…" Last year, Taric had been, if not a friend, at least someone willing to pair up with Sol in workouts. "He put on a lot of muscle."

"He stays longer at practice. Why did you stop working out with him? Why do you let him show you up?"

"He stays at practice because he lives in a trailer!" Sol said.

"He *cares*." His father growled the words. They hung over the table.

Sol lifted his head, meeting his father's brown eyes, looking down the long muzzle with the same brown top and grey sides his brother had, the same black-tipped ears, the same full cheek ruffs. Every time he looked down his own black muzzle, or at his black paws or tail, he saw the differences. Since Natty'd gone, his fur seemed even more black, his hazel eyes even more speckled and strange.

To his right, Sol's mother was so quiet she must have been sitting stock still. She said, softly, "Do you want the boy to get good grades or be a good baseball player?"

His father didn't look away from Sol. "His brother led the football team to the state finals and graduated with honors. Let the young wolf fight his own battles."

Sol couldn't bear his father's scrutiny. He turned to the empty wooden chair again, staring at the old claw-scratches marking the arms. Natty hadn't understood him, but he'd stuck up for him. Without him, the buffer between Sol and their father was gone. When they scraped against each other, Sol was the one who felt worn away after every encounter.

His father pressed. "Well? We haven't talked about baseball in weeks. Maybe months. *Do* you care?"

"I care," he said, because to say anything else would be suicide. He couldn't say, *there are things I can't talk to you about*, because teenagers can only keep secrets for as long as the parents don't know that there *are* secrets. He couldn't say he wanted to talk to his brother, because his father would tell him to pick up the phone and call, and he couldn't say why he couldn't do that now. His chest constricted around his heart. He put his paws up on the edge of the table to try to steady himself.

"You don't care that much about your grades." His father's ears were cupped forward, his fur bristled out. Not as much as the time he'd caught Sol and Natty playing with matches in the backyard, but enough to keep Sol's tail curled. "Mostly you seem to care about talking to your friends. Or is it just 'friend,' now? I haven't seen you with Xavy, or Mika, lately."

"They're *your* friends' sons," Sol muttered.

"You're always with that otter."

"Meg. She's his girlfriend," his mother said.

His father raised a large paw, held it over the table for a second as though considering the possibility, then swept it aside. "She never comes to the baseball games."

"She doesn't like baseball," Sol said. "She says it's a farce." The words were a mistake, he knew, but he was desperate to divert his father's anger.

"And no doubt you think the same." His father's grin, humorless, showed his long canine teeth. "Is she also a plant-eater?"

"No," Sol blurted out.

"Then *what* does any of this have to do with eating *steak*?"

His father's fist pounded the table, sending plates rattling, shocks up Sol's arms. The young wolf jumped. His tail curled in tighter; his paws clutched each other. His tongue rasped against his palate, trying to form words. "I...I...I..." He swallowed, dry. "Don't want to. Any more. It's cruel. They're living things."

The older wolf pushed his lip up, showing his inch-long canine fang and the ivory, glistening teeth around it. "You see this? God made us to eat other living things."

He made you *that way*. Sol's brain raced. *I'm different. Just because I have teeth doesn't mean I have to eat steak. I can make my own choices.* But all the words he could force past his dry tongue were "I...don't want to. Anymore."

"Solomon James—"

"Let 'im." His mother's quiet voice cut through the angry growl. Her softer, lighter muzzle leaned toward Sol's father, her paw covering his on the table. "It's a phase. I went veggie one year."

"That was in college. And it's not the same. If he doesn't eat steak," his father growled, to her now, "he'll never win back his starting spot."

"I'll..." Sol's tongue stuck to the roof of his mouth as his father got up from the table, walked around to him. He cringed, and hated himself for it.

The older wolf stood and stared down at him, then grabbed his wrist and held up his arm. He closed his other paw around Sol's bicep and squeezed, hard.

Sol bit his tongue to avoid crying out. His ears flattened, but he couldn't shut out his father's words. "You going to be an All-Star baseball player with this?" His father glared down at him. "You think you can build muscle with broccoli?"

His eyes held Sol's with an iron grip. The young black wolf felt tears starting and willed them back. If he cried at the table on top of everything else, his father would call him weak to his face, would send him upstairs. He licked his lips nervously, and his father released his arm and his eyes with a huff of disgust. "You'll eat steak with the rest of the family."

Sol forced words through the pressure closing his throat. "I don't—" He'd thought he was safe, but his voice cracked, betraying him. He clamped his jaw shut and stared down at the pile of vegetables on his plate.

His mother spoke up, softly. "You can get protein from beans and supplements. Mrs. Finch—the goat—buys them for her family. I'll ask her what she gets."

"You will not." His father cut a piece of his own steak. "I don't want her knowing Sol wants to give up meat. I don't want anyone knowing about it because it is not happening."

"Wha—" Sol tested his voice. It held, precariously. "What are you gonna do? Force-feed me meat?"

His father's fork clinked against the plate as it came to rest, and the older wolf rested his paws flat on the table, as if threatening to stand again. "If necessary."

"Jerius," Sol's mother murmured.

"I'll...I'll make myself throw up, then." Sol's ears came partway up. "I'll make myself sick after every dinner."

"Boy," his father growled. "Don't push your luck."

"Pretty soon I'll throw up from the taste of meat because I won't be accustomed to it."

"Sol," his mother said. "Not at the table, sweetie."

Sol's father held his fork in the air, a piece of steak on it, but he was glaring at Sol. "Is that something else you got from that bullshit psychology class? Because I will beat the psychology out of you if I have to."

"You can't make me eat meat!" Sol yelled.

"You will not eat anything at this table until you do." His father wasn't quite yelling back, but he wasn't far from it.

This was where Natty would step in and say something disarming like, "Hey, let him eat what he wants, Dad, I'll keep an eye out for him." Or maybe, "Let him give up meat, Dad. More steak for me." And his father's fur would lose that bristly look, and his mother's ears would come up, and maybe they would laugh. But Sol couldn't make that happen.

"Let him try it," his mother said. "What if he gets his baseball spot back?"

"How is he going to do that without eating meat?" His father sounded as incredulous as if she'd suggested Sol grow wings and fly.

"He'll work extra hard," his mother promised for him, "won't you?"

Sol nodded. He knew enough to keep his mouth tightly closed.

His father held up a paw, ticking off points on clawed fingers. "That means more practice. Stay late at school, work out on weekends, spend time with your teammates. No hiding up in your room with your computer."

"I…" *I use it for school,* was his standard excuse for the time he spent online looking up pictures and forums, talking to people who were more like him than the sports-obsessed, car-obsessed cardboard cutouts in his school, but he swallowed the words and nodded again. "Yes, sir."

"Well." His father's teeth still showed behind his long black lips. "The Lakeside game is what, a month away? Beat that 'yote for your starting spot by then and you can eat whatever you want. And," he said as though it were an afterthought, "you'll still get that car for your birthday and graduation."

"What?" Sol yelped.

"Otherwise…" His father shrugged. "I'm sure your mother would appreciate a new set of kitchen appliances."

His car? His *car?* He felt as though the legs of his chair had buckled, as though the floor had dropped out from under him. His appetite for even the steak he was pretending he didn't want was gone, in a stroke. Thoughts tumbled like bricks through his mind: getting away from the house, driving to Millenport, getting to see Carcy… Everything ruined, tumbling like a card house when the ace had been cruelly yanked from the foundation.

His mother bowed her head, lowering her ears. Sol knew she'd done her best, but still, he thought, she could've defended him a little more. Natty would've said something like "Aw, Dad, you don't mean that," but if Sol tried it, the words would twist and sharpen and he'd be yelled at, or maybe cuffed. Definitely sent to his room without the rest of his dinner. Sullen, he shoved his fork into the pile of vegetables and lifted a clump of them to his muzzle, ignoring the smell of the steak and his father's loud chewing.

Afterwards, in the kitchen, his paws soapy with dishwater, nose filled with the domestic scent of lemon and duty, he replayed the conversation in his mind, thinking of all the things he should have said, dwelling on the loss of his car. He had it all picked out, too, or rather, his father and Natty had picked it out for him, a sporty two-door green something. Now the image of it flickered in his mind, tenuous, obscured by his father's glare.

His mother spoke up, softly. "I can try s'more creative things with vegetables," she said. "If you'd told me…"

Sol picked up a plate and stared at it. The edges of the meat's juice lingered there in a brown pattern, like a foreign language. He attacked it with the sponge until the place gleamed white, then turned it so it reflected the greenish-grey stone walls, the lighter slate ceiling, his own black muzzle.

"Sol?" His mother touched his shoulder.

"Sure, Mom," he said. "That'd be great."

"You'll work hard at baseball?"

He rinsed the plate and set it out to dry. "If you get a dishwasher," he said, "at least I won't have to wash dishes."

"Your father didn't mean that. He was just—"

"I think he meant it."

She let her paw drop, the claws snagging his shirt and then falling free. "It won't matter," she said. "You can get your spot back."

"Taric's good." Sol found his own plate, where no stain had survived the initial rinse. He passed a sponge over it and then rinsed it again. Sooner he was done, the sooner he could get out of here. He needed to talk to Meg, about dinner, about school, about the car.

"So are you. Just…try hard? For me? You'll be off to college next fall, and it would be nice to have just a peaceful time until then."

The pleading in her voice worked its way under Sol's fur, until the idea of a peaceful few months was reasonable rather than laughable. "Sure," he said, rinsing the glasses. "I'll try hard. Can I go over to Meg's to study?"

His mother smiled, tail beginning to wag. "Long as it's just studying."

His heart quickened. "Her parents are home, Mom." He snapped when his parents talked about his girlfriend or having sex, or when they wanted to know who he was texting on his phone, which is why he didn't do that in front of them anymore. Because worse than losing his baseball position, worse even than being a vegetarian, would be having that conversation.

"I know, but they're otters."

"God." Sol turned the water off and rubbed his paws dry. "Don't worry, Mom, I'm not doing anything risky."

He couldn't see any way to get the car without devoting his life to baseball for the next two weeks, but at least he wanted to talk to Meg and Carcy, get out some of the frustration that gnawed at him and pushed his feet down the hill. At Meg's, he could have his phone out to text Carcy while doing his homework and nobody would tell him to put it away, although Meg sometimes asked to see. Also, Meg had a pool in her room, and though he didn't really want to swim (especially in her private pool), he still enjoyed lying in the humid air of the otter home. It made his fur feel thick and warm.

Their low two-story house stood amidst many other similar limestone houses at the top of Prospect Hill, which the kids in school called Wolf Hill. Sol loved the solid look of the houses; he'd learned last year that his neighborhood had been mostly built twenty-five years ago, but to him the houses looked like pale green ancient monuments. Even in this past year, with all his family troubles, Sol had never felt safer than sitting in his room, the weight of stone around him holding his scent and reminding him that he belonged there—as long as he didn't feel invisible eyes on him, a new development he hoped was not permanent. But he liked Meg's house more than she liked his (she said the heavy stone and scent-holding walls made her feel "twitchy"), which was just one of many reasons Sol always visited her.

It was only a ten minute walk, fifteen if Sol went the long way around by Prospect Park, down the side of Prospect Hill through his neighborhood of brick houses, flower gardens, and low white fences. The park tonight was quiet, though Sol could see cars on the other side of the park where a lot of his classmates went to make out, and on one of the benches was a lump that might be a homeless person. None of them paid any attention to him. He'd only ever come to the park at night to watch fireworks or to chase fireflies with his brother, years and years ago. A few hovered out of his reach as he padded down the hill; he made half-hearted grabs at their yellow-green glows out of habit.

At the base of the hill, he went on past the park while most of the fireflies remained behind. One blinked at the corner of his vision all the way down Gooseneck Lane with its cramped three-story row homes that smelled of fox and weasel, across and along the main street. Whenever a firefly seemed to be following him and Natty home, Natty would say, "Let's ask Mom if we can keep him!" None had ever followed them as far as this one was trailing Sol, though.

The distraction helped ease his frustration for a few moments. He jogged ahead, stopped suddenly, and it sped up or stopped with him all the way to the corner of Meg's street, where the smell of lake water and lily pads rose to meet him. Then he turned to look for it and it was gone. They could disappear quickly, when they wanted to.

Meg Kinnick lived in a smallish house with rounded walls and circular windows, like most of the houses along the lake. In the daylight hers stood out because of its bright yellow dome roof and lime green trim, which Sol had more than once heard called an "eyesore," but at night, the green softened and the yellow turned a lovely silver. It was granite, older than Sol's house, though they'd had the roof replaced just last year.

"Hi, Mrs. Kinnick," he said at their door, which had a huge daisy painted on it. "Meg and I have a project to work on."

"C'mon in, Sol." The skinny otter beamed up at him. Water glistened on her mostly-exposed fur and pooled around her feet as she stepped back carefully to let him in. He avoided the water and breathed in the floral, humid air of the large, open atrium. To his right, in an irregularly cut-out third of the room, was the opening to the communal pool where Meg's father floated on his back, wearing nothing but a damp towel loosely draped across his midsection that floated in the water. Sol was sure it had only just been dropped there. "Hi, Mr. Kinnick," he said.

Meg's mother slid back gracefully into the water, so smoothly and quietly that Sol's whiskers caught the motion while his ears heard nothing. Her husband raised a paw as she swam out to him. "Well met, Sol," he said. "Universe treating you well, I hope?"

"Most of it." Sol glanced upward at the paused movie projected onto the screen that hung below the roof's metal framework. "How are you doing?"

"Quite well, quite well." Mr. Kinnick looked up as his wife rejoined him, and stretched an arm out to the remote floating on the water at his side. The image on the ceiling sprang to life, resolving into splashing, singing, dancing otters.

Figured it'd be a musical. Sol hefted his book bag over one shoulder and padded across the wide atrium to the black-painted door whose silver skull glared ineffectually out at the bright pastel colors. Flower patterns in cornflower blue and marigold orange, rose and violet, daffodil yellow and grass green spattered the walls, fading in some places, streaked with Meg's clawmarks near the floor, her growth measured in the three-foot watermark when she'd given up scarring the flowers 'by accident' and had focused her decorating impulses on her own room.

"It's Sol," he called, fingers lightly touching the doorknob.

"Yeah" was as much of an invitation as anyone ever got from Meg. Sol opened the door and stepped into another world.

Black velvet hung down the walls, dotted with images of bands whose members wore black cloaks and dyed their fur black. On Meg's dresser, candles sputtered; they were white because her parents kept white candles around the house and made Meg buy her own black candles, so she only burned those on special occasions. The carpet was yellow, but covered with black t-shirts, and the bedspread was a deep black night sky dotted with stars—fewer than it had been originally. Meg took a black marker with her to bed sometimes.

This world matched his mood much better. He closed the door behind him and leaned against it, glancing down at his bare arm. Only here, in Meg's deep black sanctum, did shades and highlights really show in his black fur. He trailed a claw through the fur to see his lighter skin and undercoat.

"Stop admiring yourself," Meg said. "Fucking jock."

She was stretched out on her stomach atop her bed, one of her thousand black t-shirts draped around her torso, black canvas pants loosely defining her legs. The white underfur of her thick brown tail made a stark line across her leg, away from Sol. Silver piercings over her eyes and in her nose and ears flashed and glittered with the reflection of her laptop screen against the dyed-black fur of her head.

"You'd be proud of me." Sol didn't wag his tail, but thwacked it against the door, resisting the urge to look over his shoulder at that too. "Lost my starting spot."

"So?" She punctuated the word with a snap of her chewing gum. Away from the floral miasma of the atrium, Sol's nose caught the licorice smell, sharp across the stale alcohol in the room. "That's a relief, right? 'Less opportunities to fail'?"

"That was—" Sol flattened his ears. He wasn't in the mood to do his 'why baseball' speech for Meg right now. "I didn't want to get *replaced*. And it was Taric. That makes it worse."

Meg squinted. "Because…?"

Sol exhaled. "He's Tanny's brother."

"Is he as big a dick as his sister is a bitch?" Meg turned back to her laptop, but just for a moment. "Oh," she said, looking back at Sol. "Coyotes. Yeah, your dad wouldn't like that. So, gonna quit now?"

"Can't." He grabbed her desk chair and sat across it, letting his tail drape off the seat. "That's the other thing. I don't get the car if I don't get it back. Dad said." Saying it out loud settled the weight of his failure in his chest, made him squirm even though he knew Meg wasn't judging him.

She did snap her head up from the computer, muzzle twisted in a grimace. "Fuck him, he can't do that. How're we gonna get jobs in Millenport this summer if you don't have a car?"

"Sorry," Sol said. "I'll run right back and tell him how much he's inconvenienced you."

"You better." She rolled onto her back, lifting the laptop into the air.

"I'll get Natty to do it." Sol rested his muzzle on his arms. The back of the chair dug into them, but he relished the discomfort. "Maybe then he'd listen."

"Or you could feel sorry for yourself more." Meg's tail hit the bed solidly. "That always helps. Oh wait."

"What do you know? Your parents let you get away with anything. You and I could be having sex in here and they wouldn't care."

"They think we are."

Sol flicked his ears towards the door, where the music and dialogue of the movie filtered through, as flowery as the scent in that living room. "Really?"

"That's why they like you so much."

He lowered his ears. "If my dad—well, I guess my dad wouldn't mind if I did something normal like have sex with my girlfriend."

Meg bent her head backwards so far that it made Sol wince. Her eyes met his. "If you think that will get you the car, I'm game."

Sol stared at her and then snorted. "He'd just tell me I was doing it wrong."

"So you have to get better at baseball."

"I *can't!*" He kicked the desk behind him to feel the satisfying thump. "Taric is just better than me. I can't—I can't just become a better hitter by practicing."

Meg stared levelly at him. "Do you even know how practice works?"

"I mean…" He took a breath. "Some people are just born with better paw-eye coordination, right? I can't make that better."

"Could you practice harder than you have been?"

"You sound like *him* now."

"Could you?"

He pulled at the fur on his bare arm, until a clump of it came out with a bright flare of pain that focused his attention, cleared his mind of the turmoil in it for a second. "Probably."

"Because I'll do this whole goddamn project on my own if I have to. You go be Daddy's good little straight-boy alpha-wolf jock for another month or two."

"You don't have to do the project yourself." Sol rubbed the sore spot on his arm where the clump had come out, pushing it apart so he could glimpse the pink skin through the black hairs, then letting the fur fall back into place. "I'm not going to practice more. Just harder."

"Do more, too. Just in case. You been a lot less into the whole baseball thing this year, so you better do everything you can to get that car. And I don't mind doin' it myself, just fix my essays when we're done. You're way better at writing than I am. Hey, you know what? Maybe this whole 'get back on the team' thing can be your story."

Sol smoothed down the fur on his arm. "What?"

"Well, you're always crying about how you want to write about your life but you don't do anything interesting—true story, by the way."

"Thanks."

"So here you go."

Sol shook his head. "Baseball's boring." Even here in Meg's house, he could feel Natty's disapproval of that, as though his brother could hear him all those miles away. "I mean, it doesn't take a lot of thought to get better. So I...I take a few more swings at batting practice. I field grounders for an extra hour. So what?"

"I got news for you, champ. The real world is boring. Why do you think Ronald and Valinda spend their evenings baked out of their skulls watching crappy musicals on the ceiling? If you hadn't gotten me on this project, I'd be stoned right now too. Oh!" She rolled back onto her stomach, her body rippling with the bouncing of the bed. No matter how she tried to hide it below baggy clothes, her sinuous form found a way to shine through. "You gotta come over tomorrow night, though. My vampire fox buddy sent me some of his special absinthe. Should get here tomorrow."

Sol's ears shot up. "The green poison stuff?"

Meg's eyes, scornful, rose over the top of her laptop screen. "It isn't poison. It's mystical. It was banned because people were afraid of it, but now the government can make money off it, so it's legal again. The artists and bohemians drank it all the time back then. It'll give us the right feel for the project."

"The feeling of being wasted?"

"Not wasted," Meg said. "People had incredible visions on it. They wrote them down. It happened all the time."

"Why do we need visions if we're just doing a biography of Vincent van Gogh?"

"Because he probably tried it. He was all in that..." she circled her paw in the air, tracing lines on an invisible map. "That Mont-marter place."

"Montmartre." He pronounced it the way his French teacher did, *moan-MAHR-tr*, swallowing the end of the last syllable. On his phone, he texted Carcy. *Told my dad.*

"You can give the presentation." Meg disappeared behind her laptop again. "Mrs. Mercher automatically marks a letter grade down every time I open my mouth."

"If you didn't curse at her, she wouldn't."

"If she wasn't a stupid fat arctic fox-bitch, I wouldn't have to curse at her."

Sol grinned all the way back to his cheeks, the first real smile he'd had in hours. "She gave us this cool project."

"She gave *you* this project, which sucks only minorly less than all the other inane crap we have to do in Dickfield Senior High School Prison. She likes you because you're a wolf. And a jock."

Carcy's response beeped. *About being gay, too?*

"I'm not so much of a jock now." *No*, he texted. *Just about losing baseball spot.*

Guess he didn't break your thumbs.

Sol started typing out *I also decided I'm going to stop eating meat, starting tonight. Dad didn't like that*, and said, "So how do we have to break this up?"

"Why's your tail wagging?" Meg looked suspiciously around the side of her laptop. "What'd your boyfriend say?"

"Dunno yet." He hesitated, but he'd told Carcy now, even if the ram hadn't responded yet, so he could tell Meg too. "I stopped eating meat."

Her mouth gaped until she brought it slowly closed. "Athletic failure and rejection of cultural heritage all in one night? Did you hope Daddy Dearest would have a heart attack and spare you the punishment?"

"I just figured…I guess…get it all out at once."

Beep. *Cool*, Carcy replied. *You'll feel healthier in no time. :)*

"You sure did that. Tell him about your boyfriend, too?"

"You're kidding, right?" It was hard to think about what to type back to Carcy. He wanted to talk more about the evening with his father, the courage he'd had to muster. The ram had no idea what meat-eating meant to a family of wolves. *I thought he was going to hit me*, he typed.

"Well, why not get it all out at once?"

Sol snorted. "I'm not legally an adult for four months. He can still beat the shit out of me. Or lock me in my room, or take away my phone and computer, or send me to anti-gay Bible camp for the summer."

"Or what, ground you? You're not thirteen anymore. But yeah, Bible camp would suck, even if it wouldn't work," Meg talked distractedly, staring at her laptop screen. She tapped a couple keys on her keyboard. "So here's some background on our project. Comin' to your e-mail."

Did he? Carcy asked.

There didn't seem to be much he could say to that, except *No.*

Sol's e-mail flashed on his phone. He checked to make sure it was Meg's message and skimmed it as Carcy's next text came back. *Too bad. If he hit you, you could call Social Services.*

He didn't type a reply. Instead, he went to his phone's e-reader to see if "Confession" had been delivered yet. "I started looking at the books you recommended. Pretty interesting."

"You don't have to read them all if you don't have the time. I'll do the art research. Mr. Vandermeer says I could be an artist if I could learn to use a color besides black."

"I like your black-on-black paintings."

She looked up again, her eyes trailing along his arms and down to his tail. "I'd kill for your fur," she said. "Save me a fortune in dye."

He laughed. "Your fur is brown enough anyway." But his tail wagged, and he felt relaxed for the first time all afternoon. And when he checked his e-reader, "Confession" had loaded. His phone beeped again with another message from Carcy. **strokes your flank* You got time now?*

Doing schoolwork at Meg's.

Later, then. *licks your nose*

kisses

"You reading or sexting?" Meg sounded bored. "If you're sexting, I wanna see."

Sol tapped the book open to the first page. "I'm just…telling him about my evening."

"Hey," Meg said. "Is he interested in baseball?"

"I, uh…" Sol stared down at his phone. "I don't think so."

"He oughta be interested in your baseball, anyway." Meg realized what she had said, and pointed at him. "No 'ball-boy' jokes."

Carcy had, in fact, made one of those jokes, early on in their relationship. Sol pretended to ignore Meg's comment. "We don't talk about it that much. What's that got to do with anything anyway?"

"Ah, if he encouraged you, maybe you'd do better."

Sol had a fleeting vision of sitting on his bed with Carcy beside him, talking excitedly about what Mr. Zerling had said about him, or hearing Carcy praise his play in a game. Stupid, he told himself. Like that'd happen. But for a moment, imagining it, he'd felt that passion stir in him, the pride in putting on his uniform, the excitement of being part of the game that he hadn't felt since the previous summer.

The image faded; the excitement went with it. He stopped the slight wagging of his tail and said, "You don't think the car is enough motivation?"

"I dunno, is it? Better be. Fuck if I'm gonna spend another summer in this prison camp of a town. I'll kill myself. Maybe take you with me."

Sol sighed. He smelled the echo of steak in his nostrils again, twisting his stomach into a painful knot. "Yeah, seriously."

She stared at his phone. "Get your boyfriend to give you a car."

"He's not rich." Sol swiped his finger to turn to the first page of the book. "He just has a beat-up Yari."

Meg lifted her gaze to glare at him. "I'm not one of your car-obsessed musclehead friends. What the hell is a Yari?"

"It's just a little compact car." Sol had looked it up on the Internet because Carcy wouldn't send him a picture.

"Sounds like a winner." She lowered her head to her screen again. The reflections of the images she was looking at danced across her eyes.

"He…" The black walls of the room stifled the words before he got them past his throat. He turned to the words on his phone.

"What? Loves you?"

Meg had a "love" speech like Sol had a "baseball" speech. "Yeah."

"All love is fake. It's insecurity, it's an act we put on because we're afraid of being alone."

"You're not afraid of being alone?" Sol scrolled the screen up and down without reading the words.

"No. I know I'm alone."

He exhaled, fogging his screen briefly. "Thanks. Glad I count for so much." He watched the mark of his breath shrink and fade, revealing the words beneath.

"Don't be a twat. Hey, this is a nice picture, look." Meg lifted her laptop and turned it, showing Sol a nighttime scene of city lights reflected in a river, the blue sky dotted with glowing yellow beacons.

"Sure," he said. "Who did it?"

Meg's muzzle, perpetually fixed in an expression of weary scorn, fell into a wearier, more scornful look. "Vincent van Gogh? The artist we're studying?"

Sol rubbed a finger along his whiskers, pressing them down along his muzzle and letting them spring back up. "This wasn't one of the pictures in the assignment."

"He painted nine hundred pictures in his life." Meg lowered the laptop and turned it around. "This one was about being all alone, like I was saying."

"There's a bunch of those yellow thingies, though." Sol's phone went dark; he turned it on again. "Are those fireflies? They're not alone."

"They're stars, idiot. They don't have fireflies in cities." Her eyebrows lowered and she went back to the screen. "Let me write about the art, 'kay? You can write about love and shit if you want."

"Love is real." Sol checked the time. He could plausibly stay out another half hour or so, and he had no desire to go home. The message indicator on his phone remained blank; nothing more from Carcy. He focused on the book.

Chapter 2

"The Confession of Jean de Giverne"
(translated by Holliset Marchand, 1922)

Dear *père*, I know that this is not what you meant when you said you wanted all of Lutèce to speak my name. From the prison window, I hear the scurrilous rumors and whispers, and it pains my heart to think that you may be hearing and believing them. They make me out to be devoid of morals, the exemplar of the *bourgeoisie* and their contempt for the peasants. They call for the return of the guillotine, for my head to be mounted at Les Halles as assurance to the lower classes that the government has their interests at heart, that it is not an attempt to re-create the monarchy. As if my head could bear all of those meanings! Dearest father, my story is a love story, a story that could be told between farmer and flower-girl, between landowner and minister. That it was told between a senator's son and a common dancer is incidental to the heart of it, and to the tragic turn it took.

You may think you know the story, and that is why you have kept yourself from the proceedings. Much has been made of your silence. They say it is an admission of my guilt, a message to the court to bring forth the guillotine with your approval. But if you knew, beloved father, if you only knew! Since you will not come to hear my story from my own lips, I must write it down in these pages, and by so doing perhaps put to rest those wagging tongues with nothing better to do than revel in my fall from grace by adding their own crude embellishments, as a street peddler's dirty fur clings to the fine rugs he re-sells. I feel certain that when you have heard all the facts, you will fly on the wings of a dove to rescue your poor, maligned son.

I promise you that the night I went to the Moulin Rouge, I had no conception of the path my feet set out upon. It was Thierry Beaumarchais who brought me there. Father, I heard your warnings, and I am ashamed to say that I valued my own judgment over yours at that time. I know that when you spoke of finding a suitable consort that you would never have thought of one of the scandalous dancers from that den of sin, and yet so blinded was I by my youth and self-confidence that I believed I could redeem one of them from the terrible life they led.

As I am certain that you have never even approached the quarter of Montmartre and the bohemians and rogues that make their home there, I will attempt to describe to you the world that had such a profound effect on the young Jean de Giverne.

To an innocent chamois, as I was just two months ago, the chaos and cacophony of Montmartre is bewitching. It is an explosion of bright colors, a flood of smells, a patchwork of language from all corners of Gallia, gathered in a honeycomb of small rooms, each of which seems to have a window giving out onto the street and a fox, a badger, a rabbit, a mouse leaning out of it shouting or singing. It gives one the air of having entered a new world, and in early April, the ragamuffins sell dewy blooms of flowers just showing cracks of color through their green shells, the bohemians pull out their paintings of blue skies and vast gardens to show under the shelter of oilcloth with the light rain hissing softly atop. Father, father, can you see why I followed Thierry there?

He said that Montmartre is the only place where spring truly reveals her essence, that if I were to go at all, it must needs be on this first day of spring, and I had not the years to dispute him. We sat at a café beneath umbrellas with holes, so that the rain dripped through, but we did not mind it. We kept our cups away from the wrought-iron table, nibbled our buttered croissants, and watched the people roaming about the street. The dampness in the air soaked up their scents as they passed, so much sharper and more real than in our refined streets. There were few perfumes, only the unadorned, raw scents of food, of clothing, of foxes and goats and rats and rabbits. It took me very nearly an hour to be at my ease, with my own perfume and fancy clothes.

I was dressed in my fine silks, with a camel-hair coat to keep off the rain, and the cravat you gave me for my birthday wrapped gaily about my neck. Thierry was dressed more soberly, though he did leave his shirt open around his impressive chest. Even with the grey fur about his cheeks and the droop of his antler-less head, I was surprised to hear the shop owner refer to him as my father. Even a rat, after all, should know that the child of a red elk would in no way resemble a tan-furred, delicate chamois. Yet I suppose that to a rodent, all horned people are alike, much as I could be forgiven for mistaking a young mouse for the rat's son, should I ever suffer such a lapse in perception.

You will be pleased to know that Thierry corrected the rat's mistake immediately, and deferred to your status, introducing me as the son of a powerful politician (he was discreet enough not to say 'senator') while modestly describing himself as a 'functionary of moderate influence.' I understand that the rat has been heard to tell people that he believed the influence to be more than moderate, and of a distinctly unsavory type. You must know, father, that nothing could be further from the truth. Yes, Thierry set me upon the path that brought me to this prison, but never did he behave in an inappropriate way toward me.

I remember well that spring afternoon, the warmth we had not felt for weeks. All the people we watched on the street walked, hopped, or skipped through the rain. Ears perked, tails swung freely enough that more than once we were splashed by someone's enthusiasm. It was just the opposite of the stifling, restrained buildings you brought me to, and even though my fur was damp, I threw open my arms and laughed.

That afternoon, the rain lessened somewhat, and Thierry wished to introduce me to a friend of his. So he took us from under the umbrellas of the cafe and we made our way along the damp streets, so much narrower and more crowded than our grand boulevards. I believed I was getting a cultural education; in Thierry's work, he appraises art quite often. As we walked past the artists practicing their craft on the street, he offered commentary on each one. The artists, far from being disturbed or indignant at these unsolicited opinions of their work, recognized his status and nodded gratefully to each one. I felt quite as important as when you took me through the halls of the Senate.

Thierry's friend, a fierce Firenzan goat who signs his paintings Alazzo, creates beautiful perspectives despite being blind in one eye. He served us a sharp orange cheese on day-old bread while he and Thierry talked about the world of art. He lives in his studio, a room scarcely larger than your closet, where we all three sat on his bed. I sat beside the open window, and though I did not at first lean out of it as the other residents of the quarter do, it was from this window that I first saw the Moulin Rouge.

The clouds parted and the sun hit the red sails of the windmill. Though there was a breeze, the sails remained fixed and proud against the ragged clouds, glowing as if with their own inner light. The body of the mill, august despite its crimson color, held the ethereal sails to the world below when I could see that they ached to fly, fly, fly.

At that hour of the afternoon, of course, the only activity outside the Moulin Rouge comes from the vagabonds who always inhabit the street, the customers who sit with them waiting for the doors to swing open, and the occasional seller of food or favors, the small tokens purchased by regular visitors to bestow upon their favorite dancers. The regulars know each other, too; I saw a skunk and a squirrel clasp arms and engage in conversation, though at each pause they glanced up as though the cabaret might open at any moment.

I thought it odd that the regulars would gather in the street so early, hours before sunset. But after an hour's worth of stimulating discussion about the direction of the art world, or perhaps two hours, I noticed a flurry of activity below the scarlet mill. The dancers were arriving, and this was what the regulars had been hoping for.

The passion in them! Even from blocks away, I could see their eyes gleam, their bodies animated with a spirit unlike any other. I confess, father, I hungered for it myself, to know what could drive these quiet citizens to the frenzy with which they pursued the arriving dancers. Many dancers hurried past them, shy of attention; three remained, coquettishly accepting favors and bestowing kisses upon a lucky few. I watched them let their clothing slip, creased fabric revealing just a touch more of a curve, a glimpse of the white-furred secrets that lay below.

The dancers were graceful works of art, their admirers naked and open in their lust and admiration. It is true that I did not lust after the dancers in the way the squirrel and the skunk and their compatriots in devotion did, and yet I leaned out of the window as though I were any other resident of the quarter, the better to see the scene below. The thought crept into my mind, father, that perhaps I might grow attracted to those dancers, and thereby learn to be content with a female companion, as you have so often wished. Now I know that it is no use pretending that my tastes draw me to the female form. I am as God made me, and I have done my best to live a virtuous life with what I have been given.

"Hey." Meg had closed her laptop.

Sol jerked his muzzle up from the phone. "Huh?"

"I said, I'm going to burn one and then go to bed. You want a hit?"

"Nah." Sol got up and slid the phone into his pocket. It was warm against his fingers, the weight of it comforting against his thigh.

"Mom made some brownies, if you want. No smoke." She tapped her nose and then slid a practiced paw into her purse, coming out with a small tin that said 'Solar Mints' on it. "C'mon, after the day you've had, you could stand to relax a bit. Hang out, chill."

Sol's own nose twitched with the memory of one bite of Mrs. Kinnick's brownies, months ago. "Y'know, you shouldn't—"

Meg yawned loudly and obviously enough to shut him up as she pried the case open and tipped a small, hand-rolled cigarette into one paw. "Fine. Save it, narc."

Now the smell of the marijuana made Sol wrinkle his nose. "What if someone at school catches you?"

"You can't smell them inside that tin, right? Who at school has a better sniffer?" She had a lighter in her other paw that he hadn't seen her get out of the purse. "Last chance."

"See you tomorrow." The lighter flicked as he hurried out her door, closing it carefully behind him.

The lights in the living room had been turned down or off. Meg's parents still floated in the pool, lit only by the movie over their heads. Sol tried not to look, but in the brief glance he couldn't avoid, he saw only the dark and light of otter fur amid the reflective water, unmarred by any clothing. Mr. Kinnick's towel was certainly no longer in evidence. He lowered his head and half-ran through the dark, flower-scented space.

"Good night, Sol!" Mrs. Kinnick waved to him, or at least he sensed the motion.

He probably wouldn't be able to see anything in the flickering highlights over the dark of the pool, but he kept his head down anyway and just raised a paw. "Night, Mrs. Kinnick. Night, Mr. Kinnick."

If they said anything else, it was lost in the closing of their door. Sol walked along the street of old stone houses with the scent of algae and waterfowl in his nose, toward the dark mass of trees where fireflies blinked quietly, waiting for him.

Jean's story, now, that was a story. Young noble, being seduced into sin by an older friend, and gay as well. Sol didn't have anyone here to seduce him into sin, nobody else he even knew was gay, and nowhere in Midland to go that was as exciting as the Moulin Rouge or Montmartre at the turn of the century. They didn't have a gay club for Sol to stand across the street from and stare guiltily at. The closest they had to sidewalk cafés were the Starbucks a couple blocks from the school; the closest thing to street artists were the old ladies who made yarn puppets and sold them in the mall. No, being gay in Midland in 2012 was just an endurance test, the challenge of whether you could pretend to be normal until you got out.

Chapter 3

The lower story of his house was dark when he opened the door, except for the kitchen; from the foyer, he saw the light around the corner of the doorway. He paused and lifted his nose. The only scent on the air was that of his mother, and the sweetness of lemon. The wall held the scents of his father and brother, too; he touched his nose to the stone and inhaled once before going into the kitchen.

His mother's paws were deep in the soapy water of the sink. "Lemon bars smell good," he said.

"They're for the church sale Sunday." She looked up at the window over the sink, at his reflection. He moved his eyes to the reflection of hers. In them, he saw the destruction of his fragile good mood before the words escaped her lips. "Sol, your father…"

"I don't need the car." He said it only to annoy her, as his eyes traveled down the front of the refrigerator, mapping the familiar pattern of travel magnets and notes. He played with a Rosy Arches State Park magnet that held up a meatloaf recipe, sliding a claw under the picture and then letting it snap back.

"He called Uncle Nolan. He asked if you could work in the cannery again this summer."

The magnet clattered to the floor, the recipe drifting after it. Sol's ears lay flat back. "I can't do that! My fur gets all sticky, and it's six days a week—and Uncle Nolan is—"

"I know. But Sol, if you could just see how much this means to your father…"

"What about what it means to me?"

She sighed, and turned on the water to rinse the bowl, holding her paws under it and watching the water course over her fur. "It's only for another few months, and then the summer. Then you'll be off to college like Natty is." She stared down into the sink.

"It's half a *year*." The bravado of thinking he could endure anything had not taken into account the peach cannery. Christ. Sol stared into a vision of the hot, endless summer, trudging into the factory that was stifling even at six every morning, coming home at five in the heat of the day, the smell of peach so lodged in his nostrils that he couldn't smell anything properly. At fifteen, he'd been enticed by the prospect of having two hundred dollars at the end of the summer. Now, he would pay all three hundred forty-one dollars and seventy-eight cents in his account to escape and go live in Millenport with Carcy for the summer.

Honestly, he'd pay it just to avoid having to talk to super-religious, homophobic Uncle Nolan. Sol's cousin, the one who'd killed himself, had been Nolan's son, and he'd slit his wrists in the bathtub after being told to pack his things and get out. Sol hadn't found out that last part until Patty, Percy's sister, had cried on his shoulder two Christmases ago. *Daddy shouldn't have kicked him out of the house, even if he was...funny like that.* Sol hadn't realized he himself was "funny like that" at the time; later, he'd tried to talk to Patty about it and she'd denied ever saying a word to him about it.

"If you'll just work at the baseball. Is there another position you can play? What about outfield?"

Sol shook his head slowly. "They stick you in the outfield when all you can do is hit. There's like five guys who hit better than I do." Anticipating her objections, he said, "I can't play first or third either. Maybe shortstop, but Todd is great and all the guys like him."

"But if you practice..."

He wrapped his tail around his leg and resisted the urge to smack the magnet from Fire Beach. "I've been playing second base all my life, and I can't do anything else, and Taric is just better than me! I don't know what he wants from me. I'm doing the best I can."

She picked up the bowl finally and ran it under the water. "Your father doesn't want you to work in the cannery."

"He shouldn't be talking to Uncle Nolan. If he doesn't want me to work there, I mean."

His mother turned the water off and set the bowl on the counter. Water dripped from it, spreading across the stone countertop. Sol knew what she was thinking, could hear the words as though they were being broadcast from the future. His mother wrapped the dishcloth around her paws. "It's just, after the soccer..."

"That was five years ago!" He picked at another of the magnets on the fridge. "Cor kept knocking me down. And those kids from Summervale never let me score."

"Sweetie," his mother said, "I know. I just think if you really put your mind to it, you can do anything you want."

"I guess I can't." He turned on his heel and stalked out of the kitchen. As he walked up the low staircase, he heard his mother picking up the magnets from the kitchen floor.

The light in the upstairs hallway was off, but a thin bright line glowed beneath his father's door. He shouldered into his room and slammed the door behind him. The sound echoed satisfyingly in the silent house.

Sol put one paw on the wall near the light switch before turning it on and rested his muzzle against it, breathing in his scent and his brother's. The number of times Natty had leaned against the wall here, talking to Sol, it was no wonder his scent had stuck, even if it had faded a bit over the last few months. If he stood right by the wall, it felt as though Natty were just outside the door. "I'll kill myself before I go work in the cannery," Sol muttered.

The weight of the evening's events and threats came home to him all at once. He leaned against the wall and let his brother's scent prop him up. Before he knew it, his phone was in his paw, and he'd called up Natty's number. But then he thought about what he would say, and how everything would inevitably lead back to his brother asking the question, "why don't you like baseball now?" And Sol couldn't tell him, because Natty would see through anything he made up, and would mock him for the truth. He put the phone away and slammed his paw against the light switch.

Another switch turned on his iPod player. Heavy guitar filled the room and, he hoped, seeped out into the hallway to bother his father. But no stern knocks sounded at his door by the time he'd sent a text to Carcy, started up his computer and logged in.

Meg had updated the shared folder they were using for their project with the painting she'd shown him, plus three others in which washes of color formed dreamlike countrysides and cityscapes where light browns and blues surrounded arresting spots of bright red and yellow. He pulled up one that looked like a windmill, but it was not the mill atop the Moulin Rouge. Curious, he did a web search for paintings of the Moulin Rouge windmill and found one by an artist named Auguste Chabaud.

The night encroached on the mill around the edges, but its red paint and sails shone. Sol thought he could see what Jean had seen in it, the incongruity of the huge red windmill rising out of the old slate roofs and wood timbers. Below it, the words "MOULIN ROUGE," spelled out in flickering points of light, were barely visible, and they did not need to be; the mill spoke for itself. Sol could almost see the crowd below the mill gazing up at it, though only a few people had been painted in the picture. He imagined he was looking at it through the window from a small painter's room, the odor of oil paints and oil lamp filling his nose. That was the world their painter had lived in, and the Moulin Rouge was at the center of it.

He threw his shirt onto the pile near his closet, lay down, and opened his phone. Carcy still hadn't responded. Sol wanted to send another text, but sometimes he felt like the ram was annoyed at him, and he couldn't let that happen, not now with the car in jeopardy, when he might need to ask for even more from his boyfriend. He hadn't told Meg about that one question that he hadn't gotten up the nerve to ask Carcy, and she hadn't asked, probably because it was such a basic question that she couldn't conceive that he would start making plans without having asked it. After all, she already knew she had a cousin she could stay with.

And it wasn't that big a deal. Sol was pretty sure Carcy would be okay with him staying there. Once he asked.

He tossed those uneasy thoughts aside and flipped to the book on his phone again. Here, at least, was someone with worse problems than he had.

Chapter 4

I will confess that when Thierry told me he wished to introduce me to the delights of the Moulin Rouge, I was more inclined to accept than I normally would have been. I had been spending a great deal of time with Minon, the son of Jacques Delamarche of the *Cie. Gle. Transatlantique*; perhaps you suspected that it was with Minon that I frequently sated my baser urges. In that safe harbor, I did not fear exposure or extortion.

However, Minon had just a few days previous confessed to me that his wife, whom he referred to as "an unholy beast with the eyes of an eagle and the disposition of an arctic cod," had begun to suspect that the more-frequent bouts of happiness he was experiencing were in fact unrelated to the ever-larger bills she was presenting him with for her clothing and maidservants, and he feared the scandal should she leave him. As a consequence, he wished to completely remove all joy from his life by abstaining from any pleasant evenings with me.

I did not expect to find his replacement at the Moulin Rouge, but I hoped perhaps to find some companion whose beauty and grace might overcome the barrier of her gender. Indeed, my blood quickened as Thierry talked about the elegance of the dancers, the seduction in the music, and the heady aromas that awaited within from our private box. I am a slave to my body, and on that afternoon, it was my body that led me beneath the red windmill, and into the parlor that would prove my undoing.

If the street had been empty before, it was a mass of bodies by the time Thierry and I made our way down there. It was at the same time terrifying and exhilarating to be one with the crowd, where none would know who I was, that I could do anything they did, that I could have anything done to me. In the halls of the Senate, when I walk behind you, everyone knows who I am. There goes Jean, they say, the son of the great Austere de Giverne. It opens doors, but also closes them.

On that night at the Moulin Rouge, every door was open, and every door was crowded by the bohemian populace. Thierry took little notice of them; his bulk parts the crowd much as your esteemed presence does. Few people took notice of me, trailing behind him, or so I thought at the time. I would discover later that the small purse I carried was stolen from me, I presume in that crowd. At the time, I kept one hand on Thierry's soft royal blue jacket, while my eyes scanned the people around me. There were wolves with their fur painted in midnight blue swirling patterns, foxes with teardrops and hoops of silver dangling from each ear, rams with their horns covered in every glittering color of the rainbow, black rats with eyes like starless night, and I even saw another chamois, scarves draped around her neck in a cloud of color that shifted with every movement she took. If anything, I stood out for being too plain in this mass of dyed fur, bangles, and bright clothing.

Grumbles followed us through the queue of people and to the door, where Thierry quickly slipped a twenty-franc note to the bear standing guard. The way opened before us as in one of the tales of the thousand and one nights, and into that magical world I entered.

From the moment I set foot in the Moulin Rouge, the grumbles and growls of the outside world disappeared, to be replaced by lively music and the thump of dancing feet. Gone was the miasma of a hundred different scents; the club had filled its interiors with the sweet smells of sandalwood and frankincense, with a musky undercurrent that warmed my blood. Welcoming us from the walls as we entered, hung over the red and gold wallpaper, were portrait upon portrait of beautiful ladies of every species, clad only in the fur God gave them. For most, it was the surprising elegance of the artwork that drew my eye and quickened my blood; though I was unfamiliar with the artists, it was clear that they had poured all their passion and not-inconsiderable talent into the brushstrokes and colors that brought the ladies to life.

Thierry stopped me in front of the portrait of a young fox lady with a pure white pelt. Her eyes, a stunning blue, blazed out of the painting at us, and the snowy curves of her body, though not painted with detail, were rendered with sure, passionate strokes of the brush. Her tail curved elegantly behind her, suggestive without being unseemly, and both paws at her hips were presented outward and open toward us: a gesture of welcome, one might think, until one's gaze was drawn back up to the blaze of those blue eyes, which warned that any welcome would be a negotiation with the proud spirit within.

"It's masterful," I said.

Without a word, Thierry pointed me to the signature at the base of the painting: Abrazzo. I could scarcely believe that the goat we had spent the afternoon with, whose work I had glanced at and found unremarkable, could have painted a work like this. Even though the subject was undeniably female, I could hardly bear to tear myself away from it.

The rough carpeting of the hallway gave way to a lush, fine rug, with interwoven patterns of honey gold on a background of blood red. Upon closer study, I saw that the patterns were the sails of a windmill, and the decorations on each of the sails were small figures: sheep, goats, foxes, wolves, rabbits, rats, tigers, wildcats, deer, boars, all climbing the sails in a glorious festival. Thierry had to push me along the corridor, as I was quite absorbed in studying the pattern and we were slowing the progress of a rabbit and badger behind us. I continued to look down until we emerged into the main hall of the club, and here my eyes rose to behold a wilder spectacle by far than had been painted even in my imagination.

The main room of the club stretched out half the length of the Great Hall of the Senate. Thierry led me onto a spacious floor below a ring of private balconies. Dozens of small tables stood before us, each surrounded by two or three wooden chairs. Hardly any of the chairs were occupied, though, for though the heavy red curtain remained drawn over the stage to my right, the band of musicians in the small pit in front of it was playing in full force.

I am of course most drawn to the lovely elegance of a symphony, or the delicate beauty of chamber music. But there was a fire, a passion to this music that I had not heard before from any instruments. They had no harpsichords, nor violins, but rather blew horns and rattled on piano keys. They pounded on snare drums and struck an instrument I had never seen, an assemblage of metal bars in a scale that trilled upon my ears behind the other sounds and brought a smile to my lips. I have since learned that it is called a "xylophone," but at the time it was an exotic marvel. My feet tapped to the beat of the drum and the soaring melodies of the horn, but I was far from the only one.

I said that hardly any chairs were occupied, and that is not to say that the hall itself was empty. All the people lucky enough to have gained entrance to the club were crowding the spaces between the tables, dancing with each other or by themselves. Their eyes were closed in some cases, open and glittering with excitement in others. They twisted or shimmied in place, or jumped and hopped. They clasped hands in paws, spun each other around in tight circles. They wagged tails, tugged on tails, slapped tails against each other. Some of the dances, I will confess, were much more lewd than I had ever seen in a public place. But to my eyes at that time, there was nothing unsavory or grotesque about it. It was the freest expression of unfettered joy that I had yet seen, and God curse me for a weak thing, but I wished desperately to take part, to let my duties and cares be cast to the wind as so many of those below were doing. I wished to experience that carelessness, that giddy delight in simply being alive, that the music was drawing out of me. I wanted more than anything to share that joy with another.

Thierry, wise counselor and chaperone, would have none of it. He kept me close to his side as he handed another twenty-franc note to a uniformed polecat, and received in exchange a stack of paper notes. I saw the polecat changing coins for notes for other patrons, but when I asked what this peculiar service might mean, Thierry said only that I would find out in due course.

I followed his stately step upstairs to our private box, in which I was somewhat disappointed; we were not to have full privacy after all. Of the eight seats in the so-called "private" box, four had already been claimed by a party of what I believe were jackals, though their features and bodies were hidden beneath uniform golden cloaks with ebony trim and a glowing sheen that caught the light of the oil lamps and played it about our little box. We did not speak as we took our seats on the far side of the box. The last two seats remained vacant throughout the performance, serving as a discreet curtain respected on both sides. Only once or twice did they attract my attention by a flick of a tail, a casual adjustment of an ear. Not once did I see any of them look at us.

Even in my chair, my feet continued to dance to the music, hidden from Thierry's sight. My hands tapped the railing as I leaned over it, drinking in the activity below. The vantage of the balcony certainly afforded me a wider view, yet I regretted our separation from the dancing patrons. Thierry attempted to distract me by pointing out the beautifully rendered art on the ceiling, an enormous mural of clouds and old gods engaged in recreations of many classic stories we know from the classrooms of our youth. A row of oil lamps shed light on the art and also created a smoky black ring that ran like a frame around it. But I spared little attention to that, or to the gilding of the wood around our boxes, the simple wood craftsmanship with intricate designs delicately laid on top of it. I had eyes only for the musicians and the dancers.

And then the lights dimmed. I saw mice scurrying from one lamp to another, turning them down. The musicians ceased their playing, and the crowd's dancing slowed. They poured into their seats with some shoving and wrestling, but all good-natured. In a matter of moments, the throng that had been dancing merrily was seated, perched on their seats as eagerly as I was, all of our eyes now turned to the only place in the hall where the oil lamps still burned brightly: the scarlet of the heavy velvet curtain.

We were holding our breaths. The musicians all faced the stage: the badger who had been pounding the drums, the slender red fox on the xylophone, the elk on the horn, and the pianist, whom I later learned was a ring-tailed lemur. Every face in the crowd was turned in the same direction; every set of eyes from every box strained to see the first parting in the curtain that would signal the start of the show.

The silence dragged on. At the time, I could have sworn that it went on for an hour or more. In the times I visited the Moulin since, however, I came to learn that the longest M. Oller allows the silence to go on is eight minutes, timed strictly according to an hourglass he keeps by his side in the manager's box to the side of the stage. I have stood there with him, and have watched as he turns the hourglass on end, signaling to the musicians to cease their playing. M. Oller is a distinguished polecat, and his hourglass is crafted in the form of a female polecat, so that the sand trickles down through her waist to her legs when it is set right-side up. Before that last grain of sand drops into her thighs, M. Oller has received the signal from Mme. DuPont that the dancers are ready, and he lifts his paw to signal the parting of the curtain.

On my first visit, I gripped the railing with both hands as the two halves of the curtain split, biting my lip in my impatience to know what lay behind their mysterious folds. Thierry chuckled behind me, as well he might at my youthful impatience and enthusiasm. But at the time, I took no heed, staring only at the darkness behind the velvet cloth as it slowly retreated to either side of the stage.

My eyes saw nothing at first. Then I—and, I presume, the rest of the clientele—was blinded by the fierce glare of an electric light, like a bolt of lightning that went on and on. In its glow was revealed a shapely, buxom deer, standing with one hand behind her head and the other at her hip, one foot on the ground, the other resting on her knee with the leg bent to one side. She wore a large, thick petticoat and a tightly laced corset that must have been trimmed with gold for all that it sparkled in the electric glow. Her own coat was brushed so finely that it shimmered—at least, so I thought, until she made a slow movement and I saw thousands of tiny sparkles like fireflies hidden in her skin. Now I know that she brushed mica flakes into her fur; then, it was magical. The light revealed every hair, every layer of fur that covered her shoulders, arms, and lower legs, that conformed itself to the elegant curve of her muzzle and up the delicate cup of her ears, that hid in the shadows under her collarbone and blazed brightly along the top of her chest, down to the golden line of the corset.

She stood for a moment, letting us admire her and drink her in. Father, I have told you that I have no desire for the female form, but this dancer quickened my blood and made my lips dry. I wanted to see her move, wanted to watch the unfolding of those elegant limbs. I wanted to see where those deep brown eyes would wander in the crowd, and yes, I hoped they might catch mine.

Slowly, the music started, a quiet duet of piano and horn. Then she lifted her arms, stepped forward and turned, and the fireflies danced amidst her fur with every motion. She danced with the precision of clockwork, except that she moved with a fluidity and grace that no clockwork can ever hope to achieve. The circles described by her limbs flowed like water, the one into the other and into the next in a cascade as entrancing, as unpredictable as any forest waterfall.

The music quickened. Without any hitch or flaw, the dancer's movements kept time as the piano rubbed sleep from its eyes, as the horn stretched and blared a liquid tripping of notes. The drum joined in so subtly that I did not notice it until the dancer's foot tapped the stage in time. The xylophone, by contrast, announced itself with a ripple of sound. It became a sort of tuneful drum after that, as the deer stepped in time with the rest of the music. It was from that point on that the dancer began to lift her skirts, that the dance became the kind of dance that the Moulin Rouge is famous and infamous for.

She held up her skirts and skipped from one side of the stage to the other, lifting one knee, kicking the leg, lifting the other knee, twirling the foot in a circle, and so on. The nearer patrons half-rose from their seats looking for a glimpse of underclothes, but all observed the etiquette of the club and none rose further than that.

Thierry's breath came warm on my cheek. "Quite something, eh?" he breathed.

"Yes." I could barely form the word. I could not look at him because to do so would have been to look away from her.

He gave a long, deep chuckle. "She's only the third best of the dancers here. And she's not the one I brought you to see."

Chapter 5

Sol awoke in his shirt, his muzzle open and pressed to the pillow. His tongue had soaked the fabric, and his mouth was full of rough cotton fabric and the taste of his sour morning breath. Reflexively, he smacked his alarm off and then fell to the side of the bed. For a moment, he had the impression that he'd been somewhere else. Gold patterns floated just outside the haze of his recollection, jazzy music played, but as soon as he concentrated on the tune, it fled.

He pushed himself out of bed and his phone fell to the floor. He'd forgotten to charge it overnight. He sighed and plugged it in, then stumbled to the shower.

The one good thing about Natty being gone was that there were no more fights over getting to the shower first. He could take his time and still not have to worry that there would be no hot water left, or that Natty would have saved up a good smell to leave in there for him. But even that, he missed. The bathroom was always just as he'd left it, the small reminders of another presence gone except for Natty's old toothbrush, and the cream he'd used on the rough paw pads his football career had left him with.

Sol made it through breakfast without his father bringing up his meat-eating, because fortunately, there was no meat in grits. His mother usually made bacon and sausage on the weekend, but he would cross that bridge when it was set down on a plate in front of him. His father grumbled his way through the usual morning pleasantries and raised a paw as Sol went out to the bus. His mother gave him a kiss on either side of his muzzle and wished him a good day.

Fat chance, Sol thought. He was going to have to go back and face his teammates today.

The size of the school meant that there wasn't a great deal of competition, especially at the unglamorous position of second base. Sol hadn't doubted that Taric would take his position after this year. Then the coyote had grown from a lanky sophomore into a muscular junior, and had worked relentlessly at practice, talking to the starters, listening to the coaches. And still, Sol realized, somehow he hadn't believed Mr. Zerling would let Taric take his spot. Maybe that was his father's fault; the older wolf didn't think a coyote could take Sol's spot, and Sol had perhaps absorbed that belief, relied on it too much.

Two opossum cousins and a muskrat caught the bus at Sol's stop. None of them had much to do with him; they weren't on any sports teams, and they had long since passed the point where they said more than "Hey" at the bus stop in the morning. This morning was no different, standing in the welcome chill of the humid morning, the opossum cousins talking low over the purr of farm machinery in the distance and the scattered rings and slamming doors that signaled the slow waking up of the long row of ranch-style houses. Then the arthritic clanking Sol had heard every year for the last twelve clattered into earshot. The yellow school bus rounded the corner, lurched to a stop in front of them, and threw its doors open with the smell of overnight sanitizer, signaling—to Sol, at least—the official beginning of another school day.

Sol didn't talk to any of the other kids on the bus, but he couldn't help glancing at each one of them walking onto the bus. A few of them met his eyes, among the shuffling, tired crowd, but none of those looked like they knew about his demotion. A tenth-grade swift fox who lived down the street in a big extended family sat next to him at the stop after his, but opened her English book right away. For the next five stops, nobody said a word to him as he sat with his face pressed to the window, watching the tidy streets roll by, houses full of people whose sons were starting on baseball teams and football teams and basketball teams and even soccer teams.

By the time they stopped by the lake and Meg slouched onto the bus, Sol had allowed himself to relax. Meg gave Sol a nod of her head on her way to the back of the bus. He flicked his ears and nodded back. There was no real reason for him to remain at the front of the bus except habit, and the fact that the smoke that often filled the back few rows stung his nose. He would have endured worse to talk to Meg, but she did not talk on the school bus; it interfered with her strict regimen of being annoyed at The System.

If he hadn't been given a social studies project with her two years ago, he would never have discovered how funny and smart she was. It had taken him a while to convince her that a jock could be as smart and sarcastic (sometimes) as a disaffected goth, but it had been worth it. He'd never seen anyone else from their class over at her house, and at school they rarely talked. Meg and the other goths sat in the back of the bus and at the same silent table at lunch, content to leave high school alone as long as it returned the favor. In private, Meg confided in him that she couldn't stand the other goths, and suspected that each of them hated the group just as much, which was why they all kept quiet.

Not that Sol had many friends himself, anymore. In his two-bus, two-hundred-student school, the senior class knew each other well, but Sol's best friends had always been on the baseball team, not in classes, and this past year he'd let even them drift away. For the last six years in homeroom, he'd been seated between a goat named Cheffy and a boar named Polly, neither of which he'd said more than a couple words to in years. The seat in front of him was now occupied by a short red fox, a foreign exchange student who'd moved into the area only the previous year. Like the goths, he kept to himself, though more likely it was out of shyness and lack of comfort with the language.

And the seat behind him was occupied by Taric's older sister Tanny, which Sol knew was going to be trouble. Even when Taric and Sol had been workout partners, she had ignored him, but as he plopped himself down this morning, the pink-ribboned coyote gave a high laugh. "I heard you finally got knocked down to the bench where you belong," she crowed.

Sol ignored her. She leaned forward so he could smell her sour breath. "It's about time, too. If Mr. Zerling Fathead wasn't a wolf, you'da been off the team a month ago. Finally Taric gets to be where he deserves. And so do you."

Cheffy and Polly turned, then met each other's eyes across Sol's desk. They each gave a little sniff and turned back to their own work. Sol kept his eyes forward and pretended to be going over his math homework.

Tanny leaned back and said, louder, "I guess you'll like it better. That way you can watch all the pretty boys, right?"

Sol's tail curled under his chair. "Shut up," he growled.

"Which one do you like? Is it Xavy? He's cute."

"Shut up." His fur was rising on the back of his neck. Fear and anger tightened his paw around his pencil.

Cheffy gave him a curious look and then went back to drawing guitars on his biology textbook. Sol picked up his pencil and traced over the numbers he'd already written on his paper, hard. The angles of the mechanical pencil dug into his pawpads and he almost tore the paper. It was going to be like last December all over again, only this time it wouldn't stop with Christmas break. This time it would go on 'til the end of school.

Tanny taunted him once more. "Can you still shower with the starters?"

Sol dug the point of his mechanical pencil into his paper and snapped it off. Before he could vent the terrified fury building inside him, the bell rang, and the old bear, Mr. Fortune, called the class to order.

The classes were okay. It was in the sanitizer-scented tiled hallways in between and in the chaotic crowds at lunch that the bad things happened. Taric had a little coyote gang he ran with in the junior class: one scrawny 'yote who was famous in the school for being able to get any drug you wanted, and one who was a backup on the football team. Until yesterday, the football player had been the leader of the gang, but now when they sauntered down the halls, it was Taric in the lead.

Meg wouldn't be much help to him in school, so Sol tried to stick with the other senior wolf jocks. They didn't object to his presence, but he had to keep dodging through other groups because they also didn't make an effort to make sure he stayed with them. Normally they wouldn't acknowledge the 'yotes, but today they actually greeted Taric, just a quick hi, but the coyote stopped and told them how excited he was to start. So the wolves had to tell him that they were, too. Sol was about to chime in, to be conciliatory and congratulate Taric on winning the starting job, but the coyote spoke first. Even his voice was deeper and more impressive than Sol's, though there was a harsh, gravelly quality to it.

"Good thing we don't have to count on that weak sauce no more," Taric said, as if Sol weren't standing five feet from him, ears flat against his head. He mimed swinging a bat. "You guys are gonna have some production from the 2-B spot now. And maybe you'll actually turn a double play."

Sol bit his lip, but there was nothing he could do. If he left the group now, he would be calling attention to himself, isolated and alone in the thinning sea of students. If he spoke up, he would be inviting vicious attacks, and he was far from certain that his fellow wolves would stand up for him. Where was his Thierry? In Millenport, he remembered, and fought the urge to take his phone out and text Carcy right then and there for help.

"Hey," Xavy, the third baseman, said. "You're doing good and we're all on the same team. Leave Sol alone."

But he didn't contradict Taric. I wasn't that bad, Sol wanted to say. I got two hits in the last game. We had three double plays this year. Of course, pleading his own case would make him even weaker. "Oh," Taric said, "I know you gotta stick up for him and all. Sorry, man. So hey, you catch the Typhoons game last night?"

Two of the wolves were happy to talk about the game, while the others moved on. Sol tagged along behind them, hunched over. The scrawny 'yote was the only one who looked at Sol, and he did so with a giggle and a long, long smirk that curled into the ragged ruff of fur on his cheek. When he saw Sol looking back at him, he blew him a kiss and waggled his tongue around in his mouth.

"Jesus, Mox," Taric said, elbowing his friend. "Don't fuckin' turn him on here in the hall." They laughed as they walked on to their class.

The wolves looked after them. "We gotta play with him," one of them, a pitcher, said.

"He's just a prick. His friends are hinky."

"They're 'yotes."

Xavy shoved the wolf who'd said that. "Don't be an ass. They aren't all like that."

"Hey," the other wolf protested. "Why d'you think stereotypes happen, huh?"

"At least he can play," Xavy said.

"Yeah." And then the tallest wolf, the smooth-hitting first baseman, looked at Sol. "Why couldn't you've kept it up for just two more months, huh?"

"He kept it up okay back in December," the pitcher murmured. He chuckled, but none of the others did.

Awkward silences were rapidly becoming part of Sol's life. The other wolves, even Xavy, looked down and away. Sol flattened his ears and walked quickly on, leaving them behind. He hated walking to class alone, but it was better than having that brought up again. That was all he needed, on top of everything else.

A moment later, he was wishing he were more alone. Tanny ran up behind him, pink ribbons bouncing. "Hey, backup," she said.

Sol just walked faster, but Tanny kept pace with him. "I bet you're happier *riding* the *pine*," she said. "Y'oughta thank my brother. C'mon. I wanna see a wolf thank a coyote."

Don't react, don't give her the satisfaction. He managed to keep his muzzle shut and get into the classroom, where she had to shut up. After class, he grabbed his books and ran to the cafeteria, and she didn't follow him.

After lunch, though, as he left the cafeteria, she sprang from the hallway to his side. "Hey," she said in a venomous whisper, "was it my brother you were thinking of in the shower?"

He walked faster, but she kept pace. "I bet it was. I bet you want him to fuck you good."

The twisting in his gut was too much. He snapped back at her. "What, like he does you?"

"Shut up, fag."

"You still sleep in the same bed, right?"

"Shut *up*!"

"Does your mom—"

He didn't know what he was going to say about their mom, and he never got the chance to find out, because Tanny smacked him hard across the muzzle, blunt claws dragging across the thin fur. "Shut up!" she shrieked.

She stomped away, and even though Sol had gotten her to leave him alone, he felt no sense of pride or victory. He felt dirty, ashamed, because he'd sunk to her level, he'd made himself no better than she was. He slunk into his math class with his tail curled around one leg and slouched at his desk, wishing he could take it back, knowing it wouldn't do any good. Brooding over it, he took no notes for the first fifteen minutes of the class and spent the rest of it trying to catch up.

Tanny didn't bother him for the rest of the day, but once he'd shoved his books into his locker and walked to the gym's locker room, he had to deal with her brother. "What'd you say to my sister?" Taric demanded the moment Sol entered.

Here, Sol could no longer simply ignore the coyote. "She was giving me—calling me names," he said.

Taric stood no taller than Sol, and weighed ten pounds less, but he seemed to loom over the wolf. He poked Sol in the chest with a finger as hard as his expression, as rough and dirty as his scent. "Tanny can call you whatever name she wants. You get it?"

"Then I can call her—"

"You call her anything but 'Tanny' an' I will put you through that locker. You got that?" Again, the finger stabbed at him. Again, Sol wished for a big red elk to stand behind him and protect him.

"I—"

"You. Got. That." Taric took a step forward.

"Yeah." Sol hated backing down, hated it. *You'll make it up on the field*, he told himself.

But Taric wasn't moving away. He took another step forward, making Sol take a step back. The coyote might be lighter, but he had his shirt off and his wiry body seemed carved of lean muscle. "Damn right you got that. And lemme tell you somethin' else. I catch you eyein' me in the shower, I'm gonna rip your boner off."

At that, Sol could do nothing but nod, and that seemed to satisfy the coyote. "And if you turn around and look at me while I'm changing, I'll rip your ears off. Got it?"

Sol bit back the tears. He had to face his locker anyway to get his uniform on, so it wasn't a big deal, not a big deal at all. He stared at the gold shirt and maroon pants swinging from the hanger in his locker, the maroon writing on the shirt that said "Giants" on the front, with his name and the number 75 on the back. On the sleeve, in machine-like cursive, the sponsor

"Joliette's Auto Body" and a phone number swung back and forth. Behind him, the locker room activity slowly faded away. He sighed and reached for the shirt.

The locker room was empty when he turned around, save for two other bench-warmers. He trotted out to the field and stood up beside Mr. Zerling, watching the infielders take ground balls hit by the batting coach. Mr. Zerling, a muscular wolf with more grey than brown in his fur and a scar along his nose, was taking notes on a clipboard, looking frequently back up at the players, making it hard for Sol to figure out how to interrupt him to ask his question.

He looked out at the players, too. He wasn't one of the starters any more, but he hadn't been one of the backups before, either. Neither group seemed particularly interested in his status, but the wolves in the starting lineup went out of their way to include Taric in their calls to each other, as much a part of practice as the actual physical moves. "Nice hustle there, 'yote," they'd call, or "Shake that ratty tail, look alive." None of them even spared a look for Sol, who two days ago had been out there with them. They'd never really called to him that way even when he had been. And Taric called back, too. "I got yer back, fluffbutt," he'd say, or "Comin' at ya," when he threw to first. Sol had lost that this year, had retreated into himself, and then the shower incident had just made it worse. Watching Taric slip so easily into his role made his chest burn with envy. If he had another chance, if they let him back out there…he could do it. He could be part of the team again.

To one side of the field, the cheerleaders practiced their routines. The breeze dug cold claws under his fur as he watched them. One of them, a deer, pranced through her moves with clockwork precision. It wasn't hard to imagine her in a red and gold bustier, the sun glinting off the metal stands like electric lights. Sol could almost hear a rhythmic xylophone in his head.

He realized that he'd been staring at the cheerleaders for a full minute or more. It wasn't such a bad thing for him to do, though, was it? If he were interested in them, how long would he stare? If they were boys, showing off tight abdomens, dancing in costumes… He jerked his head to the side. That's what he'd been thinking about in the shower, last December. That image, too, had gotten pretty real.

He pushed those thoughts away and stared toward the stands. A smattering of students sat, several boys watching the cheerleaders, and a red fox and mink sitting apart from them. A steady breeze ruffled his fur, holding the last chill of winter and the moist promise of spring, as he watched the team practice again.

After a moment, the coach tapped him on the shoulder. "Go on out and take your practice, Wrightson."

"Mr. Zerling," Sol said. "What would it take to get the starting spot back?"

The coach's ears dipped. He shook his head. "Wrightson—"

"If I work really hard," Sol persisted. "If I clean up my fielding. I know I have to work on my decision-making." The coaches had used those words, *clean up* and *decision-making*, over and over for much of the off-season.

"Work on your plate discipline, too."

"Yeah, sure." In his mind, Sol pushed away the agony of countless hours spent with a bat, waiting for the machine to hurl the ball toward him. "Like, over the next month? For the Lakeside game?"

"I won't make no promises." Mr. Zerling watched Taric dive for a grounder and throw it to first, the kind of throw that Sol had heard announcers in the majors call a "frozen rope." He didn't think he'd ever thrown anything more than a slightly chilled rope. "And I'm tellin' ya, it probably won't happen. That 'yote's pretty good. Reminds me of Carquinez."

"Thanks, Mr. Zerling." Staying longer would probably reveal that he had no idea who Carquinez was, so Sol trotted out to the field. He took up a spot on the opposite side of the field from Taric, between another wolf and a deer. He fielded for half an hour, then went to the batting cages for half an hour after that.

The exercises, far from inspiring him, left him mostly frustrated. The drive to oust Taric carried him only so far without the support of the team around him. Earlier this year, when he'd first started drifting apart, he'd supplanted his real teammates with daydreams and stories. Now, when he was really trying to pay attention to practice by himself, it was horribly dull. His mind kept wandering back to Jean and Thierry and the Moulin Rouge, but he pushed the gold and red patterns away, until it occurred to him that if only the other guys could see him daydreaming about a *female* dancer, all the "fag" talk would go away. Then he snorted a laugh and swung hard at the next ball, and missed it by a mile.

He stayed on the field until everyone else had gone inside, as much to get the extra swings in as to make sure everyone else was out of the shower by the time he went in. Problem was, Taric was taking extra batting practice, too. Sol stopped to watch him.

The coyote really did have a great swing. All the things Sol's coaches had given up trying to teach him in the past year were made physical and real in Taric. He planted on his back foot—Sol could see the shift in weight—and his muzzle stayed pointed straight at the pitching machine.

He never took his eye from the ball, and he turned his whole torso into the swing. And he followed through, sometimes sending the bat all the way to the back of the cage. Sol had watched his coaches demonstrate this, but he'd never felt the fire in his gut to get it right; he'd been good enough to have fun, and better than any other second baseman for years. His swing had always been adequate, enough to get him at least one hit a game. But he wasn't going to be better than Taric anytime soon.

Taric turned, unexpectedly. Yellow eyes bored into Sol's. "If you're gonna stare at my ass, I'll come over there and take batting practice on your skull."

You used to watch me take batting practice. But Sol just ducked his head and triggered the pitching machine again, missing three balls in a row before he hit a weak dribbler back out to the machine. He wanted to outlast Taric, but the coyote showed no signs of stopping, nor even slowing down. Sol kept count of the hits from a certain arbitrary point. He got four, Taric five. Then he hit three in a row and briefly tied the 'yote's total, until Taric unleashed a powerful swing and launched a pitch into the stands. It would've been foul, but then, so were some of Sol's, so the wolf counted it.

The hour dragged on, and though Sol did reasonably well, Taric's score kept climbing. When it reached twenty to thirteen in the 'yote's favor, Sol stopped counting. Taric was better than he was; he knew that. But he could at least stay as long as Taric did. They'd both reloaded their machines twice so far, and this last load of pitches would have to be the last one. Orange was blossoming in the sky, pink glowing on the bottom of the clouds, and Sol's arms were tiring. He started missing more and more of the pitches. Coach had said that when you got too tired, practice didn't do you good any more, but Sol just had to finish the pitches in his machine. Taric's was going to run out first, and the 'yote would head in then.

Only he didn't. His machine buzzed, but rather than carrying the bat into the locker room, the 'yote dropped the bat in the cage and trotted out, as though practice had just started, to collect balls from the fence.

Sol dropped his bat. Only then did the fatigue in his shoulders make itself felt, so much so that it was an effort for him to reach down and retrieve the bat from the ground. As he left the batting cages, he caught Taric's eye, and had to turn away from the 'yote's triumphant smile. Tomorrow, he told himself. Tomorrow he'd stay longer. He'd done well to stay as long as he had today.

It was easier for Taric; he lived walking distance from the school, or at least not the ten miles Sol did, so Sol had to call his mother to pick him up. She told him his father would be leaving the office in ten minutes and would swing by the school to get him, which was not was Sol wanted to hear. "I don't want to bother Dad," he said, still panting from the workout. "Can't you come get me?"

His mother sighed. "Your father's not angry still."

Sol very much doubted that, but he didn't argue. "What's for dinner?"

"Spaghetti."

He waited. "And…?"

"Green beans."

"Thanks, Mom." It didn't erase the sting of his failure, the ache that came from knowing that Taric was still, somehow, out there smacking baseballs across the field. But it helped a little, enough to give his tail a little life, his step a little spring.

His fur was dirty and grassy, and he felt pretty warm even after gulping down about half a gallon of water. The showers were empty, so he washed himself off. By the time he was out, Taric still hadn't come in from working out. Sol had the fleeting image of the coyote as a Terminator-like machine, gleaming metal parts under a veneer of fur and muscle, standing in batting cages unleashing the same deadly swing again and again, a relentless hitting machine.

That led to thoughts about what the coyote might look like in nothing but his fur, and that led to dangerous thoughts to be having in the shower, even with nobody else there. So Sol got out, toweled himself as dry as he could, then pulled his pants on and walked out to the sidewalk.

While waiting for his father, he texted Carcy to tell him he'd be trying absinthe tonight. He ran a paw through his damp, chilly fur, turning his bare chest to face the breeze, and closed his eyes, damp tail wagging again. He didn't expect a quick response, but his phone buzzed a minute later: *It's stronger than beer. Don't get fucked up.*

I'll be with Meg, Sol replied, and then stretched his arms over his head. If there were anyone watching, he would stop, but the baseball field was around back, and most of the school had left for the day. *I'm outside the school without a shirt*, he texted Carcy. *Feels nice.*

Another quick reply: *Wish I was there!* Carcy must be bored at work.

The breeze and the ruffling had not completely dried out his fur when he saw his father's car swing around the corner. He pulled his shirt on hastily, put the phone away, and picked up his bag.

"I was staying late to finish up practice," Sol said before his father could say anything.

The older wolf just nodded. "Did you stay later than Taric?"

"Uh." Lie. Just lie. "No. But everyone else..."

The slow sigh, the flick of the black-tipped ears: Sol knew those signs well. He slumped back into the seat, stretching the seatbelt across himself. His tail hung limp behind him.

His father pulled out, onto the street. "I thought at least for today, you'd take this seriously."

"I stayed longer than everybody else!"

"You don't have to be better than everybody else. You gotta be better than that coyote."

Sol picked at the fur on his arm again, rubbing out the dampness and parting the fur. Why had he even bothered to try placating his father? "It's not gonna happen overnight."

"It won't happen at all if you don't apply yourself."

I'm trying, he wanted to say. I'm going to. At worst, he would gain his starting spot back in some other position, though he had no idea what that would be. Second base had been his last refuge, the middle ground between the demanding fielding positions on the other side of the infield and the demanding hitting positions at first and in the outfield. He wasn't strong enough for football, he wasn't tall enough for basketball, and he didn't have enough stamina for soccer.

"Listen," his father said. "There's no reason you shouldn't be better than a coyote at baseball. They might be a little faster, sure, but baseball's a team sport and you're part of a pack. No reason you shouldn't be better."

Sol squirmed in his seat. It wasn't fair. He'd made it through eleven and three-quarters years of school doing well enough to play. Why couldn't coach have waited just two months before demoting him? Even if it had happened after his birthday, he'd have the car. He could run away to Millenport with Meg as soon as he graduated. Just having that to look forward to would make the tension in these evenings tolerable. He tried to think back to when he'd been able to have a relaxing time with his father, and the last time he could remember had been when they'd gone to Natty's last football game.

"Sol? You hear me? You're part of the team."

"Yeah. I hear you." Sol choked the words out past the roughness in his throat.

Part of it was that for the last year, Sol had been terrified that he would let something slip about being gay. It had started out innocently enough, a couple weeks over the summer reading some material online, the burst of realization, the growing wave of guilt afterwards. He'd created an anonymous e-mail account to post to a forum for gay teens, where Carcy'd been one of the people to tell him there was nothing wrong with him. E-mail had led to IM had led to texting, and Sol had gotten his head around his sexuality without having to talk to anyone in his family, or at his church. Or the team.

Then came December, and the shower. Meg had told him that just getting an erection in the shower didn't mean you were gay, and he'd told her that he was, and she'd shrugged and said that in that case, maybe it did mean that, but who cared? The guys on the team cared, and though they probably knew that there were lots of other reasons a guy could spring a boner in the shower, they teased him with ferocious abandon all the way up to Christmas break. If he'd been able to laugh it off, he was sure it would've stopped sooner.

That was the only time he was thankful for Natty's absence. Had his brother been around the school, he would've told Mom and Dad in some disarming manner, and then they would've known, and there would have been Talks. But Sol kept his parents unaware, both of the symptom and the cause, and the price he'd paid for that silence had been more silence.

At dinner that night, his father regarded the meatless pasta sauce with the vegetables and garlic bread with a frown before helping himself, but remained quiet. Probably it was just because he loved spaghetti, although at the end of the meal he did remind the family about the work picnic that weekend, and he glared at Sol as he said that it was a barbecue. Which, of course, meant burgers and ribs and maybe chicken, and Sol had no idea how he was going to get through a barbecue without eating meat. He was pretty sure he wasn't going to get through a barbecue without *wanting* to eat meat, even with the prospect of life with Carcy to keep him strong. But that was days away, and rather than think about the many school days and baseball practices between now and then, he focused his energy on getting excited about trying absinthe.

He walked over to Meg's after dinner, in the chill of early evening with fireflies winking among the stars overhead. Fortunately, her parents were clothed this time, reading next to the pool in the living room. Sol greeted them and walked into Meg's room, his stomach starting to flutter with whole new worlds of anxiety. What if he did throw up from the absinthe? What if it gave him weird hallucinations, like that afternoon's, only stronger?

"That's the point," Meg told him. She was sitting at her desk, intent upon something in the focused light of her desk lamp, and she didn't turn around to talk to him when he came in. The rest of the room was completely dark; the ceiling light was off and her computer was closed. Reflections glimmered on the surface of the water in her pool in the corner, yellow-white and…green.

"But what if they're bad hallucinations?" He walked around to see what she was doing.

Over the scars Meg had inflicted on her desk (the A-within-a-circle of 'anarchy' was particularly prominent), two glass goblets sparkled. Beside them, the otter was holding a nondescript bottle, clear glass with a bright green liquid in it. As he moved, Meg lifted the bottle, passing it in front of the lamp.

Light transformed the absinthe. Around the edges of the bottle, the green liquid appeared dark and murky, but where the light shone through it, Sol's eyes hurt from the dazzling emerald glow. Flickers of green played over the two goblets and the metal spade laid across the top of the nearer one, which held a large sugar cube. "There's no such thing as bad hallucinations," Meg said. "Anything is better than reality, right?"

"Uh." He couldn't look away from the glimmering green liquid. She poured it slowly into the glass, to one side of the sugar cube rather than over it. "What're you doing?"

"You start with the absinthe and then pour ice water over the sugar. The water is what liberates the essence of the absinthe and frees the dreams locked within."

"And what does the sugar do?"

"Makes it sweeter, idiot."

Sol scowled at her, showing his fangs over his lower lip. She flashed a grin. "You have to add sugar and water or else it's way too bitter. Don't worry, it's still strong enough. This is how they used to sweeten it back in the 1900s."

She poured absinthe into the second goblet to the same level, about two fingers high, and then set the absinthe bottle aside to pick up a carafe of water, its surface clouded with condensation. When she poured, this time she poured the water over the sugar cube. It streamed through the sugar and somehow through the metal spade. Peering closer, Sol saw holes in the spade. "Where did you get that metal thing?"

"My vampire fox friend sent it to me. It's an absinthe spoon." The water spread cloudy tendrils through the glass, curling lazily into intricate swirls. They twined around one another and grew, merged, until no trace of the clear green remained.

The sugar cube had dissolved, leaving residue on the spoon. Meg tapped it on the edge of the goblet and then laid it across the top of the other glass. She placed a second sugar cube on it and tilted the bottle, letting the water stream slowly down through the sugar.

The ritual was hypnotic: the steady stream of water, the vanishing cube, the dancing emerald reflections growing fainter as the water spread and obscured the brightness.

"I saw you on the field on my way out." The sugar had dissolved. Meg tapped the spoon against the rim of the glass to shake the last of the sugar into it. The last threads of clear green turned cloudy as she mixed it in with the spoon.

Sol shook his head, looking up from the mesmerizing swirling liquid. "I stayed as late as I could."

"Just get that car." She shoved her chair back from her desk and got up, a book of matches in one paw. Humming softly, she lit each candle on her dresser. She'd added three—no, four black ones to the white ones. When all of them were flickering in a row behind her, she turned off her desk lamp and turned to face Sol. He could barely see the glint of her eyes in the halo of light that traced the edges of her head and ears.

"Are you ready?"

His stomach fluttered. "It's just alcohol."

"It is not just alcohol." Her eyebrows lowered, hiding her eyes behind deep shadows. "It is dreams and inspiration. It is pain and suffering. It is art…in a bottle."

Sol swallowed. "I don't need more pain and suffering."

"Come on, Sol. This shit's expensive." She sighed. "Look, don't you want a drink after the day you just had?"

"You said it wasn't just alcohol." But the tension in him, perhaps, was as much from his dad, from Tanny and Taric, from hours of swinging, as it was from the suspense over the absinthe.

Meg's voice got that tone that meant she was about to stop talking to him. "So-ol."

"All right, all right." He leaned against her bedpost in what he hoped was a reasonably appreciative pose.

"Now," she intoned, "prepare to receive the gift of the Green Fairy."

The candles smoked. An acrid, herbal scent tickled his nose. "What kind of candles are those?"

"They're just candles." Meg sounded peeved. "I'm burning some incense of frankincense."

"Frankincense?" Sol closed his eyes for a moment and saw the red and gold of the Moulin Rouge, the portraits of dancers on the walls.

"Yes." Her voice grew deep again. "It will allow us to commune with the spirits of the Mont-marter area."

"Montmartre," Sol murmured, inhaling. His fur prickled slightly. Silly, to let Meg's voice affect him. But even when she stopped talking, the uneasy feeling remained. He was sure there was someone just outside her window, watching, waiting to see if he would take that drink.

"Take your drink," Meg said, again in her normal voice.

Sol's eyes flew open. He managed to keep steady, to reach out and take the goblet Meg was holding out. As he lifted it to his nose, he stared at her window, but the curtains were drawn. Then he inhaled, and the powerful smell drove the imaginary watcher from his mind.

The scent of alcohol, curiously, did not overwhelm the herbal, anise smell the way alcohol overwhelmed most liqueurs. The combination of smells in the drink mixed with the frankincense and smoky candle smell to make Sol slightly dizzy. He closed his eyes again, and when he opened them, Meg was holding the goblet to her lips. The candles flickered through the glass, the liquid, her fur.

"Take us back," she intoned.

"Seriously?" Sol lifted his own glass. His stomach felt knotted, which was ridiculous. Whatever Meg said about dreams and anything else, this was just alcohol. It was a drink. He'd had plenty of drinks. But his nerves were no longer worry about the absinthe. He was, again, excited, thinking back to Jean's narrative of the Moulin Rouge. He would have this drink and then go back to the book, and he would understand it better.

"Shh." She closed her eyes. "Take us back to the Mont-mar-truh," one eye cracked open to look at Sol for approval, and when he didn't correct her, it closed again, "of nineteen-hundred. So that we can kick ass on our report."

Sol suppressed a giggle. Meg's eyes opened and met his. "This is serious stuff here. I looked it up on the web. People had visions. Artists became inspired. There was this seventeen-year-old poet, he was a weasel, and when he started to drink absinthe, he wrote the most amazing poems."

"Seventeen?"

She winked. "Maybe you'll become a poet. Or finally write something, anything, instead of just sitting around whining about it. Bottoms up, dear friend, and let us meet on the other side of dreams."

"What?" She was already drinking from her goblet. Sol hurriedly lifted his and gulped the first drink.

He had a moment of warning before anise and alcohol and a host of other herbs exploded on his tongue. Licorice stung his nose as the alcohol burned his throat. He'd had beer at home since he was thirteen, had had stronger liquor at some of the parties his teammates had thrown over the last two years, had even done a couple shots of Wild Turkey and Southern Comfort. He'd never tasted anything like absinthe.

"Prepare to receive the gift of the Green Fairy."

It burned his throat like whiskey, but without the harshness. The warmth in his stomach grew rather than faded. For a moment, he thought the candle lights in the room all flickered green, but when he looked, they were yellow again. Magic, he thought briefly, and smiled.

"Not bad." Meg sounded disappointed.

"Any hallucinations yet?"

She took another drink. "Nothing. Tastes okay, though, right?"

"Right." He took another drink as well. The anise, which had been fading, surged again.

Meg peered at him. "What about you?"

Green flickered across her eyes, though the candlelight was yellow. But Sol was not really inclined to trust his senses any more today. "Nothing."

"Maybe it takes a while."

They finished the drinks in silence. Sol sat on Meg's bed while she rocked back and forth in her desk chair. "So," Sol said. "This is what artists did then? Just sat around in dark rooms drinking absinthe?"

He was starting to feel buzzed, but it was a little different than a beer buzz. On beer, he just felt lightheaded and generally happy. Here, he felt lightheaded, but he also felt as though his words were echoing—or, perhaps, that he was hearing them a moment before he said them. Also, it now took about two and a half beers to get him buzzed. He'd gotten this from one small cup of absinthe.

"Pretty much." She paused. "I kind of feel something. Do you?"

The world felt free from its moorings, but not out of his control yet, definitely not spinning like an amusement park ride that wouldn't stop no matter how much he yelled. He remembered that spin from the last time he'd been drunk, at a party at the first baseman's house. Three bottles of beer followed by two shots of Wild Turkey had led to him vomiting all over the carpet and partly on the sofa, with all his teammates watching. That had been two months before the shower.

He tested the thought of that party, the baseball team gathered there, the white-tail and the fox, the rabbit and the weasel, even the other wolves. It did not bring with it the ache of loss he'd felt at practice. Why should he care about them? He'd never been a part of the team even when his name was on the roster. He was not a planet in their solar system; he was a bright green sun, with Meg in orbit around him.

"Sol?" she said. Her voice had a raised edge of hope. "Do you?"

"I just feel good." He sniffed at his empty goblet. "Is there any more?"

She laughed. "Not in one night. What do you mean, good?"

"Oh." He put the goblet down on the floor. It wobbled; he had to steady it with a paw. "Just…you know, who cares if I'm on the team or not?"

"What about the car?"

Car. He'd forgotten about Carcy, how grateful he was to the ram. He took out his phone to type a quick message. *Absinthe is great but not better than you.*

Meg made a noise of exasperation and craned her neck to see what he was typing. When she read the words, she slumped back into her chair. "Oh God." She moaned and turned the desk lamp back on. "It's making you one of *those* kind of poets."

Carcy wrote back, *Aww. :)*, and Sol's heart filled with love. "Maybe I always was," he said.

"Maybe now you can tell me what's so great about him. Other than that he's willing to sext you whenever."

"He's just…" Sol closed his eyes and pictured the images the ram had sent of himself, in all kinds of poses. "He's so handsome, and he cares about me."

"What does he care about?"

"Me." Sol floated happily on the wave of his thoughts. "He taught me all about being gay. He helped me when that shower thing happened. Said it was natural. Said it happened to him, too. We just click so well. I don't know what I've even been worried about."

"I didn't know you were worried about anything. What's Mr. Perfect done? Or not done?"

Sol waved a paw lazily. "I mean, of course he won't mind me moving in. Why would he?"

Meg's voice went a bit high in surprise. "You haven't asked him yet?"

"Oh, well. He'll let me. I can tell." How could he not know it? Every message Carcy sent him held the unspoken promise behind it *"when we're together."*

"Okay." Meg hesitated, then went on. "Assuming that plan, which has absolutely no chance of failing, succeeds… then what?"

"What, then what?"

"Once you live with him, then what?"

He opened his eyes, aware he was smiling. "Then…we're living together."

"God." Meg shook her head. "Okay, this experiment is officially a failure. You go home and sleep it off, and get back to practice tomorrow, because if you go out to Millenport without me you're gonna end up sleeping under a tarp somewhere."

"I love absinthe." Sol grinned and got up, and then leaned over Meg's head to kiss between her ears. "Thank you. And thank your vampire fox."

She swatted him away. "At least read one of those books I pointed you to before bed. Maybe you'll have interesting dreams."

"I already am." He gathered up his bag and danced his way to the door. "Good night!" As he opened it, he called, "Good night, Mr. Kinnick! Good night, Mrs. Kinnick!" He even looked toward the pool to see the dark shapes raise a paw to him as they returned the good-nights.

The night air did little to dispel the warmth of the absinthe. When he got home, he was careful to tell his parents how well the studying session had gone, and he thought he did a good job of sounding sober, even though anise and frankincense still lingered in his nose. His father sniffed suspiciously, but frankincense was not a drug, Sol pointed out when asked what Meg had been burning. He got the standard lecture about bringing strange smells into the house, delivered as half-heartedly as it was received, and then they let him go up to his room.

Carcy had texted him twice more, provocative texts that Sol answered as soon as his room door was shut. He lay on his bed and imagined that what he and Carcy were texting back and forth was really happening, as best he could without actually doing anything his parents would smell in the morning. The thump of his own tail on the bed made him even happier.

When he and Carcy were done, it was past eleven. Sol lay stretched out on his bed, too tense to go to sleep. So he lay on his stomach and brought up Jean's Confession again, thinking of Carcy.

It opened where he'd left it, at the florid descriptions of the next two dancers. He skimmed over them with a mix of fascination and envy, because they were neither a ram nor male, but they were beautiful and they were expressing their sexuality there in the open, in front of an audience.

Chapter 6

"And that is the one I brought you here to see," Thierry told me, stretching one long finger past my muzzle. I followed its direction to the cabaret floor, where amidst the dancers circulating through the tables there glowed a spot of russet fur. In the busy swirl of lights and colored costumes, it might have been lost, but it bore the quiet grace of a simple dress at an elegant ball, remarkable for the purity of its color and the aura it carries.

The fur belonged to the tail of a fox, trailing a white point behind it. I'd seen the fox on stage, one of the dancers between the second and third acts, but Thierry had not pointed her out to me then. It was only when he reminded me of where I'd seen her that I remembered.

I watched, intent now on puzzling out what it was that Thierry thought so attractive in this vixen. Her corset and short skirt, dark red with gold edging, did indeed complement her fur much more than the same uniform did on many of the other dancers, but there was a black pantheress who wore it even more elegantly. The vixen's feet did seem to glide, as if she were not earthbound at all, but that also was not unusual among the courtesans who made their way through the tables. The patrons did not pay her any more mind than the others; less, in many cases, and I thought I could see why. The largest clusters of attention and appreciative whistling grew around the courtesans whose corsets were the most visibly strained, and Thierry's fox had a very pleasant, modest shape in that regard.

He made a gesture with one hand as though grasping something out of the air. I followed his eyes and saw for the first time the vigilant shape of M. Oller. I did not see his response to Thierry's gesture before he descended to the floor. His sleek polecat form wound its way effortlessly through the crowds, between the tables, to the side of the fox. He spoke for only a moment, so quickly and discreetly that had I not been watching closely, I would not have seen the motion of his muzzle, nor the twitch of the fox's ear. She nodded.

I watched her excuse herself from her table, and in that short period of time, M. Oller returned to his post. The chaos of alcohol and laughter and sex continued unabated even as the vixen extricated herself from it, disappearing from my vision below our boxes. I turned, but Thierry's hand on my shoulder and his mysterious smile cautioned me to wait, so I summoned my strength and patience. You have said on many occasions, father, that those are not my most prominent virtues, and so it was quite fortunate that they were not tested for long.

The four jackals sitting with us turned in unison. Only then did I notice the sound of the door and turn, eagerly. All six of us there in the box stared at the open doorway filled with the light of the corridor outside, and the silhouette of the vixen standing in it.

Thierry turned up the oil lamp he had dimmed. In its uncertain light, I saw bright red fur over a long, slender muzzle, soft white fur on the throat and small swell of the chest, and flickers of emerald in two soft eyes. Her tall ears stood half-raised, polite and deferential, and in the light I could now see a soft black ribbon trailing down the edge of each ear. Such an unusual decoration; later I would know the reason for it, but at the time it was, like everything else about this dancer, a mystery.

Her voice was low. "You called for me, monsieur?"

She spoke well, but with a trace of an exotic accent from the east. I confess that even then I remained foolishly ignorant of Thierry's interest in her, but I found my heart and blood quickening in her presence.

Thierry did not dawdle. "Yes, Niki," he said. "Come here."

She closed the door behind her with a motion so subtle I did not register it. In three easy steps she stood behind our row of seats, her tail held elegantly behind her. "Shall I dance?"

Thierry nodded his head gravely. "Go on."

The fox put her paws together and bowed her head in return. She began a short, compact dance, lifting her legs as the dancers on stage had done, but it was not a can-can dance. Rather, she lifted but did not kick, she turned and pirouetted, her long tail flying after her, and then she did a series of *chaîné* turns, two to the side and then two back, which I would not have thought she had room for in our small box. But she was a small vixen, and though she danced with passion, she kept that passion tightly close to herself, without the wild abandon that had made the solo dancers so breathtaking.

"She's trained in ballet," I murmured.

Thierry merely smiled.

When Niki had finished her dance, I clapped politely. The door opened at that moment to admit another courtesan, a busty ermine. She strode in, letting the door swing shut, and spared hardly a glance for Niki before strutting over to face the jackals. I must confess, I was

"Show him the proper place for his appreciation."

curious about that glance. I thought that perhaps the two did not like each other.

Niki had not even turned, though I saw her ears flick. "Will there be anything else, messieurs?"

"Yes," Thierry said. "Come here."

She stepped forward elegantly, sliding between the seats to stand between us, against the railing behind which the joyful, lustful cabaret still swirled. Her tail hung down beside her leg, the tip marking time to the music that we could hear from below.

"Niki is special," Thierry said to me in a low voice, so that I had to lean closer to hear it. He extracted a paper from the pile he had paid twenty francs for, and handed it to me. "Why don't you show how much you appreciate the dance?"

You will perhaps be interested to know, father, that what Thierry handed me was in effect a one-franc note, an odd thing, but it made sense to me immediately. One could hardly tip a coin into the garters of the dancers, after all, and for the coarser people below, a bank-issued five-franc note would be extravagant; a day's wages for some of them.

Though I had been waiting for this moment, I needed a moment to work up my courage, so I studied the note. For all that this paper would never leave the confines of the cabaret, it was a lovely printing: a red-inked windmill on one side, the dignified mien of La Liberté on the verso, just as though it were a real note from the Banque. At first, the lovely Gallic dove seemed to be telling me "shame, shame, Jean!" But when I looked up into Niki's eyes, the voice of the dove was swallowed by the quiet in those green eyes, and the noise of the musicians and patrons below was as nothing to my ears. I held up the note, La Liberté fluttering uncertainly between us.

"That's not showing," Thierry said with a deep chuckle. "Niki. Show him the proper place for his appreciation."

Niki, without any other outward sign of acknowledgment, no answering chuckle at Thierry's deft turn of phrase nor wry smile at the awkward newcomer, lifted the edge of her skirt to reveal a garter below it, pressed tightly around her thigh, matting the fur around it. I confess that my first thought was that it was a rather large leg to be shapely—the perils of a life of dance. My second was that the garter looked uncomfortably itchy against her sleek and lush coat. We chamois have a fine hide that accommodates tight clothing and straps much more comfortably than some of our predatory friends, of course, but that does not mean that I do not envy them their thick, lovely coats from time to time. I ached, in fact, to undo the garter and run my hands over that soft fur and the hard muscles below it. But I saw, upon a closer look, another note tucked into the garter around the back of the thigh, and I realized only then what Thierry was pressing me to do.

Could I be this naughty? With trembling fingers, I tucked the bill into the garter on the outside of her thigh as gently as I could, attempting to smooth out the fur there. "Thank you, madam," I murmured as I did.

Thierry laughed. "'Madam,' is it? Do you not see why I asked for Niki, even so close, my young friend?"

I frowned. As I have said, the club's drinks were quite strong, and by that point my senses were somewhat distorted. But where I was sitting, my nose barely an arm's length from our courtesan's skirt, I soon became aware of what Thierry meant, a distinction that even in my slightly inebriated state, I could not ignore.

Niki's skirt hung gracefully down her thighs, but her hips did not have quite the arch to them that the ermine, dancing for our jackal companions, did. And in the front, where a gentleman does his best not to be caught staring, there was the slightest suggestion, a merest hint of something there that on any courtesan ought not to be.

I turned to Thierry, and I suppose my eyes were wide, because he said, "Niki?"

Obligingly, Niki lifted the skirt again, higher this time, and father, you must forgive me, but I was unable to look away from the snowy fields of white fur that were thus revealed to my hungry eyes. I drank them in, following the soft inward curve of the thigh up to the black undergarments, where I saw the truth that my nose and eyes had surely been telling me all along. For the undergarments, rather than lying flat to conceal the hidden flower beneath, instead showed the outward curve of a concealed staff, a sheathed and most un-ladylike weapon couched between those lovely legs.

I gasped, and Niki looked down with only a slight arch to *his* eyebrow.

The skirt fell, the performance over. "Will that be all?" His voice was soft, but I should never have thought it female had I not been awaiting a female voice.

His green eyes held me captive. Those sharp predator's teeth, kept sheathed in his velvet muzzle, entranced me. I hungered for the elegance of his dance, to hold it and make it mine, to understand this boy who danced among ladies and passed for one of them. My heart leapt, father, and I was reminded of my Pascal: *Le cœur a ses raisons, que la raison ne connaît point*. What my heart felt in those moments, indeed, had naught to do with reason.

"Dance again for me." I did not say "please," save with my eyes.

Niki stepped toward the open space behind our seats, but I reached out with a hand. I could not bear to have him move away from me again. "Here," I said. "Dance here."

The fox looked at Thierry, who waved with his fingers in the air, a gesture of permission, I suppose. And Niki began to dance.

If seeing him across the seats had been intriguing, seeing him up close was enthralling. In the confined space, he swayed his hips, he cupped the air in front of my face with his paws, he bent his muzzle to come closer to mine. His tail swung around to brush my knees from one side, then the other, a darting, quicksilver serpent that had a life of its own. When he had finished, I fumbled for my purse and found it gone, along with the twenty-franc note that I had intended to spend on a new suit for the soirée at the Justines.

I seized another of Thierry's notes and moved my fingers beneath Niki's skirt. I found the garter and traced it around to the inside of his thigh, and I left the note there, a blue and gold flag planted on that snowy field my eyes had already claimed and my heart longed to hold.

Again, he showed no reaction to my daring. He held my eyes a moment longer and then looked up at Thierry.

"You may go," Thierry said.

Niki bowed. "Thank you, *messieurs*. I hope my performance has been agreeable."

"Very much so. Eh, Jean?"

I could not disengage my tongue from my mouth to answer. A nod was not sufficient to convey the depth of my longing, but it was all I could coax from my enamored body.

And then Niki did a rare and wonderful thing. He smiled, and he reached out to brush my muzzle with a paw. "You are adorable," he said.

He swept past us, his skirts brushing the chairs. Thierry shoved my shoulder as the door closed behind him. "He touched you, little one. Not all boys who wear dresses like other boys, and not all dancers like their patrons, but Niki likes you."

"I want him," I told Thierry, once my tongue was again working. "I must have him. What can I do?"

"Come," he said, and nodded at our companions in the box. The ermine was sitting in the lap of the foremost jackal, swaying her hips. "I believe our friends would appreciate some privacy."

And so it was that Thierry introduced me to M. Oller, and I had my first conversation with the weasel who is the master of the Moulin Rouge. He is a sharp one, with beady, shifty eyes, and he knows the value of the wares he displays. Before we began negotiating for Niki's favors, he made certain that I knew for what I bargained. He did not want any incidents, he said; he was happy to cater to those who wanted their courtesans to be weapons rather than flowers, but he had no desire to surprise anyone. I appreciated this courtesy, and assured him that I valued Niki's concealed treasures. Though I desired them quite strongly, I feared I could not afford the price they would command, both in silver and in the shame that would ensue were I found out. Besides which, as I told you earlier, I had lost my purse in the crowd.

M. Oller, the polecat, quite cannily proposed a solution: he offered me Niki's services free of charge for one night, with the understanding that future nights would be paid at the full rate. I agreed, thinking myself clever because I held back my true intentions, but of course you already know about them, and I suspect M. Oller did too. I regret the fight we had about it, father, the more so because those were the last words that passed between us. I hope you may understand, the more I write, why I came to you with the request I did, and of course why I had no recourse but to take the actions I did thereafter.

Chapter 7

He sits by himself in the changing room while the other dancers shed the uniforms of the cabaret. They talk easily of their night while he prepares his change of clothes.

"A good night, good crowd, n'est-ce pas?"

"How much did you get?"

"Fourteen."

"Not bad, sister! I have twelve."

"Any night we do better than ten is a good night. Marianne, what did you make?"

"She always makes at least twenty."

"Tonight she should have twenty-five!"

"Twenty-four." The graceful hare says it shyly. She is new, but there is no jealousy toward her. When a girl comes to the club who can dance the way Marianne can, she never stays for long, and the other girls cherish this proof of escape and encourage it.

With Jean's twenty-one, Niki has made twenty-nine tonight, an unheard-of total. He fingers the blue and gold surface of the twenty-franc note he got from the young chamois. He has never held twenty francs in his paw all at once, not ever. The note feels flimsy, false, but he does not want to show it to anyone to ask if it is real. He thinks it must be, because the chamois is rich enough to ask for his company for a night, and it was more than just liquor-fueled desire; M. Oller talked to the young antelope afterwards, and told Niki the deal had been concluded. Niki never knows what price is set, because the money goes to M. Oller first. But last time, ten francs came back to Niki, and the other dancers say that at least that much also went to M. Oller.

M. Oller does not keep that much of all the dancers' gratuities; when Niki gives him the nine one-franc notes, M. Oller will give him back eight francs and ten centimes of real money. But because the twenty-franc note is real, Niki does not need to exchange it with M. Oller, and so he will keep it all. More importantly, the other dancers will think he made only nine, and there will be no angry jealousy.

The ermine who came to the same box struts into the changing room, a sheaf of bills held up in her fingers. "Twenty-six, ladies. The predators always pay best."

Unless you are a predator, Niki thinks, and sees the others in the room think the same thing, the wildcat, his friend Cireil the wolf, and the white wolf all flattening their ears, but saying nothing. There is a vixen who dances at the club, a real vixen, but she is not here tonight. The ermine has a predator's teeth, but when she dances, it is with a mouse's coquettish shyness, and she keeps her muzzle closed.

"But did you get a night off?" The other dancers crowd around the ermine. She has been here for three years, longer than almost any of them. For her to be requested for a night would mean that any of them might find a rich patron for one night, two nights, a lifetime.

"They will return tomorrow." The ermine stuffs her money into a small purse and unashamedly strips her uniform off, standing naked in the room.

The girls don't mind Niki seeing them naked, because they know he has no interest in them. They like to watch him, which makes him reluctant to let them. If only they would avert their eyes, he would feel much more at ease.

In any case, tonight he has another secret, and his nakedness does not seem as important next to concealing his money from jealous eyes. So he pulls his skirt down, ignores the lull in conversation, and pulls his pants up. When he changes out of his corset, he spends some time brushing the small false chest he wears on the floor, sliding his fingers along the thin strings that hold it in place over his shoulders and around his back.

"You must appear to be a lady," M. Oller told Niki when he accepted him as a dancer. "Here is what the last boy wore; see if it will fit you." And with some small modifications, it did. Niki supposes that any boys who want to dress as ladies and dance fit a similar physical type.

He has put on his loose shirt and taken the ribbons from his ears when the ermine, now wearing a simple blue dress, comes over to him. "Saw you with the goat," she says.

"He's a chamois." Niki keeps his voice soft.

"Lucky you. How long has it been since a cu-cu came in here?"

"Besides Niki, you mean?" one of the other dancers calls, and there is some laughter.

Cireil comes over to stand beside Niki. "Leave him," she says. "He's a specialist, that's all. More business for the rest of us."

The ermine rolls her eyes, but says, "I shan't dispute that," and she leaves with her twenty-four.

Niki shoves his twenty-nine deep into the pocket of his pants. He looks into the eyes of Cireil, the kindly wolf who has been here nearly three years herself and knows that she will end up in the alleys, not in the parlor of a rich patron. "Do you think he might take you away?" she asks softly.

"Maybe." Niki is reluctant to say it, because if he says it, then it means he believes it. But to say it is to share it with Cireil, and perhaps it will give her some pleasure. He would like that.

Her ears do perk up, and her eyes brighten. "I hope, for your sake." She kisses his nose. "You deserve someone who will treat you well, and I fear there are not many."

"I will accept whatever fate deals me." Niki cannot bear to tell her what is in his heart. He will save that for later, for his dawn return to the only person he can honestly call "friend" in this whole town.

Henri Trounoir is a rat, his fur as black as night. In places, it is spattered with the paints he lives in from waking to sleeping, when he bothers to sleep. His apartment is papered with future masterpieces that slumber, awaiting only recognition to wake them so they may carry Henri to the places he knows he deserves. He sits by the single window in his studio on the foot of his bed, because he cannot afford any other furniture. He would not have oil for his lamp if Niki did not bring him some, siphoned from the lamps of the Moulin Rouge; even so, Henri does not burn the oil until the street lights go out.

The lamp is still burning, though dawn reaches rosy fingers into the room, onto the rat, onto the canvas. Henri paints with desperate fury, or else he stares gloomily at the canvas, brush hovering six inches from it. When Niki lets himself into the studio room, it is the latter state in which he finds Henri. The fox takes a seat quietly on the bed, casting a long shadow onto the floor. But the rising sun lights up his fur with a soft touch. The tip of his tail seems to glow.

Presently, Henri says, "This piece may be my greatest failure yet."

Niki keeps his paws folded in his lap. He looks at the canvas and sees red and gold and white. "The colors look beautiful."

"The colors are always there." Henri heaves a sigh. "It is the art that goes missing." He slashes the brush at the canvas, leaving a scar of red-black. His paws move with grace and ease, guiding the brush exactly as he wishes. To Niki, the strokes of the brush looked wild and random, at first. After more than a year, he has come to see the elegant precision behind them.

"There was a chamois tonight." Niki sees the events unfold in his mind again as he relates them. "He likes…me."

"First an elk, then a chamois. All the horned cu-cus in Lutèce will know about you soon enough."

"The elk brought him." Niki shifts his paws. "He gave me twenty francs."

"Where did he put it?" Henri does not turn.

Niki stares at the painting, feeling again the thick fingers pressing the paper into his underthings, lingering there. He sees the leer on the chamois's face as the fingers grope him. "Just my garter."

"Liar."

"He has money. He wants me for the night." He hears the buzz of the chamois's whisper in his ear again, the litany of things the young antelope wishes to do to Niki's body, the wave of M. Oller's paw summoning him over.

Henri slashes at the painting again. "And you will go with him."

The crumpled twenty-franc note is light, insubstantial in Niki's paws. He does not have to answer, does not have to speak a word.

Henri turns, then, finally. "You would give up your dancing for that? For money?"

"For freedom," Niki says.

"You will not be free with him."

"He could learn to love me."

He feels the weight of Henri's gaze. The rat exhales with a soft wheeze. "Liar."

Niki stands and throws the twenty-franc note to the bed. "To call this 'dance,' what I do, it is like calling the chalkboard at the cafe 'art.' There is no dance for me, not any more. At least there may be love."

"Love." Henri sneers it. "Love is nothing more than our tragic attempt to justify the lust that animates us when we are young. Love is the name we give to the habits we have formed when we are old."

"You needn't repeat that so often." Niki folds his arms and looks up out the window, at the moon.

"So I thought." Henri looks narrowly up at him. "But it seems there may be need after all. Come, chéri, sit. There is love, but not in the way you are thinking of it. Love is between friends, not between sexual partners."

"Can the two never truly meet?" Niki looks down, remaining standing. He is aware of his long, bushy tail, which is warm even in the cool studio, which nearly brushes the floor as it swings back and forth.

"Never, Nikolai my friend. Now come, sit, and I will resume painting you."

Henri takes the canvas from its easel and replaces it with another. Niki strips slowly out of his clothes and sits on the bed, wrapping his tail around in the position he remembered. Henri shifts his position minutely, adjusts the tail, and then sets to painting.

This does not feel as shameful as dancing obscenely in front of the money-waving throng. Niki is not the most popular dancer by any means, but he has felt many paws and hands, claws and callused pads, on his chest and his sides, on his tail and under it, on his thighs and higher up. Being nude and exposed like this for Henri, knowing the rat wants only to look and paint, is relaxing, uplifting. Niki remembers, at times like this, that there is more to the world than *a dance in a cabaret. He notices a spot of red paint on his side, just by his chest, where Henri touched him. I will have to wash that off, he thinks.*

Chapter 8

Sol's radio blared to life with some electronica pop song. He jerked awake and heard the thump of his phone on the carpet. He'd fallen asleep reading again. He stumbled out of bed and scanned the floor until he found the phone. Dead, of course. Sighing, he plugged it in and shuffled out the door to the shower.

The water warmed quickly, and he stepped in, still feeling a little of the dancer in him. His tail wasn't as long, and when he tried to spin in the shower, he was painfully aware of how clumsy he was. No dancer, he, not like Niki. It was funny, that last section of the book being from the fox's viewpoint. Sol must have been really tired, because he barely remembered reading it, but it sure had been intense. And parts of it—stripping clothes off, the image of the naked fox—had been pretty good. He grinned and rubbed a paw down his side, getting the fur wet as he imagined a dancer's curves under his fingers.

A spot on his fur, just to the side of his chest, felt rough against his paw. He looked down and saw, reflected in the light, a patch of red on his side.

Against the black fur, it was barely visible, and it disappeared as soon as he moved his head. He rubbed again with his paw and thought he saw a sheen of red on the pad, but in the shower's light, he wasn't sure. There was definitely some red in the water on the floor; at least, it looked that way when he was standing, but by the time he crouched down to get a better look, the water had washed away any color that was there.

How could he have gotten red on his fur? It didn't smell like blood, and he didn't hurt anywhere that he could be bleeding from. He wiped his paw on the shower wall and saw a faint wash of pink, a bright pink.

What the hell?

The fur around the side of his chest felt slightly sticky. Or was he imagining that? He rubbed at it and the stickiness vanished beneath his paw pads. Had it ever really been there? And where had it come from?

When he got back to his room, towel wrapped around his waist, he rubbed at the bedsheets, but found no red stickiness. He turned his shirt inside out, but the white cotton was unmarred by any red. Then where—

His phone's charging light winked at him from the nightstand. Right—the story. He grabbed the phone and opened the e-book. His claws flicked through the text, back and forth. There was Jean's first glimpse of

Niki, there was his negotiation with M. Oller, and then—on the next page, Jean was talking about being eager to return to the Moulin Rouge.

Had he flipped forward somehow? Sol skimmed the rest of the book. Nowhere did the book switch points of view that he could see. But that wasn't right. It had to be in there. He called the search function and put in—what was the rat's name? Henry Troonoowar?

His claws hesitated over the keys. It was something like that, something like "True-Nwar," but he had no idea how to spell it. How could he have forgotten that? He must have read the word somewhere. How else did he know it? He didn't forget words, not that quickly. So that meant…that meant that he had not actually read the word. He'd only thought it—or rather, Niki had thought it, in a dream, and Sol had *heard* him.

He set the phone down, and sat on the bed, tail curling tightly around his hip. Had that last part of the story been nothing but a dream? The more he thought about it, the more the events felt less like an engrossing book and more as though he himself had experienced them. Sitting on the bed, sweeping his tail around a certain way…his didn't reach as far along as Niki's did, but he remembered the sensation. And the rat had touched him—Niki—right there, on the side of the chest.

Where the red in the shower had been.

Sol's paws began shaking. He clasped them together and pressed them to his stomach. Even against his fur, they felt chilled. His ears flattened and his tail shivered. Either something really weird had happened, or he was hallucinating that something really weird had happened. He wasn't sure which one was worse.

Hallucinations. Meg and her absinthe, the Green Fairy. There was an explanation, a reasonable one. Sol exhaled, relaxed. Meg would be pretty excited, and her vampire fox would be too, though Sol imagined him saying he'd known all along it would work.

He felt silly now, being so freaked out about it. It was probably just that paranoia he'd had all week. Still, it had been a creepy hallucination. The dream had been so real he'd believed it, but clearly he was just making up things about Jean's book.

On the bed, the phone showed the part of the book in which Jean talked about how shy he was placing the money in Niki's garter. In the dream, Niki's memory of the feeling of Jean's thick fingers had been vivid, not in the garter, not shy at all, and the twenty-franc note he said had been stolen had made its way into Niki's paws. Where had those images come from? Sol had felt so connected to Jean during that last part. His heart beat faster when he read about touching the dancer's thigh, finding out he was male…Sol had known he was going to have fantasies about that, but if he'd chosen to have dreams, they would have been considerably different. He would have felt shy and excited, like Jean had written, not bold and crude like the Jean Niki knew. Or that Sol had dreamed Niki knew.

He sat on the bed and closed his eyes, resting his head on his paws. Why had he had that dream in which the bright, wonderful world Jean had written about was sordid and sad? What twisted thing in him needed to turn his fantasies dark?

His mother called from downstairs to ask if he was ready. He jumped off the bed, sending his phone to the floor with another thump. Quickly, he dressed, grabbed his school bag and phone, and ran down to breakfast. Warm grits and sunshine eased his worries about his dreams. He'd had nightmares before, vivid ones in which bands of friends or soldiers were hunting him for being gay. This dream had just been a little more real than those because of the absinthe, that was all. Though the red in his fur had been weird, and still made his fur crawl when he thought about it.

On the bus, he kept rubbing at the spot on his side, tapping his paw until they got to Meg's stop. When she got on, he waved at her and pointed at the empty seat next to him. She just rolled her eyes and kept walking. A small grey wolf sat with Sol instead.

Fine, Sol thought, if she was going to be that way, he wouldn't talk to her until later. He kept pressing his fingers to his chest where the red had been, trying to make it look as though he were simply scratching under his shirt. This turned out not to be a good strategy when the wolf turned and said, "You got fleas or something?"

That snapped Sol's paws back down to his lap for the rest of the ride. The last thing he needed was for someone to start telling the school he had fleas, on top of being a perv who was no longer even as good as a coyote. He stared out the window but did not see any of the houses as they rolled by. His eyes were back in a small artist's studio in Montmartre, with a black rat and a red fox.

Most dreams faded with time. This one became more real the more he thought about it. He did not remember registering the smell of stale tobacco in the dream, but now he felt it in his nose. The textures of the clothing Niki had removed, the sag of the ancient bed under his weight, Sol felt those again overlaying the soft cotton of his own shirt, the firm bus seat.

Sitting in class, he was far too preoccupied with his dream to pay any attention to anything Tanny said. She gave up after a few minutes, leaving him staring at the red fox in front of him and wondering how similar he was to Niki.

Not at all, really. Niki was a dancer, tall and slender, with powerful legs. The red fox in front of him was not overweight, but he wasn't really slender. His tail tip could not properly be called "pure white," either; it had picked up traces from the various grounds it had been dragged across until it was, perhaps, like one of Henri's abstract paintings: a mixture of grey and brown dirt with red clay and highlights of green.

Sol squeezed his eyes shut, but that only brought back the artist's studio, vividly. He pulled out his phone to text Carcy, damn the rules about texting in class, but his phone's weak charge had already run out. He threw the phone into his bag and, with no alternative left to him, focused on the classwork.

By lunchtime, the visions of his dream had lessened, and he chased the remaining fragments away with his new lunchtime problem of how to eat vegetarian at the school cafeteria. When he dressed for practice at the end of the day, they had gone, but not the troubling emotions they'd left behind. Taric snarled at him when he came into the locker room, but Sol barely heard the words on his way to his locker. Only when he undressed, when he glanced down at his bare chest again, did he remember the red spot. He could still feel it even after he'd pulled his shirt on, even though he tried to ignore it.

The fierce determination to not think about the red spot on his fur gave him a desperate focus on the ball. To the surprise of both his coaches and himself, this improved his play. "Nice hustle out there, Sol," Mr. Zerling said as Sol leapt to his side to spear a ground ball.

In the batting cage, the extra focus did not pay off as much, but at least this time Taric was on the other side of the cages and not right next to Sol, so he only intruded on the black wolf's awareness with the occasional crack of a well-hit ball. Sol shut out the rest of the world, focusing only on the ball and his swing, and was surprised to look up after what he thought was only a few minutes to see that everyone but Taric was gone. His muscles were sore, so he shut down his machine and went in, ignoring the coyote as effectively as he'd ignored his dream.

At dinner, his father asked again if he'd stayed later than Taric, but didn't press the issue when Sol said no. There was chicken for dinner, but there was also a large side of red beans and rice, and Sol's father pretended not to notice when Sol didn't take any chicken. After dinner, his mother asked him if that had all been good, and whether he was still hungry.

"I was looking up protein sources on the Internet," Sol said. "I'll send you links."

"But are you still hungry now?"

He shook his head. "I'm full, I feel fine."

"All right." She chewed her lip. "There's cake for dessert. It has butter in it…"

"I can eat butter, Mom." Sol smiled. "I'm not vegan. Anyway, you made the beans and rice with butter, right?"

She shook her head slowly. "Olive oil. I didn't know…the Finches don't eat butter or cheese."

Did Carcy? Sol had never really asked. He just knew the ram didn't eat meat. Adding butter and cheese to his list of forbidden foods would create a whole new set of puzzles at lunchtime. He'd had cheese on a sandwich just today. "No, I think that's fine. I'm going to do homework now."

"You're not going over to Meg's?"

He paused, his tail curling and uncurling. "I…not tonight. I have a lot of stuff to do."

"Did you two fight?"

"No." He shook his head fast. "I just, I have a lot of reading to do on my own. She gave me books."

The first thing he did when he got upstairs was check his plugged-in phone. There were no messages, not from Carcy nor from Meg, so he texted Carcy to ask if the ram ate butter or cheese. Then he pulled up Meg's number, composing and discarding messages to her in his head. If he told her he'd had a dream and it had freaked him out, she would laugh. If he told her about the red spot, she would tell him he was imagining things. And while he wanted to believe that, he didn't think he could convey how eerie it had been in just a text message. He would tell her about the dream next time he went over, he decided.

So he might as well do some research. He flopped down on the bed and pulled up his e-reader. His claw hesitated over "Confession." Echoes of the dream swirled in his head. He chose one of the free books Meg had suggested and opened that. Reading about the trends in the art world at the time van Gogh was painting was not nearly as thrilling as reading about Jean's visit to the Moulin Rouge, but Sol wasn't worried it would give him crazy dreams.

It wasn't until he was yawning and putting the phone aside to go brush his teeth that he realized that Carcy had never texted him back.

Chapter 9

The next morning, his mother had made eggs and sausages, and though she had only put toast and eggs on his plate, his father scraped a sausage next to them without asking. Sol didn't say anything, just ate around it, and bore the scowl on his father's muzzle when he took the sausage and dumped it into the garbage disposal.

Even though he hadn't dreamed, he'd woken feeling more anxious about his dream, aching to talk to someone about it. He didn't want to annoy Carcy, but the ram had a calm, stable voice, and Sol hadn't heard it in a while. And Carcy hadn't answered him last night; that would be a good excuse to call. So he called on the way down to the bus stop, stopping a short distance away from the opossums.

The ram's voice, deep and smooth, sounded just a little hurried. "Hi, Solly. I gotta hop in the shower in a minute. What's up?"

"Oh, just…" Sol sighed. "You didn't answer me last night. About the butter."

Carcy laughed. "Hon, don't worry about the butter. It'll all be fine. That all?"

"N-no."

He could hear Carcy moving around, the rustle of cloth. "I'm getting in the shower, Sol. Look, call me back later, okay?"

"I had a weird dream!" The words tumbled out of him. He clutched his side and rocked back and forth.

"Last night?"

"Uh, no." Last night had been mercifully free of dreams, this morning free of strange paint spots on his fur. "The night before."

"Well, write up an e-mail and tell me about it, 'kay? I need to go or I'll be late for work."

"Okay…" Sol sighed. It was silly, and he was acting like a kid. "Sorry. I don't mean…"

"It's not a problem, Solly. Just write it up and we'll text about it tonight, right?"

"Right, right." He pressed the phone to his ear.

He thought there'd been another male voice there in the background, but it was gone and there was only silence until the ram's voice came back, loudly. "Love ya, Sol."

"Yeah." He flicked his ears back toward the opossum cousins, who were quieter than usual. "Me too."

If the possums had heard him talking, they didn't let on. They got on the bus ahead of him and headed for the back while Sol sat in his usual spot. He stared out the window and wondered who else might be at Carcy's place at seven-thirty in the morning. The ram said he lived alone, but had made no secret of his active dating life. But Sol had always thought that no matter what happened on a date, the date wouldn't sleep over. That was silly, he thought. What if they stayed up late, or had been drinking, and it wasn't safe to drive?

Did that mean that Carcy didn't love Sol? They'd never even seen each other in real life (not counting webcam pictures). If Sol didn't live in a smallish town where everyone knew each other, and where nobody else was gay, it might be okay for him to date, too. He was more worried that if Carcy had someone else living with him, he would be less enthusiastic about Sol moving in. Sol would have to make him see that he wouldn't be any trouble, and eventually it would have to work out. The fact that he'd called Carcy when he was stressed and needed someone counted for something, didn't it? What he felt whenever he talked to the ram, that wouldn't go away, and he knew that it would end happily.

His mind returned to Jean and Niki, how Jean had written about the beauty of Niki and the love he felt, and how Niki had heard Jean talking about his body. But of course, that last thing had been in a dream, not in the book. In any case, Niki's belief in love from the dream, that was what Sol felt when he thought about Carcy. He thought Carcy felt about him the way Jean had written about Niki; at least, that's what the ram had said to him in the past. Sol wouldn't know until they had a chance to talk in person; their talks over texts and even over the phone always felt too constrained; his flowery e-mails had gotten only short, appreciative responses.

Sol shifted in his seat, leaning his head against the glass and inhaling the floral chemical scent of the sanitizer, strong enough to obscure the other students' scents. He wanted more than anything for the bus to keep going, past the houses and out into the fields, onto the highway, past rest stops and across the state border, up to the smoky industrial outskirts of Millenport, past the football stadium and into the inner city where Carcy's apartment was. He wanted to run up the stairs to knock on the door and run into the ram's arms, and leave school and his parents behind. He wanted to feel the ram's love for him, strong arms around him and the warmth of Carcy's breath on his cheek ruff. He wanted to know Carcy's scent.

But of course, the bus stopped at the school, and even though Sol waited until most of the other kids had gotten off, until the bus driver said,

"Hey, wake up," the bus did not magically take him to Millenport. The only breath on his cheek ruff was the chill breeze of morning, scurrying along the golden bricks of the school to greet him.

He slouched along the tile floors to homeroom, and from there through the rest of the day. Again, he stayed late for practice, even though Friday nights were optional. Taric, of course, was practicing, as was about half the team. Nothing had changed, not even, Sol felt, his skill level. He had tried to recapture the brief moment of focus he'd felt the day before, but now Carcy had pushed the dream out of the forefront of his concerns, and he found himself daydreaming as much as he ever had.

Taric, now, was working harder than ever to show him up. Every time Sol fielded a ball and threw to a base, the coyote's next throw came to the same base, quicker and harder. Twice Taric leaped in front of Sol to cut off a ground ball, snapping it up like it was his first meal in days.

Sol stewed. *The next time he tries that, he thought, I'll jump right into him.* But the next time it happened, Taric leapt in front of Sol and knocked him backwards, scooping the ball up smoothly. The coyote pivoted and threw to first with a snap of the wrist, then trotted back to his position. The fox and the other coyote applauded, but others, including Xavy and the other wolves, looked away. Coach called out, "Good hustle, Taric, but let's be a team player."

"Sure, Coach," Taric said, but when he took his position beside Sol again, he said, softly, "I am. *I'm* playing with the team."

Sol flattened his ears. At least he wasn't being humiliated in front of a large crowd. The cheerleaders weren't even out; they had indoor practice on Fridays. And there were no other students watching, or at least, that's what he thought at first. As he trotted in from fielding to go to the batting cages, he saw a red fox and a mink chatting at the base of the bleachers that surrounded the field. Losers, he thought. Bad enough I have to play baseball on Friday night, but they have nothing better to do than watch?

For the third day in a row, he and Taric were the last ones left at the batting cages. Sol was tempted to stay until sunset, just to see how late Taric would stay, but his mother had already warned him that they were going out to dinner and that she would come by to pick him up at 5:30 sharp. When Sol went back in to clean up, Taric was still standing in the batting cage, stroking line drives out to the field with cracks like wooden boards snapping in two.

Taric's passion was baseball, Sol thought, and for the first time in hours, he recalled his dream. Niki had a passion for dance, and Henri had painting. That was one of the strongest emotions left over from his dream, that sense of purpose, even though in Niki's case it was a frustrated sense. Sol just did not feel like baseball was his purpose, not any more, not with how he'd drifted away from the rest of the team. If he worked at it, he might recapture that feeling of purpose, but it was clear to him that he would have to do it alone, without his teammates' support.

He doubted his father would accept "baseball is not my purpose" as an excuse for not regaining his starting spot. So he would just have to make it his purpose for the next month. Starting Monday, he vowed, he would stay later than Taric every day if he had to.

When he got home, his mother hurried him to dress up, and it wasn't until he was in the back of the car, leaning against the window, that it occurred to him to ask who dinner was with. And when his mother told him "the Norstons," he didn't immediately connect his father's work colleague Mrs. Norston with his teammate Xavy Norston, even though they'd gone to numerous events together. He did not process the connection, in fact, until they were walking up to the restaurant, and then Sol stopped dead.

Unless he stuck fingers down his throat to make himself sick right there on the sidewalk, he didn't think there was any way he could get out of the dinner. So he greeted Xavy with a nod and sat at the table, glad that his shirt was long-sleeved so he couldn't pull at the fur of his arm when his paw went there reflexively. Fortunately, Xavy seemed about as uncomfortable as he was, especially when baseball was brought up.

Sol's father, for one, kept talking about how well Xavy and Sol worked together, kept asking Sol if he was watching Xavy in practice. Sol, painfully aware that this was a roundabout way of telling Xavy to watch out for him, made one-word affirmations and desperately wished for a change of subject. Mr. Norston picked up on the theme, but as he joined the conversation, it became painfully clear that he had not been told about Sol's demotion.

They managed to avoid the subject until Mr. Norston raised his glass of white wine to the "wolves anchoring the infield"—Xavy played third base—at which point Sol's ears, flat against his head, were as warm and uncomfortable as he could stand. He couldn't respond, and his father didn't raise his glass.

The table went silent, while everyone looked at Sol and his father, and neither of them spoke. Finally Xavy had to be the one to tell his father that Sol had lost his starting spot, and to whom.

"A coyote?" Mr. Norston said it loud enough for other tables to turn around and look. Sol cringed.

"He's really good," Xavy said. "College good, coach says."

"I understand he doesn't have much but baseball in his life," Sol's father said. "It's hard to compete with someone when that's the only option they have in life. Sol here is going to college one way or another. Computer science," he said proudly.

"Yeah." Sol had no idea what computer science was going to mean, just that it was a degree that made someone "employable" and involved computers, which he liked well enough.

"Sure," Mr. Norston said. "That's tough luck he plays your position, son. Them 'yotes from the trailers, when they see an opportunity, they grab after it with both paws. Don't have packs to consider—barely got families, at that. You just be thankful you got a good family."

Sol mumbled a thanks, picking at the fur on the back of his paw under the long sleeve of his shirt. Sol's father laughed a fake, forced laugh. "Sol's still gonna grab the starting spot back. Just gonna be a little harder than he thought. I'm workin' with him, though. We're going to hit grounders and all." He'd offered this the day before, and Sol's noncommittal noise had apparently been taken as acceptance.

"Xavy'll help too, won't you?" Mr. Norston said. Xavy nodded with what Sol thought was at least a little actual agreement.

Of course, it was at that moment that the waiter brought the four steaks and the two plates of steamed vegetables. It didn't matter that Sol's mother had ordered the same thing; all eyes on the table were on Sol. Xavy, who'd stood up for him, stared at the vegetables as if Sol had ordered garbage brought in from the dumpster in the alley and heaped on his plate.

"Is that…all you're having?" Mr. Norston stared down at the broccoli, the carrots, the cauliflower.

Sol attacked his vegetables with a fork. "I'm not hungry for steak."

"Are you feeling all right?" Mrs. Norston leaned across the table. "Your ears have been flat all night."

The scrutiny of so many eyes was making his stomach hurt and his tail curl more tightly against himself. "I'm fine."

"Doctor's orders," his father cut in. "Sol was suffering from fatigue and itching. Doctor thinks it might be additives in meat—chemicals, you know, hormones, that stuff in the news—so we're cutting out meat except the organic stuff we get at home. It's a pain, but…" He gave a whatcha-gonna-do shrug. "We got protein supplements and all."

"Sorry to hear that," Mr. Norston said. "Hey, once you get that crap flushed outta yer system, you'll get that starting spot back lickety-split."

Xavy's muzzle bore that mix of curiosity and pity that was reserved for classmates with weird medical conditions, like the bobcat with the tic in his shoulder, or the asthmatic field mouse. Sol acknowledged the other wolf's look and then bent to the business of finishing his plate of vegetables.

It was less awkward, if not much, to hear the Norstons give the topic of baseball a wide berth for the rest of the meal. By the time it was over, Sol was aching to do his homework. They made it through dinner with no more awkwardness, and things were going well even as they all left the restaurant. Then Mr. Norston turned as his family was heading toward their car, and said, "Bring some of those organic steaks to the barbecue tomorrow. We'll toss 'em on the grill so Sol here can eat."

"Oh," Sol's father said. "Good idea."

But his brow had lowered, and his fangs showed over his scowl, and those were the last words he said all the way home. Sol texted Carcy about the awkwardness of the dinner from the back of the car, and in the middle of those texts he got a message from Meg asking if he had looked at her images or read any of her books yet. He ignored it until he got home, when she called him. He ran up to his room to take the call.

"Hey, woofer." She only called him that when she was annoyed.

"Sorry, I've been, uh, practicing baseball."

"At nine at night?"

"You said you'd do this on your own if you have to."

"Do I have to?"

He flopped back on his bed. "Sorry. No, look, I…" He searched for things to say. "The absinthe, uh…"

"Oh, God. You with your fucking purity-of-body thing. It's no worse than beer, I told you."

The dream. He wanted to tell her, but her irritation put him off. "No, no. I mean, yes, but…"

"Come over. I'm bored out of my fucking skull and everything on TV sucks."

He sighed. "Go to a movie."

"They all suck too. Come on. We don't have to do the absinthe again. I'll make, fuck, I dunno, s'mores or something."

That made him laugh. "When was the last time you made s'mores?"

"Girl scouts, seventh grade," she said promptly. "I used cardboard instead of graham crackers and Mrs. Cartinson burned the fur off the back of her paw trying to put the fire out."

"Is that why you got kicked out?"

She paused. "No, I got kicked out because I stood up at the meeting and asked why we were perpetuating an organization built to serve a fascist dictatorship, and Mrs. Beecham said that we were serving this country now, and I said that's what I meant."

In that moment, Sol loved Meg too much for secrets. "I had a weird dream I need to tell you about," he said. "I'll be over in twenty minutes."

She listened to his dream attentively when he got there, and glared at him when he'd finished telling it. "Fucker," she said. "You got awesome absinthe dreams and all I got was a headache."

The spot on his chest started to itch again. "It was really vivid," he said. "I still felt like it was going on when I woke up, a bit. I never had a dream like that before."

"Yeah, some drugs'll do that. Did you write it down?" He shook his head. Meg got the absinthe bottle out of her desk drawer. "Why the hell not?"

"I dunno." He rubbed at his chest. "It's just a dream. I want to write, y'know, my story." Like the ones he'd read online.

"Whatever. It'll be awesome for the project. Let me just get some glasses from the kitchen, and we'll be set." She got up.

Sol squinted at the green liquid, sloshing against the sides of the bottle as Meg set it down. It looked frenetic, anxious to escape. "I'm not drinking any more."

"Oh, don't be such a Sandra Dee." Meg rolled her eyes as she walked past him. Her fur glistened and she smelled strongly of pool water.

"Because I'm gay." His heart still quickened when he said it, even though he knew he was safe with Meg. "That's great. Thanks."

At the door of her bedroom, she turned and rolled her eyes. "Sandra Dee was the purity-purepure white mouse from the fifties, remember? Didn't drink?"

"Yeah, but still…"

"Oh, smooth your panties." Meg grinned at him. "*That* one was because you're gay." She slipped out the door with a flick of her thick tail that sent water drops at his face.

Sol folded his arms and fumed, and when Meg returned, he shook his head. "I'm not drinking it."

She set the goblets out and lit an incense burner on her dresser again. "You're letting me do all the work on this project, so you're damn well going to have dreams if that's all you're contributing. And you're going to include them in the project, too."

He bit his lower lip. She was doing most of the work, and all he was doing was reading a book, and not even one of the ones she'd told him to read. "I, uh, I have to go to this barbecue tomorrow…"

"Sol." Meg put her paws on her hips and faced him. "Come on, just do this with me, okay? If I can't have awesome dreams, I at least want to hear about yours."

But if he told her how much the spot of paint had freaked him out, she would laugh at him again. She would tell him he needed to try more drugs, and then a simple absinthe hangover hallucination wouldn't get to him.

A simple hangover hallucination. But it had felt so real. Of course, he'd never had a hallucination before. Maybe they felt like that. Maybe it really was like in cartoons, where the people who were dying of thirst in the desert imagined palm trees and water and beautiful oryx ladies (or guys) in robes.

He got out his phone and texted Carcy. *Should I have more absinthe?*

"Hey." Meg looked sideways at him, setting up the candles on her dresser. "Save the sexts for after."

Of course, without him having typed up his e-mail to the ram, Carcy had no context for understanding why he was asking. If it hadn't been for that spot of paint, Sol would have been happy to take another drink, chance another dream. The exquisite sadness that Niki felt, bright and bitter, was a purer emotion than any of Sol's muddled feelings about his own life. And the shy confidence with which Jean went about his life, not to mention his devotion to his father, were things Sol envied. It wasn't that he didn't want to write about them because they weren't interesting. He didn't want to write them because they were too personal.

The young wolf's thumb hesitated over the "Off" button, then slid up to the e-reader. It opened "Confession" to his last bookmark.

why I had no recourse but to take the actions I did thereafter.

"Didn't some famous guy go to jail for being gay, back in the eighteen-hundreds?"

The candles flickered, throwing shadows over the walls and ceiling. Meg poured absinthe into the goblets. "Couple guys did. Don't worry, though. Here they'll just throw stones at you."

"Or baseballs, at the barbecue."

"Bring some broccoli." She placed a sugar cube over the absinthe spoon. Water streamed down from the glass, dripping onto her paw and desk. She ignored the spill.

"I'll just eat beforehand and then I won't be hungry. I can have some potato salad."

"What if they put beef in it?"

"Don't be stupid."

She half-turned, smiling. "Your whole vegetarian thing is stupid.

Here."

He took the goblet she handed him. "Oh, and this 'gift from the Green Fairy' isn't?"

"It's an old tradition, so shut up and drink."

He lowered his ears. Meg just drank from her glass without any of the pomp and ceremony of the first time, and she didn't appear to be enjoying it very much. Sol lifted the anise to his lips and sipped, then took a larger drink. The bitterness flooded his mouth, stronger than he remembered, but leaving the same tingle on his tongue and in his throat.

They sat in the quiet, surrounded by the flickering candles and the smells of incense. Sol found his mind turning back to the red and gold of the cabaret, Niki dancing in the box. He could still see the leering chamois in Niki's memory from his dream.

His phone lit up with a message indicator, but his e-reader was still on the screen.

the actions I did thereafter.

"Thanks for the absinthe," he said. "Thank your vampire fox friend."

"I did." Meg wasn't looking at her computer, or at anything in particular.

"Glad we got to do this project." Sol rubbed a thumb across the screen of his phone without turning it on.

"Gives you something to take your mind off the mindless drone of baseball?"

"And everything else." Sol smiled. "But I just like working with you."

"Oh, God." Meg rolled her eyes, but smiled back. "Don't even start with me."

He looked at his message, finally. Carcy'd texted, *More, but not too much.*

Love you, he tapped back, and then took another long drink. The liquor and anise burned, but the strong sensation felt invigorating. "I think I'm actually starting to like this stuff."

"I don't have that much left," Meg said. "Two, maybe three more drinks. Should get us through the next week, right?"

"That's all?" Sol's ears flattened. "Maybe we should slow down."

The otter shrugged, finishing her drink. "My friend made it specially for us for the project."

Sol eyed his glass, but couldn't bring himself to be worried. "Made it?"

"Well, added something to the store-bought stuff. He wouldn't tell me what. Point is, it's for this project, so we should finish it for the project. If you just want a buzz, schnapps is cheaper and tastes better."

"I…" Sol struggled for words. "I feel different with this stuff."

Meg pointed a finger at him, goblet still in her paw. "Tell you what. Write me an epic poem and I'll get him to make us another bottle. Hell, even write me a good poem."

"All—all right." Sol finished his as well, feeding the warmth in him. He couldn't stop smiling. "It's a deal."

"Yeah, right." Meg snorted. "Stop smiling like that, you're creepin' me out. C'mere and look at some art."

She pushed her laptop open as he scooted his chair over to her desk. She was warm and her scent came to him between the frankincense and the anise, comforting and friendly. It wasn't anything like the guys in the locker room, the athletic male scent he imagined when he was texting Carcy. It was the scent of friendship and camaraderie, so familiar he wondered why he hadn't appreciated it more before now. "You smell good," he said.

She squinted sideways at him. "You're gonna lose your gay cred if you keep that up."

His ears flattened down and he ducked his muzzle again. "Sorry," he mumbled.

Meg didn't say anything more about it. He sneaked a glance at her expression in between paintings and thought she looked a little sorry. Of course she wouldn't say anything if she were. But maybe she was just focused on the paintings.

They were beautiful, ranging from delicate traceries of flowers and pastoral country scenes to busy city nights, splashes of color fighting in dark shadows. Two of the paintings featured windmills, but none the Moulin Rouge. Still, when Sol looked harder, he spotted it everywhere: in a four-petaled red flower, a reflection in a window, in a pinwheel of red smeared across a line of yellow lights. "Amazing," he murmured.

"Yeah, some of those guys were pretty fucked up." Meg lingered over one picture, a portrait of a female otter in a maid's dirty cotton dress looking out a window. The room she was in was dark, and the window bright. The otter's expression in the picture was hard to read. Sol thought she looked sad, until Meg said, "I like this one. She's totally like, fuck those people out there."

And out in one corner of the window, Sol glimpsed a line of red: a sail of the Moulin Rouge. "Right," he said.

"There was this whole other culture," Meg said. "I mean, the artists all did their thing inside and only a few people appreciated them. Most of them died unrecognized."

"She's a maid," Sol said.

Meg made an exasperated noise. "It's symbolic. You see the easel in the corner? The paintings?"

"I thought she was cleaning up after the artist."

"She is the artist. It's a statement on how art was seen as a service industry then. Artists were commissioned to do paintings the way you would pay someone to clean your bathroom. The ones who didn't want to take commissions starved."

"Unless they had friends to bring them lamp oil," Sol murmured. In his imagination, the lamp oil was a bright, glowing green.

"What?"

"Nothing." He itched to pick up the story of Jean again. Through the happy haze of absinthe, the dream now seemed exciting, not scary at all. He would photograph himself tonight, he decided, and then in the morning he could see if any spots had appeared during the night.

When Meg got to the point where she wanted to light up again ("it's Friday night!"), Sol took off for home. On Friday, his curfew was later, and he was able to wander down by the lake side instead of heading straight back to tension over his diet and now, maybe, hitting grounders. When his phone beeped with a message, he sat on a bench to answer Carcy's text, but it was the same message from before: *More, but not too much.* When he closed the message, his e-reader app was up, open to "Confession."

Sol shook his head. Stupid glitchy messaging. He looked out over the lake, where the moon's reflection glimmered, then down to his phone to read.

Chapter 10

The testimony of that loathsome badger has now painted the small boarding-house near Courcelles where I passed my first night with the dancer as a flea-ridden cesspool where only the most depraved acts take place. Despite the hotel manager's crude accounts of what he heard and smelled, I assure you that the feelings that passed between us that night were the most transcendent and sublime that I have ever experienced. Niki and I shared feelings, dreams, ambitions. I told him how lovely his dancing was, and he complimented me on my facility with words and charming turns of phrase, which I assure you I gave you all due credit for.

Apart from my sadness at the gulf that yawns between us, father, my greatest regret is that the promise of that night, a shining boulevard lined with the most fragrant flowers down which Niki and I both saw a life fulfilled, remains unwalked. That night, my spirit soared with a kindred soul for the first time, and boundless worlds I had never thought myself fit to enter opened their arms to me.

Minon, though he has refused to speak on my behalf, could testify to my joy that night, for I summoned him to meet Niki. I am certain that seeing himself replaced so soon in my affections, and to such superior satisfaction, will color his recollection of that night, but there is nobody else who witnessed the joy we found in each other. Indeed, I recall that Minon was not terribly pleased that night, his eyes more than a little green at the sight of our happiness. But such is his jealous and spiteful nature, and father, should he be persuaded to give his account, I beg you hold that in your consideration of his words.

Once Minon had left, Niki also insisted upon returning to his home, no matter how I begged him to stay for just one more hour, one more minute, one more second. I promised him that I would see him again, for longer than just one night. I promised him freedom from the life of dancing if he wanted it, I promised him a life of luxury—rash promises, yes! But I was so moved by the spirit of love that I would have promised him to hold the moon in the sky for his pleasure, I would have promised to stop the Seine in its course, I would have promised anything had only his dear muzzle, his soft paws but lingered one moment longer—

But I did promise to spare you details. I speak with the voice of my heart, and I hope you will hear its plea.

Once he had left, I sat in quite a blue mood. My heart had made promises and I was determined to see them through. I pride myself on my persistence, which you in the past have labeled thick-headed stubbornness. In the end, it was Minon's visit that inspired me, which I am sure he would gain no pleasure from knowing. He had made a remark on his departure wishing me well with the newest companion in my squalid closet. And so, I thought to myself, a creature as beautiful as Niki should not have to remain hidden so. It was then that I resolved to take him to the ball the Justines were to give. With an attractive, exotic fox on my arm, one who was practiced at passing for female, there would be no need to hide my affection. It would be acceptable, even encouraged in high society for once. I hoped, father, that you would be proud of me.

Thierry found me that morning at our usual cafe, and when I had explained my idea, he offered me whatever help he could provide. I wish to stress that although he did accompany me to Les Halles to shop for a suitable dress for Niki, he urged caution and restraint with every step we took. Too well he recognized the headstrong nature of a heart in love, and reined in my wilder impulses. I thought that a diamond brooch would look elegant on my fox's shoulder, but Thierry reasonably argued that the two hundred francs would be better spent to improve the quality of the dress and my suit.

Of course we did not spend that much money, father, although Thierry did provide some assistance to my weakened purse. I promised to repay him as I was able from the generous allowance you provide.

(I request, father, that should you care nothing for my fate, should I be consigned to prison and unable to repay Thierry, that at least you uphold the family honor and make my debt to him just.)

We spent a full day choosing a dress for Niki, and part of the next choosing the perfect accessories for him to be the most stunning consort at the ball. I confess that much of the time spent was my fault; giddy with delight, I could not choose between gowns. At each one I paused to imagine my darling's russet shoulders and cream-colored throat framed by peach-colored silk or crimson voile, wide lace frills or velvet folds, his slender hips accented by a soft curve of taffeta or satin, his tail showing through the split at the back of the dress.

Having finally chosen the dress (and I think you will agree, whatever you think of Niki, that the dress was the perfect frame for that work of art), we had to select a suit that would make me look no less striking than my consort. It was here that Thierry's tailor showed his value. I know that you did not think much of my striking white suit and crimson tie, which was colored to match the crimson dress we chose for Niki, but this fisher marten knows the latest fashions, and this summer, the waist-cut coat with black trim will be seen in all the best gatherings.

I tell you all this, father, so that you will understand my feelings and my state of mind after meeting Niki. For two days, I could think of little else but walking into the ball with him on my arm. Once we had the clothes, all that was lacking to me was my fox, and so on the following day, I returned to the Moulin Rouge to collect him.

Once Thierry and I stepped onto the streets of Montmartre again, the joy in life of those bohemians overwhelmed me. I had dressed more appropriately for the cabaret on this night, with a casual pair of trousers and the old blazer you may recall from my childhood. The crowd outside the red windmill welcomed me more openly, whether joyful from the soft weather and the spring breeze or simply judging me by the clothes I wore. I danced with two of them before Thierry pulled me inside.

I took deep breaths of the incense. Though I was hardly a seasoned visitor to the club, the warmth of its magic greeted me like an old friend. I had dreamed about it, replayed the memory countless times. And yet, the featured dancers were paler than before, their kicks and struts less exceptional, the sensuality less stirring. I found Niki in the line of dancers at the back of the stage and watched instead the precise elegance with which he moved, the small flourishes that nobody else was watching, that none of the other dancers matched. I marveled at how I could have missed such a beauty on my first visit, even distracted as I was by the opulence and spectacle.

Our box was shared by a pair of skunks in white blazers and stylish top hats; and a motley party of a mouse, a rabbit, and a fox dressed in an assortment of waistcoats and ascots. We sat at the same edge of the box as we had the previous time, and Thierry allowed me to gesture down to M. Oller for Niki. My heart quickened when the curtain of the box shifted, and Niki came again to dance for us.

This time, the other patrons of the box turned their eyes to him as well, not knowing, of course, the secrets he concealed under his dress. This time, I bought my own stack of Moulin Rouge one-franc notes, so that I might at every opportunity show my appreciation. Certainly he was emboldened by our night together, for he was far less reluctant to give me a kiss between the ears at every note I tucked against the soft white fur of his inner thigh. His beautiful black-ribboned ears flicked toward me, his emerald eyes gleamed in the warmth of the lamps. The fox seated behind me had the effrontery to lean forward, his black paw outstretched with a one-franc note of his own in it. I took the note and placed it in Niki's garter myself, quieting his objection with a glare.

By the time Niki finished his dance, it made no difference which side of his skirt he lifted; both garters bulged with notes. I whispered as he left that I would see him the following night, that I had a surprise for him. The lights of the club and the sensual beauty of the portraits on the walls were nothing to the lights in his eyes and the sensual beauty of his smile. His tail brushed my shoulder, and then he was gone. But I knew, I knew, it was only for a short time.

Sol's ears ached with the chill of the spring evening. How long had he been reading? He put down the phone and stared out over the lake. The warmth of the absinthe lingered in his stomach, in his chest, and his muzzle almost hurt from smiling. Reading Jean's devotion, Sol had pictured the chamois as a ram, curled horns rather than short stubby ones. His tail wagged, thumping against the bench.

The shine of the moon on the lake broke in the ripples from the breeze, splintering into shards of moonlight. Crickets chirped softly, and the stars glittered across the sky. Sol put his phone away, rubbed warmth into the fur on his arms, and got up to walk home.

He'd pulled the covers over his head when he remembered that he was going to photograph himself. So he got up groggily and turned his light on, then snapped pictures of himself with his phone. It occurred to him when he was just crawling into bed again that he should probably take his boxers off for the pictures, because after all, Niki had been naked for the portrait, and besides, the idea gave him a little thrill when he thought of it. So he slipped out of bed, turned the light on again, and took another series of pictures, this time with his boxers around his ankles. He reached down to pull them up, paused to look at the door. It had been years since his mother had come in to wake him in the morning. He'd slept naked only once before, when they were away. Why not now?

Boldly, he kicked the boxers into his dirty clothes pile and then climbed into bed, lying on his stomach. The fabric of his sheets, warm and rougher than his boxers, rubbed nicely against those usually-covered areas. Sol squirmed pleasantly, tail swishing back and forth over his bare rear. Did Carcy sleep naked? When Sol was with him, would they lie together like this and fall asleep without any clothes between them? The thought made his tail wag faster. He wanted to smell the ram next to him, but for now there was only wolf.

Chapter 11

It is harder to conceal the pile of one-franc notes from the other dancers than it was to conceal Jean's twenty. They seem to multiply; every time he thinks he's pulled them all from his garter, more fall to the floor. The ermine is once again monopolizing the attention of the others with her twenty-three, over small cups of coffee. But Cireil, of all the dancers, sits near Niki and sees the paper doves flutter like snow to the ground, light against the fox's black paws.

"He likes you, eh?" the wolf smiles.

"He appreciates me." His behind is sore, but it is no worse than he has known at other times, and not so bad he cannot sit.

Cireil nods. "One night already, and more on the way, yes?"

"I really don't know." Niki has gotten most of the bills into his purse, and the smell of such concentrated money is strong, musky, and not altogether pleasant. The bills are certainly not cleaned every night. Even so, he will exchange them with M. Oller later. Henri is close to finishing the portrait, and Niki is anxious to see him. He has enough money from Jean's twenty left over that he can afford to wait.

"It is not so bad." Cireil puts a paw on Niki's wrist. He flinches; it is also sore, from the ropes. Cireil notices but does not understand. "Do not scorn the man who will lift you from the gutter, even should he place you behind glass."

"Behind glass?" The ermine turns, laughing. "The only glass we will be behind is the store windows, looking longingly in. Where is our little cu-cu going to shop?"

"Nowhere." Niki hurries to close his purse, but it is too late.

The ermine's tone sharpens to a needle point. "What is all that? Where did you get that?"

"I danced for it."

Cireil breaks in. "He has a patron, who takes him to a private box."

Before Niki can stop her, the ermine has snatched his purse and opened it. "Sacré Dieu!" One-franc notes drift to the floor. "Twenty-five? More?"

"Twenty-six," Niki says.

The ermine drops the purse to the ground. The other dancers stare with green tinging their eyes. "You are not worth twenty-six," the ermine says.

"And where is a rich patron going to find another boy so pretty as our Niki?" Cireil demands.

"Any street down by the Pont-Neuf." The ermine stares down. "It is not right for these deviants to have so much money."

Niki feels increasingly uncomfortable, singled out. He can spare three francs; Jean will give him more on their next night, if he asks. So he takes three bills and holds them up for the ermine.

"I do not need your charity." The ermine sniffs.

"It is for all you have done to help me."

Cireil is shaking her head. But the ermine reaches down and takes the bills in the hand that is not holding her café au lait. "It is nice to have one's work recognized," she says loftily. She turns away, gathers the other dancers about her, and soon they are engaged in a loudly merry conversation.

"She will be expecting it from now on," Cireil says softly. "You now tithe to her and M. Oller both."

"I will not be here much longer." Niki folds the rest of the notes into his purse. He looks at the ermine and wishes for a moment that he could overturn her coffee all over her soft white fur, to stain it brown.

Cireil reaches out and touches Niki's muzzle. "We have all thought that at one time or another."

"He says he loves me," Niki whispers, and even though he is trying to be hopeful, he cannot keep the rest of the truth from tumbling over his tongue. "But only with his words."

Cireil is a good friend. "That is better than not saying it at all," she whispers back.

She does not ask if he believes it.

Henri does not ask it either, when Niki returns home with a warm loaf of bread from the bakery down the street, fresh from the ovens. Dawn is still no more than an idea on the horizon, but Henri is awake, sketching in the silver moonlight. His painting is taking shape, a dark cloud of leaves overshadowing a female mouse reclining, her arm up to shield herself from the leaves. He describes the leaves with quick stabs of charcoal, but for the mouse he uses touches so delicate that Niki marvels that they leave traces on the canvas at all.

Niki leaves the bread on the bed next to Henri. The black rat appears to take no notice of it, so absorbed is he in his painting. "It's beautiful," Niki says, eating the bread he took for himself. The warm crust gives a satisfying crunch between his teeth; the warmer interior is soft and delicious.

"Bah. The Dutchman could paint something twice as beautiful in half the time."

"Could have," Niki points out. "No longer."

"Death comes for us all." The rat says it as easily as he might comment upon the weather.

Niki sighs. "One need not be reminded of it so often."

"Chéri," Henri says, "I am only trying to make you feel at home."

Niki stretches his mouth into a smile, back along his slender muzzle. "Then you should beat me and tell me I will never be of significance in the world."

"You will not be," the rat says. "There is no need for beating."

"I can be of significance to one person, can I not?"

The rat's tongue shows between his pink lips, against his black fur, as he traces a difficult line. "If you are speaking of me," he says, but does not finish.

Niki does not want him to. "Jean has paid M. Oller for my company yet again."

"Ah, yes. Your 'patron.' How was it, that first night alone? Did he hold you tender? Did he whisper promises of love into your ear? Did he slide into you so gently—"

"Stop." Niki bites his lip where it is already bleeding. "Yes. All of that."

"Liar."

"So what if I am?" Niki cries. "Perhaps he means it. Perhaps love means something different to him. He is not of our world, he is not free as we are to imagine love. He knows only what his people have told him."

"And what have his people told him?" Henri sets the small brush down and picks up another. "That love is measured in sex-stained one-franc notes? Where did he put them this time?"

Niki feels the heat of the chamois's fingers inside his underthings, below his tail and around his sheath, the one-franc notes left there as flags marking claimed territory. "Just in my garter," he says.

Henri spares him a contemptuous look. "He is not of our world; he is only in our world. You are not of his world, Nikolai. If you attempt to enter it, it will spit you back to the gutter and your lovely tail will be soiled with Bella's rotten vegetables."

"I can live between worlds." Niki empties his purse onto the bed: a small pile of one-franc and fifty-centime coins, with some smaller change from the purchase of the bread, mixed with the one-franc notes from the cabaret. "I am not of this world either, but I exist here."

Absorbed in his canvas, Henri does not look at the small pile of money. "I shan't touch that," he says. "And you are of our world, renardeau. Our world is not merely this small ghetto on the hill. Our world is in every dark shadow where a child chooses art over money, in every lonely garret where the writer starves until his novel is done, in every discarded tube of paint scavenged and rescued so that its dregs may yet serve."

"Perhaps you should paint poems rather than pictures." Niki begins to remove his clothing.

"This chamois is nothing but a diversion, chéri." Henri's whiskers twitch, registering the movement. "As long as you view him as no more than a way to

pass the time, you risk nothing. Do not dream of freedom. He is a painted door. There is nothing beyond."

Dawn brightens the room, almost enough light for Henri to switch to paints. Niki removes his trousers, drops them to the floor. His underthings follow. "And this painting you are working on," he says, "is there freedom beyond that? Or is that no more than a way to pass the time?"

Henri stops. He stares at his painting and then puts his charcoal down. Gently, he lifts the painting from the easel and sets it on the floor. He turns his stool and easel to face the bed, and picks up the painting Niki has not yet seen.

Niki sits and arranges his tail. Henri leans forward and adjusts it, then corrects the fox's posture. "I will paint your ears today," he says. "Remove the ribbons for me."

Slowly, Niki reaches up. His fingers brush the black velvet of each ribbon, and the small loops of thread that keep them in place. He pulls them free. In his mind's eye, he sees the ragged, misshapen edges of his ears revealed. They droop to the sides of his head as they always do when he pictures their scars; he pulls them upright.

"Beautiful," Henri says, and he says it with more than just words. Niki winds one ribbon around a paw, lets the other fall to the bed. Outside, dawn's presence glows pink through the filthy window frame.

The alarm jolted Sol from sleep like a slap across the muzzle. He squirmed, lying on his stomach, then blinked at the clock. He'd forgotten to turn the alarm off.

"Fuck," he murmured into the pillow, and then pressed his hips into the mattress. Swearing, grinding into the sheets, it all felt grownup and adult, like the hard rock on his iPod. He reached up to turn it off.

Something soft trailed along his paw, brushed the alarm as his thumb hit the off button. He blinked, focusing on it.

A black velvet ribbon was wrapped around his paw.

With a yell, Sol scrambled out of bed. His foot tangled in the covers; he lost his balance and fell to the floor with a thump he barely felt. The ribbon was there, it was really there, and how the hell had that happened? He didn't own a velvet ribbon. His heart was racing. He unwound the ribbon and found the threads that would loop it over an ear.

Oh God. Oh God oh God oh God. He couldn't look away from the soft blackness that seemed to swallow up all the early dawn light in the room. It was impossible and yet there it was, and he remembered every detail of the dream, the feel of Niki reaching up to slide the ribbons free, the ragged edge of his ears, the gentle winding of one ribbon around his paws.

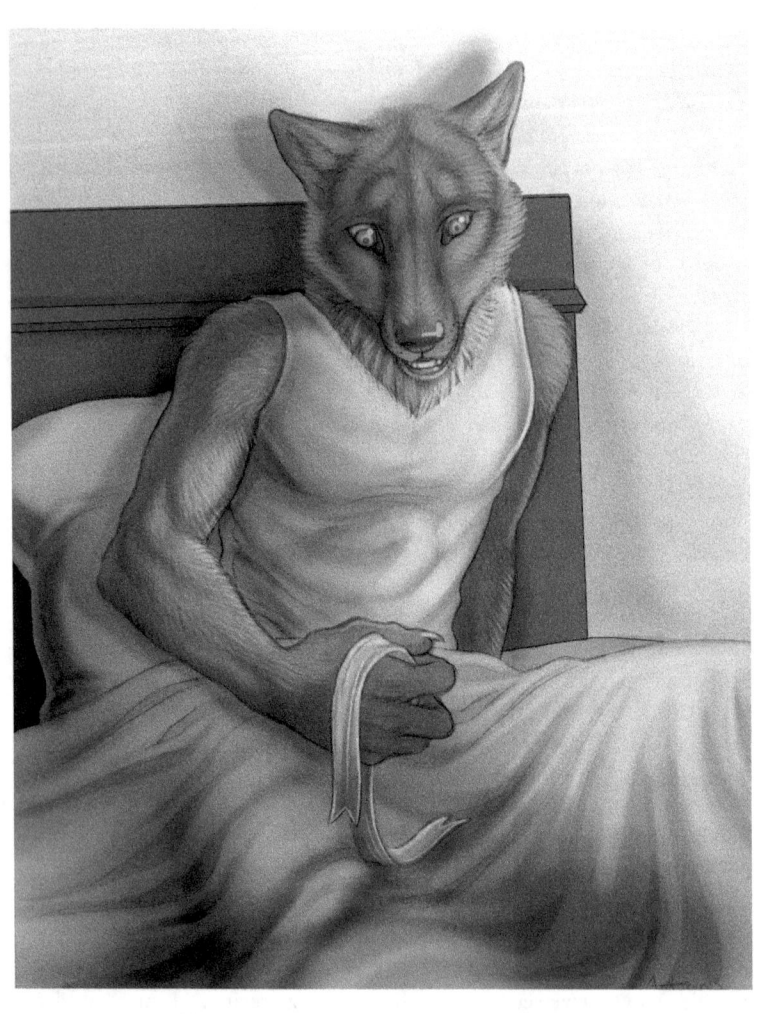

Something soft trailed along his paw.

Sol reached up tentatively and drew a finger across the edges of his ears. They were whole, smooth, unblemished. But the ribbon remained.

"Sol?" His mother's voice, followed by a knocking. "Are you okay, honey?"

He was lying naked with his shoulders on the floor, one foot still wound in his sheets, and despite the terror of the ribbon, he was still not in a condition he would want his mother to see. "Fine, fine, just a minute!" he yelled, twisting and pulling his foot from the stubborn grip of twisted linens.

"What are you doing up so early?"

His foot came free. He heard the click of the door handle. "Just a minute!" He ran to his dirty clothes, grabbed his boxers, and jammed his legs into them, pulling them up to his waist. "I just…I wanted to get up to, uh. Shower. And do homework."

"Can I come in?"

"Yes." He jumped back to the bed, sitting on the edge of it as though he'd just gotten out of it, also thereby concealing the still-too-prominent bulge in his boxers. He set his paws on his knees, and right before the door opened, he noticed that the ribbon was not in them any longer.

His mother came into the room and said something about his father while he was staring at the floor, the clothes, everywhere, searching for the ribbon. After a moment of silence, Sol realized she was waiting for him to say something.

"Sure," he said. The ribbon wasn't anywhere on the floor between his bed and the clothes pile. He must have dropped it on the clothes pile when he picked up the boxers. He didn't wear a lot of black clothing on account of his black fur, but he did have a couple black t-shirts. They were the only black he saw in the pile. Terror and his mother had made him presentable enough to get up. "Um, I'll be down in a second."

"So you were going to shower after that?"

"Yeah." He tried not to be obvious about staring at his dirty clothes. He still couldn't see where the ribbon might have gone.

His mother smiled. "Well, get your baseball clothes on. I'll have breakfast on when you get back."

"Right." He barely heard what she said, anxiously waiting for the door to close. When it did, he dove into the pile of clothes and scattered it all over the floor. He picked up every scrap of black cloth twice, and none of them were velvet.

What the hell?

A wave of cold washed over Sol. He had to steady himself on the dresser. What was happening to him? "That's it," he muttered aloud.

"No more absinthe." He slid open the dresser drawer. His paws were still shaking.

He lifted out a pair of jeans and stopped in the middle of pulling them up his left leg. Wait, what had his mother said? Baseball clothes? He groaned. At least that might take his mind off the dream. He threw the jeans back, pulled on his baseball uniform pants, and then decided he had to try to call Meg.

The phone rang and rang, and her voicemail picked up. He started to say something about his dream and then stopped. Better to tell her in person. And he still didn't know how to tell her about the ribbon. He stared again at his dirty clothes pile as he pulled on a t-shirt and ran outside.

Behind their house, the yard sloped gently down, away from the house toward the wooden gate that separated their yard from the back alley they used to pull into their garage. His father had a bat in one paw and had set two baseballs down on the barbecue grill while he took some practice swings. "Morning. How about some grounders? Thought we could walk down to the park."

Fielding ground balls was not what Sol really needed to work on; he needed to be out there with the team. But it was about all he could practice with only his father. "Sure," he said. He picked up the baseballs and followed his father down the alley to the park.

"How's that report coming?" his father asked, unexpectedly.

"Oh, pretty good." Sol scratched behind his ear, until the itch reminded him of Niki's scarred ears. He dropped his paw quickly. "Meg's an artist, you know, so she's into all that stuff. I'm helping write it."

"Not taking too much of your time, is it?"

"No, sir." He slipped through the fence surrounding the park, behind his father's bushy grey tail. "I told her I have baseball practice."

"Good." His father hefted the bat. "It's important to stay competitive in school, too, you know," he added, as though just realizing it.

They found a nice open spot among the trees. Sol trotted a baseball diamond's length away from his father and got down in his stance. He kept flicking his ears, feeling phantom scarring from his dream.

His father tapped the first ball short; Sol had to run forward to pick it up. "Guess I need a little practice, too," his father said. "It's been a while since we did this."

Sol grinned, walking back to his spot. The next ball came all the way to him. He fielded it and threw it back to his father's bare paws.

"Make that rock second base," his father said after a few more. "I'll hit you some double-play balls."

It was funny, but running to tag the bag and then throwing back to his father felt good. His father dropped the bat and stood like a first baseman, one leg back, arms outstretched, and when Sol's throws smacked into his paws, Sol felt a flush of pride.

At the end of an hour of this, his father's tail was wagging, and Sol felt almost good enough to wag his. They gathered up the bat and balls and walked back to the park gate. As they stepped through it, his father said, "Something wrong with your ears?"

Sol jerked in surprise, banging his arm on the iron post. His ears flattened, their scarred sides—no, they were fine, they were whole. "Wh-what?"

"You kept flicking them. Just wondering. Do they itch? Your mom has a cream for that."

"N-no." Sol swallowed, forcing his ears upright. He heard the words in his mind and then coming out of his mouth before he could stop them. "I had a dream." He rubbed his arm, caught in a half-second of incredulous belief that his father would understand, would ask him about the dream.

His father laughed. "You dreamed your ears itched. Go ask your mom, she'll give you that cream."

Sol trudged behind as they walked up the alley. At their yard, his father stopped in surprise. "Come on, pick up your feet!" he said, and when Sol finally reached the gate, his father slapped him on the back.

At least there was no discussion when Sol took four slices of toast, grits and eggs, and no sausage in the breakfast his mother had set out. He listened to his father talk to his mother about how well he'd done that morning, eating even after he felt full so he wouldn't be hungry at the barbecue.

The strategy worked at first. He got himself a plate of potato salad and tore off a piece of a bun so it looked like he'd already eaten a burger. Mr. Norston asked about his organic steaks, so Sol and his father said he'd had lunch at home rather than put everyone out. Sol kept rubbing the paw that had had the ribbon wrapped around it, which he didn't notice until his mother asked him what was wrong with it, and then he yanked it back against his body so fast that he dropped his plate.

He cleaned it up and walked away from the food, out to where the younger cubs were tossing water balloons and Frisbees around. The younger wolf cubs grabbed Frisbees out of the air with their muzzles, which prompted yells from their mothers not to do that, that that was why God gave them paws, but the cubs just laughed and rubbed their muzzles and went on doing it anyway. Some of the adults and older cubs got into the game, and when Xavy Norston went out of his way to ask Sol to join, Sol figured he might as well.

He was pretty good at Frisbee and was enjoying himself, lobbing easy throws to the cubs and whipping it toward Xavy and others, so he didn't notice what was going on out at the other side of the picnic until it was too late. "Hey!" one of the guys yelled, a short fox in a Peachtree Runners t-shirt. "Come on, let's pick sides for softball!"

Softball? Sol flipped the Frisbee to a white wolf cub and ignored the call, hoping they would just let him play Frisbee. But Xavy was already loping off toward the field, and Sol's father, a moment later, called out, "Sol! Come on and play!"

The white wolf cub had snatched the Frisbee out of the air with his teeth. He dropped it to his paw and threw it back to Sol. The black wolf caught it and hesitated for a moment, then tossed it to a lanky young fox cub. Sol held his paws up and turned his back deliberately so they wouldn't throw it back to him.

"Hey, don't put these two on the same team," a paunchy grey fox said as Sol stopped next to Xavy. "Aren't they both on the Richfield High team?"

"Xavy plays third," Mr. Norston said. "Sol backs up second base."

"Backing up?" The grey wolf standing beside Sol's father clapped him on the shoulder. "Thought he was starting."

Xavy looked away. Sol cringed from his father's glare. "One of those 'yotes from the trailer park," Sol's father said finally. "Tough, scrappy…just temporary, though. Sol's gonna be starting again in a couple weeks."

"Coyote, huh?" The other wolf looked sympathetic, flicking black-tipped ears. "Glad my boy's a football player."

"Sol's brother Natty plays football. He's fighting for a starting spot his first year in college. They almost never let a freshman start."

The words didn't seem to register with the other wolf. "Y'know, once those trailer kids set their mind on somethin'…" He shook his head. "Don't get between one of them and a steak, know what I'm sayin'?"

A couple of the other wolves laughed with him, though Sol noticed some wolves, foxes, and the wolverine couple shaking their heads or forcing smiles.

"Sol's taking extra practice." His father had that steely look in his eye that made Sol shut up when it was fixed on him.

The other wolf didn't feel that effect. "Gotta get him working on those leadership skills. My boy's defensive captain." He gestured out to a bulky ten-year-old cub who was examining a softball bat. "Three tackles last week."

Sol was spared from having to see any more of the argument. The fox in the Runners t-shirt put him and his father on one team, mercifully setting the wolf with the black-tipped ears on the other. Sol's team went out into the field, where he paced excitedly, eager to be part of a team again.

The game went pretty well for a while. Sol hit the ball well, though he only got one hit, and he caught three balls that were hit to him (two on the ground, one in the air). He hadn't done anything really extraordinary, though, and his attempts to bond with his teammates were met with "hey, get me another beer," or tolerant smiles, and in one case, a tousling between his ears and the remark, "you remind me of my boy before he went off to college," which became a story about how that fox was top of his class in his sophomore year. Perhaps Sol only imagined the sound of his father's teeth gritted together.

In the late innings, Sol stood behind second base, actually feeling good, feeling like it was where he belonged. There were two runners on, and his team was up by a run. He was scratching his paw again, the echo of black velvet, when the batter swung, the thud of the softball hit the air, and it came hurtling across the ground at Sol. He reached down for it—

—and just before it reached him, it hit a stone, or a tuft of grass, and spun to one side. It hit the back of his paw, and rolled along the grass to his right.

Sol cursed under his breath and dove after it. His fingers closed around it and he threw automatically around to his left, toward first base.

"Home! Home!" the short fox was yelling from the pitcher's mound, and the first baseman, too late to get the batter, threw the ball over the catcher's head and into one of the picnic tables. Potato salad exploded around it as cubs shrieked and scattered.

The batter ran past Sol and stopped at second. "Just one base?" she asked, paws on her knees and panting.

"Yeah." The short fox stood with paws on hips as the other baserunner trotted home. One of the cubs, covered in potato salad and laughing, ran the ball back to him. Sol and Sol's father, and the fox, were the only ones not laughing now. Even the first baseman, a raccoon, was laughing at his own mishap.

Sol knew his father wasn't laughing without having to turn around to look. And when they went to the bench at the end of the inning, his father hurried up behind him to mutter, "You had no chance at first. You had to throw home."

"I know." Sol's ears were already down, his tail curled around his leg. He didn't look at his father, just at his feet, one stepping in front of the other.

"Everyone gets a bad hop sometimes," the short fox said, coming up beside Sol.

"Not usually in softball," Sol's father said.

"Give the cub a break." The fox patted Sol on the shoulder. "Baseball's a faster game. Hard to adjust to the slower ball here. And it's not a perfect field. Did you see Johnson boot that grounder earlier?"

"Hey, it took a bad hop." A wolverine who must have been Johnson pricked up his ears.

The fox snorted. "Your sales proposal to CureLite took a bad hop. That was just poor fielding."

He shouldered his bat and took some practice swings while he and the wolverine commiserated over this unfortunate proposal. Sol's father stayed silent for a moment, then joined in the conversation.

Sol stayed hunched over on the bench, panting, his stomach twisting up. He kept seeing himself miss the ball, throw to the wrong base, a film loop playing over and over in his head that he couldn't change no matter how many times he watched it. He was due to bat fourth, and he hated himself for hoping that none of the batters ahead of him would get on base, that he wouldn't have to come to bat.

But the short fox got another hit. "Four for four," he crowed. "Come on, team, we're only down one! We can win this!"

His wife came to bat next. Sol knew she was going to get a hit, and he hoped against hope that she would hit a home run and win the game. But she smacked the softball over the pitcher's head, and her husband stopped at second.

"Go on, Sol." His father nudged him.

He got up. The prospect of going back out and hitting, the whole team counting on him...come on, he told himself, you've done this before. But those times it had been all right to fail. There had been someone else to hit after him, or else he'd known it was just a game. He'd never had to try to atone for an error with his father staring at him from the bench.

His paw itched again. He scratched it and then picked up a bat. As he took a swing, his stomach cramped up so tightly that he almost threw the bat. It clattered to the ground as Sol doubled over.

His father jumped up, came to his side. "What's the matter?"

"Stomach...hurts." Sol forced the words out through clenched teeth.

The wolverine joined them, and Sol's mother came running over as well. All the attention was just making things worse. "I'll be...fine," he said.

"I'll bat," the wolverine said. "Hey! Sick player, we're skipping his spot. That cool?"

Only the short fox protested, even though it was for his own team, but he gave in when everyone else outvoted him. Sol listened to the wolverine's at-bat as his mother led him back to one of the picnic tables. "Strike one," he heard, and then the thud of bat connecting with softball, and then cheers. He turned to look and saw the short fox crossing home plate, arms raised.

"Bet it was all that potato salad!" Mr. Norston, who wasn't playing in the game, wagged his tail as Sol came to sit near them, still clutching his stomach. "Xavy had two burgers."

A female wolf nearby asked why Sol had been eating so much potato salad, and Mr. Norston told her about the organic steaks, while Sol's mother stayed quiet. "Funny, Jerius never mentioned it. What's the condition?"

"It's not—" Sol's voice broke in a squeak. "I just ate too fast. I—"

"But he has a condition?" The female wolf talked over him, to his mother.

"Well." Sol's mother looked around, but his father was now batting. The game must still be tied. "We're actually avoiding all meat."

"All meat?" Mr. Norston looked surprised. "Jerius just said he was tired. If you're tired, you should eat more meat, not less."

"It's just what the doctor said." Sol's mother sounded more desperate.

"Doctor Marshall?" The female wolf had her paws on her hips, her head tilted. "I take Jimmy to him. I'll ask him next time I'm there."

"Hey, Sol, have an antacid." Mrs. Klein, a raccoon who'd known his family for years, came over with a cup of water that was fizzing. "It'll settle things down lickety-split."

He took the cup, the water warm in his paw, the sharp antacid smell cutting through the green grass and the smells of the people around him. "Thanks," he said, and looked to his mother.

"Go ahead." She smiled. "It won't hurt."

He nodded, and gulped the fizzing, tart water down. His stomach was already unclenching. It wouldn't do any harm to tell Mrs. Klein she'd helped. "Thanks," he repeated, handing the empty cup back to her.

"Now just let it settle." She bustled away, leaving Sol with his mother and, now, both Norstons.

"So, no meat at all?" Mrs. Norston asked. "How does he get protein?"

"I've been making bean salads," his mother said. "There are some great recipes on the Internet."

If anything, this was more painful than striking out would have been, but Sol couldn't escape. He flattened his ears and listened to everyone around him discuss his diet, and wished he were anywhere else.

His father didn't talk to him all the way home. His mother asked about his stomach, and Sol replied dully that he was fine. He felt sorry for himself most of the afternoon, until dinner. Then he got angry.

When he came down from his room, the table had not only been set, but portions had been served. The plates in front of his father and mother held a cut of roast chicken and a heaping pile of broccoli on each, but the third plate on the table, the one in front of the empty chair, held only chicken.

Sol just stood there at the entrance to the dining room and stared at the plate. His mother looked down at the table, but his father stared right at him. "Have a seat," he said.

They stared in silence at each other. His mother began to speak, then shut her mouth, her muzzle dipping even lower. Sol's stomach rumbled; he could smell the chicken and it was making his mouth water. "I'll just have broccoli and bread," he said.

"You need something with some substance." His father's voice was soft but unyielding. "Come on, Sol, sit down. Just this one meal."

Sol remained on his feet, tail tucked around his hip. "I'm a vegetarian now."

His father's eyes narrowed. Below his voice, a low growl rumbled. "You're a *wolf*. This vegetarian *bullshit* is making you sick."

Niki's fire, from the argument with Henri, kept Sol on his feet, made him feel there was someone standing with him, supporting him. "It's my choice!"

"Not while you're living under this roof."

"I'm not eating that." Sol folded his arms.

"Then you're not eating dinner." His father picked up his silverware and began eating.

"Fine!" Sol stomped out of the dining room, stomped up the stairs all the way back to his room.

Niki had had bread in his dream, just bread, and it was the most delicious thing ever. Sol pushed the memory of the dream away, and rubbed at his paw again. His parents wouldn't let him go to bed hungry, he was sure, but lasting the next couple hours until his mother caved in and brought him something was going to be a trial. He eyed his window, but it had been a year or more since he'd snuck out. This wasn't serious enough to warrant that.

He could call Meg again, but she wouldn't understand his talking about baseball. She wouldn't, but...Natty would. Sol pulled his phone out and called up his brother's number. It had to have been a week—two?—

since they'd talked. He thumbed the Call button and put the phone to his ear.

"Little brother!" Natty sounded rather giddy and overenthusiastic. Raucous conversations filled the space behind his voice. "How the hell are you?"

"I'm okay," Sol said. He sat back in his chair and smiled. "Actually, I'm hungry."

He told Natty about the fight over dinner, which made him talk about going vegetarian, which was skating close to an edge, but he had to talk about it. "No meat?" Natty laughed. "Why the hell would you do that?"

"Just wanted to try it," Sol said, aware of the precipice he was dancing along. "What's with all the 'hell's?"

"I mean, did you want to find some way to really piss off Dad? Because I can't think of a better one. Unless you brought home a boyfriend, ha ha. That'd do it."

The comfort he'd gotten from his brother's voice vanished. "Shut up!"

"Hey, chill, Sol. I know you're not a fag. So what's with the meatless diet?"

"It's not about that." Sol rubbed his paw. "He's already mad about the baseball."

"What happened with the baseball? Hang on." His voice grew faint. "Just my little brother," he said to someone else. "I'll be there in five." He came back to Sol. "Sorry."

He felt nauseous again, the beginning of something worse in his gut. To calm himself, he breathed evenly, in and out. "We don't have to talk right now."

"Nah, nah, it's cool. I'm just at a thing. So what happened with the baseball?"

He didn't know how often his parents talked to Natty. Either they hadn't told him or they hadn't had the chance yet. "I lost my—I lost this ground ball at the picnic. Playing softball." He related the incident.

"Dad blew up about that?" Natty laughed. "Hang in there. You got what, five months to go? College is awesome, you're gonna have a blast."

"Yeah, but..." *I need to get back on the team, and I'm having weird dreams, and...*

"Sol, I gotta go. Call me tomorrow, okay? Not too early, though."

"Sure." He said good-bye and hung up.

After that, he didn't feel like talking to anyone any more. So he played games on his computer to distract himself and texted Carcy to tell him how unfair his parents were being. Carcy, of course, was playful, and Sol got a little bit into it before realizing that his mother was likely to come upstairs at any moment with food.

But an hour ticked by, and then another. The TV went on downstairs and the news came on, and Sol got hungrier and hungrier. He tried to focus on homework, but his stomach reminded him over and over that his parents didn't really understand him, didn't really love him. If they did, they would be bringing food up to him instead of watching Saturday Night Live. At bedtime, they would bring up a plate instead of just turning off the TV and climbing the stairs. His mother called "Good night," but his father didn't say a word, and Sol didn't answer.

He'd gone from ravenously hungry to numb. Even if he weren't remembering the dream specifically, he still remembered the emptiness in Niki's stomach, the mouth-watering aroma of the bread, the fresh, firm feel of it in his paw. When he got up from his desk chair, the room spun around him in a dizzying wave, and he had to brace himself on his dresser. He'd intended to just go to bed hungry and eat in the morning, but now he thought he'd better get something from the kitchen. He opened the door to his room as quietly as he could.

The hallway was dark, the light under his parents' door out. He stepped out into the hall and almost put his foot directly onto a plate wrapped in tinfoil. The aroma of broccoli and bread rose to his nose, waking his stomach from its stupor.

He grabbed the plate and pulled it into his room, before his hungry rumblings woke his parents. Door closed, he ripped off the tinfoil and devoured the broccoli with his hands. The two dinner rolls on the plate were slightly stale, but the butter was soft and perfect. He closed his eyes as he chewed them and imagined that they were warm and fresh, from the window of a small bakery just down the street.

Sunday passed with some tension, but no more plates of meat. They went to church, and then Sol went down to the batting cages at the park to work on his hitting. He had what he felt was a good session, over two hours in the warm afternoon. By the end of it, he was seeing the ball really well, and the smell of the dirt and the grass made him happy, not stressed. He couldn't wait to get back to the team again.

At home, he pulled out his homework for Monday, for all the classes except his art class. He didn't pick up "Confession" again, because whenever he thought about it, his mind started asking what the hell was with the red paint and the ribbon, and he had to stop thinking about it. Besides, he found that when he was actively not thinking about it, as he had done after the red paint, he was able to focus better on baseball.

Still, the one thing he couldn't get out of his mind was what Henri had said about their world, about writers starving for their work, and artists working in lonely garrets. He wasn't starving—last night aside—and he didn't really work on any pieces of art. But he felt lonely and isolated, and Meg was working on her art (she claimed; he'd only ever seen two paintings). That counted for something, didn't it? As much as the ribbon had unnerved him, there was a seductive attraction to the passion present in that world that Sol envied and cherished for himself. His passion for Carcy wasn't quite the same; it felt more physical than the almost-spiritual desires of Henri and Niki. Perhaps baseball would be what he could rediscover his passion for, but now he worried about what he might have to give up for it.

Sunday dinner was a chicken casserole, but his mother had made a large salad and some bean soup for Sol. His father glared, but didn't say anything, and Sol didn't press his advantage. He even waited to say, "Thanks, Mom," until they were in the kitchen cleaning up. That night, with a growing feeling that things were looking up, he locked his room door so he could text Carcy in private. He started to ask about whether he could move in for the whole summer, but Carcy was not in a mood to talk seriously, and Sol didn't press. It wasn't like what Carcy wanted wasn't enjoyable, and they still had a couple months before he *had* to have the question answered.

Sol got on the bus on Monday with renewed determination. This week he was going to stay later than Taric every day, and he was going to get better, and he was going to show Mr. Zerling that he was determined. Being alone in the batting cages, not worrying whether the coyote thought Sol was staring at him, had helped. He could carry that over to regular practice as well, show the rest of the guys that he wasn't scared of the coyote, that he was one of them. What's more, his determination was more solid this week. The softball game could have ruined everything, but he'd spent Sunday telling himself that softball was not baseball, listening to what the short fox in the baseball t-shirt had said about the game being different. Softball was different, and he was a baseball player.

The day started poorly. He first became aware that the news of his stomach cramps and therefore his new diet must have spread throughout the baseball team when Tanny greeted him with "How's your tummy, leaf-eater?" He gritted his teeth, sat down, and ignored her, wondering how she'd found out. Xavy, to the baseball team, to Taric, it must have been.

Tanny went on about salads and leaf-eating faggots, but it was only when she said, "That hippie poser slut probably wants you to give up *eating meat*," that Sol clenched his fists.

"Better than being a wanna-be poser slut," he muttered back, and he almost added "living in a trailer." Almost.

At the bell, Sol took off for class, heart thudding. If Tanny knew about his vegetarianism, then most of the school did. He dashed through hallways, not wanting to give anyone time to make a remark to him, and thereby avoided confrontation until lunch.

Taric and the other coyotes walked into the cafeteria ahead of him, so Sol let a bunch of other students go between them before getting in line himself. None of the students around him really knew him, so he relaxed, walking past the rigatoni with beef sauce and the suspicious-looking meatloaf. He'd picked up two salads and reached out for one of the rolls, which was not fresh-baked, nor even his mother's dinner rolls, but still smelled good.

A hard shove between his shoulder blades almost sent his muzzle into the counter. He smelled Taric behind him and tried to hurry along the line, but the scent followed him, and then the coyote's scratchy, deep voice. "Come on, have some meatloaf."

The spell of the bread scent shattered. Sol turned, apprehensive. The three coyotes had finished and come back around to the line, specifically after him. "I'm not…Not in the mood."

"What, not in the mood for meat?" Taric feigned incredulity. "A wolf? Not in the mood for meat?"

"Leave me alone." Sol turned back, pulled two rolls onto his tray, and walked away.

Taric, amazingly, followed him, and so did the other two coyotes. Sol sat near one of his sort-of friends, a mule deer one grade below him, but at the sight of the coyotes, the deer shoved his chair back and picked up his half-finished salad, mumbling apologies. Taric took his spot and the other two coyotes sat around them at the table, one on the other side of Sol, one across from him.

"Didn't believe it," Taric said. "But it's true. Little faggy wolf is a leaf-eater now. Tell me." He leaned in closer. "You given up eating all kinds of meat? Or just the kind that ain't attached to your boyfriend?"

Sol tore a hunk out of one of his dinner rolls and chewed. He prayed that someone would notice, that Taric would get bored, that there would be a fire and the whole school would have to be evacuated.

But Taric kept nudging his arm when he tried to eat, as if they were ten years old and not almost legally adult, as if eating salads was some big crime. Sol finally snapped, "Leave me alone, okay?"

"Leave me alone," Taric jeered, showing back as many teeth as Sol had shown him.

He hadn't wanted to get up and leave, because that would mean they would win, and also they might follow him. But every time he took a bite of his salad, one of them would bump his arm or his tray, and finally in exasperation he stood up.

"Yeah," the coyote who played football said. "Take that leaf-eating shit somewhere else." And as Sol turned to do just that, he punched the underside of the tray hard enough to send one of Sol's salads spilling across the tray and onto the table.

Sol couldn't help himself. As the tray came back down from the punch, he let it keep going and going. His other salad and drinks slid to the edge, and still the tray dropped. And then, while the coyote was still smirking, Sol let go, sending lettuce leaves and grape tomatoes, vinegar dressing and water and milk all over the coyote's polo shirt and jeans.

The tray clattered to the floor. The coyote jumped out of his seat as Sol backed away. He heard snickers from around him, so at least some people had been watching. Taric didn't get up, just watched with one arm slung over the back of his chair as his friend took a step toward Sol.

Sol hadn't been in a serious fight since eighth grade, but he knew when a situation was heading in that direction. The little laughs that kept bubbling up from his throat at the dripping shirt and pants of the furious coyote weren't helping at all. The saving grace was that Taric and the other coyote mostly looked amused, showing no inclination of getting up to help.

"What is going on here?"

Sol flicked his ears back. He'd never been so glad to hear the shrill voice of Mrs. Mercher.

The short arctic fox walked up between the two of them, glaring at both of them. "Well?"

"Wrightson dumped his leaf-eater lunch all over me," the coyote said, shaking his paw at Sol.

"From where I was standing, it appeared that you struck his tray and brought this upon yourself," she said.

The whole lunchroom had turned to watch them now. The coyote glared at Sol but didn't say anything. Mrs. Mercher went on. "Normally, I would insist that you apologize, but it looks like you've already gotten as good as you've given. Go clean up, and perhaps from now on you'll allow Mr. Wrightson to eat his lunch in peace."

The coyote's first words when he sat down were to Taric, saying, "You just sat there? Not backin' me up?" But Sol felt, with the same certainty that Niki anticipated the hostility in the cabaret's changing room, that his life was not going to get any easier.

In fact, he was fairly certain that practice was going to be worse than usual, and he was right. To his surprise, though he did get shoved and called "leaf-eater" a few times, a mouse and deer actually came up to him and said, "Hey, cool." And in the locker room, when Taric called him "leaf-eater," the rabbit who was starting in left field leaned casually in and said, "You got something against leaf-eaters?"

Taric looked about as surprised as Sol was. "That's different," he said, ears back, "and this ain't none of your business."

"Don't see as it's yours neither," the rabbit said. "Let Sol eat what he wants."

"He's…" The big coyote waved a disgusted paw. "Forget it."

Miraculously, Sol thought that might be an end to it. But when he went out to practice, the coaches and the other wolves, even the coyotes and foxes, all of them were looking at him a little funny, like he'd been diagnosed with some disease or something. He barely got any grounders hit to him, and none of the other players threw to him. By the time warmups were done, Sol was only panting a little, mostly from the afternoon heat rather than the exertion.

Mr. Zerling came up to him as the players were leaving the field. He didn't look at Sol as he said, "Hey, a couple of the guys said you're off meat? Some kind of condition? Is it something that I should know about?"

"No," Sol said. "I'm fine."

"But you're not eating meat." Now Mr. Zerling was looking at him, and Sol didn't feel any better, because the wolf's brow was lowered, like he was trying to figure out what to tell the batter to do with two outs and two guys on base.

"It's just…it's just a thing I'm doing, and I'm fine, and it's nobody's business."

Mr. Zerling shook his head. "No, no. Course not. But are you going to be able to go a whole practice?"

"I started last week," Sol said. "I'm fine. I just want…" *I want them to include me.* But he couldn't say that, because it sounded like a whiny cub's demands, and what could Mr. Zerling really do? "Just want to be left alone."

"Sure. I'll tell the guys not to bother you," Mr. Zerling said. And then, before Sol could correct him, he walked off yelling at some other player who didn't appear to be doing anything wrong.

Sol bit his lip. He had never before had the feeling that he could just walk off the field and not be missed. And it was all because of what he'd chosen to eat? Even after the shower incident, though he'd lost a lot of respect, he'd still been one of the team. This was different, dismissive and cold. The horrible thing was that Sol could feel the faint echoes of the wolf he'd been a year ago, when he hadn't been "funny like that" nor vegetarian, and that wolf would have been mystified if one of his friends had stopped eating meat. He hoped he would have been more understanding, but if the other wolves had turned their back, would Sol have had the courage to try to understand his friend?

Of course he would. The problem wasn't his diet, it was that he was already alienated from the team. Well, fine. If he had to work twice as hard to prove he belonged, he would. He stalked over to the footwork drills and practiced until his feet were sore, alone, while the other players were doing other drills, throwing the ball back and forth, catching and throwing, catching and throwing.

When his legs were burning, he picked up a bat and went to the batting cages. He deliberately chose the one all the way at the end so that he wouldn't have to talk to any of his teammates, wouldn't have to see anyone except the random smattering of people who always sat and watched, today a mouse and a fox. The machine spat balls at him and he lashed out at them, the sounds of contact more satisfying than they'd been at the softball game.

Dumping the tray in the coyote's lap—he hadn't even thought about doing it. It seemed bold for him, and he was sure he was probably going to pay for it at some point, but there had been something so satisfying about the coyote's expression, the vinegar dressing covering his shirt, the milk and water dripping down his front. Where had that come from?

Unwillingly, he thought of the coyotes as the jealous dancers in his dream. He was trying not to think about the actual events of the dream, but the emotions persisted. In fact, Sol felt more outraged on Niki's behalf than he did on his own. Whatever else people thought about his vegetarianism, he was doing it of his own volition to be closer to Carcy. He hadn't been forced into it.

Still, he couldn't imagine what would happen if the school actually found out he was really gay, and not just the closest thing to it that they knew. So when Taric yelled at him, "Hey, Fagson. Get out of the cage, the starters need to practice," Sol's ears went back.

He turned and saw that the rest of the cages were full. Of course Taric had probably let everyone else claim one first, so that he could be the one to kick Sol out. "I'm…almost done," Sol said.

"You're done now." Taric came around the side, gripping the chain link with one paw. "Do I hafta come in there and take you out?"

Sol smacked the button to stop the pitching machine. He could only leave the cage in one direction, and that direction took him past the coyote. Even though he moved as quickly as he could, Taric was faster, pushing his shoulder against the chain link and growling into his ear. "I'm always gonna be better than you," he said. "Dumpin' salad on my retarded friend don't change nothin'."

Whatever, Sol wanted to say, but couldn't make his mouth form the word, which was probably just as well. After a moment, Taric let him go.

"Don't you fuckin' watch me, either," he said, stepping into the cage and starting up the machine.

In half an hour, Sol knew, the cages would be empty, except for Taric. So he just took his bat and practiced his swing. It was easier without worrying about the ball; he could focus on where to plant his leg and work on his follow-through. And soon enough, the cages did empty, and Sol took one of the vacant ones to hit some more balls. Tonight, he swore, Taric would go home first. Nobody else on the team would see. Nobody would know for sure. But Sol would know, and if he could keep that up for a week, he felt that would really prove his dedication to the team.

The coyote seemed just as determined to outlast Sol, even if he didn't look at him once. But the black wolf kept hitting even after his arms were exhausted, after he'd reached the point last week where he'd quit. He just looked down the row of cages at Taric, and every time the coyote lifted his bat, Sol did the same. He refilled his machine, casting an eye down to see if Taric noticed, but Taric was still swinging away, his hits still loud, but not quite as sharp now.

Sol's and Taric's shadows grew longer, and Sol had to take longer breaks between hits, sometimes letting two balls go by without swinging. His muscles ached, but in what Mr. Zerling called "a good way." And Taric, he noticed, wasn't swinging at every one any more either. The coyote's ears were swept back, listening for the crack of Sol's bat. Once, when Sol let three balls go by, Taric half-turned, smirking. The smirk disappeared when he saw Sol watching him, and he went back to hitting.

The sun wouldn't go down until almost eight, and there was a point, probably around six-thirty, when Sol wondered if they would both be there until then. But it wasn't quite seven o'clock when Taric kicked the side of his cage and just left, walking from the cages back to the locker rooms. "It's not like you're going to get better," he snapped as he passed Sol, and he hit the chain link fence with his bat just to emphasize the point.

"I'm getting a little better," Sol grinned. He felt rejuvenated. He wished Xavy and the others were there to watch.

Taric turned, muzzle open to respond, and then shut it with a click and a shrug. He walked away, tail swaying behind him.

The next ball came flying out of the machine, but Sol was watching Taric, and only returned his attention to the batting cage at the jingle of the pitch smacking into the chain link. On the next, he unleashed a perfect swing and connected, sending the ball sailing over the pitching machine and into the field.

So it went all week: practice late, rush home for dinner, homework, bed. During the days at school, Sol did a good job of avoiding Taric and the other coyotes, although he noticed that the other wolves from the baseball team didn't particularly like him around either. Xavy was the most favorably inclined, and he still wore that expression of pity, as if Sol were mentally handicapped rather than just vegetarian. Maybe that's what he thought. Sol didn't care; he didn't need to talk to any of them. By Wednesday, he felt as though he were moving in a fog where the only things he could see were his next class assignments, like baseballs shooting out of the future at him.

He did not see Meg, except for briefly on the bus, and though she sent him e-mail messages reporting her progress on their assignment, he didn't respond with anything more than a quick "Cool." She asked him about coming over again, and he told her that baseball practice was taking a lot out of him. Jean's book and Niki's dream were not so much memories as a conflicting tug of emotions. He missed them, but he could still feel the velvet of the black ribbon on his fur in idle moments, and that made his fur stand on end and his heart race. It wasn't something that seemed to belong to his real life: either it was something that had come out of his dream into the real world—ludicrous—or he was having serious hallucinations. Baseball was real and physical and undeniable, and he could lose himself in it without fear that he would wake up with infield grass under his claws or a batting glove in his bed.

Friday night, his dedication paid off. They had a home game against a high school that was 4-0 on the year, and Mr. Zerling put him in to hit late in the game. He made good contact and got a single, and got pats on the back from the deer and mouse and even Xavy and one other wolf. They lost, but Taric didn't play spectacularly well, and that lifted Sol's spirits. Another week like this, of showing his dedication to Mr. Zerling and the team, and he might start again.

And if he got his spot back, he would get his car, and if he got his car, he would be on his way to Millenport this summer, and that reminded him that he had best start to work on Carcy, who was also real and undeniable, if not yet physical to Sol.

Chapter 12

"You know what time it is, Solly?" was the first thing the ram asked when Sol called him Saturday morning.

"Sorry," Sol said. It was after nine, but he guessed the ram could've been up late. Carcy did sound tired, his normally smooth voice gravelly. Sol rubbed his paw. "It's okay for me to call, isn't it?"

"It's okay. So what's up?"

"Well…" Sol hesitated. "You know how you said I should come see you this summer?"

"Course, Solly. We been talking about it for a couple months now."

"Yeah." There was no reason this should be so hard to say. "What if I came for, um, a little while?"

"More than just a weekend? Sure, like a week?" The ram sounded very casual. Almost as if he were distracted and not paying complete attention to Sol.

"A week, yeah. But I was thinking about trying to get a summer job in Millenport."

"I remember you said that." Carcy sounded amused. "So you could come by more often."

"Thing is," Sol said, "the thing is, I don't really have a place to stay."

The phone got quiet. "You were thinking about staying here," Carcy said when Sol didn't go on. There was no doubt now that Sol had his full attention.

"Kind of." Sol waited.

Again, he thought he heard another voice in the background, just for a moment. Then it went quiet, and Carcy spoke again. "Look, Solly, it's not that I don't love ya."

Sol interrupted before the rejection could become final. "I know it's a lot to ask. But it'd be a really good way for us to get to know each other. And it'd be just three months."

Carcy's breathing sounded like the ocean in Sol's ear. "Maybe. There's some stuff I'd have to work out."

"Anything I can help with?"

"No." This time the response came quickly. "No, I just need to work out things."

Sol didn't quite know what to say to that, but at least Carcy hadn't said no. "I can see if I can find another place. In case it doesn't work out."

"That might be a good idea."

The matter-of-fact tone lowered Sol's ears and curled his tail around his leg. "I'll look around, I guess."

"Can you cook?"

As fast as his ears had lowered, they came up. "Sure! I mean, I can make salad."

Carcy laughed. "Anything else?"

"I'll work on it." Sol's tail wagged. "My mom is looking up vegetarian recipes."

"Okay-dokay." The ram had gone back to being casual. "So what was up with this dream? Was I in it? Was it a naughty dream?"

"Oh." The ribbon had been a week ago, the paint days before that. Sol hoped that the dreams and hallucinations only came the nights he drank absinthe. Even so, it wasn't something that happened to most people; it was weird and different and scary. He imagined telling Carcy, and the ram asking, *So some morning there'd randomly be ribbons and paint in bed with us?* There'd be no chance of him moving in then. "Yeah, no, it was just one of those, those horror dreams, y'know? It freaked me out and, and I wanted to talk to you."

"That's sweet, Solly."

And they talked a little longer before Carcy had to get going, though the ram said he would be around that night for some texting. Sol hung up and paced his room for a little while, and then he called Meg.

"Hey, jock," she said. "Wanna come over and hang out?"

"Maybe," he said. "I'm not going to smoke any pot."

"I wasn't going to ask. Though you really should."

Sol sighed. "I can't…it'd mess up my baseball…"

"Oh, bullshit. Those major leaguers are all on drugs. But whatever. How's your work on the project going? Read all those books yet? Written reports on them?"

"Um."

"Just kidding. How's Operation Wheels coming along?"

His tail wagged. "Hopes are high. Hey, I was thinking, what would you want a potential roommate to do?"

"Stay the fuck out of my room and my life."

"No, I mean, if someone wanted to move in with you. What would make you say yes?"

"Financial obligation."

He laughed. "Really? You wouldn't live with me unless you owed me money?"

"Honestly, Sol, you're kinda uptight. You're a good friend, but once in a while you need to unclench."

"Unclench."

His father knocked on the door. "Sol? You wanna catch some grounders?"

"It's not a bad thing," Meg said. "Just I wouldn't want to live with it."

"Fine. Just a minute," he called to his father, then said to Meg, "Sorry, I can't come over. I gotta go practice."

"Goddammit, Sol, if you don't come over I'm going to be so bored I'm going to smoke right away. You don't want to contribute to the delinquency of a minor, do you?"

"I'm a minor too. Anyway, you'd light up as soon as I left."

"Maybe not tonight."

"Well, sorry. I have to practice with my dad. The one thing I don't get to do so much after school is field. Nobody wants to hit to me anymore."

"Probably because you're so uptight. No, wait. Jocks like that. I dunno what it is."

"It's that I went vegetarian," he said.

"Seriously?"

"You're not a wolf."

"Goddamn."

He snorted. "Kind of like, I dunno, if you said you didn't want to swim anymore."

"That's different. We all swim with relatives and everything. Who cares what you eat?"

"That's what I'm trying to say. We all eat meat. If you don't, you're like…you're like a rabbit, or a mouse."

Her tone got sharper. "Or an otter?"

"You eat meat." He sighed.

"Mostly fish. So am I like a, what, like a pelican?"

"You don't have packs like wolves. We all stick together. Do something different, and you're not quite part of the pack any more."

"Good thing they don't know you like boys, huh? Or is there a gay wolf pack, too?"

"It's not funny."

"It's kind of funny."

Sol felt irritation like a whine in his head. The argument was pointless and Meg would never understand anyway. "I gotta go."

"Wait! At least do some reading this weekend, okay? I'm getting stuff together for the report, I can show you next week. If you have time, you can make it better. But you gotta know what we're talking about. When does all this practicing end?"

"Next week. We have a game Friday and then after that Mr. Zerling will set the starters for the Lakeside game."

His father asked about the same thing when they went out to the park, and Sol told him the same. He shared how optimistic he felt, and was glad when his father's ears perked up at the news. "I stayed later than Taric every night this week," he said, slipping through the park gate behind his father.

"You tell the rest of the team that?" his father asked.

"No…I mean, they're gone by then, and school is busy with classes. I don't want to brag about it or anything."

"That coyote would brag, you'd better believe it. Do they ask at lunch? They must notice you stay until they leave, right?" His father hefted the bat, holding one of the baseballs.

"They…don't really ask." Sol trotted across the grass, to avoid having to tell his father that he ate alone all week. That would bring up his salad lunches again. His father was happy about his baseball, so Sol was going to focus on that.

He finished his homework Saturday night, so Sunday after church, after his father had hit grounders to him for another two hours, Sol settled down to do some reading for his project. He read some of Meg's books, but every mention they made of the artists' community recalled the small studio of Abrazzo, every painting brought back in his imagination the fine figure Henri had been painting in his dream. The words he read were black and white; the images in his head were in color. He missed those images, wanted to return to the world again.

He wouldn't drink absinthe. That way he could go back to Jean's narrative and not have to worry about bringing anything back from a dream. Heartened by that logic, he opened "Confession" and found the spot where he'd left off, just after Jean's second visit to the Moulin Rouge and his second night with Niki.

I returned home that night in high spirits. My fingers remained warm with the touch of his fur, and the anticipation of seeing him again in two nights carried my feet high above the paving stones. Thierry remarked that he had rarely seen me so gleeful. You must understand: the first night alone with him was the brightest of my life. To have experienced an echo of the night had brought me such bliss as to make me spin and dance in the street, and the promise of a future night was more than I could have hoped for.

Of course, I had hoped, and had bought a dress and suit upon the strength of that hope. But one never knows, in these times, and especially in the poorer quarters, how long any of us have. I had twice woken from nightmares of returning to the Moulin Rouge to find that Niki had been claimed by another, had been struck by consumption, or had been killed. Your many lectures to me have driven home the danger of public expression of affection for another male, but Niki had no such instruction. He seemed to believe that in his blissful haven of Montmartre, he was safe from persecution. How naïve! With only a few more days, I would be able to extend the protection your station affords me to the lovely fox, but until then, he existed on the sufferance of those around him, subject to the whims and vagaries of fortune that have taken so many fine artists from us before their time.

So on that night, I was able to dispel those morbid thoughts and devote myself entirely to rejoicing in the good fortune my life had brought me. I slept but little, and the following morning found me in the same good humor. Bertrand de P— and Charles L— joined me at Galerie Beaumont for our regular luncheon, and it took them the entire span of two minutes to remark upon my mood. I modestly confessed the reason for it, that I had found a date for the ball at the Justines' mansion, and that news met with their enthusiastic approval. I told them that "Nikky" was a red fox dancer of modest talent but great beauty, and as Bertrand is a red fox himself, and Charles of Rhonese wolf descent, they were quite impressed. Later, I would learn that they immediately contrived to part me from my fox if "she" were as lovely as I claimed, but those schemes—well, you know how they ended.

The luncheon carried on for some hours, as these things do, and Bertrand and Charles of course prated on about all the lovely ladies they had bedded, or wanted to bed, or knew that someone else was bedding. Bertrand expressed his relief that I had found a lady to bring to the ball who was not one of my father's friends (you will excuse his rudeness), and Charles asked if this meant that I was finally discovering an interest in ladies myself.

I rarely complained about this, but this topic of conversation was not uncommon, most especially when Bertrand and Charles and I were dining in the company of other peers, whom Bertrand and Charles wished to impress by calling out my flaws, as they saw them. I had friends of my own, but they would not join me, Thierry because he thought himself too old, Minon because he did not appreciate my lighthearted teasing of him in front of the others. Still, it was important for me to continue to dine with Bertrand and Charles. You understand that they were and are of a different class. You have told me upon many an occasion how you put aside your personal feelings in order to place yourself in select company, how by so doing you raise yourself up. I admire that quality in you, and my luncheons with Bertrand and Charles, however tedious they may have been upon occasion, were my attempt to emulate your skill and manners in my own social circle. I am sure they viewed the luncheons as a droll amusement, or else an act of charity: what other predators would dine so frequently with a mere chamois?

I suffered through that afternoon with a smile, because I knew that come the ball, Bertrand and Charles would be the ones with their tongues lolling after the beauty on my arm. And so I turned the conversation to the classical beauty of the ladies they chose to accompany them, and did my best to subtly suggest in whatever ways I could the manners in which they were lacking, manners in which, of course, my Niki would shine far above them. Bertrand and Charles, well-mannered sons of privilege that they are, were only too happy to join in my deconstruction of their consorts, never guessing my true intent behind it all.

Their consorts, they said, were like living works of art. Bertrand and Charles had each of them experienced phases of their life during which they sang the praises of a certain artist, or style of art, and these phases coincided most closely with the favor those artists enjoyed in society circles at the time. Their families bought paintings as mother buys dresses, according to the current fashion, and the paintings that fall out of favor are sold at auction or quietly stored in secluded rooms that are never visited by guests.

Similarly, the wolf and fox could be seen with a new consort at each new event. I had supposed for a short time that their fickle nature could be attributed, as mine was, to the search for a partner in life; I soon found that their likely marriages were being arranged by higher powers, and they treated their companions as accessories to their mood and fashion. So it was that when white was in fashion, Bertrand could be seen with Valerie the arctic fox, and Charles with a lovely white wolf from the northern countries. When wide skirts and bodices dominated every gathering, Bertrand and Charles arrived at the Justines' ball that year accompanied by a pair of plump tigresses who spoke very little of the mother tongue. And this year, when ladies find it more fashionable to be seen in trim dresses that accentuate their feminine lines, both my luncheon companions would be escorted by the slender, pretty wolves visiting from the Iberian court.

My fox would outshine them all, even had I not purchased the finest dress for him to wear. I could not have been more certain of that, and I held in my favor the added advantage that my family had long since given up attempting to arrange any sort of union for me. I was free to marry for love, and love I had found, even if I could not marry it.

He didn't remember putting his phone away, but he woke in the morning without any dreams, no spot of paint nor black ribbon nor crumbs of a 19th century luncheon clinging to his muzzle. The peaceful reality of the morning was a relief, but Sol's heart felt a small twinge. He wondered what Niki had really thought of his second night with Jean, wanted to know what Cireil thought, wanted to see Henri's finished painting. Stupid, he thought. It's just a dream. But the small ache, like a slowly healing scar on his ear, persisted despite all his logic.

When he arrived in homeroom that morning, there was a pile of rotten salad on his desk. Tanny, stretched out at her own desk, perked an ear at his approach but did not turn away from chattering with her friend. Sol stopped halfway across the classroom when he saw it, then turned back and grabbed the trashcan from the front. The fox who sat in front of him walked up while he was shoveling the rotten salad into the trash. His black ears flicked as Tanny said, "Throwing away your lunch, leaf-eater?"

Sol had no intention of replying, but the fox had other ideas. "You should be more polite," he said in a light Siberian accent that belied his thicker frame.

Tanny turned all the way forward to face them, her eyes widening. "Stay the fuck out of this, Ivan."

"My name—"

"I don't give a fuck what your name is." Around them, some of the other students were watching avidly, others turned away in embarrassment, though even their ears stayed focused on the mounting argument.

The fox shrugged, but his grey eyes were narrowed. "Not nice to put garbage on desk, is all."

"Yeah, well, he's been keeping my brother down for a year now, and my brother is way more talented and finally gets his starting spot, and this faggot wants to steal it back. Is that nice?"

"If he is allowed to play, it will be the coach decision."

Sol didn't quite know what to do. The only times he'd been present for an argument about him in which he wasn't involved had been at home

"You should be more polite."

with his parents. Reflexively, he'd adopted the same posture and attitude, muzzle and ears down, but he realized that he didn't have to. Tanny started to reply, but he cut her off. "We'll just let the manager decide who's more talented," he said.

"You fucking wolves," Tanny said, and this time she said it loudly enough to reach Mr. Fortune, at the front of the room. The old bear didn't notice much, but he lifted his head at that remark.

"Detention, Miss Winston," he said. She opened her muzzle to protest. "And another one if you continue this conversation any further."

Tanny glared at Sol, folded her arms, and sat back in her seat.

Sol exchanged a look with the fox, murmured, "Thanks," and then took the trash can up to the front of the room. When he returned to his seat, he tried his best to ignore Tanny kicking his chair by looking at the fox. Sol realized he didn't know much about him, didn't even know the fox's first name. When Mr. Fortune called the roll, the fox answered to Tsarev, and that was all Sol knew.

He didn't have time to ask anything before they were being quieted for morning announcements, and the Pledge of Allegiance, and then the bell rang and they were off to class. Sol didn't see the fox in any of his morning classes, nor in the cafeteria at lunch, though to be truthful, the black wolf's attention was distracted. He'd sat by himself at the end of a table, and though he didn't notice Taric and the other coyotes immediately, he was soon made aware of their presence by the pieces of food being lobbed at him. The main course was spaghetti and meatballs, and it looked as though the 'yotes had grabbed more than their share of meatballs, because three landed with red splats on Sol's tray and plate, and then another hit him in the back of the head before Mrs. Marcher walked by, putting an end to it.

If the coyotes had moved from openly harassing him to launching projectiles from a distance, that was a step forward in that it was easier to ignore. The meatball that had hit him on the head lay on the floor in a small splatter of tomato sauce that he glanced at as he took his tray to the back. He cleaned up in the bathroom and then went to social studies.

Tsarev had that class with him as well. Sol walked in and paused by his desk, but the fox had barely looked up when the teacher said, "Take your seats." After the class, Sol was called up to the front to discuss his assignment from the previous week, which had been decidedly subpar. He promised the teacher he would do better, ran out of the class, and barely made it to his next one in time.

In last period history, Sol had enough time to say, "Hi," to Tsarev before the bell rang, and when history was over, Sol had to rush out to baseball practice.

The afternoon was the warmest they'd had all month. All the canids panted within half an hour of taking the field, and the deer glistened with sweat. The air felt thicker, but Sol felt an extra spring in his step. Emboldened by his weekend practicing with his father, he charged ground balls more aggressively, taking them even when they weren't hit directly to him, until one of the coaches yelled, "That's good, Wrightson, but let someone else get one." Then he stepped back, but he was encouraged to see Xavy flash him a quick smile across the infield. He focused on the ball and its movement, but his ears kept picking up Taric's chatter, as the coyote constantly congratulated the wolves on plays or called out how easy his own had been.

Sol hadn't thought anything of it before; the coyote just wouldn't shut up, that was all. But in light of what he'd read, he noticed that Taric only complimented the wolves. The one time he complimented a deer was when Xavy said, "Good grab," and Taric jumped in with, "Yeah, lookin' sharp." The way his dad and a lot of the other wolves talked about coyotes had always just been part of Sol's life. He'd never really thought to examine them from the other side. But the stark lines of Jean's world in Gallia of a hundred years ago were recognizable in the softer brushstrokes of today: diffuse, but like Henri's charcoal strokes, no less powerful.

Again, Sol ran for the batting cages before everyone else got there, and again, he took the one on the end. This time, though, when he glanced out at the bleachers and saw a fox sitting there with a notebook on his lap and writing in between looking up at the players, he recognized Tsarev. Had the fox just come out to see him practice? That would be weird. He missed the next two balls, thinking about it.

"Hey." Taric rattled the chain link. "Starters need to practice, Fagson."

Sol considered arguing, but he wanted to talk to the fox anyway. So he shouldered his bat and left the cage without turning off the machine, walking past Taric and out to the bleachers. The metal bleachers, hot from the sun, stung his feet as he hurried up them and sat down a foot away from Tsarev. He let his tail flop down and leaned back, lifting his panting muzzle to the scant breeze.

"Hello," Tsarev said. His tongue, too, lolled out, just from sitting in the heat.

"I should've told him to pretend it was a meatball." Sol stared out at Taric.

The fox inclined his head. "Excuse me?"

"They were throwing meatballs at me at lunch. Sorry, it was a bad joke." Sol turned. "I wanted to thank you for this morning."

Tsarev's brow lowered. "It is very rude, what she did. I do not understand the..." He waved a paw. "Vegetarian. Meat tastes so good! But it is not my business, yes?"

Sol stretched his arms as he talked. He'd have enough energy to go do some footwork and take more batting practice. "I didn't think it would be such a big deal," he lied. "Who cares what I eat?"

"Eating less meat makes you less strong? That is what they think?"

"Seems to be. It hasn't yet."

"I have Internet friend." The fox waved a paw. "She eats no meat, no fish, no egg, no milk...this is 'vegan,' I think she says?"

"Vegan, yeah." Sol shook his head. He kept his ears turned toward the fox, but the cracks of bats hitting baseballs still sounded explosive beats, like muted fireworks on the field. "I'm not there yet."

"She says even tame animals are people. Fur like us, faces like us." Tsarev peered curiously at him. "Why did you stop?"

"Same thing." Sol curled and uncurled his paws. One of the batting cages was vacant. "Moral issue."

"I think it is very courageous."

Sol turned. "Thank you," he said, with a broad smile. "You enjoy watching baseball?"

Tsarev ducked his muzzle. "Any sport," he said. "Nice day, sunshine. I can do homework, I watch sport."

"You play anything?"

"Football."

"Really?" Sol didn't believe that—Tsarev wasn't nearly tall enough to be a wideout or cornerback, and his vulpine build wasn't bulky enough for about anything else. "What position?"

"Defense." The fox hesitated, then opened his notebook and pointed to a picture on the inside front cover. "This is Feodor Lysavitch. Best defense, Siberian team Novosibirsk."

The picture showed a short fox wearing a red and blue uniform with white Cyrillic characters, a round white ball with drawn yellow lines around it exploding off his foot. "Oh, soccer!"

"Yes. Sorry!" The fox took the notebook back, his tail wagging a little. "I forget."

"It's okay. I used to play, years ago, but I wasn't quick enough." Sol glanced down at the field, where a couple of the batting cages were now empty. "I should get back to practice."

"Thank you for coming to talk to me."

"Thank you again, for…this morning, you know." Sol held out a paw, and the fox, after a moment of hesitation, shook it.

"Hey," Taric said as Sol walked by his cage on the way to the footwork drills, "you wanna beat me, you better practice instead of hitting on guys in the stands."

"Tell your sister to stop leaving her lunch on my desk," Sol shot back as he passed.

He walked a little more quickly, but all Taric said was, "Stay away from my sister." He didn't leave the batting cage at all. So Sol did his footwork exercises until his paws were sore, by which time most of the other players had left. And then he went back to the batting cages and hit baseballs until the shadows stretched across the field, and everyone else, all the coaches and Tsarev (who waved) and Xavy and the other players, everyone except Taric, had left.

And this time, Taric didn't go home. He stayed in the batting cage, matching Sol minute for minute. With every pause between balls, Sol looked over at Taric's muscular form and easy, sweeping swing, so precise, so powerful. Then the wolf picked up his bat, held it just off his shoulder, and waited for the next ball. He thought that Taric was watching him, too, between swings, but he never caught the coyote at it. Every time Sol glanced over, Taric was either swinging his bat, or still as a statue waiting, staring at the pitching machine.

With each swing, Sol tried to feel the passion he'd felt in his dreams, tried to keep his form as strong and perfect as Taric's. He kept a scorecard of hits again, and this time he stayed closer to Taric's total over every span he counted. The more he hit, the better he got. But the more Taric hit, the better he got, too, even if that was hard to imagine. Sol waited for the coyote to leave, figuring he could pick up at least ten or fifteen minutes of practice after that, but Taric remained in the batting cage. Shadows crept along the field toward the bleachers, and then over them, and then the sun dropped behind the school and it was really starting to get dusky and hard to see.

Sol bit his lip. He would be late for dinner if he stayed much longer. His machine had run out of balls, so he trudged up to it and turned it off.

His ears caught what might have been a small 'ha' from Taric, or it might have been just a grunt. In either case, he didn't look back; he hurried to the locker room and dressed, and Taric hadn't come in by the time Sol left at a run to catch the town bus, panting all the way.

Fortunately, his father didn't ask, and Sol was only five minutes late to dinner, so there was no heavy drama that evening. But the next night, Taric again outlasted Sol, and that night his father did ask.

"He's staying 'til sunset," Sol complained. "I'll be late to dinner."

His mother spoke up. "You can't expect Sol to stay for the entire night."

"We'll find out this weekend," his father said. "Eh, boy?" Sol chewed a mouthful of mayonnaise-y bean salad and nodded. "You talk to Mr. Zerling?"

Sol shook his head. "But I'm doing everything he told me to." Except working on his decision-making, and how could he demonstrate that if they wouldn't give him the chance?

"All right, then. As long as you're giving it a hundred and ten percent." His father let it drop there, and Sol quelled the flutter of trepidation as best he could.

The week passed in a rush of classes and hot, humid afternoons. Tanny and the other coyotes let Sol be, plus or minus a few projectile carrot sticks, and his conversations with Tsarev and Meg were brief and distracted. The impending game occupied more and more of his mind, kept his tail wagging and his foot tapping, and his pencil chewed to pieces. He barely thought about Niki and Jean, and only had time for short, quick bursts of affection with Carcy.

By Friday, he was barely able to focus enough to write down his homework for Monday, let alone pay attention to the lessons or think about Tsarev. He and the rest of the team missed their afternoon classes anyway, to get on the bus and drive the forty minutes to Huxley.

Traditionally, the starters got on the bus first, then the backups. Sol had to walk past all the starters sitting in front before sitting halfway back with Jeremy, the armadillo whose main talent was catching fly balls. Fortunately, Jeremy didn't seem to mind Sol's foot-tapping or tail-wagging; in fact, he didn't even comment on it. After an initial attempt to talk to Sol about the Typhoons, he gave up and just stared out the window.

Sol rubbed the back of his paw. The closer the game got, the more he wondered if he really had a chance to gain his spot back. In the thick of practice, immersing himself in the world of baseball, he'd not given much thought to what the end result would be, finding in himself some optimism that he'd found a way back out of the hole he'd dug himself into. But he recalled again the whipshot cracks of Taric's line drives, the chatter of the coyote with the players, and the way the ball seemed to leap out of his paws. The best Sol could do was point to his dedication and improved hitting—if he'd improved.

But Mr. Zerling would see that, would appreciate Sol's dedication. If he got some chances in today's game, Sol would definitely show the old wolf how much he'd learned, how much he deserved to have his spot back. The team had seen his dedication, Xavy was his friend again, sort of, and they would all see through Taric's transparent attempts to win their favor with insincere compliments. They'd see Sol's hard work and they'd know how much he could mean to them.

Besides, Carcy and Meg were counting on him. Most importantly, he was counting on himself. This game was going to get him out of his home, out of this small town, away to the big city where he could be gay without looking over his shoulder, where Carcy wouldn't care if he ate vegetables, where they could go to clubs like the Moulin Rouge and live in small, dirty apartments, sharing the comforts of love and art.

The more he thought about that, the more nervous he got; his tail stopped wagging and just twitched against the seat, and he rubbed the back of his paw harder and harder. Just relax, he told himself, relax, because if you tense up, you'll just make it worse.

Still, he was so nervous, pacing around before the game, that he had to excuse himself, go to the bathroom, and text Carcy, sitting on the tank behind the toilet.

Big game coming up. Got to do well or might not get starting spot back.

And no starting spot meant no car, and no car meant no visit to Carcy. The ram had to care about that, didn't he? He always sounded unruffled when they discussed it, which Sol had taken for Carcy's faith in him. But for all his confidence over the past week, now that the moment had arrived, his own faith in himself could use a boost. He rocked back and forth, staring at his phone. He only had a few minutes.

His phone stayed dead. If he waited one more minute, the coaches would come banging on the doors looking for him. Of course, that had been when he was starting. It occurred to him that it would be worse if they did not.

So he slid off the tank and out of the restroom, getting back to the dugout in time to avoid any reprimand other than a glare from Mr. Zerling. Then he had to turn his phone off for the game, and the national anthem was playing, and he was on the edge of the bench, watching the game.

The bad part was, Taric was outstanding. The way he leapt for each ball, the way his throws slammed into the first baseman's glove, and his aggressive stance at the plate all looked to Sol as if the coyote, too, were fighting for escape. He rubbed the back of his paw and curled his tail around his hip and thought, just, please, give me a chance. When the other players on the bench joked about their opponents, about the field, he was too tense to join in the first time. Then he thought of a good line and couldn't keep it in, and the ensuing laughter relaxed him, to his surprise. These were his teammates too, after all. So he made an effort to talk to them throughout the game, all the while keeping his eye on the field, and Taric in particular.

The good part was that Huxley High's team was terrible. Their pitcher gave up six runs in the first inning (Taric hit a double and then stole third), and two more in the second before their coach replaced him. By that time, the game was pretty much out of reach, since Richfield had a lion pitching who was on his game, shutting down Huxley's lineup. So in the fifth, Mr. Zerling took Taric out (with a pat on the butt and a generous "you done a game's work already") and put Sol in.

He felt transformed. Xavy stayed in at third and threw the ball to Sol before innings, just like he'd used to. Crouched in the field, watching the batter, Sol felt the weeks of practice behind him as confidence in his ability, assurance that when he dove for a ground ball, he'd come up with it and throw out the batter. And he was part of the team again, in the field.

Between innings, he stood with the other players, ears perked, and listened to the coaches. They told him about the upcoming batters, where to shift to field for the different hitters; they told him about the pitcher and what kind of pitches he threw. Sol absorbed the information, and it made sense to him out on the diamond, and he danced over the field with (he thought) grace and confidence.

He got three chances in the infield, all routine ground balls, and none of them challenges. He made the putouts at first as quickly and efficiently as he could. Blue-grey clouds blanketed the sky out of nowhere, which made it easier for Sol to see the ball, and he took advantage of Nature's gift. Both times he came to bat, he hit the ball well; once it dropped for a hit, and the second time the center fielder made a spectacular leap to rob him.

"Good hit," Mr. Zerling said as Sol jogged back to the dugout. "Nice hustle out there." Xavy gave him a pat, and so did a couple of the other players. The batting coach told him he'd really improved his swing. Taric, leaning back on the bench chatting with the pitcher, didn't even spare Sol a look. Didn't matter; it wasn't the coyote's approval he was looking for. He gulped down a full cup of water and rested back in the shade, listening to the coaches talk, tail wagging against the bench. His teammates elbowed him, joked with him, and he joked back. Nobody mentioned his vegetarianism, even when they talked about getting hot dogs after the game. Sol grinned and panted and relaxed, thinking not only about the team, but about his summer and Carcy and all the rest of the year ahead of him.

They won the game, and piled onto the bus in high spirits, even though it was hot inside and they were all overheated and panting or sweating. On the way back, someone much nearer the front than Sol asked Mr. Zerling about the Lakeside game, and the grey wolf stepped out into the center aisle, tongue hanging out. "We've got Harmony next week and then Lakeside the week after that. I talked to the coaches, and we've decided who's going to start at Lakeside. We're going to go with Stew here," he gestured to the lion, "to start."

The bus generally murmured approval. Sol half-stood to look over the bus, his tail still, his blood now much colder than the hot, sticky air on the bus. Mr. Zerling nodded to a raccoon two seats behind him. "And of course, Chuck starts next week." The wolf raised a paw. "Good game, team. Get some rest. You earned it."

Sol bit his lip. His paw shot in the air before he could stop it, before Mr. Zerling could turn around. "Yeah, Wrightson?"

"Um." Everyone in front turned around to look at him. Taric's eyes, dark grey, bored into him. "We talked about…" Please, please, don't make me say it out loud on the bus.

The team fell silent. Sol expected to see at least a few encouraging smiles, some of the team looking back at him or giving him thumbs-ups, but not one of them looked up. Taric, a few rows in front of him, talked in a low voice with the fox who played center field. Sol couldn't hear their words, but the coyote's muzzle was stretched in a lazy grin and he was paying no attention to Sol or Mr. Zerling, though his ears were up and flicking back and forth.

"Oh, right." Mr. Zerling rubbed a paw over his muzzle. "We're going to stick with this lineup for the Lakeside game. You guys are really coming together as a team."

Just like that. With those few words, it was over.

Chapter 13

All the work, the two weeks of practice, of fooling himself that he could play baseball, of ignoring everything else in his life, it was all for nothing. The disappointment lodged in his throat, thankfully never rising to the pressure of tears.

He sat on the bus until everyone else had left, and then he got up and trudged out. Xavy and Taric and a couple of the other wolves were standing around talking. Xavy raised a paw to Sol and said, "Nice game," which was nice, but on the whole, Sol would have preferred that he keep quiet, because that made Taric turn around and laugh.

"Better," the coyote said, "but a long way from the best, am I right?"

His smirk twisted the knot in Sol's throat, turning up the pressure. The black wolf just raised a paw to Xavy and kept walking, Taric's laughter echoing in his ears all the way to his father's car.

On the way home, his father asked him about the game, and Sol rattled off his stats, heading off any question about the lineup for the Lakeside game as long as possible. His father might have sensed something, because he just said, "Sounds like Mr. Zerling gave you some good playing time and you made the most of it."

"Tried to." Sol knew he wasn't doing a good job of disguising his mood. His ears were back and his tail was tightly wound and he was staring down at his lap. He shouldn't have looked that way after a great performance and a win.

"Typhoons are at home next week. Think you might want to go?"

"Sure." Even that one word was hard to choke out, because he knew that by the time that game came around, he would have to have told his father the bad news. After that, his father wouldn't want to take him down to the park, let alone to Vidalia for a baseball game.

Dinner was a series of silverware-on-china clinks punctuated by short questions and monosyllabic answers, as Sol headed off any conversation that might lead to baseball, even the discussion of the Typhoons game. His father happily shifted to the upcoming football draft and who the Millenport Orcas needed versus who they would stupidly pick, which conversation did not require participation from Sol. And then dinner was over, and Sol practically leapt from his chair. "I gotta go to Meg's and work on our project," Sol told his parents as he was clearing his dishes.

"There's raisin spice cake," his mother said brightly.

"Maybe when I get back." Sol grabbed his bag and walked out the door. While it was true that he had to go to Meg's, it was more because he couldn't bear to stay a moment longer in his comfortable stone house, where the confrontation with his father loomed overhead every moment, where he couldn't escape the scents of his parents anywhere.

It had started to shower lightly, but not enough to bother Sol. The rain suited his mood, and so did the darkness, with the clouds blotting out the moon and stars. No crickets sounded; the only noise was the hiss of rain on asphalt and grass, and the splash of his footsteps through the wet night. Even if it started to rain harder while he was at Meg's, part of him relished the idea of arriving home soaking wet. His mother would feel sorry for him; the moment when he had to admit his failure would be postponed still further.

Nobody else was out on the street on the way over, but Meg's parents were in the outdoor pool, enjoying the rain. Meg herself came to the door to let him in. "Hey, stranger," she said. "How's the Jock Quest going?"

"Over." Sol followed her to her room and kicked the door closed. He dropped his bag with a thud and brushed water from the fur on his arms. "Mr. Zerling isn't going to start me in the Lakeside game."

She turned and stared. "Fuck me."

He dropped to the floor, knees up, damp tail curled around his hips. "I did everything I could. Two weeks just isn't enough to make up for months of..." The knot pushed at the walls of his throat, his failure lodged below his tongue. He sighed. "Or to beat that coyote."

"He still giving you shit?"

"Some. His sister—"

"She's a bitch. Glued my locker shut in ninth grade."

Sol's ears flicked. "Why?"

"Because she's a psycho bitch. Listen, the real question is, how the fuck are we getting to Millenport without a car?"

Sol shrugged. "Bus?"

"We're gonna lug everything we want to move to the city with to the bus stop and then carry it to my cousin's and your boyfriend's place? You can do that if you want. Why don't you just get him to come down and pick us up?"

He sighed. "I still don't know if he'll let me move in. He said there were 'things he had to work out.'" And Carcy hadn't texted him back—oh. He'd never turned his phone back on after the baseball game. He dug it out of his pocket and mashed the power button.

Meg snorted. "It's just for a summer. Then you go off to Charleton

College to become a computer nerd, which, by the way—"

He knew what Meg thought of his major, and the fact that he mostly agreed with her didn't mean he needed to hear it again. "Any chance your parents would take us?" The phone came up slowly, and then buzzed with a text message from Carcy. *I'm sure you can perform. :)* Sol closed it without answering.

"To the evil center of corporate greed and the murder capital of the southeast? Fat chance." Meg rolled her eyes. "I don't guess your parents would."

Sol stuck the phone back in his pocket. "Mom's already crying about me leaving in the fall, and Dad won't even drive me across the street once he hears how I...how I fucked up the baseball team." The swear made him feel uneasy, but once he'd said it, the knot in his throat released somewhat. The problem was, what it was releasing felt like it might turn into tears. He fought to hold them back, because he didn't want to upset Meg any more than he already had.

She stayed quiet after that, tapping on her keyboard. Whether she was giving him time to collect himself or just searching for some other way to get out of Midland, he didn't know, but he stared at his knees and breathed evenly, until the pressure on his throat decreased further. Summer seemed a long way off, and college an eternity away. All he could think about was this next night, and the next two months, going back into the school where everyone scorned him, where he would forever be a second string, with no friends who could do anything for him but commiserate. If only Carcy could come to the school, could walk up to Mr. Zerling and point at Sol and say, "I want him," and take Sol away from all of this.

"We'll figure it out," Meg said. She slid down to sit on the floor with him, holding the bottle of absinthe. Her smile was a bright line in her black-furred face.

She started to say something else, but when she'd moved to the floor, the bright screen of her laptop drew Sol's eye. On it, a hollow-eyed fox with ragged fur stared back at him, one ear scarred and mutilated, and Sol thought of Niki, all in a rush, and jerked forward before he realized that the fox on Meg's laptop had brown eyes, that he was older, that he was, in fact, Vincent van Gogh and not a Siberian fox dancer.

"What's wrong?" Meg craned her head back toward her curtained window. "Ronald and Valinda making noise in the pool outside?"

"No, just..." Sol looked down from van Gogh and rested his head back against the wall. "Sorry, I thought I saw...I mean, that van Gogh picture is creepy."

"All the pictures of him are creepy. But you jumped like you saw a ghost or something."

Sol shook his head. "It doesn't matter. Anyway, I don't know what there is to figure out. I don't have a car, I don't have a team, I don't have anything."

"You got me. And you promised to get me to Millenport and I ain't gonna let you slide out of that just because you don't have a car. Right?"

"I guess."

"You guess. You better be sure. Come on, who are the two smartest seniors in the whole damn high school?"

"Tara Soben and Rob Carter?"

Meg play-swatted at his face. "They're the best memorizers. They can vomit back anything a teacher says onto a test, and that's all the teachers grade on. I mean, who are the best at—oh, fuck it, you know what I mean. You and me, we'll beat this fucking town or die trying."

Sol eyed the bottle. "Better problem-solving through chemistry?"

"Figured you could use a drink. Want this, or something from the liquor cabinet? The folks have kelp wine and cooking sherry."

Sol stuck his tongue out. "That's all, really?"

"I can get you the good pot if you want it."

"Jesus, Meg."

She shrugged. "Suit y'self. Though it'd really help."

The paint and the ribbon surfaced in his memory, but he remained numb. If the dream world wanted to carry him away, then it could have him. It couldn't be any worse than what was left for him here. And he missed Niki. The fox, at least, was escaping from his own prison, and Sol wanted to watch. "Can you do the ritual?"

Meg gave a little snort of laughter. "Now you want the ritual."

"You said we can't drink it out of the bottle."

"You want me to light the candles, too?" She got to her feet. "Scoot, I need to get to the kitchen to get the sugar and the goblets."

Sol stood too, and stepped back out of her way. "I'll light the candles."

He found comfort in the small, fragile flame, the way it held on to the candle wick as he touched the small match to each one of them. Out of Meg's window, he could see sparkles of light as the rain hit the pool, but he didn't want to look too closely for fear of seeing her parents. The darkness beyond the pool was absolute: no fireflies, no moon, no stars. Sol looked away from it, back at the steady flame of the candle, and he forced himself to breathe more evenly.

Meg returned before he was done. She said, "Don't burn anything," as he lit an incense stick and the smell of frankincense filled the air.

"Like you couldn't just throw it in the pool." Sol closed his eyes and breathed in the fragrant spice. He sat back on the bed and let the rich, sharp scent take him away from the memories of the day.

"That's not the point," Meg said, but Sol barely heard her. His muscles still ached, but for the first time since the game had ended, his chest didn't feel like a coil of barbed wire. Anise wafted toward his nose, joining the incense; he opened his eyes and saw Meg holding out a goblet of milky green liquid to him.

"Prepare to receive the gift of the Green Fairy," she said. "May she show us the solution to our problems."

"Someone has to." Sol raised his glass to Meg's.

To himself, he said, *may she show me more of Niki.* As afraid as he had been of another spot of paint, another ribbon, at least they were his experiences. He didn't have to wait for Mr. Zerling or his father to tell him he could have them.

They sipped the absinthe, and Sol waited for the warm feeling to steal over him again. Meg sat and watched him. "That help?"

"Some," Sol said.

Meg swirled the drink before taking another sip. "You know, artists used to sit around and talk about philosophy and art with this stuff."

"Life sucks. Does that count as philosophy?"

"Take another drink." Meg shook her head, and draped one arm over the back of her chair. "You know, you get like one night to be like this and then you better snap back to your regular goofy self. It's fucking exhausting being the cheerful one. I dunno how you do it."

"I don't know how I did it either." Sol filled his mouth with absinthe, let the sharp smell sting his nose, let the liquid burn his throat. It seared away the pressure, distracted him from thoughts of peach canneries and Bible-thumping uncles and frustration at a four-hour separation from Carcy. That made him think of Jean and Niki, and his paws tingled with the urge to see them again.

"Can I read on the bed?"

Meg's eyebrows lowered, and her grin soured. "That's it? That's your big discussion about art? 'Can I read on the bed?'"

"It's for the project."

She looked at him a moment longer, then shrugged and assumed her usual weary scorn. "Knock yourself out."

He stretched out on her bed and pulled up his phone. A blinking light indicated he still had not answered Carcy's message. *I know,* he told it silently, and pulled up "Confession."

Chapter 14

You may criticize many things about my predilection, father, and many of them would be true. But for all of those, there is one point which you may not challenge; namely, that I have had a far wider experience of partners, and by that I do not mean to imply some crude tally of marks in a ledger. I mean that as a young buck, when you attended balls and soirees and searched through the forest of high society for companion, your choices were limited to a small segment of the population. Marriages are arranged, yes, but even when you seek only a dalliance, a consort for a short span of mutually enjoyable evenings, you cannot pick and choose. Take Minon, for example. His father found a lady squirrel for him to marry, but in the years before that marriage, when he was still making his desperate attempts to be accepted by our peers, he was never successful in his courtships of any but mice, rats, and, once, a shrew whom he insisted had a lovely personality. He walked with me among the chamois, the stately Rhonese elk and Anglic red deer, and none of them gave him so much as a second glance. Just as I, father, walked among the vixens and the wolves, the exotic lions and leopards, and even the less haughty weasels and stoats. They happily shared my conversation, at which I am somewhat more gifted than the unfortunate Minon, but even that facility of manner would not have been enough to persuade any of those lovely ladies to spend an hour alone with me, let alone an entire evening.

And yet, for as small a sum as you might spend at one of our second-best restaurants, I was blessed again with the company of a fox as lovely as any of those vixens, at my beck and call for the entire night. He was quite patient with me, that night; I was so eager to show him off to Bertrand that I fear I became quite over-excited with him. His quiet dignity in the face of my enthusiastic plans only set my resolve that he would be my consort for the night of the ball.

He had asked if he might go, and I prevented him, but had not told him my plans. While I made my ablutions, he complimented my chambers, my taste in decorations and artwork. Of course, father, my tastes in artwork had their roots in my upbringing, from the playful murals in my nursery (I still recall the bright red sunset and the design on the shields of the chamois warriors) to the paintings I grew to love and appreciate in our salon as I myself grew. I would not have developed the discerning eye I now possess were it not for your guidance, both in instruction and by example.

I believe I have made you proud in my artistic taste (if nothing else) and created of my own chambers a monument to the finest artistic styles and movements of our time, and so I hope you will trust me when I tell you that even *déshabillé* (perhaps especially so; forgive me), Niki himself shone out among all the paintings I had collected. He kept his tail not only elegantly brushed and clean, but always at a flattering curl against his body, and I swear that Renoir himself, did you place him in my chambers and provide him with a palette as wide as the Seine, could not have captured the delicate and natural beauty that sat on my *chaise-longue*.

And yet, the fox seemed unaware of his own beauty, the power he possessed over me. He smiled when I paid him compliments, he submitted willingly to my pleasure, and yet I could see that he felt that it was all a charade, a play that was being put on for the benefit of some unknown audience. I hoped that my proposition would convince him, that in bringing out the dress I had bought, showing him the value I placed on his presence at my side, that then perhaps, finally, he should awake to the possibilities that stretched between us. I have told you that I saw a future, and I firmly believe that the failure to find that path rests with me, that if only I had found the right words, the right gifts, our fates might have ended differently.

As it happened, Niki's reaction to the dress was wholly unexpected. He told me politely that it was lovely and said he hoped I would not be offended if he said that he grew quite tired of passing for a female on five nights a week, and had little wish to assume the guise for a sixth. I assured him that at the Justines' ball, there would be nobody reaching under his skirt, that the only eyes upon him would be respectful and admiring, that he would be as safe as a painting under glass.

Still he demurred. I could not force any reason out of him other than that he would feel ill at ease, out of place in such a world. Over and over I assured him that I would be his guide, that my arm would never leave his side. I showed him the elegance of the dress and how beautifully it set off his fur; I brought him all the perfumes at my disposal with which he could mask his barely masculine scent; I pleaded with him to believe that the evening would not only pass without the kind of incident he feared, but that it would be possibly the most enjoyable evening he had passed in his life.

(He did not speak much of his early life, father, but a perceptive chamois such as you or I can tell from the bearing of a person, from his naïveté in matters of society and the wideness of his eyes at the fine carpets and polished marble of my chambers, from the respectful cant of his ears even when unnecessary, what experiences he is accustomed to having. Believe me when I tell you that Niki had never been to an occasion even as elegant as a dinner with Mme. Beaumarchais, much less the Justines' ball.)

I resorted at last to one of the basest temptations I could muster. Niki had not spoken of any specific friends of his, but his words on the general poverty and squalor that dominated the neighborhood had not escaped my notice. If he would not seek out my company for its own sake, then I could still tempt him with lucre. If he did not wish it for his own sake, then, I cajoled, think of the good he could do for his less fortunate friends. If he did not wish to profit from the gifts nature had bestowed upon him, at least he could render them useful for his friends.

He seemed unable to decouple the idea that he would dress as a female from the prospect of dancing—not dancing with me, as would of course be expected at a ball, but I believe he thought he would be expected to perform. It took me well over an hour to convince him to agree, and then only by inviting him to attend a dinner the following night, an event with fewer expectations and fewer attendees, so that he could feel more certain of himself.

Yes, father, I hope that you will now have a clearer understanding of why I asked Niki to accompany me to M. X—'s dinner. I think you will agree that no lasting harm to your business dealings came of that impulsive act, despite your harsh accusations afterwards. In fact, Mme. X— and Niki were engaged in conversation for most of the evening, and she complimented me on my way out for my choice in such an attractive and well-mannered consort.

Niki and I celebrated our new agreement in the short time we had before the dawn brought our tryst to an end. Then he had to return to his life in Montmartre, but I swore it would soon not be so.

He can still feel its confines, the starched monstrosity of taffeta and frills that Jean claimed had belonged to some female relative. More likely, Niki thinks, it was a drunkenly impulsive gift for some unfortunate female he was courting that had been roundly refused, and many months later, he, poor wretch, is the one forced to bear the burden of the chamois's inebriated lack of taste. And yet, still, Jean's delight at seeing him in the dress softens the humiliation. It is even enough to make Niki's smile not altogether false. And Jean repeatedly insists that the unbearably gaudy affair Niki will wear two nights hence is far more comfortable, that it makes less noise at the slightest movements, that it does not smell of must and mildew beneath the expensive perfume.

The food at the dinner was exquisite and rich, sauces and fresh baguettes and roasted fowl that fell off the bone; butter and honey and small, soft rolls; piles of vegetables whose green skin and scents burst forth amid the browns of the bread and fowl. Still, Niki had difficulty eating too much of any one thing. He has subsisted on small, plain fare for years, and this embarrassment of riches, no matter how it tantalized and delighted his nose, did not agree with his stomach or his mind. He twice stopped himself from asking for a small basket of the rolls, or a small jar of the honey, to take back with him.

Now, though he still feels the weight of the food in his stomach, he wishes he had asked. He is coming back to the room with nothing but the promise of payment, no token of affection nor souvenir to share the life of Jean and his family with Henri or Cireil. The sun creeps over the shingles atop the houses on Niki's street as he passes the bakery and lifts his nose to the smell of bread. He has left Henri money, and although he knows there is little chance the rat has bought any bread himself, Niki will wait to be sure before spending any more money.

Many familiar scents meet Niki's nose outside the small house where many of the dancers live with artists and musicians, and one familiar muzzle, coming along the street from the opposite direction: the ermine. She apprises Niki as they stop facing each other. "And where have you been spending your free night, little cu-cu? Off with your chamois patron?"

Niki lowers his head and tries to walk past. But the ermine stops him, her dark eyes intent on his muzzle. "Your lip is torn."

"I'll have it seen to before tonight."

"No plasters." The ermine releases him. "Your boy plays rough, does he?"

Jean's fingers clenched around his muzzle, holding it shut; Niki's lower lip caught between his long canine teeth. His paws, tied, unable to move. "I bit it. By accident."

"Ha." She laughs. "The swelling will go down. It always does, petit. And then the cut will heal, in time."

"Already I barely feel it." Niki focuses on the smile he remembers from Jean, after, and the pain does indeed lessen.

The ermine smirks. "Do not fret. Most of the girls will not get two nights from the same gentleman."

"This was my third." Niki stands straighter. "He is taking me to a ball in two nights."

"You are working in two nights." The ermine's eyes narrow.

Niki shakes his head. "After the ball, he wants me to stay with him."

"Of course he says that." But the ermine's pure white fur might be turning a light shade of green in the reflected light from the limestone buildings. "If you leave the Moulin, M. Oller will not take you back."

This might be true or it might not; some girls have left and returned, but there are whispers of what they have had to do to be allowed to return, and Niki is not certain that he has anything to offer that M. Oller would want. "I will have no need to return," he says.

"And we will be better off. Perhaps the deviants will stop frequenting our cabaret, stop bothering us with their disgusting demands." The ermine turns on her heel and marches away.

Niki watches her go, the sunlight tinting her back, her feet loud on the paving stones. The quarter is just waking up now, the smells of people joining the aroma of bread through the damp morning air. He lingers, closing his eyes and inhaling. The smells of the quarter surround him, infuse him, the honest scents of simple food and paint, of wood and the musk of the inhabitants. This is his world, and yet, how can he turn his tail to Jean's world, with its rich food and rich people, with its carpets and polished marble and money shared as easily as fleas?

He mounts the stairs slowly to his room, through the scents of his neighbors and their debris. The door creaks as it opens. He calls a cautious, "Allo?"

There is no response. Henri lies curled up on half the bed, his eyes closed and his head resting near the open window. Niki closes the door behind him, at least, as well as the ancient door will fit into the warped frame. Henri does not wake.

The morning sun is kind to the paintings. Looking down on their creator, they shimmer and breathe, glowing with warmth. Niki takes a moment to bask in their glow, letting their shapes and hues wash over him. He pads slowly across the room to the bed and sits on the other half, drawing his knees up to his slender muzzle as he removes the ribbons from his ears. He clasps his paws around his shins and lets his tail swing free behind the bed, looking over at the easel. The reclining female mouse, fully painted, smiles back. Around her, a haze of bright autumn reds and yellows swirl in large brushstrokes, but Henri has described with charcoal lines where he intends to finish the work, add more definite outlines of leaves. Niki feels that the outlines are perhaps more beautiful than the finished work, but he is not the artist.

The other portrait, the one Niki has not seen, is propped against the wall. The stained cloth over the canvas has slipped, exposing one corner. Tempting, but he is tired from his long night, and he respects Henri too much. When he *leans against the wall, he can see out the window, past the shingled rooftops of Montmartre to the gleaming spires of the palace, to the center of the city and the ancient majesty of Notre Dame and, perhaps, the house from which he has just walked this past night, where Jean lies asleep in his enormous bed, sated amidst his ropes and his oils and the smell of fox. Niki's eyelids, heavy, shutter his eyes against the day, and he, too, sleeps.*

When he wakes, Henri is seated at his easel, and the light is muted, the sleepy glow of afternoon. Niki watches the brush dance across the canvas, dip to the palette and back to the canvas, leaving traces behind it in brilliant crimson and gold. The oily smell of the paint fills the room. He rubs sleep from his eyes and cannot restrain a yawn.

"Awake from your revels," Henri says without breaking a stroke. "I would say it is nearly time for you to report to your drudgery at the cabaret. If, that is, your cher chamois, your cherois, has not yet liberated you from the shackles that bind you to this dismal life."

"No." Niki stretches his legs. "He has promised me money, but—"

"Bon Dieu." Henri dips to his palette. "In three nights you have earned nothing? Your courtesan skills lag far behind your dancing skills."

"He wants to take me to a ball. He promised me after." Niki crouches, extending one leg and then the other.

"You shall be the prettiest of the ladies at the ball." Henri sighs. "And then what? He will tie you to his bed? You exchange one dance for another."

"The money from the cabaret, it is enough to live." Niki sits on the bed, grasping one foot. "But for how much longer? I thought that after, I would—"

"Spare me the details. I am certain I can fill them in. Is it so bad, this life? You at least make a pretense of dance."

"I—"

"You may enhance the tawdry with the graceful, even if the usual patrons cannot notice any distinction. In your own way, you are following your art. And this you would give up, all for the chance to eat pickled ostrich eggs and drink Bourgogne wine."

"Cireil understands. She does not think less of me." Niki stands and fastens the ribbons over his ears. He wanted to tell Henri his plan, but now the rat is being unreasonable and Niki thinks that if he does not allow himself anger, he will find himself overcome by tears. "One must live, no?"

"Yes." Henri throws his brush down and turns, his eyes bright. "One must live. And art, this is where one finds life. Existence is nothing without art, as you will find, renardeau."

"I am not a cub." Niki glares stiffly back at him. "I have lived without art for a long time. I shan't miss it."

Henri stares, and then he straightens his back. He turns, slowly, but does not resume painting. "You will," he says softly.

"Good-bye," Niki says. He breathes in paint, and rat, and fox, and paint.

He is at the door when he hears Henri say, "I notice you have not mentioned love."

"Sol."

Someone was shaking his shoulder.

"Sol!"

He blinked, his eyes crusty with sleep.

"Hey, if you're gonna sleep in my bed, at least take your clothes off so my parents can 'catch' you."

He yawned hugely and rubbed a paw against his eyes, smiling. An oily smell filled his nostrils. "Sure, if you want. What smells?"

"Thanks." Meg punched his arm. "Look, I'm gonna light up to chill out and I didn't want you waking up to a room full of smoke. Also you're drooling on my pillow."

"Uh." Sol propped himself up on his elbows and rolled onto his side. He wiped his muzzle. "Sorry."

"No biggie." Meg flipped the pillow over. "It's raining harder. You want me to get Ronald to drive you home?"

"What are the chances he's sober?" Sol sat up slowly, taking his time. He could still smell the thick, oily scent, even over the taste of anise in his muzzle. The lonely, hollow emotions of the dream hung in his head, battling with the feeling of well-being left from the absinthe.

Meg wiggled her paw. "Sober? Pretty good. Not baked?" She shook her head.

"I'll walk." He yawned again and rubbed his nose. "You don't smell that? Smells like…like paint?"

The otter shrugged. "Still smells like frankincense to me in here, but you're the one with the sniffer." She got out her tin of mints and pulled a joint out.

Sol stood and walked around the room, his nose high. The scent stayed strong everywhere he went, unnaturally. It should be stronger in some places than others. If he weren't still feeling the warmth of the absinthe inside, it would probably worry him, because scents that came from nowhere usually came from you. Smelling things that weren't there got you a trip to the doctor.

But after one circuit of the room, the smell didn't seem so important. What was a hallucination compared to questions of life and art? He felt the echoes of the dream not only in his nose, but in the stiffness of his legs and arms. He stretched while Meg rummaged in her desk for another incense stick.

She lit it—sandalwood, not frankincense—and Sol breathed in. The oily paint smell lingered, but weaker. He walked over to Meg and draped an arm over her shoulder, almost knocking the joint out of her paw.

"Careful!" She held the joint away from him, but didn't shrug him off.

Sol breathed in the spiraling coils of incense smoke and Meg's scent and marijuana and still, below it, oily paint. "Sorry. This is just nice. It's just what I needed."

She took her lighter out. "I swear, this fuckin' project. Where else could you get buzzed and call it homework?"

"Yeah, it's pretty cool. Okay, I'm gonna walk home." Niki's loneliness made Sol want to hug Meg again, to tell her how much he valued her friendship, but she was already bringing the cigarette lighter to the end of the joint.

"Mmkay." She flicked the lighter on. "You going to be okay, walking home?"

"I'm fine. I'm chill. Everything's good. See ya Monday."

Even the chilly evening rain felt right. The warmth of the absinthe, though fading, kept him feeling light inside, even as his fur gradually soaked up more water. It dripped into his eyes and ran into his nose, light drops that he blew out as he walked. He kept his ears folded back and his tail curled beneath him, and he hurried along the sidewalks. The moon's light described silver edges of the huge masses of clouds overhead. Every time he looked up, he hurried faster. The air smelled like ozone and storms, like thick and warm, as though the clouds themselves were about to break.

When he turned the corner to start up Prospect, wind rushed down to meet him. It flattened his fur, drenched it, and pushed him back down the hill as he gritted his teeth and struggled up. Even though the full fury of the storm remained in abeyance, Sol was, if not drenched, at least very wet by the time he walked in the door. He shed his jacket and wiped down his fur in the foyer, at which point his mother came out from the kitchen. "You're soaking wet!"

"I walked home from Meg's," he said.

"Go dry yourself off—"

"I was going to!"

"—and I'll get you a piece of raisin spice cake."

He stood dripping on the floor at the base of the stairs. The cake smelled exquisite and rich. He shook his head. "I'm...no, thanks."

His mother's ears lowered with her frown. "Are you feeling okay?" She leaned in to smell him.

"I'm fine, Mom." But her nose was already wrinkled, her head tilted.

"Meg was burning incense again?"

"Yeah, it has to do with our project. I'm gonna dry off and then I'm just…" He put one foot on the lowest stair. "I'm gonna go to bed."

"Sol?" Her tone, high and worried, stopped him. "Are you doing drugs?"

"Mom." He shook his head. The absinthe high had mostly, mostly faded. "No."

"You smell a little like…and Meg's parents encourage her to experiment."

He shook his head again. "You told me how you feel about that."

"Your father thinks…the way your baseball fell off…"

"I had two hits in the game today. Or as good as." He wanted to ask where his father was. It was late, so he was probably in the den, because the TV wasn't on in the living room. "Were you just waiting up for me?"

"I'm making a roast for tomorrow."

He couldn't smell the meat over the cake, which must be sitting out on a counter. "Sounds good. Potatoes and green beans?"

She nodded. "If that's all right?"

"Sure." He exhaled. "Thanks, Mom."

His tail uncurled as he walked up the stairs, dripping behind him. He rubbed himself dry with a towel as best he could, and then tossed the towel onto his bed and flopped down on it. Back home, he couldn't forget that he wouldn't be getting a car, that he would be stuck here through the summer with Carcy effectively on the other side of the world. He'd be lucky to manage a bus ride for one weekend visit.

Two more months of school, two more months of being a backup on the baseball team, getting taunted by Taric and ignored by the others. Two more months of getting shit for vegetarianism, of doing homework and not having a car, of going over to Meg's once or twice a week and texting Carcy, two more months of uncomfortable dinners with his father. Well. Five more months of those. He closed his eyes and pressed his muzzle into the pillow.

Chapter 15

He is dancing in the line behind the ermine, two dancers away from Cireil, in perhaps the next to last show he will ever dance in at the Moulin Rouge. Perhaps. Niki's timing has been off this whole evening, not so much that anyone but him would notice, because of what the ermine and Henri had said to him.

It is not so bad, here in the cabaret, now that he thinks of leaving it. There are no patrons who watch him and only him the way Jean does, but there have been before and will be again. What worries him is that Jean is the first to have requested him for more than one night; Jean is the first to offer him money and freedom. But is it more freedom than he has now? He kicks his legs at precisely the right height, he moves his feet in precisely the right steps, and though the movement is not difficult, the dance makes his blood pump faster, each well-placed (if a half-second slow) step is a success. In moments like this, he feels as though the Dance is animating his body, as though even if he ceased moving of his own volition, his limbs would continue to describe their patterns, his body would twist and turn. He feels a part of something greater than himself.

He has felt that way with patrons, sometimes. Not with Jean, not yet, but he takes such pride in the chamois's pleasure that it is almost as good. Jean has suffered, that is clear, at the hands of his family and his society, and that is a pain Niki is only too happy to help ease. His tongue finds his swollen lip, holding it away from his teeth. It is not so bad, he thinks. And Jean may come to learn gentleness, in time.

So it feels selfish for him to wish to continue dancing here at the cabaret. Even if he can only help one person, is that not better than simply dancing for his own sake?

He moves with the girls, back and forth. Though the ermine takes the front stage, Niki searches the audience and finds one or two patrons whose eyes linger on him before moving on. He makes note of them for after the show. Cireil taught him this, he knows, but he cannot remember a time when he did not know how to do it.

The line of dancers moves behind the curtain, gathering backstage while the ermine finishes the show alone. In the few minutes before they move out onto the floor, Niki talks quietly with Cireil.

"Did you pass the test of the dinner?" the wolf asks him.

Niki smiles. "If I have not yet been poisoned by the food, then I believe I have."

"So, the ball. You will go?"

The fox licks at the tear in his lip. "Do you think I should?"

Cireil reaches up and turns his muzzle out of the shadow. She stares at his lip. "Were you any other girl, I would say yes." She releases him. "But you love dance, and it shows so much in your movements."

"I will never be at the front of a show." Niki does not attempt to keep the bitterness out of his voice.

"No. But not through the fault of your performance. And does that matter?"

"I can make him happy," Niki says.

Cireil smiles. "And he? Can he make you happy?" When Niki does not answer, Cireil says, "There will be others who can make him happy. But who will do that for you, if not him?"

Niki takes a fold of the velvet curtain in his paw and slides the fabric through his fingers. There is the dance, there is the performance, and there is the elegance of the club, no matter how M. Oller tries to hide it behind gaudy gold paint. "To not have to be touched again..."

"My dear," Cireil laughs, "we will all reach that point soon enough. I say this: if you truly love him, then go to him."

The ermine has come strutting back from her dance in time to hear this. "You're a fool, old wolf. You simply want company in your last days here at the club."

"My days are not so short as you might think." Cireil's hackles fluff around her neck.

"Ha." The ermine turns to Niki. "You see how deluded she is, cu-cu. Listen to her at your peril."

"And you," Cireil says calmly, "wish only to see Niki gone so that you may be assured that M. Oller will not give him your show."

The ermine laughs, loudly enough to draw the eyes of several other dancers. "My show? To that Siberian môme? Come, let us suggest it to him. I have not heard his laugh in many weeks."

"You see?" Cireil turns to Niki, who has not dared say a word. "You must stay, if only to prove her wrong."

The ermine waves a paw. "Stay. Go. I promise you I shan't notice, and nor shall our patrons." She waves a paw airily and strides past the pair of canids.

"They all hate me," Niki says in a low voice, looking over Cireil's shoulder at the other dancers, all turning away slowly.

"They do not," the wolf snaps, "and so what if they did? You dance for dance, not for their love, not for your chamois's nor for anyone else's."

Niki's tongue curls around his lip. The pain flares lightly and subsides. "And for what do you dance?" he asks.

"Come," Cireil says. "Let us go earn our wine."

She says that every night to Niki, although he has never seen her drink a drop of wine. It would be nice, he thinks, to bring her to his apartment, to sit with her and Henri and talk about dance and art and life. Perhaps Henri would like to paint her. Cireil has no grey in her fur, but her ears often slide down from fully upright, and her eyes are weary. Henri would appreciate the depth in her muzzle, and Niki would appreciate the chance to talk to Cireil when he is not dressed as a female dancer.

Niki follows her out onto the floor, where they dance among the tables. Two of the dancers are immediately called to tables. Niki and Cireil dance together over to the bar, where they separate and search out the patrons who watched them during the show.

By now, the floor is familiar to him, the sharp scents of rodent, of fox, of wolf, of deer, of mustelid, all different in species but all male, all aroused to different degrees. Niki floats from one scent to another on the sharp fruit haze of wine that soaks the air. He knows how to keep his tail curled behind him just so; he knows how to place his feet and lift a leg to show his shapely thigh, feminine enough to fool even most of the sober patrons (there are not many sober patrons). He can tell, now, which tables will never be interested in him and which tables will show interest if he stays near. Sometimes it is the species: the rabbits, rats, and mice can rarely resist the allure of commanding a fox, of claiming their ownership of him with their fifty-centime notes (Niki rarely gets one-franc notes unless he goes to a private box; the well-off tables are claimed by the more senior dancers). Sometimes it is clear from the way the patrons are sitting: careless and bored, muzzles drooping over half-full cups of wine. When they have come to drown sorrows amid gaiety and debauchery, then Niki can lift their muzzles and spirits, and coax a franc or two out of them.

But the patrons who watched him during the show, those are the first he visits. Tonight, it is a short rabbit in a plain white shirt, but as Niki approaches, he sees the rabbit's pocketwatch chain, and his spirits rise. He dances around their table, and from the rabbit and his two companions, Niki earns three fifty-centime notes, tucked into the waist of his dress. None of them even tried to reach beneath his skirt, none of them even looked askance at him, as the foxes and wolves sometimes do when they catch just a whiff of his male scent and think they must be mistaken.

He moves on. There was a table of goats in artist smocks whose eyes lingered on him, who pointed him out to each other, but they were being entertained by a ewe the last time Niki looked. Now the ewe is dancing for a pair of jackals, and the goats catch sight of Niki again. He smiles, swishes his tail, and dances toward them with little kicks. In each kick, he remembers his training, and he feels a little bit of the joy of the dance.

On the way, he passes Cireil, but she is intent on her next table, moving even without the sashays and hip-turns that she taught Niki to use. He wants to tease her about it, but there will be time for that after. He has a table to dance for.

The goats are more drunk, or perhaps just more aggressive, but not in a dangerous way. They press bills into his garter, they contrive to brush his false chest, and by now his reaction to that is ingrained: even though he does not feel it, he acts. He jumps and then coos and presses against them, then slides away, as though he enjoyed it but knew he was not allowed to. One of the goats, bold, squeezes his rump, and Niki gives him exactly the same reaction, with a flick of his tail across the chair.

He makes another three and a half francs at this table, then sees the other wolf—not Cireil—heading for the table, and graciously he steps aside, teasing one of the goats with a finger across his horns before spinning off to another table. His body feels the touch of the goats' hands still, but he must go on; there is another hour yet to be danced.

A commotion near the bar stops him and the two dancers nearest him. They start dancing again immediately, for fear of M. Oller's wrath, but keep their eyes on the small knot of people. Niki dances his way around to where he can see a small mink, teeth bared, staring venom at Cireil.

When he sees the wolf, he hurries to her side. "…places to put your paws," Cireil is saying.

"I pay for my paws to go where they like," the mink snarls.

M. Oller appears, somehow, at Cireil's side as the wolf says, "The club has rules."

"I have money," the mink says, and the appearance of the polecat does not diminish his fury. He shakes a pile of notes at M. Oller. "What did I buy these notes for if not to take my pleasure?"

"I do apologize," M. Oller says. "Please tell me what's happened here."

"He—"

M. Oller holds up a paw to silence Cireil. Niki shrinks himself to hide behind the wolf. If M. Oller notices him, he will send Niki away to continue dancing, and Niki wants to remain to support Cireil. Fortunately, the polecat does not seem to notice the fox. "Sir," M. Oller says to the mink, "please go on."

"I was enjoying the dance," the mink says. He glares at Cireil, yellow eyes narrowed. "I pulled this whore into my lap, and she was enjoying it, don't try to deny it."

Niki bristles on Cireil's behalf. The wolf's tail curls beneath her but otherwise she maintains her dignified stand. She does not respond. So the mink snarls at Cireil. "And then I placed some notes in her garter, like always—"

"Not in my garter!" Cireil snaps, and again M. Oller must hold up a paw. He indicates for the mink to go on. Niki sees the effort it takes for Cireil's ears to remain even partially upright ("never flat," they are instructed by M. Oller, "never down").

"And she struck me!"

The wolf draws in a breath, lifting her muzzle. "I—"

M. Oller turns to Cireil, cutting off her protest. "Did you strike a patron?"

"No." She meets his stare, then drops her eyes. "I struggled to get off his lap. My elbow may—may have brushed his muzzle."

"You bruised it!" The mink leans forward, showing his eye to M. Oller. "See where it is already swelling?"

Niki can see nothing under the mink's eye, but M. Oller considers. Before he can speak, Cireil leans close to him and whispers something into his ear. Niki's large ears bring the hiss of the last few words to him, carried by Cireil's desperation and hurt. "…inside me!"

The polecat's eyes widen. The professional respect he always carries for his customers drops from him in a moment. "Did you?" he demands, and Niki sees that the mink does not need to ask what M. Oller means.

"My fingers slipped." This sullen admission from the mink is followed by anger, a pointed claw at Cireil. "She begged for it! She rubbed herself against me—"

"Our dancers are encouraged to include our patrons in their dance." M. Oller's voice is as cold as winter, as cold as the trains from the east in January.

"Dance! Filthy foreplay, more like. Why do—"

With all the grace of M. Oller himself, the two boars who provide security for the club appear behind the mink. Each one grasps an arm. The patron is shocked into silence, and then as he is forcibly pulled through the crowd, he unleashes a stream of invective. But, Niki thinks, he has not the experience nor passion of a Siberian father whose cub wants to dance.

M. Oller straightens the sleeves of his waistcoat. "Go backstage," he says to Cireil. "You are finished for tonight."

She bows her head and walks back through the bar. The patrons and dancers part before her, allowing her the space to walk. Some dancers touch her shoulder or back; Niki would like to, but he is too far already, and M. Oller is staring at him.

"And you," he says, "you are not dancing."

Niki bows his head rather than speak, and lets the dance spin him through the crowd as the patrons slowly resume their conversations. He is heartened to hear them speak of the mink as a "boor" and a "lout," but he cannot keep the sadness from his throat as he watches Cireil's noble bearing in her march to the stage door.

He dances for another hour, but the mood in the cabaret is sour, the patrons tentative. The mink is discussed many times in Niki's hearing. By the end of the hour, he has heard a wine-slurred badger mutter that "they will throw someone out for the crime of appreciating the dance," and a thick-set marmot warn a friend, "don't put a finger on them or you'll be on the street," with a jerk of his thumb. Niki wants to correct them, but the rules of the club also state that the dancers are not to engage the patrons in conversation; they must wait for the patrons to engage them. So he dances and attempts to entertain the badger and marmot, knowing that they will not be putting any bills into his waistband.

By the time he returns to the locker room, Cireil has already left. He does not speak to the other dancers. The ermine watches him, especially when he presents his eight and a half francs out to M. Oller. The polecat counts out seven and seventy-five centimes in return.

"Perhaps you are not leaving after all," the ermine says to Niki, at the doorway. She smirks, licks a finger, smooths the fur on her small ears.

Niki lowers his head. "I... have not decided yet."

"It is not such a bad life, the dance." The ermine smooths the other ear. "There is no other life for you, you know." She turns her head back to the other dancers. "A girl may find a patron who can afford to keep her as a servant, perhaps as a mistress. But you... there is no cu-cu out there who will keep you."

At that, Niki lifts his muzzle. Now the other dancer is watching him with a mix of pity and satisfaction. "Yes, not even this rich chamois. The risk, the danger if he is discovered to be keeping a boy! And why would he need to keep you? The streets are filled with boys desperate for one night. They can be had for one of those coins in your purse."

"You do not know him," Niki says.

"Neither do you."

Niki steps out into the back hallway of the club. He shakes his head, knowing there is nothing more to say to the ermine.

"A demain, cu-cu," she calls after him, amused.

Perhaps you will see me tomorrow, he thinks, and perhaps the day after, but not for the reasons you think. It is not because Jean is insincere. It is because here there is the dance, and there... who knows what is there. Love, perhaps, but there is love here, too, even if it is more diluted.

These thoughts bring him through the hallway to the back door. He pushes *the reluctant wood hard with his shoulder, letting in the cool, damp night air. Automatically, out of courtesy, he holds it for the ermine walking behind him while he turns to his right, looking down the dark alley he takes to the Rue Blanche.*

In the darkness, there is a heap of clothes the size of a person.

The door slips from Niki's fingers, striking the ermine. She cries out angrily, but Niki is two steps toward the body, and the ermine's words clatter to the ground and fall away as she sees what Niki sees. And by this time, Niki already smells wolf.

"No," he whispers, but he cannot hold his feet still. They take him closer and closer, and the scent of wolf fills his nose, so that he can detect the distinct and familiar character of it as well as the sharpness below it, the coppery-bright tang that sends his tongue to his bitten lip in sympathy. And then he is kneeling beside it, the thing that once held the spirit of his friend Cireil.

Her body is on its side, turned away from him. She might still be alive, he thinks, though he knows it is only hope speaking, a small light powerless against the darkness. His paw hovers over her shoulder, not wanting to extinguish the flicker.

The ermine's scent rolls in behind him as she approaches. "I will fetch M. Oller," she says. Not the gendarmes, of course. M. Oller will do that; they will come for him more quickly. She runs back to the club, while Niki extends a shaking paw to Cireil's nose.

No breath warms his fingers. He cannot bear to touch her muzzle, but even at a finger's distance away, he can tell that it has no more warmth. He leans forward and catches a hint, just the barest hint, of a mustelid scent. Something fierce and angry, like… like a mink.

M. Oller will be here soon. But the scent tantalizes him, and Cireil is turned away as though keeping the secret from him. From him, with whom she shared all she knew. His paw grips her shoulder and pulls. She resists; he pulls again, panting with exertion or emotion or both. Her body shifts, and then rolls in one clumsy motion toward him onto his toes.

He yelps and jumps, losing his balance and falling backwards. When his tail hits the ground, his teeth snap closed on his lip right where it is already swollen. Blood drips onto his tongue, the scent of blood fills his nose, overwhelming any faint mustelid scent he might have thought he'd smelled. The stain on the front of Cireil's plain yellow dress looks black; but then, the dress looks white, and Niki only knows it is yellow because he has seen it in the light. Here beneath the clouds, meters from the closest gas lamp, the color is gone from it, and though he can replace the yellow of the dress from memory, the blackness of the stain does not become red when he does so. It is dark and deep, a hole without bottom stretching from just below her breasts to her waist, sending tendrils out along the side she was lying on.

Her eyes are glassy grey, and there is nothing behind them. Niki reaches down to close them, and closes his own against the pressure of tears. He presses his tongue to the fresh bite in his lip. No dance is worth this price: to watch his friends waste away and die, to know that the end of his road is more likely an alley than a bed. Not when a hand is extended to him.

He takes Cireil's cold paw in his. He will hold it until M. Oller arrives.

Pain flared through Sol's lower lip. He jerked awake and brought a paw up to his muzzle. His eyes were wet, his chest tight. *Christ*, he told himself. *It was just a dream. Don't be—don't—*

But when he sat up in bed, when he saw his paws, the dream flooded back to him again and he couldn't hold back a sob, and then another. His paws shook and his body shuddered, and small squeaks forced themselves past the thick blockage in his throat.

It took him a good ten minutes to stop shaking, wiping his eyes, wincing at the pain in his lip. He must have bitten it in the night; he could taste blood on his tongue even after he'd finished crying. And his tail was sore, too, as if he'd slept on it poorly. Or fallen back on it in a stone-paved alley.

Even after he stopped the tears, Cireil's blank, grey eyes haunted him. Grief welled up inside him, denied the release of tears, a tension that shook his paws until he clasped them together. It was a dream, just a dream, he told himself. He hadn't even known Cireil that long, only two years—

Two *weeks*. Two weeks since he'd started dreaming about her, of course. He squeezed his paws together and then pressed them to his muzzle. That mink, that damn mink, how could they let him get away with that? Just because she was a dancer, he thought her life meant nothing. He had no idea how many other lives he had scarred with that savage, bitter action.

Sol focused on calming himself down. Deep breaths, paws on his knees. Finally, mercifully, the knot of grief loosened. Cireil's blank eyes still tugged at him, but Sol pushed the image resolutely away. It's just a dream, he told himself over and over again. It's just a dream, nothing more, why are you crying over a dream?

The smell of buttered eggs and bacon floated up to his bedroom and his stomach rumbled. Breakfast was downstairs, and so were his parents, and if he went down on the verge of tears, there would be questions. He could tell them it was a dream, but once he told his father that he was definitely not starting the Lakeside game, they would think he was crying over that. His father would think he was a sissy, even if his mother stopped him from saying the word out loud.

Maybe he could put off telling his father. Maybe if he fell down the stairs and got a concussion and had to be taken to the hospital…or maybe Natty would call to tell the family that he was going to start in the football game this afternoon, and his parents would pile into the car and go.

Or maybe Sol would have a nervous breakdown as a result of a weird, scary, absinthe-induced dream. Of all the possibilities, that seemed the most realistic.

But already the grief felt more manageable, more distant, as though he were no longer mourning the loss of his own friend, but of a friend's friend. He still felt the bleakness in his chest and throat, but his eyes were dry and he was only sniffling a little. So he pulled on pants and a t-shirt. He crept down the stairs, taking care not to fall down them. By this time, he hoped, his father might have finished his breakfast, leaving the kitchen empty for Sol to sneak into and eat.

No such luck. His father looked up as he entered the kitchen. "Morning," he said, and tore a chunk off the end of a strip of bacon.

Sol mumbled, "Didn't sleep very good," and headed for the grits on the stove.

"Didn't sleep well," his mother corrected him, but neither parent said anything more to him until he was sopping up the remnants of his eggs with a piece of toast.

"You want to catch some grounders this morning?" his father said, laying down the sports section of the paper.

Sol stared down at his bowl of grits. "It's raining."

"Not that hard." His father leaned forward on the table. "Did Mr. Zerling make a decision?"

Here it was. Blank eyes staring into a cloudy sky. "No," he said, and then saw himself a week in the future, two weeks in the future, his father yelling, *how long have you known?* "I mean, not really. But kind of. I guess it's not definite but…"

His father's voice was even, measured. He knew, but he wanted Sol to say the words. "Did you win your starting spot back?"

Sol's mother stood beside the table, reaching down to take her plate to the sink. She froze, her muzzle pointed down at Sol. If not for the tick of the kitchen clock, Sol would have no idea that time was passing. The hiss of the rain and the gurgle of water through the gutters made Sol feel that the house was awash, floating down the street; normally he enjoyed the feeling of adventure that brought, but this morning it just left him even more unmoored. He could smell the rain even though all the windows were closed, a lightly damp, earthy smell beneath the toast and grits and eggs.

"Sol?" His father leaned closer.

"No." Sol lifted his head. "No, I didn't. Taric's still playing really well and Mr. Zerling doesn't want to mess with chemistry so I'm on the bench for the Lakeside game." And when compared to dying alone in an alley, how bad was that, really? He glared at his father, keeping his ears up with an effort.

His father didn't look angry or upset, though. He just raised his eyebrows slightly. "Well. What more could you have done?"

There was nothing he could have done. Anger at his father kept the grief about Cireil and the frustration about himself at bay. "I did everything I could! I stayed until it was dark, I worked my tail off for two weeks, I caught grounders with you…"

"Wolves are supposed to be leaders. Did you work to gain the confidence of your teammates?"

"I did it by playing as hard as I can." He fidgeted on his chair.

"And by not eating meat?"

Sol shoved his chair back from the table and folded his arms. He swiveled his ears back so they faced the kitchen window, making the sound of rain louder. "What does that have to do with it?"

"Norston came to my office—Xavy's father. Asked about your health. What do you think his son's tellin' the team? That you're weak, that you can't do the job, that it's good that they got a replacement for you!"

"He's just…he's just stronger, and faster. And the guys like him better."

"They should like you." His father's finger jabbed at him across the table. "You're a wolf."

"I'm not like you!" Sol yelled. He stood up. "I'm not like Natty! I'm just me!"

His father leaned back in the chair. "Yes, you are. Well." He turned to Sol's mother. "Would you like to go to Sears today?"

Sol shoved his chair in against the table and stormed out. "Solomon James," his father called after him, but he didn't stop. He marched up to his room, slammed the door, and turned his music up as loud as he could stand it before dropping onto his bed. His own scent, worn into the sheets, enfolded him; guitar riffs slammed his ears and shivered through his body; his tail lay trapped under one leg, the ache from his dream pulsing along in time to the music.

Beneath the guitar, he heard pounding on his door, his name called in his father's deep voice. He flicked his ears that way, but didn't move. There was more pounding, and then the door opened and his father came in.

"Hey!" Sol sat up in bed. "You're not supposed to come in unless I say it's okay."

His father shut the door, walked over to Sol's stereo, and turned the music off. Sol grabbed the remote from beside his bed and turned it back on.

"Turn that off." His father glared across the room.

Sol folded his arms. The band Dragonsbane wailed angrily about the injustice of the world. "Fine," his father said. He grabbed the iPod out of Sol's stereo and put it in his pocket.

"That's mine!" Sol yelled. He jumped off the bed and stood, paws balled into fists, four feet from his father.

"You want to act like you're twelve, you'll get treated like you're twelve." His father leaned against the dresser. "Why don't you tell me what you think you've done to deserve a car."

"I did everything you asked me to!" Sol hated the "tell me what you think" game. He couldn't keep his voice down. "I worked and tried and stayed late and I didn't think of anything else."

"For two weeks," his father said.

"That's all the time I had!"

"You think you'll get the starting spot back by the end of the year?"

Hope sparked for a moment. "I can! Yes!"

His father looked levelly at him. "Really? If I called up your manager, would he tell me the same thing?"

Mr. Zerling, always diplomatic with parents, could say anything. But the flare of hope had already gone out. Sol licked the swelling where he'd bitten his lip. "He…he might. I could try for another position."

"When I promised you the car, Sol, I thought you knew you had to earn it. Finish your classes, keep up your athletics as well. If you'd only slipped a bit, maybe in two weeks you could've shown some commitment to the team. You do that, your manager would be able to trust you to start again. He could always move the coyote to another spot, if he's really that good."

Sol's paws ached, but he didn't release his fists. How had he not earned the car? He'd stayed on the team for years, and just because he'd lost his starting spot, all that meant was that someone better had made the team. But deeper down, in the parts that squirmed below the surface of his thoughts, he knew: he hadn't cultivated friendships on the team, he hadn't gone out with the guys in…a year? More? Not since December, that was for sure. And he hadn't worked out any harder than he needed to, and sometimes not even that much, in longer than that. "You were never going to give me a car," he said.

His father's frown deepened. "Of course we were. I didn't help you pick one out for my own amusement."

"Whatever." Sol's claws dug into his paw pads. "Sorry I couldn't be perfect like Natty."

"Don't bring up your brother. This isn't about him."

"Yes it is! You want me to be like him, you wanted me to play football, and when I picked baseball—"

"When you lost your spot on the football team, you mean."

"—you said it was *almost* as good, and you keep telling me I'm not doing everything I should! What else can I do?"

His father shook his head, slowly. "Graduate, keep your grades up, stay on the team. Then we'll talk at the end of the summer. Your mother thinks you need a car for college. I'm not convinced. Yet."

Sol lay back his ears, but refused to submit. The tears still felt dangerously close; he raised his voice to drive them back. "So, what? You want me to keep practicing until all hours of the night? You want me to magically make all the wolves on the team think I'm awesome?"

"Don't raise your voice to me." His father stepped forward, glaring down. "You know what you need to do. Just decide if it's worth it to you to do it."

Some of the girls had returned to the cabaret. Sol opened his mouth and the words just came out. "Maybe I should suck Mr. Zerling's dick. How about if I got back on the team that way?"

The room went silent. Sol held his father's eyes, aware he'd gone too far. His father's brow lowered, his ears flattened. He pointed at Sol. "You're grounded for two weeks. You come right home after baseball practice. No going to your hippie friend's house, no going anywhere."

"But—"

"But what? You got something else to say?"

The cold fire in his father's eyes matched his own. Sol lowered his ears. "No," he said.

"Good." His father stalked out of the room and slammed the door.

Sol sank down on the bed and unclenched his fists. For several minutes he lay there, trying to hear the angry music in his head again. Grounded for two weeks. A whole summer working in the peach cannery, with crazy homophobe Uncle Nolan, all with the lure of maybe, maybe a car at the end of it, which Sol would bet his phone, computer, and iPod (if got it back) would not happen. And then college, where he would be a computer science major not because he wanted to, but because that's where all the good jobs were and he was reasonably okay at it. The problem was that he didn't love anything else enough to make an argument for not majoring in computer science.

He'd thought that at least he could play baseball in college, but it looked like even that was a pipe dream. All he really had to look forward to in his life was Carcy, and Carcy would come through for him. Wouldn't he? The ram said he loved Sol, well, now Sol needed him, needed that love.

At least his father hadn't taken the phone, like the last time a couple years ago. Though maybe he just hadn't thought of it yet and was on his way up right now to take it. And Sol had a phone call he was going to have to make if that might happen.

He dialed Carcy quickly. The phone rang and rang, so long that when the ram did pick up, Sol thought for a moment it was a recording. Then Carcy said, "Solly, what's up?"

"I got grounded."

Carcy said, slowly, "For the whole summer?"

"No, but my dad sometimes takes my phone, so…don't text me 'til I tell you it's okay, okay?"

"Sure, Solly. You okay?"

Sol breathed deeply. His father's strong, furious scent still hung in the air. "I'm fine. I talked back to him is all. I'm not getting my car, that's for sure."

"Game didn't go so well?"

"The game went fine, I just…I didn't get my spot back."

"Ah well. So…" The ram paused. "What's going on with this summer?"

Sol bit his lip. "What's going on is that I'm going to be stuck here working at the peach cannery and I'm going to smell like peaches and machine oil all summer." His voice cracked a little on the last word, so he stopped, but then couldn't keep quiet. "I can't do that, Carce, I can't, I can't. I'll kill myself."

"Whoa, hey, calm down there, wolfy."

Kill himself? That was way, way over the top. Grief and desperation returned in force, between the dream and the fight with his father. When he rubbed his eyes, his fingers came away damp. "I'm sorry. I didn't mean that. I wouldn't…wouldn't even think of something like that."

"Well, good." Carcy talked slowly. "I'd be real upset if you did."

Sol inhaled, trembling. He forced himself to say the words. "So, if I find another way to Millenport…can…I stay with you?"

Another long silence. Carcy's breathing sounded slow and measured. "Here's the deal. You could stay, but…" Pause. Slow exhale into the phone. "I have another roommate."

The words "you could stay" had excited Sol so much that he almost didn't hear the rest of what the ram said. "That's okay! I can stay in your room. I won't take up space and I'll clean, and I'll cook sometimes, and I won't be any bother—"

"Solly." Carcy cut him off firmly. "We only got the one bedroom."

"Oh, well…" Now the implications of what the ram had said worked their way through his excited haze. A slow, creeping coldness prickled his fur. "Is he…your boyfriend?"

"Not…really. He's just a friend."

"With benefits?"

There was another pause, a short one. "Sometimes."

The word came out defiant, like he was challenging Sol to call it off. And part of Sol was telling him to do just that, that same small squirming part that said the things he didn't want to hear. But it was buried below the feel of peach syrup in his fur, the sickly sweet smell of fruit, the anger he still felt at his father. "I won't get in the way," Sol said. "I gotta get out of here, Carce. I'll do anything."

"I knew you were a good wolf, Solly. Bucky said you'd be a drama queen."

"That's his name? Bucky?"

"Uh-huh. He's a good guy. You'll like him when you get to know him."

An uneasy thought surfaced. "Do, uh. Do I have to do stuff with him?"

Carcy laughed. "Nah. I mean, once you get to know him, if you wanna…"

"Okay. I just…I can't wait to be with you."

"Me too, wolfy." The ram's tender tone melted Sol's doubts. After all, they were far apart, and if Carcy had a roommate, a bedmate, to save money…of course Sol would be imposing, but it would work out. And he'd be with his ram.

"So…do you think you could pick us up?"

"It's a day trip, there and—wait, 'us'?"

"Me and my friend Meg. She's gonna stay with her cousin, but she needs a ride too."

"How much stuff we talkin' here? I only got a little car."

"It won't be much." Sol looked around his room. "Two, three boxes and a couple bags."

Carcy sighed. "I could get one of you no problem. I dunno about two."

"Maybe we could just take her stuff and she could take the bus?"

"We'll see. You work it out and let me know, and I'll…yeah, I'll see if I can free up a day to drive there and back."

Warmth replaced the coldness in Sol's chest. "Thanks," he said. "I love you."

"Love ya too. Hey, I gotta go. Bucky and I are running out to lunch. Send me an e-mail."

Sol hung up the phone, which his father had not yet returned to confiscate, and just sat on the bed forcing himself to smile. It was going to be okay. He'd get a ride to the city, and he and Meg could hang out, and he and Carcy would grow closer and eventually Bucky would move out, of course. And he'd go to college or he wouldn't, and Carcy would come with him if he did. It was all going to work out. It was going to work out fine.

He called Natty next, just to complain. "I didn't make it back to the starting lineup in two weeks. Like anyone could do that."

Natty, who had been eleven the last time he hadn't started a game in high school, said, "What happened with you, anyway? Spend too much time in school?"

"It was just…" Sol sighed, tail curled around his hips. "Taric's better, that's all."

"Dad should understand that."

"He's talking to Xavy's dad and he thinks the whole vegetarian thing had something to do with it."

"Sure. I mean, why wouldn't you eat meat? How you getting protein?"

Sol felt the conversation eroding under his feet. He stood up, walked to the door frame where he could smell the faint trace of his brother. "It's not—I feel fine. I feel great. Anyway, he's not getting me a car and then I mouthed off at him and now I'm grounded."

"Why are you not eating meat, again?"

"Look, it's—" Sol paced back and forth. "It's not important, it's just a thing."

"Just hang in there," Natty said. "It gets so much better in college. And have a burger." And then he had to go, to lunch or practice or something, Sol didn't really catch it because he was too busy thinking about how Natty just didn't *get* it.

He texted Meg to let her know he couldn't come over for two weeks and to ask her what he could do for the project, and she asked if he wanted her to bring him anything at school. At first he said no, and then he brushed the sore spot on his lip again and texted her: *Absinthe?*

Meg didn't reply, and Sol didn't feel like chatting much more anyhow. Doing homework now would have felt too responsible, so he just brought up some torrent sites to look for TV shows and movies. But his teeth scraped the bitten part of his lip again, and a burst of grief accompanied the small pain. He scratched his paw and pulled up a search site to look up, "absinthe hallucinations."

He got a lot of links to people eager to debunk absinthe hallucinations, found an article about the poet Meg had talked about, and read about the banning and re-legalization of absinthe. So he tried searching on dreams, and on vivid dreams, and on hallucinations, and on hallucinations following dreams brought on by absinthe, and got nothing more interesting. Nobody had experienced the sort of waking hallucinations he had, or at least, nobody who then felt compelled to record it on the Internet in some form.

Then again, he thought, he hadn't recorded it at all either. Where would he write it? People would say he was crazy. So quite possibly there were other people out there who'd had these sorts of things happen to them, who just wanted to live quiet, normal lives. Maybe that's what he should do.

But he had to know if Cireil was real, if he should be mourning her death or just forgetting it. He had no idea how to spell her name, and he couldn't find a list of Moulin Rouge dancers from the turn of the century anyway. He tried to look up "murders in Lutèce," but he didn't know the year, nor even the time of year other than that it wasn't cold enough to be the dead of winter, nor hot enough to be the summer. And "murdered Moulin Rouge dancer" didn't yield any useful results either.

The dull ache of frustration had set in when he came up with another idea. Henri, the artist, was the other recurring character in his dream who had a name but had not appeared in Jean's book. An artist, a black rat who'd painted alongside some of the artists Meg was studying: that he could look up. He just had to figure out how to spell the name.

"Noir" was easy enough. After sounding it out in his head, he typed "Henri Trunoir" into the search engine.

No results came up. But the search engine helpfully asked, *Did you mean **Henri Trounoir?***

Sol clicked on the link, fingers trembling.

A short page of links came back, along with some image results. He clicked on the Wikipedia page.

Henri Trounoir (?-1901?) was a painter in the Montmartre area toward the end of the 19th century. Very little is known about him. Three paintings survive, one dated 1889, the other two dated 1901, along with a portfolio of sketches. His preferred subjects were nudes in front of colorful, intricate backgrounds, like the more famous examples of Auguste Renoir, although Trounoir's style is more reminiscent of van Gogh. He may have been a student of Fernand Cormon's with van Gogh in the late 1880s, according to some records from Cormon's studio which show an apprentice painter named "Trounoir" working there for three years. However, at van Gogh's Lutèce exhibition on the Blvd. de Clichy, no Trounoir is listed as participating.

His surviving paintings display talent similar to the middle years of van Gogh. His last known painting is dated 1901, when he is presumed to have died.

And one of the images on the Wikipedia page was a female mouse, reclining before a background of red and yellow leaves rendered with short, sure brushstrokes.

Sol's nose knew the oils that covered the canvas. He stared at it. The background had been less defined in his dream, but it was the same female mouse. At least…now he was sure it was. The other two paintings looked familiar, but they hadn't held his—Niki's—attention in the dream the way the mouse had. And neither of them was of a nude fox.

The other links all had the same text from the Wikipedia page: *Very little is known about him…he is presumed to have died…* The images were all of the same three paintings.

Nobody had images of the portfolio of sketches. Where would one go to find something like that? Probably Sol would have to go to Montmartre itself, to ask around one of the museums there and do some detective work. And he didn't speak the language—not when he wasn't dreaming, at least— and right now he wasn't even allowed to walk down the street, let alone cross an ocean in search of a sheaf of hundred-year-old drawings that would show him…what? A sketch of Niki, perhaps?

For the heck of it, he searched for "Niki Moulin Rouge" and got no results, even though he knew that Niki and the Moulin Rouge were mentioned in Jean's book. The failure just frustrated him further, the thought that the answers he was looking for might well be out there on the Internet, but buried too deeply for him to find.

At least, he thought, he felt more sure that Cireil had been real, and that the emotion he'd felt for her had been for a real wolf who died on the street a hundred years ago. That made him feel better about his grief, less silly than if he'd been crying over a dream.

When he closed that browser window, an old one popped up: the one showing the car he was supposed to have gotten. He stared at it for a second and then closed that window, too. Henri was more real than his lost car, and so, he was sure, were Cireil and Niki.

Carcy, too, was very real, and he would rescue Sol from this. Over the weekend, Sol spoke more to Carcy via text than he did to his parents in person, grunting in sullen monosyllables when asked a question. His father said, over Sunday dinner, "You'll lose the attitude or you'll be grounded another week."

Before Sol could reply, his mother said, softly, "Jerious, give him time."

"He's had two days." His father turned back to him. "I'll pick you up from school after practice tomorrow at six-thirty."

Sol couldn't resist the taunt. "What if Taric stays later?"

His father glared at him until Sol set his ears back. "Six-thirty. Sharp." And those were the last words they exchanged.

Monday morning on the bus, Meg stopped at Sol's seat where the swift fox's nose was buried in her English book again. "Hey, bookworm," she said. "Go sit back there."

"I'm sitting here," the fox said.

Behind Meg, a lion said, "Siddown or get out of the way."

Meg ignored him, leaning over. "I'm gonna sit down and talk to my friend here in about five seconds, whether you move or not."

"Take your seats," the bus driver yelled back.

Meg swung her thick otter tail around to whack the side of the seat. The swift fox jumped. "Three," Meg said. "Two."

"Jesus Christ," the lion said. "Get out of the fuckin' way already."

"Stoner bitch," the fox muttered, and collected her bag, sliding back two rows to a free seat.

Meg grinned. "Scoot," she said to Sol.

He slid closer to the window. Her tail landed on the seat between them and she followed it. The lion said, "About fucking time," so she gave him the finger.

"What's up?" Sol said. He glanced toward the back of the bus. "Out of drugs?"

"Shut up, asshole." Meg glared at him. "I sat here to talk to you, since you can't come over. What'd you do, tell your old man that baseball is a huge waste of your time and a sissy sport?"

"I told him you said that." Sol lowered his voice. "I told him the only way I'd get a starting spot is if I gave Mr. Zerling…oral…you know."

Meg raised her eyebrows. "Good for you. Got some spine in you."

"Did you bring the…" He glanced at her bag.

Her brow lowered. "Yeah, I brought it," She tapped her bag, so Sol's ears could catch the clink of glass. "When we doing this? Want to ditch history?"

"After practice."

Meg scowled. "You mean I gotta stay after school? You're the one being punished."

"Stay after school and drink." Sol nudged her. "Think that's punishment?"

"Can we sit under the bleachers where the spiders are?"

Sol tilted his head, not sure whether or not Meg was serious. "I was thinking the park across the street, but…"

"Too bright."

"You're serious."

She raised an eyebrow. "You can't drink absinthe in the sunlight in a park. What's wrong with you?"

"I don't like spiders in my drink?"

"Besides which," she said, "if a Responsible Adult sees us, you'll be grounded more than just two weeks, and I'll get suspended. Third strike, or some bullshit like that."

"All right." Sol shrugged. "Under the bleachers it is."

"Great. What time?"

"I dunno." He thought about it. "Mr. Zerling calls practice at five-thirty. Quarter to six? I need to be done by quarter after so I'm not late for my dad picking me up."

"Done." She squinted at him. "You sure you want to be buzzed for dinner?"

"They never noticed when I came home from your place. Maybe it'll make it more tolerable."

He was glad he had that to look forward to, because the school day was pretty terrible. Tanny started in right away with the "bench-riding" and a new nickname, "meatless," and though she hadn't brought any props, the constant chatter was annoying enough to fold his ears back. In his classes, his homework from the previous week, when he'd been killing himself at baseball practice, was returned. His grades definitely showed the lack of attention. At least he didn't have to bring that home to his parents.

And at lunch, where they were serving clam chowder, Taric's football-playing friend dumped a bowl of it down Sol's side and on his lap. Because the teachers were right there, Sol couldn't retaliate, and the coyote apologized, smirking the whole while. "At least you can lick it clean, meatless," he said, low, as Sol made his way to the bathroom.

He wiped up as much as he could, but the rest of the day, he smelled like clams and cream. It was a relief to get into his baseball uniform and take practice—but being free of the smell was the only good thing about practice. Sol didn't complain to Mr. Zerling or talk to his teammates. He caught grounders mechanically, and only batted until Taric came over and rattled the cage. Then he ran laps desultorily, panting from the heat, imagining that he was running down the hill of Montmartre, through the streets of Lutèce, or along the freeway to Millenport. When Mr. Zerling called practice done, Sol happened to be near the batting cages.

He rested his paws on his knees while the others left the cages, and then walked off the field, ignoring Taric's sharp laugh behind him. Tsarev waved to him from the bleachers. Sol waved back with a tired wag of his tail, but he wondered if Meg would still want to drink under the bleachers if the fox were sitting there.

Fortunately, by the time he emerged in his chowder-scented clothes, Tsarev had gone. Taric was still in the batting cage, smashing line drives across the practice field with the regularity of a hammer driving in a nail. He didn't object to Sol watching him this time, or maybe he didn't notice. Or maybe, because Sol was in his schoolclothes and not competing any more, the coyote enjoyed it.

At ten to six, Meg appeared around the side of the bleachers, hissing at him. Sol almost jumped, and ran around to the corner where she was. "How long have you been here?" he asked.

"Long enough to watch you jumpin' through hoops with the rest of the Stepford Sons."

"You brought it, right?" If nothing else, at least the lousy day had distracted him from the dream. Now that Meg was here, though, his heartbeat quickened and his tail twitched with anxiety.

Meg gave him another squinting look. "Jesus, yeah, I brought it. Come on, I got it all set up."

She led him under the bleachers to where she'd set her bag against a post. The earthen smell mixed with the sour smell of garbage, which always lingered despite the school's attempts to keep the bleachers clean. Sol wrinkled his nose and squinted. Fat stripes of sunlight showed dust particles swirling lazily around him; the contrast between light and dark made it hard for his eyes to see anything clearly. It took him a good while to make out the shapes of the two red plastic cups on the cement support at the base of the pole. "I brought the knife and the sugar. Sorry, I tried to find green cups."

Sol leaned over and caught the familiar anise smell. Cloudy green liquid swirled in the cups. "You're the best," he said.

"I know." Meg sat cross-legged beside the cups and grinned at him. "Come on. Ready to accept the gift of the Green Fairy?"

"I need it today." Sol sat across from her. "This day's been shitty."

"I saw you get a clam chowder bath. That coyote's a piece of shit. Vicki Reis says at football practice he's such a suck-up to the starters that it makes all the cheerleaders sick."

Sol paused, cup in paw. "You talk to Vicki Reis?"

"You kidding? But I listen when she talks shit about guys. Never know what might come in handy." Meg lifted her cup. "Now, Green Fairy, please bestow upon us your gift of inspiration. Let us see by your light, let us breathe your inspiration."

She was about to drink when Sol added, "Bring us your dreams of… art."

Meg's face, already black under her makeup, was nearly unreadable in the shadows. "You still having dreams?"

"Yeah." Sol felt himself on the edge of telling her, but she lifted her cup before he could.

"Then bring us dreams." She tipped the edge of the cup to her mouth.

Sol did the same, felt the now-familiar scent of anise and the warm tang of the alcohol on his tongue. He drank down half the cup and set it back down, keeping a paw over the top.

Meg set hers down. "I was kidding about the spiders," she said.

"I know." Sol glanced up. "Y'never know."

They sat in silence, while Sol let the warmth of the absinthe blossom inside him. "Thanks," he said, "for bringing all this."

"Now I can say I snuck under the bleachers with a boy." Meg leaned against the post. "If anyone ever asks. You can pay me back by gettin' me a ride this summer."

"Oh yeah." Sol's ears perked up. "I talked to Carcy. He says he'll come down and get me, and that we can bring your stuff in the car. So if you can take the bus, we'll hold your stuff at his place until you get there."

Meg squinted. "I dunno if I trust your boyfriend to not smoke all my pot."

"Then don't pack it." Sol reached for his drink again. He'd thought Meg would be happy that he'd worked something out.

"He have a big place? Lots of room?"

"One bedroom. And another boyfriend." The words came out before Sol could stop them. "I mean, not a boyfriend. Just a friend." He took another drink to stop himself from talking.

"Just a friend." Meg nodded. "A friend he sleeps with?"

"Hey, just because we're gay doesn't mean we're promisku—." His tongue tripped over the word. "Promis-cue-us."

"Maybe you shouldn't finish that." Meg nodded at his cup. Sol met her eyes as he lifted it to his muzzle and drained it. "All right then. Maybe you shouldn't listen to me."

Sol put the cup down. "Yes," he said. "He sleeps with him. Sometimes. But he says they're not boyfriends."

"Guys'll say anything to get you in bed." Meg held up a paw. "That's all guys, not just you queers."

"How do you know that?" Sol put his empty cup down.

"Alison Damarcus says so."

"You talk to Alison—oh." He nodded as she tapped her ears. "Well, he says—he says it'll all work out."

"Sure he does." Meg finished off her own cup. "So when do I have to be packed by? Finals? Two months?"

"Two months. Christ." Sol closed his eyes and again saw the days of baseball practices, the games sitting on the bench, the dinners with his father.

Meg laughed, softly. "Yeah, don't you wish we could go next week?"

"Damn!" Warmth bubbled up through Sol's throat in a laugh. "That'd be awesome. Get out of here, get the rest of our lives started."

"Except you wouldn't graduate from Midland Hell School. Wouldn't that screw up Charleton College?"

Sol's tail wagged lazily against the cool ground, stirring up dust and other less appealing smells. "Who cares? I don't really want to go there anyway. Carcy dropped out of college and he's doing fine."

"Great role model. In a few years you can start hitting on high school boys."

"And who cares about computer science anyway? I don't want to do that."

Meg leaned forward. "What do you want to do?"

"Don't know." Sol waved a paw. "I'll figure it out. What about you?"

She laughed and leaned back, resting on her tail. "Don't need a high school diploma to be an artist."

"Well, I don't need a high school diploma to be…" He closed his eyes and searched for a word. "Happy."

"So call your boyfriend. Tell him next week."

"But I'm grounded." It made sense when he said it, and then at Meg's expression, Sol just started to giggle. "Right. So, what, play hookey from school?"

"Pack in the morning, leave in the afternoon. Would it take you that long to pack?"

He thought about it. "No. But...you're serious." She just looked back at him. "Next week?"

"You were going to leave anyway."

"Yeah, but..." He sighed. "I was gonna talk to them at least, like, the week before."

She didn't need to ask who he meant. "So they could try to talk you out of it? Write 'em a note from Millenport. Call them at their jobs before you go. You can say goodbye."

"I guess..." He was feeling more buzzed, more confident. "What about your parents?"

Meg zipped up her bag. "By the time they notice I'm gone... y'know, they wouldn't let me go to the city, but they'll be thrilled that I'm making my own decisions. Striking out against authority. Know what I mean?"

"Not really."

"I'll send them a postcard. Just be thankful you have normal parents. God." She stood up. "Speaking of which, you'd better get out there and get changed."

"Right. Thanks." He stood, too. "Thanks again. I feel a lot better."

"Sorry you have to put the clam chowder ensemble back on. Another reason to take off next week."

"No kidding." It made more and more sense the more Sol considered it. Get out now while he had the opportunity. If someone was extending a hand to him... "I should just call him right now and ask."

Meg raised her eyebrows, but didn't say anything as he took his phone out and dialed Carcy's number. The ram picked up quickly. "Hey, Solly. I'm at work. What's going on?"

"Sorry." Sol couldn't keep a big grin off his muzzle at the sound of the ram's voice. "Listen, uh, would you be able to come get me and Meg next week?"

"Next week?"

"I know. We're just sick of this. We need to get out now." Meg nodded, but kept the skeptical expression.

Carcy sighed. "I work, Sol. You know, I can't just drive four hours... hang on." Faintly, he said, "Will that be all?" and then an amount. A moment later, after a quick, "Thanks for shopping Save-Plus," he was back. "Sol..."

"I can't wait to see you," Sol said. "Please, hon." He didn't even feel self-conscious about the endearment, not until he saw Meg's finger stuck down her throat, mock-gagging.

Carcy sighed. "Can't it be this weekend, or next?"

"My parents are home on the weekends."

"This is a big pain in the ass, Sol. You sure you want to do this?"

"I know. I'm sure." Carcy would do it. Sol's grin stretched wider. "I want to be with you."

"Yeah. All right. Let me see what day I can get off here."

Sol giggled. He wasn't quite buzzed enough to say "so you can get off here" in front of Meg, but Carcy got his meaning anyway.

"Ha. Right. Listen, I gotta go. I'll text you the day."

"Love you," Sol said, prompting another round of gagging from Meg.

She shook her head as he put the phone in his pocket. "On account of he's going to drive us to the city, I'm not going to say anything. But God, Sol."

"Someday you'll find love and you'll understand." He wanted to skip out from the bleachers, sing his way to the locker room.

"I might say the same about you." She raised a paw. "See you tomorrow."

His father wrinkled his nose when Sol got in and closed the passenger door. "Spilled some chowder?"

"There was an accident at lunch." Sol leaned back in the seat and stared straight ahead. His eyes drifted closed. The movement of the car buoyed him, floated him along the road.

"How was practice?"

The words took a moment to travel from his ears to his brain. He composed the response carefully. "Great. It was great, yeah."

"Good." That was it. He didn't show any interest in anything else, which Sol resented even though he didn't want his father to ask any more. The idea that he would only be living with his parents for another week kept intruding on his mind. It was a big change, but a necessary one, he knew that. And it was only a couple months before he would be leaving anyway. It didn't mean that much to them, and it would make a huge difference to him. Besides, they'd grounded him—grounded him, like he was fourteen again. Well, this would prove to them that he was grown up.

He repeated that refrain all through dinner and the evening, for as long as the absinthe buoyed his spirits. His parents didn't seem to notice his mood, but then, they didn't talk much all through dinner (roast chicken with spinach and rice; his mother didn't make a special bean salad for him, but they didn't force the chicken on him either), and after dinner he went up to his room to catch up on homework. He got tired around ten-thirty and stretched out in bed with his phone. "Confession" opened, but the words blurred. He forced himself to read the first few lines.

Another night with my darling approached, and the ball the day following that. I was in a state of high excitement for that entire day, wishing nothing more than for the sun to set. I checked Niki's dress every hour, checked my own suit no less frequently, and took two baths—that is the day I wanted to dismiss the mouse Valoir for failing to adequately clean the bathtub, and you told me I could not.

Sol imagined Carcy that excited about seeing him, could just picture the ram checking his—well, his car. He smiled, without even realizing that he was no longer reading.

Chapter 16

Clouds hang low in the sky and there is no moon, at least, not that Niki can see. He has no idea what time it is, only that it is not quite night and not quite dawn, that in-between time when the world is so quiet that his ears catch the ticking of the clock in the heavens. The soft white robe, made of fine cotton from the south, hangs almost weightless from his shoulders and coats his fur in a cloud. It is too short for him, but Jean liked it that way, liked how the black fur of his forearms and lower legs sticks out below the cuffs and hem of the robe, as if Niki is a child grown out of his clothes.

Few people are on the streets to see him. The dancers will not quite have left the Moulin Rouge, the bakers are only starting their morning bread. No smell but flour and the past and future rain comes to him until he enters the building, climbs past the dirt and garbage in the stairwell. One floor below his, someone has urinated on one of the stairs. His nose wrinkles as he steps over it, and he wonders if there was a time when he did not mind. He keeps the sleeves of the robe carefully away from the walls of the narrow stairwell, away from the door frame as he opens the aging wooden door.

Oil and rat reach his nose, and the rancid smell of starvation. Henri has not been eating the food Niki brought for him; a half-baguette sits on the floor near the bed and shows evidence that some of the smaller inhabitants of the room have been enjoying it. The sour smell comes not from the food, but from Henri himself, stretched out on the bed. He is not wearing a shirt, so Niki can see the ribs showing as faint lines in his short black fur.

"Tch." *He closes the door behind him. First things first: he removes the robe and sets it aside, exchanging it for an old pair of cotton trousers, worn and dirty, but with comforting weight. Only then does he walk to the bed and look down at the rat, ears perked.* "You needn't pretend to be asleep," *Niki says.* "I can hear your breathing."

Henri cracks open an eye. "I am not asleep. I am dead."

"You will be. Why do you not eat?"

"Art is my food." *Henri rolls onto his back, stares at the ceiling.* "It sustains me."

"Here." *Niki picks up the bread, carefully gripping it around the parts that have been eaten. It is disgusting, but it is food. He holds it out.* "Eat something."

By way of reply, Henri reaches under the bed, comes out with a clear bottle half-full of a cloudy green liquid. He gulps down two, three swallows, then holds the bottle out to Niki. "Drink something."

Niki sighs and replaces the bread on the plate. "You should not be drinking."

"Inspiration!" Henri shakes the bottle at him. "You are leaving me for him, so come, share one last drink with me."

The fox hesitates, but Henri's arm, thinner than the baguette he scorns, does not withdraw. Finally, Niki takes the bottle, as much to drink as because the rat's arm is trembling and he fears the bottle may drop and shatter.

"I am not leaving you," Niki says. The absinthe in the bottle is un-sugared, which Henri relishes but Niki finds undrinkable. So he pads to the small shelf near the door and picks up a wooden cup. Next to the cup, behind the absinthe spoon, half of a sugar cube sits covered in dust. He brushes it as clean as he can, places the cube on the spoon on the cup, and pours the diluted absinthe over it.

"When will you be back?" Henri looks his way.

"When I can." Niki brings the cup and bottle back to the bed, where he sits on the floor, knees drawn up, and curls his tail back around his hips. "When he allows."

The fox tips the lip of the cup to his muzzle, lets the warm green liquid spill over his tongue and down. Even with the sugar, the searing bitterness makes his eyes water, but he takes another drink, then sets his cup on the floor, the bottle on the bed.

"What would you have me do? Dance for brutes in fear for my life every night? End my days like—" Her name calls the image and the scent; the pain and the grief. "On the street?"

"You already know what I would have you do." Henri sighs. He stares at the ceiling again.

"It is a rare chance, for one like me." From the fox's seated position, the window past Henri's prone form shows nothing but the low, grey clouds. "There are not so many patrons who like boys, fewer who will spend the money to keep one, with all the boys by the river so cheap."

"Of course. It is practical. In a few years you will be one of those boys yourself, and you will not command as high a price."

Niki has never seen these boys, but he imagines them standing in the cold shadows by the Seine, desperate, lonely for any loving touch. He sees the fat purse of paper francs Jean dangled before him, enough to pay for a year of rent and bread for Henri. "I have been receiving instruction for the ball. Whom I may talk to, what I must say. I am to behave as a wealthy foreign lady from Siberia. If all goes well, then—with Jean's money, I can do good, perhaps. I can help—people. I can support dance, and art."

"I am certain your lover has chosen you because of the good you can do with his money. Will he tie you up before the Société Nationale des Beaux-Arts, as well?"

I can help people, Niki repeats stubbornly to himself, and he takes another drink of absinthe. The bitter wormwood makes his tongue curl, but the drink warms him. "I will find a way to bring money to you, one way or another."

Henri waves a paw. "Money is not what I need."

Niki stands, looks down at the rat. "To make art, one must continue to live."

"And when one can make art no longer, then what?" Henri reaches for the bottle. He drains it in two swallows and holds it up in the air. "When inspiration is gone, then what?"

"Inspiration never truly leaves the artist." The bottle is between Niki and the window; grey clouds show through the clear glass. The sky outside is the same color as when Niki entered the building.

The rat's arm wavers. The fox reaches out, takes the bottle before it drops, and sets it on the floor. Henri turns to the window and stares out. "It may be gone for so long that it amounts to the same thing."

Niki looks at the easel, where the portrait of the female mouse appears to be finished. "I have spoken to M. Oller. He will buy that painting from you."

"I did not offer to sell it."

"No. I did."

Henri closes his eyes. "He has not seen it."

"I described it well."

Dawn may be here in a moment, or an hour. Henri turns back from the window and then shakes his head from side to side. "So it may hang in his gaudy hallways next to the pornography whose only purpose is to prime his patrons before you come to pump out their francs? So that your chamois's friends may walk past it and think to themselves that the breasts are not as big as on the painting next to it? Is this the gallery worthy of my talents?"

Niki shakes his head. "Even the Dutchman sold his work, you will recall."

"And he died insane."

"Do you revere him so much?" Niki stares; the rat turns away. "It is money," Niki says softly. "It buys bread, it pays Mme. DeGris for the room."

Henri fixes him with a reddened eye. "Of course. Selling art as sex for money. It is your life now, is it not? I should not find fault with your haste to push me down the same road. Learned behavior, the Pavlovian reward. Your countryman, eh?"

"I do not know a 'Pavlovian,'" Niki says.

"Is it so ingrained now?" Henri asks. "Do you hear the rustle of francs and

168

pull your trousers down without knowing why? Let us experiment." He turns his head lazily to one side, then the other. *"Did you bring any francs? My hoard appears to be missing."*

Niki rubs his eyes. His paw comes away moist. *"At least I will survive,"* he says. *"At least I will not lie in bed starving within easy reach of food because I picture myself slave to some higher calling that does not know my name."*

"Art never knows your name." Henri's voice gets stronger. *"You must know its name. You must cry at its feet as you mewled to your mother, you must beg its attention for just one moment so that you may push the grandeur in your mind out onto the canvas. It is fickle, it cares nothing for you, and you must give it your all for that one moment, in the hope that the one moment will be followed by one more."*

"And how is that different from Jean?"

The rat sits up, coughs. He glares at Niki. *"You knew, once. You talked about the dance, about how you would dance your dance and how some noble patron would take note of you and would lift you up to the ballet, and even if he didn't,"* he coughs again, harder, *"even if he didn't, all that mattered would be that you were being allowed to dance. And now, now look at you. Away all night being bent over silken sheets and down blankets."*

"Love is as important as art." The protest is weak, but it is all he has.

"Tell me, does the pillow taste better when it is finely threaded cotton?"

Niki kicks the small plate with his foot, tipping the vermin-nibbled hunk of bread and its crumbs to the floor. A shower of white crumbs sprays over the black fur of his foot. *"It tastes better than empty air."*

Henri wheezes. He looks directly at Niki. *"Liar."*

Niki sets his jaw. He marches to the easel and takes the painting of the mouse. *"I will bring this to M. Oller,"* he says. *"In that way perhaps at least something of you will survive the month."*

"If all you wanted was survival, you could have become a soldier of the tsar. He would not have used you as harshly, nor promised you so many illusions."

"I have no illusions!" Niki's fingers grip the canvas so hard that one of his claws digs into the edge. *"I know the life I go to—"*

"Then go!" Henri's yell is scratchy. His claws dig into the bed. *"Go to your noble who cherishes the lovely facade of you and cares nothing for the soul that withers and dies within. Go, and leave me here. You do not see art, you do not live art. You have given up."* He falls back onto the bed. *"I have nothing more to say to you."*

"Eat something," Niki says. *"I will bring fresh bread tonight."* The crumbs of the stale bread still show on his fur; he leaves them there, not attempting to shake them off.

Henri makes no response. His eyes stare up at the ceiling, reflecting the sky filled with dark clouds. Dawn must be approaching by now, but one would not know it. Niki leaves the building and closes the door, the painting clutched safely under one arm.

Chapter 17

Sol blinked awake into the haze of morning. Outside his window, clouds covered the sky, eerily similar to his dream. He stared at his clock, trying to make sense of the numbers; it was five-thirty, forty-five minutes before he had to get up. He squeezed his eyes shut and pressed his head back into the pillow, but he could not get Niki's anger out of his head. The friend turning his back, Henri's stubborn refusal to understand, his blind adherence to this idealistic life of art…

At least he hadn't woken up with a painting under his arm. He shifted under the covers, and felt a rough grit against the pads of his foot. He exhaled, and lifted the blanket.

Against his black fur, specks of white showed like snow. Crumbs.

He stared at his white-speckled foot. It had been days since the ribbon, and though he'd had the oily paint smell and the bitten lip, he'd forgotten the cold chill of seeing something tangible return from his dream with him. His heart pounded with the urge to collect the crumbs, to hold them and keep them as proof that his dreams were real.

Of course, they weren't proof. He was being silly about this. He'd had bread last night, for sure, even if he couldn't quite remember what kind. So that was all these were, just remnants of dinner rolls. Their scent, weakly yeasty, only registered when he leaned forward and sniffed at them, but it was the same familiar smell of modern-day bread, not the rich fresh baguette smell he remembered from his dreams. At least, as far as he could tell.

"Pretty weak," he said. Saying the words out loud reassured him that the crumbs were perfectly normal. Must be because he'd had the absinthe so early, it had time to wear off and not give him weird hallucinations in the morning. Briefly, he wondered how the crumbs had gotten onto his foot, when he'd never woken up with crumbs in his fur from dinner before. Well, he told himself, you never ate dinner buzzed on absinthe before, either.

He yawned and got up to go to the bathroom, where the crumbs persisted. He brushed them off against the back of his leg, dismissing a small urge to taste them. Whether they were stale crumbs from last night or dream-crumbs from 1901 (he felt a little foolish for thinking that now, seeing them cold and real on the tile floor), he didn't think they would be very appetizing.

It was probably just because he was thinking of the crumbs, but when he walked out of the bathroom and turned off the light, he saw a sprinkling of white, like hard snow, on the hallway carpet.

Sol stood and stared. The small patch of crumbs didn't go away. He hadn't walked by there on his way from the room to the bathroom, so they hadn't come from his foot. As he watched, a small speck of white fell to land amidst the other crumbs.

His eyes tracked it backwards, up to the trap door that led to the attic. He walked over to the door and lifted his paw to the ring dangling from a string. It was only two years ago that he'd grown tall enough to reach it without jumping. The plastic felt cool to his pads as he slid his finger through it and tugged gently.

The door didn't open. The silence of the house grew oppressive. Of course it wasn't crumbs from his dream in the hallway. It was just dust from the attic that looked like crumbs.

Another crumb—piece of dust—floated down past his nose. Sol rubbed the back of his paw across his muzzle. Then he pulled, hard, and reached up to stop the clatter of the ladder falling as the door sprung open. With only a little noise, he eased it down, ears perked for any sound from his parents' room.

The house remained silent. Sol lifted his muzzle, but the attic was darker even than the hallway, and he saw nothing. He put one foot on the bottom rung of the ladder, still staring up. He felt as though at any moment, something might tumble (or jump) out of the darkness at him. But when he shifted all his weight to the foot on the ladder and lifted the other one, the darkness remained still, silent, waiting until he arrived at the top.

With his head immersed in it, his eyes adjusted more quickly. He scanned the ground slowly, but there were no more crumbs anywhere to be seen, only the grey trails of cobwebs and an even layer of dust. No smell of bread reached his nose, only old scents from his family, from older relatives, from insects and mice and squirrels. Sol frowned, his breath shifting particles of dust, and looked around again.

There, in the corner, small white specks lay around the base of a long cylinder propped against a box. The cylinder, a roll of something, had one corner peeled back to show a dark color. Sol stepped up into the attic, took a deep breath, and immediately coughed out a mouthful of dust. The roll did not move. He crept forward through the warm, musty air, as though the roll were a coiled snake. Two more steps through the dust, and he had to stop to sneeze, but even that did not disturb the roll. It stayed where it was until he was close enough to reach out and touch it.

It was thick between his thumb and forefinger; canvas, not paper. A rolled-up painting, as he'd known it would be. He pulled; it unrolled slowly, reluctant and stiff with age. Leaves, bright gold and sultry red, glowed on the canvas against the soft brown ground. More leaves and the grey of stone, as he unrolled it, painted in thick brushstrokes, familiar brushstrokes, short and sure, and then...a splash of pure white.

Sol dropped the canvas, which snapped immediately back into its roll. He backed two steps away from it, ears flat, tail wrapped tightly around his thigh. It stayed on the floor, not moving, not mysteriously uncurling to reveal the female mouse. For all that he could see, the canvas looked entirely normal up here in the dusty, musty attic. He smelled cobwebs and small creatures and insulation, saw the lazy trails of dust in the air in the half-light that filtered down through the grimy window, and felt the cool floorboards under his feet. The painting was just there, it was real, and it was normal.

And when he went back downstairs, it would be gone, wouldn't it? Like the ribbons, like the paint. He rubbed the back of his paw and kept his eyes on the roll. His ears flicked back to the open trap door; the rest of the house was still silent. Slowly, his tail uncurled and swung slowly behind him. Even if the painting weren't gone, he could just ignore it, if it remained up here in the attic.

But Niki wanted so badly for something of Henri to survive. And if Sol ignored the painting, left it up here to molder—though who knew what it was doing up here in the first place—then what would that be doing for Henri?

Of course, the rational part of Sol reminded him, Henri was all part of his dream. He had a Wikipedia page, but that didn't mean that what Sol was dreaming was true. But even if so, even if Henri was only part of a message from Sol's own subconscious, well...it was still a message.

The black wolf strode forward. His paw closed around the roll and lifted it from the floor. He resisted the temptation to unroll it again, just keeping it in his paw as he hurried back down the ladder. It would have been difficult to close up the ladder quietly even with two paws free; with only one, it was impossible. It clattered up, and Sol lost his grip on the ring as the trap door flipped upward and slammed shut.

His ears rang with the noise. He stood staring at his parents' door for a moment, then darted into his room. Carefully, he leaned the rolled-up canvas in the corner, then ran into the bathroom to shower. Rustles of movement came from his parents' room, but they did not look out in the brief time he was in the hall.

When he came back, the canvas was still there. It looked so normal in the morning light that if he hadn't known where it came from, if he couldn't still feel the itch of crumbs on his foot or the smell of dust in his nose, he wouldn't have given it a second thought. Twice while getting ready for school, he walked halfway across the room, his paw shivering, and stopped, staring at the rolled-up cylinder. He wanted to know, wanted his dream to be real, but to unroll the canvas fully and see Henri's painting would also irrevocably place him in the middle of it. The questions about how it was all happening were bad enough without adding the question of why it was happening to him.

Those questions consumed him all through the morning. Meg didn't talk to him on the bus, and Tanny smacked him once on the back of the head in homeroom, but the visions of crumbs and canvas persisted. Tsarev turned to talk to him, but only got as far as hello before they had to stand for the Pledge of Allegiance. In each class, Sol traced horrible sketches of his memory of Henri's painting in his notebook, then ripped them out and threw them away.

At lunch, he sat by himself again. The cafeteria's offering today was stuffed tomatoes, supposedly filled with some weird vegetarian tomato-saucy rice mix, but when Sol poked through the stuffing, he uncovered suspicious-looking brown-grey lumps in it that he thought might be sausage. That was where Tsarev found him, trying to pick the unidentifiable lumps out of the undercooked tomato.

The fox sat next to him, startling Sol, who'd been sniffing his tomato closely trying to figure out what the grey lumps were. Tsarev laid his ears back. "It's okay that I sit here?"

"Sure, yes." Sol smiled. "Sorry, just…not sure what this is."

Tsarev leaned to sniff at his own tomato. "In Siberia, we call this *taina.*"

"Tie-nah?"

"Nobody knows what it is."

Sol laughed. "I'm glad I'm not the only one."

"I think it is not meat." Tsarev lifted his muzzle. "It smells not like meat."

"I'm just not sure I want to eat it, whatever it is." Sol picked another lump out of the tomato.

Tsarev shrugged and scooped a lump of rice, sauce, and lumps onto his fork. "It is not so bad." He chewed and swallowed. "You did not stay long at practice yesterday."

"No." Sol sighed, and told him about not being selected for the team, about the fight with his father, and almost about being grounded. You barely know this guy, he chided himself. He doesn't want to know about your home life, especially not about being grounded like a little cub. But the lure of a sympathetic ear was stronger than his courtesy, and Tsarev listened attentively.

The fox nodded. "I am sorry to hear that," he said. "You saw an otter after that?"

"Uh. Yes." Sol tilted his muzzle. "You saw me?"

"I was not looking," Tsarev said hastily. "Not, um…" He mimed using a telescope.

"Spying?"

"Not spying. I came back out, I see you go under seats with her."

"Right." Sol's fur prickled with guilt. Was the fox going to turn him in for drinking?

"She is…girlfriend?"

"Oh!" The wolf realized what Tsarev probably thought they'd been doing. Making out was better than drinking. "Yes, yes. That's right."

The fox's ears lowered and he took another bite of his tomato. Sol wondered if maybe Tsarev felt he'd intruded on Sol's personal life. Maybe it was a Siberian thing.

"Don't believe him," jeered a voice behind them.

Sol turned, Tsarev turning a moment later. Taric and his two friends stood behind them staring down. Nearby, Xavy and one of the other wolves had stopped eating to watch. The coyote in back held a tray, but Taric and the football player didn't. Taric spoke again. "See, meatless, you made the poor guy sad. He wanted to suck your cock. Tell him the truth."

"Shut up," Sol snarled, but the fox talked over him.

"You may leave us alone," he said.

"Oh, may I?" Taric adopted a mocking tone before going back to his sneer. "See, I know he lied. Cause you don't know about the time we caught him in the shower with a boner, staring at the *guys*."

Sol's ears flattened, uncomfortably warm. He looked at Tsarev, but the fox didn't react with disgust—at him, anyway. Tsarev was definitely leaning away from Taric. So Sol said, "Nobody cares. Just go away."

Taric laughed. "You want people to believe you like girls, you should pick a pretty one, not an ugly goth bitch."

Sol kicked his chair back and stood, paws balled into fists. "Shut up!"

"Sit down, backup," Taric said. He stepped forward and shoved Sol back down in his chair so hard that the wolf's tail was caught between his butt and the seat.

The ache from his dream flared. Sol restrained a yelp, with difficulty, but before he could spring up again, Tsarev was on his feet. "I said, you may leave us alone. I am not interested in what you—"

"You sit too." Taric pushed the fox, hard, with one arm.

Tsarev fell back onto the seat of the chair, overbalanced, and landed heavily on the floor, his tail puffed out and askew. The three coyotes nearly doubled over laughing. "See you, fags," Taric said, and led the others away.

Sol looked around for a teacher, but none were in evidence. He kicked his chair back, eyes fixed on Taric, all the anger from his dream coming back to him. "Hey, asshole!" he yelled, and grabbed the tomato from his plate.

Taric turned, still laughing, and had only a moment to change his expression. Sol fired the tomato, a frozen rope of a throw. It sped straight and true, and caught the coyote square across his muzzle.

The missile exploded in a shower of tomato and rice and unidentifiable grey non-meat. Pieces rained down Taric's shirt, sprayed his friends, splattered all around. His tan muzzle looked gruesomely bloody, smeared with red sauce and bright red fragments of tomato skin. Sauce dripped red from the end of his muzzle as he stared, disbelieving, at Sol.

The whole cafeteria echoed with the rattle of forks falling onto plates, and then went dead silent. Even Tsarev, struggling to get to his feet, stopped with his muzzle open, staring between the two of them. Then Taric said, "I'm going to kill you," and covered the ground between them in three long strides.

Sol heard the far-off cry of a teacher, but ignored it, bracing himself. He had time to get out, "Bring it," and then the coyote was on him, snarling and punching. His eyes stayed fixed on Sol's, and he moved with alarming speed, his muscular arm as fast and hard as a baseball bat. His scent and breath at the close quarters smelled of meat and rage, and he kept throwing words like "fucker" and "shithead wolf" and "fag" as if they were punches themselves.

Around them, students formed a circle and chanted, "Fight! Fight!" Sol got his arms up against the rain of blows, trying to angle himself in closer so Taric didn't have as much leverage. He punched back, keeping his arm low, and then grabbed at Taric's arm to stop the punching. He missed and took a blow to the ribs; grabbed again and slowed the coyote's arm.

And then Taric ripped at his shirt, and Sol felt teeth in his shoulder— the coyote was *biting* him? He wrenched at the thick tan-furred neck, keeping his own muzzle well shut even in the face of the tempting brown ear in front of it. While Taric tried to keep Sol's arms pinned, they staggered and shoved at each other, slamming into the table and one of the chairs. The students around them yelled indiscriminate encouragement.

The biting was more annoying than painful, but it was enough of both that Sol twisted his shoulder more and more desperately. Finally, he planted both paws on Taric's chest and shoved the coyote away from him. They both stood, panting, and Sol, needing to gain any advantage he could, took advantage of the brief respite to lash out.

His punch, a wild, sweeping right hook, missed Taric by a country mile. As the coyote laughed at him, Sol brought his fist back around, and this time, he didn't miss. The back of his paw connected with Taric's muzzle in a loud crack, snapping the long tan muzzle to one side.

Taric staggered, looked shocked first and then furious. He leapt at Sol again, muzzle open, and the wolf jumped back reflexively—not quickly enough. Taric's fist slammed into his cheek just under his ear, knocking him into the table again. He grabbed at the table's edge to stop himself from falling, and was only vaguely aware that Taric had jumped after him when a tall bear burst between them, shoving them apart.

"Stop it, stop it!" Mr. Fortune held the two of them apart. Sol, his head still ringing and full of rage, launched a kick at the coyote and caught him on the thigh, sending him a step back. Taric renewed his struggle to get to Sol, and Mr. Fortune had to get bodily between them. "I said, stop!"

Another teacher, a lion, joined them and grabbed Sol while Mr. Fortune grabbed Taric. "Principal's office, both you, right now. Terry?"

Mr. Fortune nodded, keeping one large paw on Taric's shoulder while the lion steered Sol behind them. Taric swaggered through the cafeteria, though Sol noticed that the strut was particularly pronounced when they were passing Xavy and the other wolves on the team. "Pick a fight with me, will he?" the coyote muttered, and the wolves looked up with wide eyes, first at him, and then at Sol.

Sol spent the next ten minutes replaying the fight and kicking himself for all the things he knew and hadn't done. Taking advantage of a guy who bites by hitting the head, which is harder to defend. Going in low when you grapple with someone, keeping your center of gravity below his. In the heat of the fight, all the academics of it vanished and there was only instinct and survival.

They both got detention for a week and a lecture about fighting, to which they both nodded and mumbled insincere apologies. "Nice job, Fagson," Taric said as they walked out of the principal's office. "Mr. Zerling is gonna kill me if he can't get me out of it. It's your fault anyway."

"Leave me the hell alone." Sol let a growl into his voice.

"You wanna finish this outside?"

Sol shrugged. "I'm not the one got a starting spot on the team to lose."

Taric turned and poked him in the chest. "Yeah, well, you're my backup, so I ain't worried 'bout losing it."

"It's second base," Sol said. "Don't take a rocket scientist to play it. He'll get a backup outfielder in. Maybe Reggie." The fox who backed up in right field was not very agile, and was generally considered one of the slower players on the team.

"Fuck you. Like he could take my place."

"Yeah well. Someone will, and it sure as hell won't be me."

"Fuckin' right it won't."

And then they split off to their separate classes, and Sol didn't see Taric again until it was time for detention. Sol passed the stifling, excruciating hour by rubbing his side, watching Taric rub his muzzle, and replaying the fight over and over and imagining Carcy pulling up outside the school with an open door and a smile. Only the tick of the clock and the slow droning of flies against the window broke the silence, coupled with the occasional shuffle of paper when the teacher watching them moved on to the next paper she was grading.

When they were finally released, they ran together to the baseball practice field, jogging at first, and then running harder, teeth clenched. The afternoon was dark already, the air thick with the smell of rain, but Sol drove everything from his mind except the rangy coyote running beside him, then a step in front of him, then two steps.

Sol ran flat out, but Taric beat him to Mr. Zerling by a good ten feet. The older wolf was looking at the thick black clouds overhead and talking with one of the assistant coaches, but they broke off when Taric ran up and launched immediately into his explanation. Sol skidded to a stop a step behind, panting, close enough to hear the coyote's surprisingly accurate account: "I was just giving him shit, you know, the way we do, and he threw a tomato at me. Couldn't let that stand."

Sol stood apart, kept from getting closer by Mr. Zerling's posture; the wolf was focused on Taric, both ears forward, arms folded. "You need to learn discipline," he told the coyote. "Getting detention doesn't help your standing on the team. We need to practice as a team, work as a team. When you're gone for an hour every day, even just for a week, it doesn't help. Okay?"

"Yes, sir." Taric folded his ears back and lowered his muzzle.

"Right." Mr. Zerling punched his arm. "Go take some swings. We'll arrange for you to have some practice this weekend."

When Taric was on his way, the older wolf turned to Sol. "I'm disappointed," he said, unnecessarily, since the frown, the tilt of the ears, and the gruff voice said that all for him.

"He left out the part where he pushed a smaller kid down," Sol said. "And called me a faggot. Again. Is that okay?"

Mr. Zerling sighed, but his ears didn't come up. "I hated having to bench you. You were a good kid, always did what I asked. But some guys respond better than others. I thought last week, maybe…"

"I stayed 'til it was dark!"

"Yeah, you did." Xavy and one of the other wolves paused on their way back to the shower, listening from a few feet away. Mr. Zerling didn't notice them, or didn't let on that he did, anyway. "You worked real hard. But the thing with your diet, and you didn't work with the team…you were working for some individual goal. And this team ain't about individual goals. So I'm suspending you from the team 'til after the Lakeside game."

Sol gaped. "Suspending…? Like, I can't even practice?"

Mr. Zerling nodded. "Go get your head on straight, do what you need to do, and you can come back for the last month of the season and the playoffs. You're a good kid, and you can help the team, but not if you're getting one of my best players into fights and detention."

Suspending me from the team won't stop me getting into fights in the cafeteria, Sol wanted to say. How does that make any sense? "Fine," he said, ears flat.

Mr. Zerling looked down at his clipboard. Sol waited a moment, long enough for his watching teammates—ex-teammates—to disperse. Then he walked away, because there wasn't anything else to do.

"Hey." Xavy had caught up with him, the other wolf trailing a bit behind.

"Oh, hey." Sol slowed and turned, wary at first, but Xavy didn't look aggressive; his ears were up, and he wasn't frowning. Nor was his friend.

"Sucks," Xavy said. "I mean, you gettin' suspended."

Sol shrugged. "I guess."

"Taric's a good player, but he's kind of an asshole. The guys were sayin' they didn't think you'da been the one to take him down."

"I didn't." Sol laughed, and winced. "My face is still sore."

"Yeah, but still. Y'know, he wants to be one of the wolves." Xavy laughed.

Sol didn't laugh, though he knew Xavy was trying to tell him that he would always have what Taric couldn't. That should have made him feel better. Instead he thought of Jean's account of the luncheon with the wolf and fox, their contempt for him so clear that even in his own writing, he could not completely conceal it. "Thanks," he said to Xavy, because that seemed like the right thing to say. "He's a better player, so you guys are gonna have to deal with him. Sorry I…" He touched his lower lip where it was bitten. "Sorry I couldn't stay better this year."

Xavy patted his shoulder. "Look, I don't get the whole vegetarian thing. But, uh, I guess we'll all be headin' off to whatever after this, so… good luck with it."

"I'm not gonna be standing with a goat on a street corner screaming about how 'Meat is murder.'" Sol grinned, which only caused him a little pain. "Just…I didn't wanna do it anymore."

"Sure, okay." Xavy still didn't understand, but at least he was polite about it. "Hey, you coming to the Senior Night party next month?"

"Uh…" Next month, Sol hoped to be in Millenport. "Probably not… I'll see what Meg wants to do."

Xavy nodded. "You should come. It'll be good. Take care, huh?"

Sol raised a paw and watched Xavy hurry off to the locker room. The idea of not practicing was so strange to him that he wondered for a moment if Mr. Zerling would let him use the batting cages for forty-five minutes as long as he didn't talk to the other players. He snorted; what would be the point of practicing? To get better at something he wasn't ever going to do again? By the time his suspension was over, he'd be four hours away and out of school.

Once he was around the corner of the school, he kicked small stones along the path, and then chased after them as though they were ground balls he had to retrieve. He lunged after them, grabbed them, fired them into the school's yellow brick wall. He had just kicked a small pine cone when footsteps hurried up behind him, so he came to a dead halt and then walked forward as though he'd just been walking the whole time, while the pinecone skittered to a stop on the grass. Then Sol caught the smell of fox, and relaxed before Tsarev came up level with him.

Sol turned to greet him. Tsarev was smiling, but his ears were partly down and his smile looked a little bashful. "I did not get to say thank you," he said all in a rush.

"Oh, don't mention it." Sol waved a paw. "He had it coming. I've wanted to do that for a while."

"You wanted to throw tomato? Because cafeteria only serves every two weeks. Is a long time to wait."

"No, I meant…" Sol paused, and then stopped, folding his arms. "Are you being funny?"

Tsarev's ears lay back flatter. "Is not funny?"

"No," Sol grinned, and then rubbed his cheek. "I mean, yes, it is funny. It just hurts when I smile."

"Sorry!" The fox cheered up. "I will try not to be funny."

"It's okay. I don't mind."

"So." Tsarev looked back at the field. "You are not practicing, not meeting girlfriend?"

"No. Meg's at home, and…I'm suspended from the team."

"Oh." The fox looked away from Sol, down at the ground. "For fight? For defending me, you are suspended."

"Yeah, but…I mean, no. I wanted to do it. And you were sticking up for me, anyway."

Tsarev heaved a sigh and slumped forward. He rested his elbows on his thick legs. "Is difficult. Fate, I think? Fate is difficult."

Sol suppressed the urge to put an arm over the fox's broad back. "Fate's a bastard."

"I am sorry to ask about the otter," Tsarev said. "Your girlfriend. I believe you, of course."

"Thanks." Sol stuck his paws into his pockets and turned the corner to the front of the school. There was nobody there, would be nobody there for at least half an hour. He leaned against the painted yellow bricks and let his tongue hang out of his muzzle. It felt good in the still, warm air, under the thick, low clouds. "Anyway, it doesn't matter."

"Your girlfriend does not matter?" Tsarev stood near him.

"Baseball." The faint shouts of team practice echoed from behind the school. Sol closed his eyes and leaned his head back, suppressing the pang in his chest. He might miss baseball, but it didn't miss him. "I'm getting out of here."

"At the end of the year." The fox tilted his muzzle. "Yes?"

"Next week."

"You will not finish school?"

"What's the point?" Without baseball, Sol felt as though the last artificial tie holding him to the school had blown away. The yellow brick walls, the big silver letters reading "Richfield High School," who cared whether he left them in two months or in one week? They held nothing for him anymore, no friends except Meg, no use, no happiness, nothing.

Tsarev scratched the side of his muzzle, and frowned as though he'd never thought about the question before. "Graduating? Diploma is the point, no?"

Sol felt wonderfully rebellious. "I can take an exam if I need to. I don't know what I want to do yet, so I'll take a year and figure it out. I don't need to go to college right away."

"What will your girlfriend do?"

"She's coming with me." Too late, he thought that maybe he shouldn't have given away Meg's plans, but Tsarev didn't seem likely to run and tell tales.

The fox just nodded. "I hope you will be happy," he said.

"Thanks." Sol wagged his tail slowly.

Tsarev's musky scent had sharpened, as though he were afraid of or nervous about something. The fox fidgeted from one foot to the other, but all he said was, "I would like to have talked to you some more. I am sorry there was not more time."

"Well," Sol said, "We can stay in touch. If you come up to Millenport I'll show you around."

"All right." Tsarev brightened, bringing his phone out. The sharpness eased from his scent and he relaxed, his long bushy tail swinging easily behind him. He and Sol exchanged their e-mail addresses and then the fox bid him good night. "My host family is strict with time of dinner," he said.

"So's mine." Sol watched the fox walk off and then leaned back against the bricks, closed his eyes, and waited for six-thirty.

The first thing his father asked him when he got in the car was, "How was practice?" and Sol didn't have the energy or desire to soften the blow.

"I got suspended from the team," he said. "For two weeks, including the Lakeside game."

His father didn't respond until they were stopped at a red light, and then he turned on Sol. "Suspended? What did you do?"

Sol looked straight ahead, holding the end of his tail in his paw, rubbing the back of that paw with the other. Tension coiled tight in his chest. "Got in a fight. With Taric."

His father examined him. "You picked a fight with another player."

The light turned green. They drove on, and when Sol didn't say anything, his father kept going. "You remember that movie, where the guy told the pitcher he always, always had to be thinking about what arm he was using even when he got emotional? You remember that, Sol?"

A variation on the "what do you think" game. Sol ground out, "Sure," between clenched teeth.

"You need to think like that when you're on a team. Always, always, think about what your actions mean to the rest of the team. Did Taric get suspended too?"

"No."

"So Mr. Zerling thought it was your fault. So you've become the kind of player who's so destructive to the team that he'd rather you just go away than give you another chance."

He'll get his wish, Sol thought. "Guess so," he muttered.

"I can't begin to express how disappointed I am in you." His father slammed a fist into the steering wheel. "Eleven years of team sports, and you haven't learned a thing."

"No," Sol said, turning to stare out his window.

"Dammit!" His father's yell made him jump. "Don't you even care?"

"I care," Sol said. *Just about a lot of things you don't understand.*

What was surprising was that he did not get in trouble for fighting. Even his mother, when told the whole story, said that as long as he was defending someone else, he was in the right. "Not that we want you to make a habit of it."

And his father mostly sounded upset that he hadn't finished the job. "You let him get you in the muzzle? You didn't try to bite him, did you?"

After Sol had assured his parents that he knew better than to bite in a fight and that he would not be making a habit of it, the fight was not mentioned again. But the suspension, that was brought up over and over again, until Sol was released upstairs to do homework.

There he texted Carcy. *Did you get a day yet? I can't wait.*

He tried to do homework while waiting for the ram's reply, but found himself working the same math problem out over and over again. Finally, his phone beeped, and he grabbed it before the third beep had even sounded.

How's Tuesday?

Works great, he typed, relieved. *Thanks.*

He sent two e-mails right away, one to Carcy with his address, the other to Meg. She texted him right away to talk details, and they agreed to pack the night before and go to school in the morning; if they didn't show up in homeroom, their parents might be called to see if they were ill. They'd duck out over lunch and take the city bus back home. Carcy would arrive at Sol's place around one, they'd load the car, and then drive over to Meg's to load her stuff. If there was room, Meg would come with them; if not, they could get her to the bus station somehow.

He lay on his side on his bed, and his eyes came to rest on the rolled-up painting in the corner of his room. When he'd come home to his room, he'd walked over and touched it, to make sure it was still real. And now, preparing for sleep, feeling on the edge of a grand adventure, he regarded it with a smile. It would come with him for sure. He'd take it along, and he and Meg would look at it and it would remind them of the project and the absinthe during the hot summer nights in Millenport.

The rain still had not come, but the clouds continued to crowd the sky. Sol felt his dream strongly when he looked out at them, so much that he could smell the oily paint, the rancid smell of Henri's self-imposed starvation. When he closed his eyes, he could see the old, smelly room where the rat painted his pictures, the bed where rat (and fox?) slept. He could feel Niki's longer, flowing tail behind him; the aches and pains in his lip, cheek and side mirrored the fox's in his dream. But he, like Niki, was leaving, was taking the rat's painting and moving on to a better life.

For the rest of the week and most of the weekend, he packed as stealthily as he could. There was very little he was going to take, so mostly he sorted through his things and decided which were necessary and which weren't. He had never really wanted to keep many things from his childhood; his trophies from competitions in younger days didn't have much meaning to him, and he had all his photos and music on his computer. What's more, he was hoping he could pack lightly enough that there would be room for Meg on the trip. He hated to think of her taking the bus alone.

At school, Taric ignored him, both in the cafeteria and sitting across the room in the silent detention period. Tanny didn't, but her taunts didn't bother Sol as much when he could picture himself slugging her brother every time she talked to him. And he had the unexpected pleasure of eating lunches with Tsarev.

They didn't talk about Sol's leaving, only about baseball and soccer. Sol was surprised to find out how ignorant he was of international soccer, but the fox didn't seem to mind; he was happy to tell Sol about the various teams and players in exchange for the old baseball and football stories Sol had grown up on.

Sol hadn't expected to use the fox's e-mail address until after he'd left, but on the weekend, he read a story about a baseball player who had hit a home run in his first at-bat back after two years, a player everyone had said would never play again. Sol sent Tsarev an e-mail with a link to the story, and got an enthusiastic response about how wonderful life could be sometimes. It was nice, amid the upcoming uncertainty, to look forward to exchanging e-mails, to having a virtual friend when the real-life world had shrunk to just him, Meg, and Carcy in Millenport. He didn't think he would be having many conversations with his parents, nor with Xavy or any of the baseball team, once he left.

All day Monday, the feeling of being watched returned in force. His ears flicked around as if he could catch people talking about his imminent departure, and his tail twitched constantly. Every time he walked into a class, he thought, this is the last time I'll be walking into this classroom.

This is the last time I'll be sitting in math, in physics, in history. But nobody treated him differently, nobody said anything, even though he felt sure they all knew. It was exciting, and scary at the same time.

Niki, in his dream, had loved parts of the Moulin Rouge, and though his home hadn't been comfortable, he had a friend there. Sol had a comfortable home, a routine at the school that he was used to, even if he didn't like it, and a group of people whom he could call friends, if perhaps not close friends.

But he also had a boyfriend and a new, exciting life to look forward to: exploring the big city, living on his own, finding a job, and doing something he was interested in. Even if he didn't quite know what that was, yet, he was much more certain to find it there than here.

Chapter 18

He thought he might dream about Niki Monday night, but his dreams were gone the moment he woke, leaving only an uneasy residue in his muzzle that he tried to erase with toothpaste. Walking down through the cloudy morning to the bus stop, Sol had to force himself to breathe normally. Talking to Meg might calm him, so he sat by himself, but Meg didn't slide in next to him when she got on, just walked right to the back. Sol's tail kept twitching against the seat, until the possum who did sit next to him looked down at it for the fourth time. The black wolf held his tail in his lap after that, though it wriggled against his fingers with all his nervous energy.

In between his first and second classes, right around nine, he got a text from Carcy. *Leaving now. Seeya soon.* The reality of the words stopped him cold. A raccoon bumped into him from behind, and he shut the phone off and put it away quickly, paws shaking. By the time Sol got to class, he was sure the raccoon had seen the message, was sure everyone in class was staring at him and that they knew they wouldn't see him again after today. The morning felt like a dream to him, as though he were already lying in a bed in Millenport, dreaming of the Sol he used to be. Would it be like this for Niki, he wondered, leaving the Moulin Rouge? If the fox had the strength to change his life, then Sol could too.

At lunch, he hesitated at the doorway to the cafeteria, then broke away from the crowd of students. Alone, he walked down the hallway to the school's entrance, and there he stopped dead. Mr. Fortune stood in front of the wide glass doors, his bear's bulk imposing against the grey light of the afternoon. He peered in Sol's direction over his wire spectacles. "Something I can do for you, Mister Wrightson?"

Meg came up behind him. "We're going to meet my mom for lunch. We've got a note."

She walked past and handed a folded paper to Mr. Fortune, who examined it, looked up at Meg, examined the note again, and finally said, "All right."

"You brought a note?" Sol hissed to her once the door had closed behind them.

"You didn't?" She rolled her eyes. "They always keep a teacher by the front doors. How long have you been going to this school?"

"Almost four years." He looked back over his shoulder, at the long, low, golden bricks. "Almost." The rain had finally come, a light sprinkle. The clouds promised more soon, but for now it wasn't even enough to notice.

"Good riddance." Meg hitched her bag over her shoulder.

They caught the bus back to their neighborhood and parted with a hurried wave. "See you in about an hour," Meg said, and Sol, increasingly nervous, nodded quickly.

He let himself in and ran up the stairs quickly, putting aside the thought that this would be the last time he would be in his house for who knew how long. The house's silence unnerved him. He wanted music.

His iPod lay where his father always stashed it when it was confiscated, right in the top drawer of his dresser. Next to it were six pairs of t-shirts, neatly folded. The scent of his father came strongly, not from the clean shirts, but from the room itself. Sol paused to look around. There were photos in the room: a picture of his mother and father from their wedding, years ago; pictures of Sol and Natty as cubs, individually and together; a family picture from three years ago, on vacation to the amusement park outside of town. The smiles, the love and happiness in the pictures, stopped Sol and fed the butterflies in his stomach.

He was doing the right thing, the best thing for himself. He weighed the iPod in his paw. *They still treat me like a cub. They won't let me be myself. I'd be leaving in five months anyway, and I didn't even pick out the college. I need to get away.*

Anyway, there was nothing he could do about it now. Carcy was on his way, almost here, and when he got here, he would be taking Sol away. Nervous jitters were perfectly normal. Sol took the iPod back to his room and put on some hard rock while he finished getting everything into bags.

At five to one, he ran downstairs and paced by the front door. He didn't quite want to bring his bags downstairs, because what if his parents came home unexpectedly? What if Carcy didn't show up? As the clock ticked over the hour, his worries multiplied.

At five after, he became convinced that Carcy had brought Bucky with him, that that was what had delayed him.

At ten after, he knew the ram had decided he was too much trouble. Probably Bucky had told him not to bother with the high school wolf, had called him a whiny, weak cub. Without even knowing him. Sol imagined Bucky as a coyote, telling Carcy that they didn't need another roommate in their place, that Sol would just screw everything up. He imagined Bucky telling Carcy how weak a vegetarian wolf was, not caring how much effort and strength it had taken for Sol to make that change and stick to it. Sol's fists clenched. He'd gotten Taric good; he'd get Bucky, too, if the coyote—or whatever he was—made any trouble for him and his ram.

But at twelve past one, a small car pulled up outside. Sol hurried to the window in time to see a big, muscular ram get out and stretch, alone, then check the number on the house before walking up to the door. It had to be Carcy, though it didn't look exactly like his picture. So he opened the door and stood there grinning, tail twitching.

The ram's face broke into a smile. "Hey, Solly," he said, in a familiar, deep voice. He wore a t-shirt of the band Def Match and an earring in his right ear, below the majestic, curling horns atop his head. His fur was white and thick, in waves along his head and tight curls at his chest, poking out over the top of the t-shirt.

"Hi," Sol said. "Uh, come on in."

Carcy walked through the door, and after Sol had closed it, wrapped his arms around the wolf. "Good to see you," he breathed against Sol's ear, which flicked ticklishly.

"Mm, you too." Sol hadn't hugged a non-family member in a long time. Carcy was warm and solid in his arms, and he relaxed for the first time that day. He pressed up against the ram, and then Carcy shifted to press his groin firmly into Sol's leg. Sol let him, then felt weird about it and tried to shift himself away, without much success. "Uh," he said, heart pounding, "did you have a good drive?"

"Rained for the first half of it. Seems to be all to the north, though." Carcy finally let Sol disengage from the hug, and they stood and looked each other over. Carcy in person loomed over the ram of Sol's imagination, a few inches taller and broader in the shoulders than Sol was. He smelled of sweat and beer, and when he talked, cheese and oil on his breath. He'd told Sol he was twenty-two, but there were creases in the short fur around his eyes that made him look older. "I tell you, if I didn't know which town was yours I'd still be drivin' around. All these little backwoods bumfuck towns look exactly the same. Don't blame you for bein' anxious to get out."

"You want something to drink?" Sol took a step toward the kitchen. "We got milk, um. And beer."

"Are we gonna be here a while?" Carcy grinned. Before Sol could answer, the ram said, "Sure, a beer would be great."

Sol hurried to the refrigerator and pulled out a beer—one of the cheap ones, for company. He reached in to get one for himself, then changed his mind and grabbed a can of Coke instead.

When he came back out to the living room, Carcy had dropped himself onto the sofa. It was weird seeing him there; heck, it was weird seeing him, period. Sol was still reconciling this large ram with his boyfriend, whom he knew mostly across a phone. So he handed Carcy the beer and then sat on the edge of his dad's recliner, tail flicking nervously, looking down at his Coke.

"Don't wanna sit next to me, Solly?"

"Um…" Sol pressed his tongue to his sore lip. "I'll be sitting next to you all the way back."

"Yeah, but there's a lot we can't do then. I'll be driving."

Sol gulped down his Coke and then burped. "Excuse me," he said.

Carcy laughed, downed a good third of his beer, and let loose a belch that dwarfed Sol's. "No 'scusin' necessary," he said. "Come on, sit over here, relax."

On the family couch where he and Natty had tussled? Where he and his parents had watched TV, played games? But Carcy was staring at him, waiting, and Sol didn't feel able to come up with any more excuses to stay away. He got up and walked past Carcy, then sat himself on the sofa with about a foot between them. The thought of the Moulin Rouge dancers keeping a distance between themselves and their patrons made him relax a little, then tense up again when Carcy slid over, closing the distance between them.

"You're cuter in person," the ram murmured. His weight pressed in on Sol's shoulder.

"Th-thanks." Sol took another drink.

"Got those cute ears. God, I love wolf ears. They're so…" Carcy's breath warmed Sol's ears, ruffling the little hairs in them until they flicked around, out of Sol's control. The ram chuckled softly and brushed his nose into Sol's left ear.

Sol jumped, then forced himself to sit still. He was trembling, nerves and arousal warring in him. In their texting sessions, Carcy always played with Sol's ear, and that was awesome to imagine. And now the ram did it for real: he closed his lips around Sol's ear and tugged.

Sol squirmed back against him, a little embarrassed at how quickly he was responding. The ram's arms held him tightly, one hand sliding down his back towards his tail. "Uh," Sol said, "I'm not eighteen for a month yet, I mean, we could, you could get in trouble…"

Carcy licked his ear as he let it go. "Nah," he said. "I'm only nineteen. Two years difference isn't illegal."

"Didn't…" Sol licked his lips. Carcy's eyes met his. "I thought you said you're twenty-two."

He thought Carcy might get angry, might ask if Sol was implying he was a liar. But the ram just laughed. "Aw, Sol, I guess if I said that, I thought you wanted someone older to look up to. What's the matter? You didn't seem too worried about age last week."

"Oh." Sol swallowed. He put the Coke can down on the coffee table, now aware of a more urgent scent from the ram. "Um. We should get my stuff."

"We got time. I wanna relax a little." The ram stretched an arm back across the couch, right where Sol would be sitting if he leaned back now. "Y'know, I thought drivin' four hours would be better than standing behind the counter, but it's exhausting. Your folks ain't comin' home 'til five, right?"

"Yeah, but…" He cleared his throat, trying to keep his voice from breaking. "It's…it's just up in my bedroom. It'll take a minute."

"Oh, okay." Carcy grinned. "I'm cool with going upstairs."

"I can get it." Sol stood. "It's not a problem."

The ram's grin widened a bit. "I'm here to help, Solly. Besides, I wanna see your bedroom."

Sol walked up the stairs slowly, giving his heart—and other parts of him—time to settle down, though his whiskers twitched with the ram's movement behind him. He was painfully aware of what Carcy expected of him; that made it difficult for his heart to slow. He wanted what Carcy wanted, so why was he being such a baby about it? The ram wasn't going to hurt him. He touched the side of his muzzle, where his lip was sore.

At the top of the stairs, Carcy said, "You have a really cute tail," and brushed it. Sol curled it away, around his hip. He hurried to his room, where he paused to inhale his brother's scent.

He only got a sniff of it before Carcy pushed his way past. The reassuring stability of Natty gave way to the beer and increasing arousal of the ram. "Nice place. Cool tunes," Carcy said, because the iPod was still going.

Sol walked over and shut it off, tossing it into the nearest bag on the bed. "We don't have to bring the player if there's not room."

"I got one," Carcy said. He sniffed around the room, then stopped at the small pile of three bags on the bed. "This everything?"

"That and the…" Sol waved a paw toward the rolled-up painting. "Poster."

"Cool." The ram hefted the two largest bags.

Sol felt a wash of relief. They were just going to go to the car, they would get Meg and be on their way. He picked up the painting. "You think there'll be room for Meg? My friend?"

"Depends what she's got." Carcy set the bags on the floor by the door, picked up the third one, and set it beside them. He pulled the iPod out of the bag and set it back in the player. "Got any Trisha on here?"

Sol shifted his weight. The poster tingled in his paws, just for a moment, like the jolt he got from licking a battery. He jumped and nearly dropped it. "Shouldn't we, uh, get going?"

"Look, I know you're real anxious to get out of here. Trust me, we got plenty of time, and I don't wanna get right back in the car. You seem real tense, anyway, and I can help relax you a bit. Haven't you been looking forward to this?" Carcy found a soft rock album and backed up to sit on the bed. He patted his lap and raised an eyebrow.

"Sure," Sol said. He didn't move, but he couldn't look Carcy in the eye. "I just…"

"Just what?" The ram's tone grew darker. "Look at me, Sol. What, don't like the look of me in RL?"

"No, no!" Sol took a step closer. "You look great. I mean, really awesome."

"You do too. So c'mon, let me see the rest of you." Carcy reached down to his own waist and pulled his shirt off in one fluid motion, revealing a nicely shaped chest and thick, muscular arms. His scent crowded its way into Sol's nose, thick and forward. He grinned at Sol. "Your turn."

"I don't know if I'm ready now," Sol blurted out.

Carcy raised one eyebrow. "We don't have to do nothin' you don't want. I just wanna get to know you a little better. I mean, we're gonna live together."

Sol twisted his paws around the canvas roll. It felt warm, but it didn't deliver any more shocks. "I'm sorry. I know we're going to, I know we…did stuff over text…but…I'm just feeling weird now."

Carcy stood. "Listen, Sol, this is a big deal for me, too. We'll be having sex—that's what it's called—sooner or later, right? Might as well be sooner, get that first time out of the way. You know? I don't want to get you to Millenport and have you 'feelin' weird' and start cryin' and wantin' to go home and calling the…your parents or something. You said you loved me."

"I do," Sol said, automatically and desperately and no longer, he was aware, completely truthfully. He loved 290-418-3831, the entry in his phone labeled "Carcy," with whom he'd exchanged confidences and thoughts and amorous texts, but this person in his house, half-naked in his bedroom, bore only a passing resemblance to that phone entry. "Please, can't we wait 'til tonight?"

"Will you be more ready tonight? If you're not ready now, I dunno. Maybe I should just head back and fuck Bucky. I know he's ready." Carcy reached out, as if for his shirt.

It seemed to be waiting for something.

"Please," Sol repeated. "I'm just really stressed about moving."

Carcy didn't pick up his shirt. He reached instead for the painting. "It's not like I'm askin' you to do anything we ain't talked about."

Sol pulled the painting away. He didn't want to set it down, but Carcy was going to take it from him if he didn't, so he set it against the bed. "I know we talked," he said.

As soon as his paw was free, Carcy grabbed it and pulled the wolf closer. "Did more than talk, too, right?"

He pressed Sol's paw to his groin. Sol closed his eyes. "I…I guess…"

"See?" Carcy rubbed Sol's paw up and down. "Ain't so bad, is it? You want to stop?"

Sol didn't answer. If he just went along with it, it would be over soon, he thought. And then Carcy's other hand cupped his own groin, started rubbing there, and Sol's eyes flew open. It felt good, but it didn't feel right, not here. This wasn't the way he'd imagined things going at all, but his treacherous body did not seem to care.

Natty's scent flickered past his nose. He made a noise in his throat, but Carcy just said, "Shh. It's gonna be good, just trust me. You can trust me, right?"

Sol's free paw brushed the painting. He looked down at it and then up, across the bed at the mirror on his closet. In the reflection, he saw Carcy moving both hands up and down, saw the desperation in his panicked hazel eyes. He looked trapped. And then he saw the flicker of movement, a shadow behind Carcy.

The wolf's eyes flicked forward, but there was nothing there. He flicked back to the mirror. Definitely, a shape behind the ram, a shifting shadow with a long, flowing tail, whose ears showed in ragged silhouette against the light of the hallway through the open door.

Carcy's eyes closed. He lifted Sol's paw and pressed it to his bare stomach, forcing it down inside his underwear.

Behind the ram, the shadow lifted an arm. It seemed to be waiting for something.

Sol's fingers brushed something, and he curled them away from it. "Please," Sol whispered to the shadow.

"Sure, Solly," Carcy said, and moved his fingers to Sol's waistband. "Y'see? I—"

The shadow moved, its arm whipping across Carcy's muzzle in the reflection. In front of Sol, the ram's head snapped to one side.

He let go of Sol's paw and pulled his other arm back, eyes open and blazing yellow anger. "What the fuck?"

"Sorry!" The word came out cracked in two through Sol's bone-dry throat. "I'm sorry, I just don't…I'm not ready…"

Carcy cracked him hard across the muzzle, catching him right on the swollen part of his lower lip. "You *hit* me? Jesus, you've got some fucking nerve!"

"No," Sol whined.

"What the fuck did I drive all the way down here for? So I could haul some kid back to Millenport and *not* have sex?" Carcy shouted in Sol's face, his broad white chest looming over the wolf.

Sol staggered back, one arm flailing. It struck Carcy on the shoulder; the ram pushed it aside easily and elbowed him in the chest, knocking him backwards onto the bed. Pain exploded in Sol's ribs; he curled around it, wheezing to catch his breath, and cringed as Carcy raised an arm again. "I thought you were more grown up, Solly. The whole running away from home, I get it, I been there. You know what I did after that? I took responsibility for my fucking life! I had a boyfriend, I went to his place, and we fucked! I was sixteen and he was twenty, and you know what? I was grown up enough to handle it. I know how much you hate all this baseball shit and high school crap you didn't want to be a part of, I was taking you away from that and showing you what real life is all about. And what do I get?" He leaned over and smacked Sol on the nose hard enough to bring tears to Sol's eyes, though not only from the physical pain. "'I'm not ready! I'm not ready!' And then you have the fucking gall to hit me! After I drove four hours down here and took a day off work, which by the way I can't fucking afford."

"I thought you loved me," was all Sol could bring himself to say. He hated the way his voice cracked, hated the way he felt everything slipping through his fingers, hated the way Carcy was looming over him and the way he felt paralyzed.

"Bucky said I was being an idiot, falling for a cub again. He said, 'he's too young.' But I told him how you went vegetarian, told him 'bout what we talked about. I thought…" The ram lifted a hand to his eyes and rubbed them. "You know what, forget it. Just forget it. When you grow up—don't call me."

Sol watched him walk to the doorway, where he turned around, his curved horns and small ears in silhouette, eyes glaring with reflected light. "I can't believe you fucking hit me," he said.

"I didn't." Sol pressed his fingers to his own eyes. "I didn't."

Carcy shook his head and walked out. Sol listened to him descend the stairs, and it occurred to him that his last chance to get out of here, his last chance to escape months of misery and then a college he didn't want to go to, his last chance was walking out the door in about ten seconds. He struggled to get to his feet. "Wait!" he called.

His paw brushed the painting again as he got up. His head snapped around of its own accord to look in the mirror. There he saw the silhouette again, standing in his doorway, the ragged fox's ears and the long fox's tail, and more: gleaming green eyes, fixed on him.

Slowly, the figure shook its head. It made a kind of choking, keening noise. Sol's ears flicked forward, and he realized that he was the one making the noise. He tore his gaze from the mirror and ran to the hall, then to the top of the stairs.

Carcy stood there, still shirtless, one hand on the door. "You bring my shirt?"

"No, I…" His muzzle stung; Carcy had hit him right where his lip had been bitten. He put a paw up to it. Like in his dream, like Niki's aches that the fox had dismissed as unimportant, that he'd regarded as the price to be paid. Sol swallowed. "No."

"Fine. Keep it. Fucking cub. Don't call me again." He opened the front door. Sol heard him mutter, "four *fucking* hours." The door slammed, and he was gone.

Sol stared at the door for a long, long time. Then he turned on shaky legs and made his way back to his bedroom.

The mirror held only his reflection. He brushed the painting with a paw, but no spark touched his fingertips, nothing magical happened, no figure appeared from it. "Why did you stop me?" he whispered. "I just needed some time. I panicked."

The only sound was his iPod, still playing that soft rock album. Sol grabbed the remote from his bed and stabbed at the power button until the stereo shut down with a click. "Why?" he said, louder. "Now, I'm… screwed."

His mother would be home soon. His father would be wondering why he wasn't at the school. Meg would be wondering where he was. And he would be here, in this stone house, always, eating vegetables under the disapproving glare of his father, working in the peach cannery over the summer, taking the bus until the fall when he would go off to some small college to learn a subject that barely interested him.

He jumped when his phone rang. His first thought was that Carcy was calling him back, that the ram had gotten ten minutes down the road and realized that Sol was just scared and didn't mean it. But it was Meg's voice that came through when he answered. "Hey. Save the happy sex time for when you're back at his place and get your tails over here."

Her expectation just made the reality that much harder to bear. "We're not—I'm not coming. It's not..." He wiped his eyes, which seemed to be filling up again.

"Not coming?" Meg's voice got louder. "What the fuck? Did that asshole back out?"

"No," Sol said. "No, he was here, we just—we just fought." He pressed the back of his paw to his eyes, feeling the tears soak into his fur.

"You fought? With your boyfriend?"

His throat tightened. "He's not—I don't think he ever—just forget it, we're not going."

"Sol?"

He hung up the phone and dropped it on the bed, and leaned against the wall near his door. His brother's scent was still there, but not comforting now. He could only think about how disappointed Natty would be in him: *Geez, Sol, you can't even run away right,* he'd say. So Sol staggered over to his bed, where he sat with his knees drawn up to his chest, his tail curled around them. The mirror showed only the black wolf on the bed, rocking gently back and forth, no shadowy figure with a paw on his shoulder. All around him, silence gathered and grew, broken only by the small noises he couldn't stop himself from making.

When the door opened downstairs, Sol scrambled off the bed, running for his bedroom door to slam it shut. He pulled open his bags and threw the clothes into the dresser frantically, until he heard Meg's voice calling, "Sol?"

Sol stopped, exhaled. He walked to his bedroom door and yanked it open. "In here," he called, but Meg was already coming up the stairs.

"You okay?" she asked when she got to the room. "What happened?"

He found he couldn't meet her eyes. "He got here, and...he wanted to..." He picked up Carcy's shirt where it lay on the edge of the bed, balled it up in his paws.

"He wanted to fuck."

"Uh. Yeah."

"Jesus." Meg took the shirt from Sol. "This his shirt? He just left it?"

"He was pretty mad."

She stared at the shirt. "Def Match sucks. Fucking posers." He watched her claws pick at the fabric, methodically, until they'd created a small hole. Then she grabbed the shirt on either side of the hole and pulled hard. The shirt ripped; the hole grew large enough to stick an arm through.

"Fuck him. You know? Let's go get a burger or something down at Clark's."

"Not hungry." Sol sat back down on the bed. He glanced again at the mirror and then back at Meg. "Let's go to your place."

"All my parents have is sunflower seeds and tofu." She pulled at the hole in the shirt and stared down at it. "Oh, right. Come on, Clark's has veggie burgers too."

"No, I mean." His paws curled. For a moment, he almost told her about his dreams, about the shadowy figure that had hit Carcy. If anyone would understand, Meg would. But the words caught in his throat. When he'd been on the bed, terrified, the shadow had made perfect sense. Now, feeling safe and miserable, when rescue was not as easy as a smack to the head of a ram, the shadow and his dream sounded crazy. He would almost have thought that he had imagined it, that it really had been his paw that hit Carcy except for one thing, the thing he couldn't escape, and that was that if he had really hit Carcy hard enough to snap his head around, that thick head with the bony horns, his paw would have felt it. His paw, right now, would hurt. And it didn't.

"What?" She squinted at him.

He took a breath. "I just want to have some more absinthe."

"Christ, Sol."

"Not like that, I mean—"

"You know, I'm not a 'Just Say No' kinda gal, but Jesus, smoke some pot. Don't go booze, and especially don't go boutique booze."

"I just need it, just one more time."

Meg folded her arms. "Listen to yourself. Come on, let's go outside, I've got a joint in my bag."

"I don't want pot! I need the absinthe, I need the...the dreams!" He scrabbled for words, something that would make Meg understand without making him sound crazy—or crazier. "It's an escape, it's this other world..."

"You've been having more of the dreams?" She glared at him. "You're not imagining you're a bird or something, are you?"

Sol got up off the bed, stalking across his room. Meg backed away from him, but he didn't touch her, just turned around and paced back and forth. "I have these weird dreams and it's only after I drink the absinthe, and I...I need to get back there. I need to ask something."

"Ask something?" Meg shook her head. "Jesus, you sound like my parents, talking to your dreams. Forget them. What do you need to ask them anyway?"

"Why...why." He stared at the corner of his room, at the poster. "Why I'm having them."

"I'll tell you why you're having them. Because you're drinking and you're working out a lot of shit in your head. Okay? Let's go to Clark's already."

"You don't understand!" Sol flattened his ears. "I need the damn absinthe."

"No, you don't! You need to chill and talk this out with a real person." She grabbed his shoulders.

He stared right into her eyes. "I don't need you."

Meg froze. Then she let go, and slowly straightened up. Her eyes stayed locked on his for another minute and then she stepped toward his door. "You know what, I'm not gonna just be your absinthe dealer. I'm sorry I ran over here. Give me a call when you get your head on straight."

"No, wait!" He grabbed her arm, but she shook him off and stalked out to the hallway.

He followed her down the stairs, trying to apologize, but it wasn't until she got to the bottom of the stairs that she turned and said anything to him, though her words came haltingly. "Listen, I—I know this sucks. You don't mean what you say. You wanna sit down and talk about it, come find me. But I'm not gonna give you absinthe, and if you can't think of anything else to say to me, then I'm leaving."

Sol's jaw worked. He couldn't free himself from the obsessive need to figure out what had happened, why the shadow had helped him. If Meg was such a good friend, why did he feel like she'd just laugh if he told her about the shadow? "I...I don't know what I'm going to do."

She pointed up the stairs. "You're going to unpack. You're going to tell your parents you felt sick and they sent you home. You're going to delete that fucker from your phone. And you're going to go to school tomorrow."

The sick part wasn't going to be hard. Already his gut felt clenched and twisted. "And then what?"

Meg shrugged. "Then we figure out something else. Right? We got months."

"Months. I can't wait months." Sol sagged against the wall. "I thought he loved me. I thought that's what this was all about."

"I told you, boys'll say anything."

Sol pressed his fingers to his eyes again. It was all a jumble in his head: the reality of Carcy, the shadow of Niki, the who-cares attitude of Meg. "Go," he said roughly. "I'll be fine."

"You don't look fine," she said.

"Then get me some absinthe!" he yelled, and that did it.

Her expression grew as black as her fur. "See you in school," she said, and walked out.

Chapter 19

Sol's footsteps echoed in the house, his claws click-click-clicking on the hallway before he stepped on the carpeted stairs. All around him, the stone threw his movements back at him in echoes and air currents, his whiskers twitching. Every time he tried to think of what tomorrow would be like, or next week, or next month, he came up with the same emptiness. Meg had run out on him, taken her friend's absinthe and her ritual, and he would never get to see the end of Niki's story. He wasn't going to move to Millenport, he wasn't even going to have the hollow pleasure of baseball. He'd be lucky to see any time off the bench, the way things were going. Tanny would torment him every day, and Taric would fight him again, and his father would force him to eat meat.

He took out his phone and pulled up Carcy's number. It was hard to believe that he couldn't just text Carcy and tell him all about the asshole who'd just come by pretending to be him, that if he did, Carcy wouldn't text back with a smile and tell him that it was all okay, that he still loved him. But really, when it came down to it, when had Carcy really been interested in him, or in anything other than a good sexting session? Those had been the times when Carcy was really engaged with him. When Sol told him personal stuff...not so much.

Because those were the times when Carcy would roll his eyes and say to Bucky, "it's that whiny wolf again."

Sol selected "Delete," and hesitated only a moment when the phone asked him to confirm that he really wanted to erase Carcy from his People. Then he shoved the useless phone into his pocket, stomped his way into the kitchen, and threw open the refrigerator door, sniffing inside for what had to be there. The beers, the Cokes, he ignored, trying not to see them. There, on the second shelf: a cold piece of leftover steak. The fat on it was solid white, thick and greasy, and the meat was clammy to the touch. Sol didn't care; he wrapped his paws around it, brought it to his muzzle, and tore off a hunk with his teeth.

The grainy texture of the meat and fat were barely noticeable behind the wave of the taste, the rich beef he hadn't had in weeks. The first taste of it disgusted him, but then its sweet flavor overwhelmed his mouth. "Mmm, God," he moaned, and ripped off another hunk, chewing the cold, greasy meat only a couple times before swallowing the whole lump. It was terrible and it was amazing. He gnawed at it, sank his teeth into the flesh, swallowed great bites because he couldn't wait long enough to chew them, and in minutes was left ripping scraps from a bone.

He was licking his paws clean when he felt the churning in his stomach. He'd thought that the twisting, empty feeling would go away when he ate something, but it seemed to be getting worse. Just the meat settling, he thought, but after five minutes and a glass of water, it wasn't getting better, and after ten minutes, his skin felt very cold and his fur was prickling all over in seemingly random patches. He made his way up the stairs, which was much more difficult than it should have been. The walls of the staircase felt cold even through his fur, and he couldn't make out any smells from the limestone, though he was sure he was leaving his own scent there. When he stopped to lean against the wall, the reek of meat on his breath accumulated around his nose, feeding the roiling in his stomach, and he had to move on.

Still, he made it to his bathroom with several minutes to spare, which he spent bracing himself on the sink and then, when the determination of his stomach to empty itself became more apparent, on his knees in front of the toilet. It seemed to take him a very long time to vomit; his head felt warm and his breath came in short bursts, and finally he coughed and heaved, and the half-digested steak came up, brown half-chewed masses forcing their way up his throat. He vomited into the toilet, then almost splashed the seat with the next wave when he recoiled from the reek of it.

When he was done, he reached up weakly to flush the toilet, and the remains of the steak swirled away. Then he lay back against the wall and cried. Because now he couldn't eat meat, he'd ruined himself forever just for this stupid ram who only wanted sex, and the noble thing he'd done in going vegetarian looked like the foolish act of a foolish child. He was not properly a wolf, nor properly grown up, nor properly anything.

Carcy was right. He was going nowhere. He had nothing left; he couldn't talk to his parents or his brother, had driven away Meg, wasn't mature enough yet for Carcy. The smell of vomit hung thick in the air, oppressive and sour. His head swam, his stomach lurched, and he threw himself forward in time for the second wave of vomit to land on the side of the toilet. Most of it landed in the bowl, but a brownish-orange smear stained the white porcelain on one side and dripped slowly down to the floor.

Sol watched it dully. He couldn't even throw up properly. And the jackknife forward had aggravated his ribs, which were now complaining sharply. Probably broken.

He fell against the side of the bathtub and let his head loll to the side, looking down into it. The cooler, damp air there smelled less of vomit than the rest of the room. He could climb into that. His cousin had done that, too, poor "funny" Percy, had just climbed into a bathtub and run warm water and opened his wrists. Patty had told him they found a kitchen knife on the floor. She told him that even her God-fearing homophobic father had cried. Sol's parents would cry over him, too, would regret the things they'd done. He put his paw on the water tap.

His fur prickled with the feeling of eyes on him again. His head turned the other way, toward the full-length mirror on the door. There he was, a pitiable creature, sprawled against the side of the bathtub—and standing over him, a dark silhouette with ragged ears and bright green eyes.

Sol yelled and tried to jump to his feet, slipped on the tile, and smacked his already-sore jaw on the toilet. Stars danced before his eyes, but through them he saw the shape reach down, and then he felt himself hauled to his feet and thrown roughly against the door, his muzzle pressed sideways against the mirror.

In the mirror over the sink, he saw the ragged-eared shadow holding him to the door. His legs felt like jelly and his heart was racing. "Don't hurt me," he whimpered, but although the eyes of the shadow gleamed with a hard, angry light, and he could feel the rage in the room, it just held him there. "Why are you angry? What did I do?" His voice was high, and it kept cracking.

Like a gunshot, the image of himself in the bathtub appeared in his head, followed by a surge of rage.

"I won't!" he squealed. "I wasn't serious, it was just…I promise, I won't, I won't!"

The pressure vanished. He stared wildly at the mirrors, which showed only a terrified black wolf. The haze of anger that had filled the small bathroom was also gone, leaving only clean white tile and the smell of vomit. He ignored the taste of it in his mouth as he stared into the mirrors, mouthing the words, "Come back." When no shadow appeared, he screamed, "*What do you want from me?*"

Still there was no answer. Sol rinsed his mouth and then stumbled down the stairs, wrapped himself in a blanket, and sat on the couch, ribs throbbing, jaw sore. When his trembling had subsided somewhat, his heart had stopped racing, and his head no longer felt as if it were burning, he tried to close his eyes and sleep, but he could not get the shadow out of his head.

He pulled out his phone, automatically, thumbed through e-mail, but nothing there would help, nothing meant anything to him. The shadow wouldn't answer him, and he couldn't make himself dream. The only way he could reach out to it was to read more of "Confession." At least then he could see more of Niki.

His fingers fumbled as he called up the reader and skipped ahead to where Jean had taken Niki to the ball. The words sometimes blurred with tears, but on the whole they remained legible. Mostly.

It was the night of the ball that ruined everything, father. Had you remained longer, I have no doubt that your wise and even temperament could have prevented the events from degenerating as rapidly as they did. Alas, we cannot always foresee where our presence will be most useful, nor even when as simple a decision as not attending a ball may affect two lives. I do not blame you for it; the fault lies equally with Niki, if not more so.

It all began so splendidly. The Justines had decorated their mansion as befits the season, with dried flower garlands as pleasing to the nose as to the eye, with the latest works of art, with concert pianists paid to provide chamber music for we privileged guests. Of course, those trappings perfectly accented the venerable oak and brick walls and the Firenzan marble floor of the grand ballroom and reception room, and even if one looked up, the reliefs that adorned the ceiling gave the eye no respite from beauty.

The service prior to the ball, impeccable as always, brought the most delightful delicacies—the Justines still employ Frederic deGuigne, whose hors d'oeuvres are as transcendent as his tenderly cooked entrees. His pâte de foie gras, his braised duck breast in raspberry glaze, his spanokopita each one is like a small morsel of heaven melting on one's tongue. And yet, the most delectable morsel at the ball was the fox whose paw sat lightly on my arm.

He wore the clever contraption made for him at the cabaret, to increase his chest to a respectable size. Over that, the crimson fabric of his dress flowed like water over the curves of his body, in silken ripples down his chest, gathering in at the waist before breaking like a wave over his slender hips, cresting in elegant whitecaps at the hem of the dress. His dark-furred legs were not visible, but his paws set off the crimson fabric perfectly, as did the flow of his perfectly-groomed tail (I insisted he spend an hour brushing it out). And of course, his muzzle was brushed so neatly that not a hair was out of place, his emerald eyes matched by an emerald brooch at his throat. Even the black ribbons on his ears had been replaced by ribbons from our own household; Mme. Roche was kind enough to sew a set that covered the full ear, less visible and less likely to be remarked upon.

I make no exaggeration, father, when I tell you that for the first two hours, all eyes were upon my fox. Bertrand and Charles had brought consorts who paled like the moon at sunrise before the work of art I had created. The two of them spake courteously to me and to Niki, but in private I could see their eyes on him, nearly as green from jealousy as his own beautiful eyes were naturally. I took full advantage of every opportunity to parade him nearby, and I did not conceal the glee I took from their humiliation.

You would think, would you not, that any consort would take great joy in bringing such happiness to his—or her—companion. But Niki kept his cool expression all evening, as though all this were beneath him. This suited me, as I had introduced him as Tsareva Sveta Romanov, second cousin to the tsar himself, and his naturally high voice and native command of Siberian served him well in that role. Only once did I fear that our charade would be uncovered, when the former ambassador to Siberia introduced himself with a deep bow and apologized for his unconscionable lapse in forgetting the name of such a remarkable young thing. Niki carried himself well, very loftily forgiving, but then the ambassador asked where her retinue had been housed in the city as he wished to call on them.

I endeavored to change the subject, but Niki answered him with a neighborhood and a name that I am certain he invented on the spot. Such a bright, quick mind; alas, had I but known then that something so sharp can cut the wielder as well as the opponent, I would surely have ended our evening after that near-disaster. I reprimanded Niki afterwards, telling him that the ambassador would surely attempt to find the Siberian traveling party in that area, and he told me that it did not matter because the ambassador was not about to do so this very night, and so it was not worth worrying over.

I should not have allowed him to quell my worry so easily, but his seductive manner charmed me into staying longer. Besides, I believed that when the dancing started, there would be no further use nor even opportunity for conversation. He would have no role other than to look attractive.

For the first hour of the dance, he did just that. If his body and his muzzle had attracted eyes, the elegance of his dance attracted twice as many. We spun through waltzes, danced formally to minuets, and Niki even accepted dances from both Bertrand and Charles, the first time either one of them has requested a dance with my consort. That meant that I had the opportunity to dance with their consorts, and I enjoyed that greatly—more than the young ladies did, but the dances are not for their pleasure, after all.

Bertrand requested a second dance, and this is where the trouble started. I was not present for the beginning of their discussion, but as I understand it, it began over a comment he made regarding one of the paintings the Justines had acquired, something to the effect of "it is a passing fancy, a placeholder for next month's placeholder." (This is Bertrand, always trying to sound rather loftier than he is; he has no knowledge of art.)

Niki inexplicably took exception to this. I suppose that he thought he knew something of the world of art, as a mouse nibbling rinds of Edam in the corner of a cheese shop may fancy itself an expert on the noble art of cheesemaking. He challenged Bertrand to find beauty in the painting, and Bertrand tried to distract him with the compliment that he need not look for beauty in the painting when it was staring into his eyes. I might have been offended at his attempt to steal away my consort's affections had I not been certain of Niki, but as it happened, Niki was not put off. He gave Bertrand quite the lecture about the role of art and the duty of the observer, and it was from this moment that I became aware of what was transpiring.

I attempted to extract Niki from the proceedings, but he established himself in front of one of the Justines' paintings and proceeded to render a fanciful opinion as to the message of the painter, as if one need concern oneself with what the creator of a work of art thinks. Do we ask of the builders of the palace what message they wished to send in its design? Do we even care to learn their names? Do we ask what Mozart wished to express with his minuets? No; we simply dance, and that is all the respect we need pay the artist. The art is the gift; we are the recipients, and we make what use of the gift we will.

All around, people shuffled and looked uncomfortably at each other. Mme. Justine made a valiant attempt to humor Niki, but before their discussion could progress very far, Charles made a remark about the poverty of most artists and asserted that were the artists more well-off, their opinions would count for more.

This seemed a popular position among the younger set, but Niki's eyes darkened, and had I been Charles, I might have feared that his claws would find my eyes. As it was, his verbal claws were sharp enough; Niki told Charles that the poorest painter had more to contribute to society than this room full of strutting peafowl, at which point I was obliged to seize his wrist and explain to the company at large that Mlle.

Romanov was suffering from a fever brought on by the warmth of our springtime and the proximity to the river. And as we were leaving, I overheard Charles remark to Bertrand, "Not very feminine. There's always something wrong with the prettiest ones," and Bertrand reply, "Leave it to Jean to find the prettiest *boy* in Siberia."

The ball had been ruined, father, ruined, and I daresay Niki was surprised at my fury afterwards, being still somewhat choleric from his confrontation with Bertrand. I attempted to make him understand what had transpired, how he had undone my careful work and undermined my reputation among my peers, but he stubbornly insisted that I needn't care for the opinions of a set of careless popinjays. I found myself getting more furious rather than less, and so I called upon his other skills to ease my temperament, at which he succeeded as well as ever. I will say only that his resemblance to Bertrand allowed me to vent many of my frustrations in a most enjoyable fashion.

It was perhaps my error to leave him restrained for the remainder of the night with the promise of payment in the morning. I swear that I had every intention at the beginning of the evening of paying the agreed-upon sum, but how could I render full payment when he had behaved so abominably? He argued that he had never once let slip his true sex, which was my sole condition, and I replied that he had hardly comported himself as a lady was expected to, with Bertrand's final comment as my evidence. Still in a temper, though subdued from my attentions, he told me that Siberian ladies were expected to have opinions about art and were unafraid to express them, a nice piece of subterfuge that might have worked had I not made the acquaintance of Maria Elena Dimitriova last year and seen for myself how perfectly proper she was.

And when I returned from using the necessary, as dawn broke over the rooftops, I found my fox vanished, my purse empty.

Chapter 20

His mother arrived home at five after five, surprising him out of his reading. His explanation that he'd been sent home sick, bolstered by the smell of vomit that still hung around him, satisfied her. She bustled him up to his room, and if she noticed the bags on his floor or the iPod in his stereo, she did not say anything. "Stay here," she said, "and I'll get you some chicken—er, vegetable soup." Her brow creased and her ears lowered.

"Mom," Sol said, and she leaned closer. "Chicken...chicken soup is okay."

She rested a paw between his ears, smoothing down his fur. "Sweetie, you don't have to—"

"It's okay," he said. "I wanna try." He couldn't bring himself to tell her about the steak, but maybe chicken soup would stay down.

She found out about the steak, anyway, after looking in the refrigerator. When she came out with a glass of water and no chicken soup, she sat next to Sol on the couch and took his paw. He felt so guilty that it was hard to look at her, but she spoke softly. "Honey, did you eat the steak? Did you think you were getting sick from being vegetarian?"

"Sort of."

"Oh, Sol." She squeezed his paw. "You don't need to eat meat for us to love you. Even your father."

"I know." He choked the words out. "I was an idiot. I thought...I thought it would be different."

"When I went vegetarian, you know, I felt weak the first month, but after that it was okay. But I just missed the taste of meat. And I didn't have a real reason to keep going with it." She rubbed the back of his paw. "I know it'll make your father happy if you eat meat again, but that's not the reason you should do it."

Sol shook his head. "I don't want to be vegetarian any more," he said. "It was a stupid thing to do."

"It wasn't stupid." His mother leaned over and kissed his head. "But I'll get you some chicken soup anyway. You feel warm."

It tasted good, salty and warm, and it did stay down. It made him hungrier, actually, so he asked his mother for something more solid, and she brought him bread. It wasn't fresh-baked, but it was still good. While she was gone, he put his bags away, and was pleased to find that his ribs didn't hurt quite as much. He didn't want to risk putting the iPod back, so he left it, but didn't turn it on. Carcy's shirt remained on the bed. Sol kept it at arm's length so he wouldn't smell it and hid it in the bottom drawer of his dresser, where hopefully he'd forget about it or throw it out later.

When his father came home, his mother intercepted him. Sol heard them talking downstairs and then his father walked up, his tread heavier than Sol's mother, and opened Sol's door. "Doing okay, there?"

He was smiling, and his ears were up. Sol kept his up as well. "Yeah. Just stomach problems."

His father's eye fell on the bowl by Sol's bed. "Chicken soup?"

Sol nodded. His father's smile widened. "Hope that makes you feel better," he said, and withdrew.

It did and it didn't. His stomach settled, his fever and chills subsided, but the one thing Sol could not get out of his mind was the shadow in the mirror. These dreams had started with a drop of paint, then a ribbon, a painting, and then a shadow that could hurt people, throw them into doors. Part of him was afraid to find out what would come next; part of him was excited. After reading Jean's account of the party, he wanted to know what Niki had really said and done. Most of all, he wanted to know something the story could not tell him: whether Niki was a ghost who had a particular interest in him.

What if the absinthe magic was growing stronger? What if Niki could possibly be brought forward to live in this time. He would be happier here, where it would be easier to find work, where male dancers, even gay ones, could live fulfilled lives.

It was crazy, of course it was crazy, but after the day he'd had, he found himself clinging to the belief that it could happen. But in order for it to happen, he would need to get more absinthe, and that meant going to Meg's house, because she was not going to bring it to school again, he was sure.

His parents came in to wish him good night around eleven, turned his light out, and shut his door. As soon as they were gone, Sol slipped out of bed, threw on jeans, and opened his window. The night was warm enough that he didn't need a shirt.

The footholds he'd scraped in the joins of the stones of the house so many years ago were still there, though he slipped halfway down. He scrabbled at the stone for several seconds, dislodging a small chunk of limestone, and then fell to the soft dirt edging the house with an impact that caused his ribs to flare with pain again. He waited for a moment, paw pressed to the sore spot, and fortunately, the pain subsided. He brushed himself off and hurried down the hill, excitement growing with each step.

Clouds still obscured the moon, but the air smelled like past rain, not future rain. He sped past the soft glow of fireflies in the park, ran in front of the distant glow of headlights across the streets, turned toward the smell of the lake, even thicker tonight with the recent rain. The town was still, this late on a Tuesday night, streetlamps glowing, only the occasional car breaking the low scrapes and chirps of insects. Nobody Sol knew was out, or at least nobody who stopped to ask what he was doing out at eleven-thirty, which was almost what time it was when he got to Meg's.

Sol snuck around the edge of the outdoor pool, sniffing for their scents, but only caught the warm, herbal smell of the pool, which the Kinnicks kept chlorine-free. Flickering candlelight showed between curtains at Meg's window, overlaid by its faint reflection in the double glass. Sol bent for a pebble and flicked it at the window.

It made a crack that sounded like a gunshot. Sol cringed and ducked instinctively, even though there were no bushes to hide behind. His heart hammered out the seconds. It was impossible that Meg hadn't heard it; maybe she'd heard it and knew it was him and was ignoring him. He reached for another pebble, but as he did, the curtains shifted to one side, and the flickering light brightened.

The window slid up, revealing Meg's silhouette, gleams of silver sparkling around her ears. "Are you insane?" she hissed, but as she moved the candle in front of her face, Sol saw that her expression was almost pleased. "Wait for school tomorrow, we can talk about what we're gonna do then."

"Do? You mean for the project?"

"To get out of here. Just because your dickhead Def Match ex-boyfriend fucked us over doesn't mean we give up, right?"

Give up? Get out of here? "You still want to go…what? Where?"

"We're still going to Millenport, right? Look, I e-mailed my cousin, I asked if you could stay with us for a couple weeks. I'm sure it'll be okay. Maybe you and me can find a place together."

Millenport was more than four hours away from him now. "I don't want to go to Millenport," he said.

Her eyebrows lowered, her tone flattened along with her ears. "Then what? You need to talk about Dickhead some more? Come around front. And put a shirt on. Wait, on second thought, don't bother."

"I don't want to talk! I just need to get back into the dream."

"The dream, your fucking dream again." She glared at him. "You know what, Sol? When you go hide in your dream, reality keeps going on around you. It doesn't stop. You want me to go to Millenport without you?"

"I found a painting in my house. It's real, I saw a…" *A ghost.* He couldn't make himself say the word.

"So I could be gone tomorrow, and you'd never see me again, and you wouldn't give a shit as long as you have your dream."

Sol shifted his weight. The ground below his feet was damp. "Meg, come on. You're not going…you're being a drama queen. I'm just asking for help here."

"So am I," she snapped. "What are you going to do for me?"

"I'll…" He groped for something. "I'll finish the project work. I don't have baseball now, I'll write up the reports, I'll do all the work. Please, I just need to get back to the dream."

Her eyes narrowed, the reflected light in them vanishing. "You'll finish the report," she said. "Fine. That's great. You think that's what I wanted to hear from you?" She disappeared from the window, and returned holding the bottle up. "Here, you want it so bad, take it. Don't worry about the report. In fact, don't worry about talking to me again. I'll figure out my own way to Millenport."

She threw the bottle out onto the grassy verge leading up to the cement around the pool. Sol looked up at her, taking cautious steps toward the bottle. "Thanks, Meg," he said. "I'll do the report, I promise."

She stared out and after a moment said, "Fuck off," and closed the window. A moment later the curtains swept back across it.

Sol's tail swept back and forth over the ground. He stayed in his crouch, eyes on the bottle. Meg hadn't meant it, of course. She was upset, and she always said things she didn't mean when she was upset. Anyway, there wasn't anything he could do about it now except take the bottle. If he tried to rap on her window to apologize, she'd ignore him.

So he padded forward and closed his fingers around the bottle. He tucked it under one arm, the green liquid splashing around inside it, and ran home.

Climbing up to his room without dropping the bottle proved the most difficult part of the whole experience. He scrambled up, switching the bottle from one arm to the other, sometimes holding the neck in his teeth; he nearly dropped it once and had to wait a full minute for his heart to stop pounding, pinning the bottle between his chest and the wall. When he reached his window, he put the bottle inside and then clambered in himself, shut the window, and stood there just looking at it.

His desk lamp shone down through the green liquid, still restless from its journey. Sol brushed his fingers down the side of the bottle. He fidgeted from one foot to the other, tail wagging faster, watching the magical reflections, emerald on his fingers.

It occurred to him that he would need a glass, water, and sugar, and that only two of those three would be found in his bathroom. He padded quickly to his door, listening to any noises in the hallway. His parents were still awake, but usually they went to sleep around midnight. Could he wait ten minutes?

He got back into bed and tried reading more of "Confession," but the next bit was Jean talking about his luncheon the following day with his friends and how they teased him about picking up unstable ladies that acted like boys, and Sol couldn't focus properly on it. He read the same paragraph over and over again, and when his eyelids started drooping, he had to close the book. There was a shooting game on his phone that he could play for a little while without getting bored, and that kept him awake until finally, at quarter past midnight, he heard his parents climb the stairs and go into their room.

Quickly, he crept out of his room and down to the kitchen, where he poured some sugar and water into a glass and hurried back upstairs. It wasn't going to be quite the same as when Meg had done it, but he felt sure it would work.

In minutes, he had a glass full of cloudy green liquid. There wasn't much left in the bottle, but Sol thought he'd only need the one more. "Prepare to accept the gift of the Green Fairy," he breathed out, and without taking another breath, brought the glass to his lips.

He hadn't added enough sugar, or maybe he'd added too much absinthe. The drink stung his tongue, bitter anise crowding in with the herbal flavors, leaving the chemical-anise aftertaste. Sol swallowed, drank the rest, then placed the glass on his desk. He breathed in and out, trying to relax as he stripped to his boxers and got back into bed. Warmth, familiar and welcome, blossomed in his stomach and worked its way up to his chest. He closed his eyes.

A feeling of well-being and calm followed the warmth. Everything was okay, it was going to be fine. His parents still loved him, and Meg would forgive him, and in a week he'd be playing on the baseball team again, and Taric would get in good with the wolves and stop bothering him…

Where had that thought come from? Sol yawned. He would sleep, he would dream, and in the morning something would happen. Something, anything.

Chapter 21

It is already light in the streets of Lutèce. There are some who look askance at Niki, in his formal red dress, running along the pavements, making no effort to avoid the refuse in the streets. His feet are filthy and sticky by the time he labors up the hill of Montmartre, drawing more and more curious looks. The clothing worn by those around him is no longer neat and once-fashionable: it is untidy and never-fashionable, stained cotton shirts, thrice-patched trousers worn without a hint of self-consciousness, cloth caps over splayed ears that keep the light rain from the eyes. Sometimes an ear sticks out from one side or the other, but nobody corrects the wearer. Everyone is greeted with a smile and a wave, though both falter when the greeter takes a closer look at Niki. I belong here, Niki wants to tell them as they clear a path for him, but he is not certain that is true, not anymore.

The quarter feels strange, different. Maybe it is that people are seeing him as a lady out here in the open, that the disguise he wore in the cabaret has broken out to the real world. Perhaps it is the hour; he is unused to walking the streets after the sun has risen. The smells are different, bread and coffee diluted with the smells of the people, the wood of the houses and the rain-moistened refuse in the streets.

The alley behind the Moulin Rouge is empty. Niki knows there is no wolf lying in a heap against the brick wall of the restaurant opposite, but he can not make himself look in that direction. At the back door to the cabaret, the fox works the old lock on the door the way Cireil taught him to, and slips inside without anyone seeing. He eases the door shut behind him; the creak of old wood and rusted hinges is louder in the quiet of the empty club. He walks on the balls of his feet, keeping his claws elevated, first to M. Oller's office, then to the dressing room, which is as empty and silent as the rest of the club. There he throws down the small purse of paper he has been carrying onto a bench, closes his eyes, and breathes the air.

It is full of the scents of the other dancers. Even Cireil's has not had time to fade, not yet. But though Niki's scent here is as strong as any other, he still feels out of place. He trails a paw down his side, snags the red fabric with one claw. The dress is probably ruined by the rain. Niki can feel the moisture soaking through it to his fur, and he does not look down; he knows what water-damaged silk looks like. He has no time to care for the dress, and he will not be returning it to Jean in any case. He strips the thing off him, tearing at its laces and impossible knots that took so long to fasten. He holds it in front of himself, looks at the dark streams and spots where rain has warped the silk and bled the dye. Then he lets it fall to the floor.

He stands naked for a moment, brushing black fingers down his red-and-white side. There is room, here, with the other dancers away, to recall the steps of his childhood: he lifts his left leg in front of him, attitude devant, *though his toes are not strong enough for him to perform* en pointe *any longer, even if he had the proper foot-caps. He rises to* demi-pointe, *does two* chaînés *turns into a small side leap, his tail flowing out behind him. Closing his eyes, for a moment he is eleven again, in his father's barn, imitating the movements he has seen at the ballet so many times. Smells of straw and manure replace the smells of incense and dancers, even when he opens his eyes again.*

Simple steps flow easily into patterns. His body knows the bends and the pushes, the leaps and the twists, and follows their music in the silent room. He hears the words of his teacher telling him that he can be a great dancer. Every movement brings him closer to his bright future, to attending the Imperial School, to performing with the Imperial Ballet. The joy he feels in his movement is echoed in the audience, in the wonder of the people watching the heart and passion he pours into every gesture, every step. He moves as he has not in years; he performs turns, arabesques, jétés. *The pains in his wrists and muzzle and back vanish, and Niki dances.*

A single pair of paws clapping stops him. He opens his eyes to see M. Oller leaning against the doorway watching him. "Very nice," the polecat says. "Should I ever open a ballet, I will know who to sign. In the meantime, you should take your things and go, before the employed dancers arrive."

Niki drops his paws to his sides. He walks stiffly back to the small locker that holds a pair of trousers and a plain shirt, and rubs the sore spot on his muzzle. "I suppose you would not be in need of another dancer, so soon."

M. Oller straightens his narrow bowtie, then slides his paw down his side, into the pocket of his sleek black suit. "I am already interviewing several lovely young things."

"Do they have experience?" Being naked would be an advantage for Niki were he negotiating with Jean, but M. Oller does not look at his naked body with the same hunger. The fox pulls on trousers, and the polecat's expression remains the same.

"Experience is overrated." M. Oller examines the claws of his other paw.

Niki pulls his plain shirt over his head, shakes his ears and head. "I can bring several more paintings to the club."

"Paintings." The polecat scoffs. "I might walk out into the street and return with several paintings stuck to the soles of my feet."

"Not such as these. The one I brought you two days ago, you remember? He will be a great master."

M. Oller feigns, or perhaps genuinely feels, indifference. "Well, bring the paintings to an interview tomorrow," he says. "You may dance with some of the other applicants and we shall see."

"Thank you, sir." Niki holds up the purse. "I wonder if I might exchange these notes."

The polecat frowns, reaches out a paw. Niki hands him the purse, but looking at the notes does not erase his confusion. "What is this? You have been hoarding tips?"

Niki shakes his head. "My…patron paid me in those notes. I believe he must have purchased them, been saving them…" It had been quite a shock to see that the purse of francs Jean had promised Niki was filled with the currency of the Moulin Rouge, an artless reminder of Niki's standing in the world. Still, there were fifty of the one-franc notes there, and although it is not what they had agreed upon, it is close. It will be enough for him and Henri to live for several months, when added to the previous tips Niki has received from Jean.

"Well." M. Oller weighs the purse, then nods curtly. He reaches into the pocket of his pants and takes out two twenty-franc notes and a five. He hands them to Niki, with narrowed eyes. "Your patron is a curious one. I hope you have found what you sought."

"Do any of us?" Niki takes the money, and then gathers up the dress. He imagines Henri's face upon hearing that an unknown benefactor has purchased five of his paintings for the Moulin Rouge. Perhaps he will have to change the number to four, since the amount is somewhat less than he'd anticipated. He will describe the benefactor as a mysterious mouse, in honor of the servant who took pity on him that morning and loosened his bonds.

M. Oller holds the door to the dressing room for him. "I saw that you left the harness in my office. Thank you." For the first time, the polecat shows the trace of a smile. "It is always delightful to come to one's work and find a pair of tits on the desk."

Niki smiles, too, stepping out of the hall. "You have been very kind to me. I hope to be able to repay the favor in time."

"For future reference," M. Oller says, "I prefer the tits to be attached to a live body. No matter the species."

"Yes, sir." Niki swishes his tail, which also has a painful kink in it, but the pain is less. When he leaves the club, his step, like the air, has more spring in it.

The rain feels cleansing, nicely cool on his muzzle. He stops at the bakery and gets a loaf of bread, and next door buys a small round of a Camembert cheese and a bottle of wine to accompany it, a celebration for Henri's sale and

The smell is what he notices first.

for his return to the dance, whenever that might happen. When he emerges from the small grocer, the rain is coming down harder, so that even in the short half-block before Niki reaches his apartment, his tail is soaked through and water flows from his ears in streams.

He sets his bag of groceries down to shake himself, picks it up again, and climbs the stairs. "Henri," he says cheerfully as he pushes the door open, "you were right, dorogoï—"

The smell is what he notices first, the wrongness of it; even though the window is partly open and the rain is coming through, it cannot completely clear out the smell. Niki knows it from his childhood in western Siberia, from the time the plague ran through their town and everyone remained indoors, but there is no plague here, no plague save for the thin cord knotted at one end around a rafter in the ceiling and at the other around the neck of the black rat.

He spins very slowly, back and forth, eyes bulging. His protruding tongue is now purple, or perhaps blue; Niki cannot bear to look at it very long. The fox drops his bag with a thump (the wine bottle is solid; it does not break) and walks over to the body of his friend, so slowly. There is no rush.

The rain lashes harder at the closed half of the window and sprays the bed through the open half. The air feels colder than when he was outside. Niki runs a paw along his friend's arm. Beneath the fur, the skin is cold. Henri has been dead for a day at least. The fox steadies him with a paw on the paint-stained cotton, to stop the horrible spinning, and then searches the apartment for a knife. He knows there is one here, but it is nowhere he looks, and he is sobbing now, and everywhere he looks, Henri's dead eyes watch him and tell him it is the wrong place.

Finally, Niki climbs up on the bed and takes the rope in his paws and gnaws through it. It is possibly the worst thing he can ever remember doing in his life. The smell is terrible and the rope is thick and tastes of dirt and Henri's body swings gently against him. And when the rope finally parts, it slips through his paws and Henri lands with a stiff, undignified crash on the floor.

Only then can Niki clamber down and pull the stiff body of his friend into his arms; only then can he let out all the tears that have been leaking from his eyes, the howls of anguish that bring curious neighbors to the door and send them away, shaking their heads sadly.

When his sobs subside, he just sits, holding the emptiness like a precious thing inside him. Beneath the death and rain, he can still smell the acerbic rat, and he imagines what Henri would say, if his dead lips could still form words.

Silly fox, to cradle this lifeless husk. You abandon your muse and your friend and yet cannot abandon this empty shell? Do you so require the reminder of what you have left behind?

"You were wrong," Niki says. "You were wrong. I came back."

But did you come back for your art, or because your chamois strikes you? Because you cannot bear to be shackled, or because the shackles were more confining than you had imagined?

"I came back for you," Niki says.

In his mind, the rat laughs dryly. Liar, he says.

Niki lifts the rat to the bed easily; he weighs nearly nothing. It is only then, lifting his eyes to the room, that Niki notices the white cloth covering the easel. It is the robe he wore from Jean's, the one he left here, and it is covering a painting.

The fox walks slowly to the easel. He knows what lies below the cloth. His fingers grasp the edge, black on white, rough pads on soft cotton, and he lifts it away. On the canvas below, against an autumn background of red and yellow, sits Niki, tail curled demurely around his side with the white tip curved just away from him, one paw supporting some of his weight on the bench, his one visible eye focused somewhere far away. Henri has captured the pose perfectly, the fox on a stone bench in a park poised to stand, about to get up, but forever caught in the moment before he leaves. Niki touches the canvas, half-expecting to feel his own fur beneath his fingertips, but it is only the rough brushstrokes and the oily texture of paint. He stands there staring at the image, wanting the painted fox to turn around and meet his eyes.

The hazy leaves in the background seem to shift in his peripheral vision, but the fox remains static. His coat shimmers, like a reflection of the leaves around him, all oranges and yellows and browns with red highlights, and even the black of his paws and the white of his muzzle and chest are luminous. The painting is bright and awake, a marvelous memorial not only of Niki, but of Henri himself. And yet, Niki cannot look at the picture for long without his eyes filling with tears.

There are many things one might see in the painting. The fox's nudity and demure pose suggest romantic meanings: as he is caught between staying and leaving, perhaps love is always in such an unsettled state. As the fox's bright green eye is staring off beyond the autumn trees, perhaps love is always looking toward that which is unattainable. As the red and gold leaves show the autumn and the dying of the trees, perhaps love is arriving just before the moment of death. But Niki sees in it a message for him, and him alone: You are about to leave me, and so I am leaving you first.

And yet, it is the loveliest thing Henri has painted, and Niki finds wrapped around the emptiness in his heart a gladness that his friend completed it before he died.

Chapter 22

Sol woke with a heaving sob, his pillow wet. His eyes were sore, the fur around them as wet as the pillow, and his throat felt scratchy and raw. His alarm was silent; the whole house was silent, but the light outside bathed his room in a soft glow. The dream enfolded him as surely as did his soft sheets, the taste of the rope against his tongue, the weight of his dead friend in his arm, the question howling through his mind: *why, why, why?* And, worse than the question, the answer, in the painting itself.

Sol clutched his pillow to his face. He saw the paintings all around the studio in the daylight, awake for the first time, but he could not remember details of any of them, none except for the painting of the fox. There had been soft colors and landscapes, faces, and the dead eyes and slack jaw of Henri. The chill of the artist's studio worked its way into Sol's fur, adding shivers to his sobs. He pulled his sheet around him, but the chill was inside him, and the sheets did nothing to warm him. Grief filled his chest, broke through his throat in a keening cry no matter how he tried to muffle it with the pillow.

He'd thought the grief of Cireil's death was bad; this was a hundred times worse. There was no questioning the reality he was grieving, not when the smell of death curled through his nose, the chill of the rain lingered on his skin, the anguish burned all through him. His chest heaved, sending sparks of pain through his ribs as he sobbed against the fabric, sheets clutched in his fists. He heard Henri's words from his dreams, the rat's passion for art and for Niki: gone, gone forever now. *Death comes for us all.* Sol could see the rat placing the noose around his neck, thinking himself alone in the world, despairing, falling, dying.

Yesterday, he had looked at the bathtub with that same thought, with no regard for the people in his life. That was when Niki's shadow had come and stopped him, and the fury made sense now. Niki had been through this before, had lost Cireil and Henri in the span of a few days, and he would not let Sol make the same mistake Henri had. Sol felt hot, his nose running and eyes still streaming tears, and this was what he had been about to inflict on his mother, his father, Meg and Natty. Uncle Nolan's howling grief over losing his son did not seem ironic, nor desirable, nor anything but pitiable now. Even though Sol hadn't really been thinking of killing himself, not more than a passing image, he had been serious about running away from home. What would his mother have thought when she came home and found him gone without saying good-bye, without telling them where he was going or why or that he loved them? Look at how Tsarev had reacted, and he barely knew Sol.

The young wolf rubbed at his eyes and nose again. Grief and hurt still wrapped around his chest, tightening a vise around his lungs. His breaths came shallow, and still came with sobs. Every time he closed his eyes against the blur of tears, he saw the body of the black rat in his arms—in Niki's arms. And then he thought, what came back from the dream this time?

He wiped his nose and sniffed the air, looked around his room. There was no red dress, no white robe, no filthy rope. There was no smell of rat, of rain, of paint. Had the absinthe not given him any hallucination this time? Why would this time be any different?

Perhaps the story was over, and this was how it ended: with Niki alone and cold amid the smell of death. Nothing had come back because there was nothing left to bring back.

A different grief sent Sol into another paroxysm of sobs. He rubbed tears from his muzzle, tried to take deep breaths to calm himself, and finally the constriction around his chest loosened, just a bit. He felt he was gaining control of himself, until the worst thought of all occurred to him: what if the thing that had come into the world from his dream this time was death?

He sat up in bed, eyes wide, paws clasped together. He squeezed his muzzle shut, trying not to let the tears out again, telling himself he was being crazy, irrational, but then he saw the rolled-up painting and he couldn't hold it in. He made a strangled half-sob and grabbed at his phone so roughly that he knocked it to the floor. The image from the dream remained clear, but changed: now he saw Meg's face on the body cradled in Niki's arms, felt the stabbing in his heart as though she were the one who was gone.

He dove to the floor, hanging off the bed, and called up her entry to send a text message. He mistyped the simple message, *Are you OK?*, four times before he got it right. She wouldn't be up yet, but hopefully she'd answer. Of course she was all right, though. She had to be.

But if Meg was all right, then—then what? His parents? He braced his arm against the floor, ignoring the twinge in his ribs, replaced his phone on the nightstand, and was just contorting himself to get out of bed when his mother knocked on his door.

"Sol?" she called softly.

"Mom!" he yelled, unable to help himself. Relief washed over him, so welcome he tried to jump out of bed and got tangled in the sheets again. This time, at least, he didn't fall, but when his mother came into the room, he was hopping on one leg, pulling his other foot out of the sheets.

"Are you okay?" she said. "I heard—"

He leapt across the empty duffel bags still lying on his floor and threw his arms around her. She wore a thick terrycloth robe, not the soft cotton of the robe in his dreams, but Sol pressed his muzzle against the shoulder and rubbed his eyes on it anyway. "I'm sorry, I'm sorry, Mom."

"For what, honey?" Her paw came up to stroke his ears, the other arm holding him. Her scent washed over him, loosening the last of the tightness around his chest.

His breathing slowed and his tail relaxed from its tight curl. "I…" He looked down at the empty bags, and the words spilled out of him. "I was gonna run away."

Her eyes widened, but she didn't say anything, just kept him in her embrace, cupping his ears and rubbing at their base. He swallowed. "I was just so frustrated, and I hate the peach cannery and Uncle Nolan and the fight at school and the baseball team and they're always picking on me…"

He stopped, aware that he was starting to feel like a cub who couldn't handle his own problems. But his mother nuzzled him and kissed him on the bridge of his nose. "I'm glad you didn't run away," she said softly. "I know it's hard, and I know it seems like forever, but it'll get better."

"I know." Sol hugged her tighter. "I just didn't want to wait."

"Oh, honey." She rocked him back and forth. "Why don't you stay home again today? I'll tell your father you're still feeling sick."

It was a little humiliating, being coddled like a cub. Stay home, avoid all your problems, and Mom will take care of them. But it was also another vast wave of warm relief to have his mother caring so strongly for him. "Okay," Sol gulped.

"I'll call in and see if I can stay home with you. If not, I'll leave you some chicken soup. Okay?"

"Yeah."

He loosened his hug. She stepped back and wiped the fur around his eyes delicately. "Promise me something, though." He nodded. "If you really, really can't see any solution but running away, come talk to me. We'll work something out."

"Wh-what about Dad?"

"We'll handle your father." She smiled and patted his shoulder. "Promise?"

He gulped and nodded. "I promise."

She paused and looked him in the eye. "Is there a reason I should be worried? If something happened to you, you'd tell me, right?"

He almost did, but his legs were still shaking and he felt weak all over. Besides, Carcy was gone, well gone, and telling his mother one thing would open up too much more for right now. "No. I mean, I would, but...I'm okay."

"Okay. Now go back to bed. I'll bring you up some toast."

"With honey?"

"Tch." She smiled, and as she walked out of his room, her tail wagged slowly.

Sol climbed back into bed, still feeling shaky. Of course she would have noticed his bags, anyway. Not to mention the clear bottle with its finger-height of green liquid, sitting on his desk next to the cloudy glass. But she hadn't said anything. Maybe, maybe, she hadn't noticed.

He was glad his mother hadn't asked questions about how he'd planned to run away. That was the one thing he still could not bring himself to tell his parents. There was no need to, after all. He still felt ashamed of himself for how he'd been duped, how he could have let someone like Carcy into his heart. It hadn't taken much time at all to figure out that there wasn't much love there; the ram just wanted a young guy to fuck, and Sol'd almost let it happen. He would have, if not for Niki.

His mother brought toast with honey and some tea, and if she noticed the absence of the absinthe bottle, she still said nothing. "The office says I can work from home today, so I'll just be downstairs," she said. "Call me if you need anything."

Sol reached for his phone to text Meg, just as his father looked in briefly to say, "See you, champ. Get better soon," and Sol smiled, with a thumbs-up. When the door closed, he picked up his phone again. Meg still hadn't written back, and he knew she had to be awake now. Probably she'd be on the bus. He called her phone directly, and got no answer.

She was ignoring him. Of course that was all it was.

To convince himself, he went over the events of the previous night, the way he'd treated Meg to get the absinthe from her. He'd stalked to her house in the middle of the night, acting crazy and obsessed. She, too, had been looking forward to getting away and now was stuck here in Midland, stuck through no fault of her own but only through his actions. She'd wanted to talk about getting out, and he hadn't spent time commiserating with her, asking her what she would do, caring at all about how she felt. He'd only demanded the drug that would make *him* feel better. She already had to deal with parents who were stoned all the time, who left her to her own devices, and then he'd left her just as alone.

She would be in class by this time. He sent her another text, which also received no answer. She was ignoring him, she was right to ignore him. The cold core of his dream was his and his alone. He had not brought back Henri's fate to her, he had *not*.

As penance, he applied himself at his computer, spending hours reading passages from the books Meg had recommended. When he'd read so much his head was buzzing, he wrote short essays on the world of Montmartre in 1901: The Lively Community of Artists, The World Outside, and The Struggles To Survive, including the squalid atmosphere he'd seen in his dreams. That was the most difficult part to write. He set down a vivid description of Henri's cramped studio, writing that many artists shared rooms to save on rent, and sometimes used their roommates as subjects. And sometimes, he wrote, sometimes the world seemed so forbidding that they could not bear it.

Twice he tried to write an essay about a fictional black rat artist, made up as an example. Twice he reached the end and sat staring at the screen for five minutes, unable to write any more. No words he set down adequately conveyed the horror of the stained old rope, the gruesome body dangling from it, the spirit that had animated so many beautiful paintings gone, the paintings themselves lost forever. If Henri had been real and had painted so much work, how many other artists had lived and died and been forgotten? How many lives had ended with no-one to notice them, no-one to care for them? Sol wrote some maudlin closing paragraph and then erased it and lay on his bed staring at the ceiling for fifteen minutes.

It was five in the afternoon when he had written as much as he thought he could, taking a break every hour to text Meg even though she did not respond. The tightness in his chest had lessened but by no means gone, and Sol did not think that going downstairs to watch TV would help. He had to tell her about his dream so that she would understand.

But when he opened a blank document intending to write her a letter, the first words he wrote were, "Once there was a fox named Niki, who wanted to be a dancer. His father wanted him to be a soldier, and so Niki ran away from his family and his home."

Sol rubbed the back of his paw over his eyes. He had meant to start by telling Meg about the world of his dreams and introducing Niki. He read the words he had just typed, and he did not erase them. When he set his fingers back to the keys, he felt the words come to him. He let them come, typing until his parents came home.

After dinner, after another text to Meg that went unanswered, Sol saw his e-mail indicator blinking. Tsarev had sent him an e-mail message.

Dear Sol,

I guess since you were not in class today that means you have gone. I wanted to wish you very good fortune. I am sorry that I did not get the chance to talk to you more often. I think you are nice wolf but you are lonely like me sometimes. I have host family here, and I have one friend in Samorodka, which is my home, but I do not have friends to talk to here. Many people are nice because I am not from here, but being nice is not like being friend.

It is difficult to talk in person about this. I do not know how to find people who might be okay to talk about it with. You were very kind and in the problems you were having with other boys, I saw problems I used to have in Samorodka, and I thought you will understand. Also I thought that it is easier because you are not here now. I am sorry I could not talk to you before. I hope you will understand me.

Here I stay quiet and nobody notices me. I am a stranger. But it is different with people you grow up with, because they know you all your life and when you change, they see you change. I applied to exchange program to see your country as well as to leave my own, and I am lucky my English is very good, and I am accepted.

But I am matched in program to small school in small town, because Samorodka is in small town, and so I find many of the same things. It is different because I am not known, and also because in this country, a boy who likes boys is not very unusual. Small unusual, but not big unusual like in Samorodka.

Yes, I am like that.

I think maybe you are too, but then you tell me that the otter is your girlfriend. But you do not act like boyfriend to her, not mostly. But even if you are not like me, I think maybe you will understand being me, not like other people here. I can not even tell host family and I can not tell other students. I am ashamed to say that I am almost glad you are leaving because it is easier to tell you now.

So I know it is difficult, but maybe you can write back to me. Maybe where you go there are other boys like me and you can tell me it is better here than in Siberian small town. Or just be my friend. From far away, nobody will see us being friends and it will be okay. I have many friends on the Internet but none I know nose to nose.

Again, I wish you very good luck in wherever you go.

Your friend,

Alexei

Sol stared at the phone. He wanted to kick himself. Tsarev—Alexei, that nice fox, he was gay? He'd been sitting in front of Sol for the whole year and Sol never knew? He started typing out a reply, but the words never sounded quite right—"I'm gay too!" "I do understand, because I am like that too." "Awesome!"—and after the fourth try, he canceled the message. No words felt adequate to convey Sol's delight and amazement, his eagerness to talk to Alexei and to listen to him, the doors he saw opening before him. That the second gay person he'd met would already be a friend of his felt astounding and miraculous, and it made him even more grateful for Niki. Think of all he would have missed if he'd left with Carcy, or if he'd hurt himself.

But at least he should send Alexei an e-mail of some sort, so the fox didn't worry that Sol was ignoring him. He typed out, *Thanks for telling me. Actually, I ended up not going, so I'll see you in school tomorrow. I hope we have time to talk.* That didn't sound too bad.

Maybe this was Sol's reward for sending Carcy away. He spent a moment imagining his arms around the fox, kissing him on the muzzle, but that fantasy did not feel quite right. Alexei was just a friend, not a boyfriend, but—he was gay, too! He was someone Sol could talk to and not be afraid, and Sol would be the same for him. Of course, he'd never talked to a gay person nose to nose before Carcy's visit, but he already knew Alexei, already knew he liked him. Would they talk about their fantasies? Whether he had a boyfriend? Sol had no idea. But they might be the only two gay students at Richfield High. They were going to have to stick together.

And Meg. He had to talk to Meg. He spent several minutes looking at his desk, thinking about the absinthe in it. He wanted very badly to take another drink, to find out what happened to Niki. He had only one drink left, and he hoped that would be enough. But perhaps if he took just a taste of it tonight, that would be enough, and the magic would still happen.

The bottle felt warm to his paws. He poured just a splash into his glass and then drank it, and immediately nearly spit it out. The anise taste was overpowering, as bitter as mouthwash, without water or sugar to temper it. Sol gulped, fast, but the taste didn't leave his tongue and palate.

Oh, he'd forgotten. "Prepare to accept the gift of the Green Fairy," he mumbled quickly, and then breathed in, bringing the taste up into his nose. The tickle built and built until he sneezed, and even then his head felt terrible. He stripped off his shirt and fell into bed, opening his phone to "Confession."

There was some extended recounting of the fallout from the night at the ball, but that wasn't what Sol wanted to read about. He stopped where he saw Niki's name, but it was just Jean yelling at his friend Thierry and throwing him out when Thierry told Jean to forget the fox. Sol skimmed the book to the point where Niki's name came up again.

You may well imagine my surprise when the thief reappeared at our door the following day. My spirit smarted still from the taunts of Bertrand and Charles, no matter how well I concealed it, and I confess that that evening I had already finished half of one bottle of wine, tired of it, and started on a second. My sobriety had no bearing on my comportment during that evening, I hasten to add. I have nothing but contempt for those who blame their actions on humors, on alcohol, on the stars, on anything but themselves. I am as I was born, as I was raised to be, and no mere bottle of wine is sufficient to alter that.

The sun had set; the moon was out. I sat by the window watching the reflections of the gas lights on the Seine. The night was quiet and still, so that there was nothing to trouble my thoughts on the last day. I could not see a way to restore my standing in the eyes of my peers. Thierry would no longer take me on adventures. Your dismissal, too, hurt me. Though I know you may not believe it, father, I spent many hours thinking upon your advice, and I concluded that you were right. It was time that I leave behind the games of youth and find a proper job, proper friends, a proper wife.

But no wife could compare to the elegance and beauty of Niki. No chamois or elk, no exotic impala or oryx, could be so graceful, with a predator's disposition subject to my will. And none of the boys I knew would be able to dress so convincingly as a lady, to the approval of my peers. My fox was like nothing I had seen before, and would never see again.

I believe that was my thought at precisely the moment that François announced that I had a visitor. Before I could tell him to turn the visitor away, Niki pushed his way into the room.

I told François to leave us, and stood to confront the fox. He had brought the robe he'd been wearing when he left the previous night, but I did not care; my attention was set entirely on the fox. My heart leapt to see him, and yet of course I could not rejoice in his appearance without also dreading his departure.

I asked his business, presenting myself as coolly as possible so that he might not see the power he held over me. He had come, he said, to return my robe. Our association, he said, would thereby end.

His manner was in all ways resolute, but I detected below it a deep sadness. I have learned from you to read the tail and ears of our predator peers, and in Niki I saw that he did not truly wish to leave me, but that he had convinced himself—or been convinced—that it was for the best. Whether it was a result of the well-deserved scorn of the good people at the ball, or my over-excited attentions following, Niki had concluded that he had no place in my world.

How I attempted to persuade him otherwise! I pointed out that had he but kept his opinions to himself, he would have passed admirably and there would have been no frustrations for me to vent upon his person. I flattered his comportment, his elegant grace, his skill in movement, all so ladylike on the outside, and yet with the steel core of masculine presence inside for those who might take the time to appreciate it. I asked him, in all that he had sated my desires, had I not cared for him as well?

He remained impervious to my pleas at first, though I worked upon him. I could see him weakening at the idea that he could live a life of luxury and ease in my apartments—I meant for him to live in the apartments that Uncle Remy recently vacated—if only he would abide by some simple rules. And I believed, fool that I was, that he felt some of the same emotion for me that I felt for him.

In the end, it was a delicate mention of the money and the dress he'd taken from me that broke his will. Even such a creature as this courtesan had some sense of honor; after all, he had returned my robe. His affected ignorance of any existing debt between us was no obstacle for me. He had not fulfilled the agreed-upon obligations and therefore was not entitled to the compensation I had promised without rendering further services. I hoped, father, that in enticing him to stay one night so that I could show him my tender side, I would thaw his heart, show him that submitting to my extravagant gifts would be a demonstration of love and not a shackle to his pride.

And I promise you that that is how the evening began. I used every lesson of my years to demonstrate the affectionate companion I could be, how great was my charity and love for this mean creature. I was willing to kneel down and extend a hand to raise him up, and I thought that thereby I could win his heart.

Alas, father, I fear that your appraisal of my romantic nature was correct when you observed that I attend too closely to romantic plays of the stage. In such plays, whenever the kindly lord raises up the lady from the gutters, she proves to be a devoted and entirely suitable companion. And I believe that for the brief span of my acquaintance with the fox, I was blinded by the bright future promised by those plays. Curse the playwrights, for it is by their pens that I stand here pleading my case with you, father! Curse them for the bright colors in which they painted their world, colors so vivid that I could not believe them false, could not see the stains and imperfections they concealed. I learned my lesson, alas, too late, and my only hope is that some playwright might set down my story to the stage, that some young romantic might experience reality in the theater before he need experience it for himself. There, the knife is dulled, the wounds healed by the following morning. But here, father, I still feel the sting of that night.

For no matter how gently I treated the fox, no matter what heartfelt verses I poured out to his ears, he submitted only physically to me. And when we had finished, he laughed at me, said I had no more appreciation for him than for the paintings that hung in the ballroom of the Justines. He said that he would seek out Bertrand and Charles and show them my secret, and share their laughter, for a courtesan may prefer his own gender without sanction, but a senator's son would be ridiculed and mocked for his nature, over which he has no control.

I fell to my knees, father. I had thought that the previous day had ruined me, but here, here, I saw my life laid out and shattered by this heartless prostitute, this fox whose predator's nature revealed itself at last, who even though his physical teeth might be bound, still had fangs to sink into my heart.

Chapter 23

Sol startled awake at his alarm. He stared at the clock, disoriented for a moment until he remembered he had to go back to school. It was only when he was stretching that it occurred to him that he had not dreamed of Niki. He shot a baleful look at the desk and the hidden absinthe bottle. So he needed the full glass and perhaps the ritual after all, and he would have but one more look.

He'd learned by now not to trust Jean's account of events, but the chamois's words about those who would blame their behavior on "anything but themselves" stuck in Sol's head. He'd already made up his mind to apologize to Meg, and though he'd apologized to his mother, he felt he owed her more of an explanation. Not today, not tomorrow, but someday. There was still a sore spot when he thought about the events of two days ago, a pressure that built behind his eyes and down into his nose, but it was over, over, and he had to keep telling himself that. Carcy would answer for his own actions, somehow; Sol had his own mistakes to make amends for, starting today.

When he got on the bus, he sat toward the back and stretched his legs out so nobody would slide in next to him. And when Meg got on the bus, last of all the students at her stop, he reached out and grabbed her paw.

"Lemme go," she snapped, and walked on toward the back of the bus.

Sol watched her go, then slid out of his seat and marched back to join her. "Siddown," the bus driver called, and at that, Meg looked up and saw Sol. She'd sat in a seat by herself, and now she slid to the outside as Sol walked up to it.

"Get lost," she said.

A porcupine behind them lifted his head. "Ooh, lovers' quarrel."

"Fuck off, Cory," Meg said without turning.

"I need to talk to you," Sol said. "I'm sorry. I'm really sorry."

The bus driver looked in the mirror, back at Sol. "Siddown!"

"You better go sit down," Meg said without moving.

"Fine." Sol plunked himself down in the aisle and looked up at her. "I'm gonna stay here, then."

"Hey, Sol!" The bus driver was half out of his seat now. "Find a seat or we're gonna be late to school."

This sparked interest around the bus. "Stay there, Sol!" "Yeah, don't move!" a couple students yelled.

Sol looked up at Meg. "Please," he said.

"Oh, God." She slid over. "This is only because I don't want to be the center of attention here."

"Thanks." He scrambled up and into her seat, and the bus struggled forward on its way.

"I told you we're done," she said, but he cut her off.

"I know, just give me a chance, one chance. 'Til we get to school."

She rolled her eyes and let out a long, exaggerated sigh. "Fine. You're lucky I'm a fucking softie."

"Yeah, you're a regular Ma Teresa." He dug into his bag as Meg snorted, and came up with a thumb drive. "Here, first of all."

"What's that?"

"I wrote up some essays for our project. Figured you could use it when you put it together, if you're doing that by yourself."

She took the thumb drive between thumb and forefinger, looked past it at him. "You're not helping?"

"I will if you want."

She held up the small plastic drive and then stuck it into her pants pocket. "We'll see. That all?"

"No." Sol took a breath. "I'm really sorry for ignoring you. I still want to go somewhere with you. Maybe not Millenport, but…" He twisted his paws together. "You remember I told you I got dreams? Well, I felt like I needed to go back to the dream to figure out what was going on in my life."

Meg shook her head. "I told you, you want pot. Relaxes you, chills you out, shows you that nothing is that big a deal. Dreams are just confusing puzzles of shit our subconscious throws at us."

"I was dreaming about this guy…"

"Oh, I get it." She smirked.

"Not…not like that. But he was going through some of the same things I was. I wrote it down to show you…"

Her eyes held a small spark of interest now. "So did he fix your problem?"

"No." Sol stared down into his lap. "But I kinda figured out I need to do something about it myself. Like forget about…you-know-who, to start with."

"I told you that."

"And I need to apologize to you about something else, too."

Meg frowned. "I already figured you'd drink all the absinthe. It's okay, you can pay me back."

"Not that." He lowered his voice, even though the bus's clattering engine drowned out most conversation, and the two cubs in front of him were small-eared, a squirrel and a mouse. "I almost…I was gonna kill myself."

She watched him patiently. When he didn't go on, she said, "And?"

"Well, I didn't."

"I figured that out, Lord Peter Wolfy. What else?"

Sol frowned. He felt like sticking his tongue out at her. "Isn't that enough? Did you hear me right?"

"Sure. I think about killing myself once a week, twice during fucking Woodstock anniversary week. So what's the big deal?"

He stared at her unconcerned expression. Silver glittered from her fur, reflecting the sun. "You never told me that. Are you okay? I didn't know…"

"That's why I didn't tell you. I don't tell you who I have sex dreams about, either. You're a great guy, when you're not being an asshole, but there's some things a gal keeps to herself. What's going on here?"

Sol stared down at his knees. "I guess it doesn't matter, but the thing is, y'know, when I was thinking about how shitty a thing it is to do, I was thinking about what you'd feel like when you found out."

"Aw, Sol, that's sweet. Look, tell ya what. You feel like killin' yourself again, come on over and we'll do a suicide pact."

"For Christ's sake."

Meg laughed, softly. "How were you gonna do it?" He refused to look at her. "Come on, how? Let me guess. Ma's sleeping pills."

"Bathtub," he said.

"Drowning yourself? Oh, no, Sol, you weren't going to cut your wrists?" She put a paw on his wrist when he didn't answer, drew a claw down it. "Probably weren't gonna use any topical anaesthetic, either."

"Topical what?"

"Numbing cream," she said patiently. "Otherwise you'd get a shallow cut in one wrist, it'd sting, and knowing you, you'd bleed all over the bathroom and chicken out."

This was not at all how he'd envisioned this conversation going, but then again, he'd never really been able to accurately predict a conversation with Meg. "Well, how would you do it?"

"Sleeping pills." She didn't hesitate. "Got a stash of them from when I was 'troubled.'" Her fingers made air quotes.

"'Was'?" Sol asked, making the air quotes back at her.

Meg shook her head and then laughed, leaning into him. "Just got better at hiding the symptoms."

"You're crazy," he said, but his tail flicked between them on the seat.

"For the record." Meg kept her voice low. "I'm glad you didn't try to cut yourself. Prob'ly they would've decided I was a bad influence on ya. Go read up sometime on what they do to attempted-suicide kids. And if you'd managed to do it—which I don't believe—that woulda sucked."

"I'd miss you, too." Sol leaned back against her.

"I didn't mean that." She didn't lean away. "I mean that you'd manage to kill yourself before me. I'd lose all my goth cred. My vampire fox friend would never talk to me again."

Sol rolled his eyes, even as his tail tried harder to wag, pressed between the two of them. Meg shifted away from it. "Hey, tell your tail to stop molesting me."

"Sorry, it has a mind of its own."

"Glad one of you does." She leaned against the bus window and affected boredom. "So what stopped you?"

Here was the moment. She'd brushed off his dreams enough times, but she was asking, she was listening. Sol took a breath. "I think it was... the guy I was dreaming about."

Meg's expression didn't change. "Because. you wanted to have more dreams about him?"

"No, I mean literally." The bus stopped at the traffic light outside the school. The scenery behind Meg wasn't moving, and neither was she. "Something picked me up off the floor and threw me away from the bathtub. And I think it was the guy I was dreaming about, who lived a hundred years ago."

"So a ghost stopped you from killing yourself." The bus struggled forward, creaking around the turn. "You know, Sol, you might want to keep that story to yourself."

"You don't believe me." He'd expected as much, but hoped for more.

"I believe that you believe it." Meg shrugged. "Ronald and Valinda believe in mystical powers and it never brings them shit. But it makes them kinda happy. So if you want to believe it, I won't stop you."

"It was real! It hit Carcy to get him off me, and then it dragged me away from the bathtub. It had the same ragged ear, the green eyes..." He lowered his voice. "I don't make up stuff like this."

"No, you don't," Meg said. "But you were pretty freaked out when I saw you that day. You'd be amazed what people can imagine when they're freaked out like that. Well, I guess you wouldn't. Look, Sol, the problem is that getting rid of Def Match Dickhead, stopping yourself from getting into the bathtub—that's stuff you should be proud of doing. If you put it all up to some ghost, then what are you gonna do when the ghost isn't around?"

Sol bit his lip. "I wasn't imagining it," he said.

"And if there were ghosts, then why you? Why come across a hundred years just to slap around some cub rapist?"

The bus doors opened. Students near the front began filing out. "That's what I want to find out," Sol said. "That's why I needed to go back into the dream."

"Well, do what you have to do, I guess." Meg watched the students around them leave. "Just promise me you're gonna try to keep some hold on reality, okay?"

"I'll try." Sol picked up his bag and stood. "We can keep talking about Millenport."

"I said *keep* some hold on reality."

He smirked, sliding out into the aisle. Meg walked behind him to the front and down the steps, and as they walked toward the front doors, he said, "What stops you?"

"What? Oh, from offing myself? Spite, mostly."

"Spite?" He held the door for her.

"Yeah. Because fuck if I'm going to let this shitty universe win." She grinned, brushed him with her tail, and walked on ahead of him.

When Sol walked into homeroom, Tsarev—Alexei, rather—was bent over his desk doing some last-minute assignment on his netbook. Sol slid into his desk, and the fox's ears flicked back. He turned quickly, eyes wide, ears flat. "Hi," Sol said. "Look, it's cool. Don't—"

Tanny threw a crumpled paper at his ear. "I did not think you would be here," Alexei whispered.

"It's okay," Sol said.

"Hey, meatless," Tanny said. "Save the luuuuv talk for after school. Nobody wants to see you two make out."

Alexei leaned back and whispered, past Sol to Tanny, "I have heard that when a girl opens her muzzle to a boy so much, it is because she wants his cock in it."

Tanny looked shocked for a moment, and then she said, loudly enough to make Sol's ears flatten against his head, "*Fuck* you, Ivan!"

"Detention," Mr. Fortune called from the front of the room.

Sol stared at Alexei and the fox winked back. The bell sounded for opening announcements, and all through them, Tanny muttered, "Goddamn commie bastard fuckhead." But she didn't say another word to Sol.

Alexei and Sol went off to separate classes; Sol wouldn't see him again until lunch. He submerged himself in the comfortable normality of Physics, and it was while walking from Physics down to Social Studies that Sol ran into Taric, Xavy, and a few other wolves from the baseball team talking in the hallway. One of Taric's coyote friends hung back, leaning against the locker and checking messages on his phone, or maybe playing a game on it, though his ears were perked toward the conversation the others were having.

Taric was talking up a story about some female fox he'd fucked. The wolves looked only somewhat interested. As Sol walked by, Taric said, "But meatless there wouldn't know nothin' about that."

Sol half-turned. The insult didn't sting as much as it would have, because he no longer cared what Taric or anyone thought. Rather than getting angry, he could laugh it off, could come up with a return insult, like, "In what cemetery did you dig up a fox who would let you fuck her?" Xavy particularly, but the other wolves as well, looked sympathetic or uncomfortable, and probably would cheer him standing up for himself. But as he opened his mouth, he felt the pain and frustration in Jean's account of his friends the wolf and the fox, their scorn and derision. Jean was a complete douche of a person, to go by Sol's dream, but it was in those moments that Sol thought he was most honest, and it was then that Sol felt most sorry for him. So on the spur of the moment, Sol walked up to the coyote and stuck out his paw.

Taric looked at it as though Sol were offering him a clump of manure. But before he could say anything, Sol said, "Hey, I never congratulated you on winning the starting spot at second. You're good and you work real hard, and the team's better with you there."

The coyote's ears flattened. "What the fuck is this?"

Sol saw Xavy smile, out of the corner of his eye, but kept looking steadily at Taric. "Congrats," he said. "That's all. You're a great player. I bet you'll get a minor league contract when you graduate."

"I don't need no meatless asshole to tell me I'm a great player." Taric snarled.

Xavy said, "Seems like the proper thing to do'd be to shake his paw."

The coyote looked around at the wolves. Even his friend had looked up from the phone and was watching. "Fine." Taric grasped Sol's paw for a moment, then let go.

"Good luck," Sol said. "I mean it."

"Yeah, whatever." Taric stabbed a finger at him. "I ain't forgot you landed me in detention."

"Well, keep your paws off my friends and that won't happen again."

"You threatenin' me?"

Sol shook his head slowly. "Nope. Just saying. You leave me alone and I'll leave you alone and nobody needs to go back to detention."

The coyote squinted at him. "What the fuck is with you, meatless?"

"His name's Sol," Xavy said.

Sol shrugged. "It's okay." He was trying not to smile at how off-balance Taric was, at how strange and wonderful it felt to have Xavy stick up for him, at how even more strange and wonderful it felt to realize that he didn't need Xavy—or any of the other wolves—to stick up for him. He needed a pack, but not their pack; he had his mom, and Meg, and Alexei, maybe, and...and Niki, too, however real he was. So Sol looked Taric right in the eye and said, "See you in detention," and the coyote said nothing as Sol walked away.

At lunch, he got the vegetable stew because the turkey looked gross, and he ate with Alexei. "You were amazing," he said.

"It sounds right, yes?" the fox said.

On the spur of the moment, Sol walked up to the coyote.

"It sounded awesome. Where did you hear that?"

Alexei grinned. "We have girls in Samorodka, too." He looked past Sol to another table, and his grin dimmed. "The mail I send you…"

Sol turned and saw the coyote and his two friends, one of whom appeared to be pointing at Sol, but Taric didn't turn. "Let's talk after school," he said. "And don't worry about those guys. I think that's over."

He didn't follow Taric over to the baseball field after the silent hour of detention, just wandered out in front of the school to wait for Alexei and the late bus. He was leaning back against the yellow brick, breathing in the warm air with his eyes closed, when he heard a quiet, "Hello," and opened his eyes to see Alexei.

The fox's ears were back, his tail down. He shifted from one foot to the other. "Why did you not go?" he said.

"Didn't work out." Sol was able to say that without thinking about the events of two days ago, at least not very much. His muzzle still ached a little, and his side hurt, but after a day of school, it all seemed much more remote. "I guess I'm stuck here a little longer."

Alexei looked around. "Thank you for answering my e-mail."

Sol smiled. "It was really cool of you."

"Cool? Of me?" For the first time, the fox didn't look scared. He tilted his muzzle to the side. "Why cool?"

"It was really brave. It's hard to tell someone something like that about yourself, especially here."

"It is easier to type." Alexei gave a bashful smile. His eyes, when he looked up, were a lighter grey than Sol remembered. Niki's eyes were green, Jean had said, and the shadow in Sol's mirror had had bright green eyes. But Alexei was not Niki; he was Alexei, and Sol wanted to get to know him, too.

"I guess so." Sol looked down at his paws and rubbed the back of his right one. "I…I kinda prefer saying it in person, myself."

He looked up in time to catch Alexei's transition from confusion to surprise, and then to caution. "I am not certain my English is correct, but…"

The fox's eyes were wide, almost pleading, ears splayed to either side of his head. Sol knew exactly how he felt. He checked to make sure nobody was listening, unable to stop himself, and then said, "Your English is fine. I'm…I'm gay."

Alexei smiled so widely that Sol thought he might injure himself, then he clapped his paws together. "This is wonderful!" His tail arched and wagged, and he took a step forward toward Sol, then back. "I am very happy that you did not leave."

"Yeah," Sol said. "I think I am, too."

The rattle and growl of the late bus interrupted them. Sol stepped involuntarily forward, waiting at the curb as the bus pulled up. But when the doors opened, he looked back at Alexei. They could talk tomorrow, of course, in homeroom or at lunch, or after school again. But they were here today, and the sun was breaking through the cloud cover and the ground smelled fresh and new.

Sol waved to the driver to go on without him, and stepped back to Alexei's tilted muzzle. "I'll call my parents to pick me up," he said.

They sat together cross-legged on the lawn out in front of the school. Sol told the fox about Carcy, about their relationship that had built up online and how false it had all been. Telling someone out loud, without having to be on guard against Meg's cynical assurance that of course the world was a terrible place and what did he expect, kisses and candy, was a great relief. Alexei listened attentively, made sympathetic noises at the right times, and his eyebrows creased in worry when Sol talked, hesitantly, about the ram coming up to his bedroom and taking his paw.

And then, Sol paused. "Do you believe in ghosts?"

"Ghost?"

"The spirit of someone who used to be dead."

Alexei smiled. "I know what 'ghost' means. I...yes, I suppose. In Samorodka, we say there is haunted house. Old man died many years ago, still hates cubs." He smiled. "My friend Vasily says he has ghost in his attic. Mother of grandmother..." He searched for the word, then pulled out a netbook while he continued to talk. "Her spirit remains in house, sometimes watches over family, sometimes gets bored and makes noise. Sometimes frightens chickens. Ah! Great-grandmother." He smiled and closed the computer, his tail flicking. "You see a ghost?"

"I...I might have." Sol flicked his tail against the grass. "I felt like there was a spirit...stopping me from giving in to him."

"A spirit of an ancestor, perhaps." Alexei flicked his ears. "Often our ancestors may remain to protect us."

"I don't think it was...I mean, it was a fox." Sol rubbed his muzzle and laughed. "You aren't descended from a ballet dancer who lived in Paris, are you?"

Alexei shook his head slowly. "Why do you ask?"

"That's who he was in my..." He stopped himself from saying *dream*. "In my head."

"My ancestors live in Siberia always." The fox's whiskers twitched. "But I am happy I reminded you of him."

"To be honest…" Sol looked steadily into the fox's eyes. They weren't green, and his build was stockier than a dancer's. But he could easily envision Alexei cheerfully bringing food to a sick friend, could imagine him playing soccer with the fire and joy of a ballet. Perhaps the resemblance did go beyond merely being a fox with a Siberian accent. "You do remind me of him."

Alexei smiled at Sol, his tail wagging. "What happened with your— with the ram?"

"Oh." Sol brushed the back of his paw against his muzzle, against his whiskers. He looked up in time to see his father's car pulling into the parking lot. "He left. I don't think I'll be seeing him again."

"I'm sorry to hear that."

Sol nodded toward the car as it pulled up to the curb, getting to his feet. "My father."

Alexei scrambled to his feet as well. "I will see you tomorrow?" His tail swished.

"Yeah." Sol grinned and extended a paw. Alexei shook it, and then watched as Sol got into his father's car. Sol waved through the window as they pulled away.

"I don't remember him from the baseball team," his father said.

Sol shook his head. "He plays soccer." He leaned back in the seat.

His father snorted. "Soccer." His wide grey muzzle inclined slightly in Sol's direction. "You feeling better?"

"Uh-huh."

"Started eating meat again?"

Sol shifted in the seat, freeing his tail where it was trapped behind him. "Sometimes."

"Little late for it, but I guess you learned your lesson."

He'd learned his lesson, all right, but even if he couldn't tell his father the whole story yet—maybe ever—he couldn't just stay quiet, either. "It didn't have anything to do with baseball."

His father half-turned, keeping one eye on the road. "Don't argue for the sake of arguing."

"I'm not." Sol looked his father right in the eye. "It was my decision to start, and it was my decision to stop. I just didn't want to do it any more."

His father raised an eyebrow and then turned to face the road. "All right, then."

The atmosphere in the car was relaxed, his father's tail not wagging exactly, but swishing, and Sol ventured a request a few moments later. "Dad, Meg and I have this school project…"

"So work on it at school."

His father spoke carelessly, but without irritation. Sol plunged forward. "It's a big project, and I wasn't going to ask to go over there, but if maybe she could come over just for tonight and maybe tomorrow night if we need the time. It's due Monday."

His father sighed. Sol leaned forward. "I'll leave the bedroom door open." Partly, he told himself.

They turned onto the main street, heading west. Sol and his father reached for the sun visors at the same time, to block the glaring sun. "Get it done tonight," his father said. "Mom and I are goin' out tomorrow night."

Sol called Meg when he got home. "You can come over," he said, "but we have to finish the report tonight."

"Your house smells funny," she said. "Let's do it over the 'net."

"I want to show you this thing I found. It's from the dream."

She sighed. "Fine. I'll get my things."

"See you in a bit."

"Hey," she said, "You're not going to make me watch you dream, are you?"

"I'll wait 'til you leave. I promise." He grinned and set the painting on the bed, sat next to it, and began reading "Confession" where he'd left off.

You will see at this point how cruelly the world conspired to leave me with no other course of action. If I were to defend our good name, if I were to continue with my life in any sort of respectable manner, well, this courtesan—nay, such a title bestows more honor upon him than he deserves—this blackmailing whore could not be allowed to continue with his plan. You will recall, I hope, the case only two years ago, in which M. De R— was acquitted upon the revelation that the rabbit had been blackmailing his family, threatening their livelihood. Or if not acquitted, I believe the court showed leniency, allowing him to live in his quarters under house arrest. Of course, I would willingly submit to such a fate, for while I do believe my actions justified, I understand that to preserve the appearance of equality, some punishment must be levied. Much as we appreciate the privilege we have earned, the power in this country rests with those who would abolish born privilege as they abolished the King. And so I know that my only chance at clemency rests in throwing myself upon their mercy.

First I had to convince myself that my love was but a phantom, pledged to a creature who did not exist. My love for Niki was true and pure, and he took it with his fangs and devoured it whole. It was only when I realized how cruelly I had been used that I was able to bring myself to do what needed doing.

I swear to you, father, he did not suffer. He was laughing, and I struck him once with a candlestick—one of the set given to us by the Marchands, not one of the good set, but I believe it has already been entered into evidence, and you know this. He collapsed, insensate, as a rag doll might fall, or a marionette whose strings were cut. I fell to my knees, horrified by what I had done even though I understood well the necessity of it. It was but a moment, but the life had already fled from him. I clasped my hands together and looked to our Father, beseeching Him for mercy.

Sol stopped reading, staring at his phone. Jean had killed Niki? *Killed* him, beaten him over the head? No, no. Niki hadn't died that way, he couldn't have. His gorge rose. He read the paragraph again, but the words didn't change. Sol scrolled ahead, skimming the text as it went by.

—the Seine being so close, it naturally suggested itself—
—my poor fortune that the night watch was present on its rounds this of all nights—
—my attempts to explain the body they had seen me push—
—the restraints found on him were placed there prior to the blow—
—dead before he was thrown into the Seine, father, I swear—

And then the book ended:

I ask you, père, to believe in your son. Have faith that I acted only in the best interests of our family, and that it breaks my heart even now to think of what I was driven to, as much for the loss of my beloved fox as for the trouble and calumny I have caused to you and mamère. I beg of you to bring this document to the court and intercede on my behalf. I swear that from this day forward I will live a chaste and respectable life, I will follow your wishes to the letter, I will not stray from the path you have tried so hard to guide me on. I have learned my lesson, that love is not for those such as me. All my aspirations of romance lie cold and dead at the bottom of the Seine, and will trouble me—and you—no longer.

If you need proof of my feelings, you need only look so far as the painting: all my love was poured into it, and there I preserved my fox as I remembered him, as the ghost of my love wished him to be. In that painting he is my faithful companion, all the good of him without his base nature. I beg of you, consider the painting and the depth of feeling it demonstrates. If you approach the court, certainly they will hear you as they will not hear me; certainly if you vouch for my character, they will listen; certainly if you ask for clemency, they will grant it.

I place my heart, my honor, and my very life in your hands.

I remain always,

Your faithful and obedient son,

Jean

There was an afterword, which noted that Jean de Giverne had been tried and convicted of murder. He had been apprehended on the bank of the Seine after throwing in the body of a fox, which had been recovered but never identified. This pleading letter had remained locked in his father's desk for twelve years; only after the elder chamois's death had it been discovered and published.

The afterword did not mention the painting Jean alluded to, but Sol knew instantly what it must be. He ran to his computer to search, but as he sat, he heard the clump of Meg's footsteps on the stairs.

She tossed her backpack on his bed, then sat down beside it. "Looked over your essays. Not bad. What the hell are you doing?"

Sol tapped some terms into a search engine. "Just looking for something. Give me five minutes. The thing I wanted to show you is there." He gestured backwards at the painting, rolled up on the bed.

"You painted something?" In the reflection of his computer screen, he saw her black-furred arms holding the white roll of canvas, unrolling it.

He'd just gotten an image result from a search on "Jean de giverne painting": a male fox, nude, seated on a stone bench in a park in autumn. It looked instantly familiar from his dream, *the fox on a stone bench in a park poised to stand, about to get up, but forever caught in the moment before he leaves*. Sol clenched his fist.

"Trying to figure out who painted your painting?"

Meg had come up over his shoulder. "I *know* who painted it." He stabbed his finger at the screen. "It wasn't this asshole. This is the guy who wrote one of the books I read. It said at the end that he'd painted something, but he didn't, he just took credit for it after…" Sol took a breath and forced himself to relax. "Anyway, it's not the one I have."

"Sure it is," she said, and he saw that she was holding the rolled-up painting. "Well, it's not a painting; it's a giclée."

"A what?" He stared as she unrolled the painting, and he realized that he had never opened it all the way. He'd assumed it was the female mouse, but as Meg unrolled it, Sol saw that the white fur he'd seen was the tip of a fox's tail. Sol's mouth felt very dry. There it was, unmistakably: the painting of Niki. Sol reached out, but hesitated before touching it.

"Giclée. A reproduction. Really nice. These days they kinda roll them off like on an assembly line, but this is a good one. Painting's not bad either."

"It's beautiful." Sol traced a finger down the edge.

"Well, I know why you think it's beautiful. And yeah, he's not bad. But they always exaggerate in paintings."

"Not this one," Sol said before he could stop himself.

Meg arched an eyebrow. "Found a photo of the model? Or a, whatsit, a daguerrotype?"

"Not really." She kept staring at him. "This is the guy from the dreams. I found this in the attic and it's the same painting of him from my dreams. I mean, that's…that's weird, right?"

Meg stared at him. "You sure you never saw this before? I mean, it was in your attic. Maybe you were like five…"

"Maybe." Sol looked at the giclée in Meg's paws as she let it curl back into a roll. "But the book was written by the guy who claims he painted that painting! How did I start reading that book, then?"

"It's a little out there, but…" She sighed and rubbed her ears. "A hundred-year-old ghost reaching across time and space to a high school student?"

Sol set his ears back. "You're the one with a vampire friend."

"He's not a real vampire, moron."

"Does he know that?"

"Of course he knows that! Look, we're just trying to make the world a little more interesting than it is. He doesn't go out at night and bite people's necks. He just wears a cape." She paused. "And eye makeup. Sometimes."

"Does he sparkle?"

"Don't ever ask him that." She shook her head and unrolled the painting again. "Who did paint this then? Van Gogh? You said it's not this guy." Her finger rested on a little scrawl that read "J. de G."

Sol rubbed at the name with his thumb, to no effect. He looked away. "It was this artist named Henri Trounoir. He was really good. He was Niki's friend."

"Oh God, you named the fox."

"He's in the book," Sol said sharply.

"Is he? What happened to him?"

Sol followed the curve of the fox's back up to his ears, to the bright green eye. "He died. The chamois killed him."

Meg stared at him. "Seriously?"

Sol nodded. "Smashed in his head with a candlestick and threw him in the river."

"He...wrote about this?"

"He got caught. So he wrote a confession hoping to show extenuating circumstances."

"Extenuating circumstances for bashing in someone's head. This oughta be good. So?"

Sol shook his head. "He was executed."

"Well, good. At least *their* justice system got it right."

The black wolf let his eyes wander over the painting again before rolling it up. "I guess so. That didn't bring him back to life, though."

Meg put a paw on his shoulder. "Okay. Look. I will admit that something is going on here, something weird and maybe pretty awesome and cool. I mean, I still don't believe in ghosts. But if it's good for you, then it's cool. And it's good for you, right?"

"I guess." Sol didn't want to tell her he'd cried more in the last two weeks than he had the two years previous. That didn't seem like it would be a mark on the positive side of his story. "It's been exhausting, too."

"Promise me something." Meg tapped his computer. "Write that shit down."

"I already started."

"Then finish. And let me see it when you're done." She sat on the bed and eyed the half-open door. "Okay, now we need to finish up this report before your dad kicks me out."

They sat down at the computer and put together the work Sol had done with the impressive amount of work Meg had done. More than once, Meg praised the level of detail and realism Sol had put into his essays, and said, "You dream some cool shit." Sol, looking over Meg's collection of paintings and touching up her essays on the artistic movements, found himself understanding better the background of the work Henri and van Gogh had been doing.

After an hour and a half, Meg pronounced herself satisfied with their progress. "Which is good 'cause it's about time for me to go." She looked around. "Where's the gift of the Green Fairy? Let's get this over with."

"Um. Yeah. It's in my desk. I'll get some glasses."

Meg called as he was heading down the hall, "Just one. I don't get fucked-up ghost dreams."

"Doesn't matter," Sol said. "You started this with me, you can finish it with me." He hurried down the stairs and called, "Just getting a glass of water," to his mother and father in the living room. In the kitchen, he stacked two glasses and filled the topmost with water, took a small cup of sugar, and ran back upstairs.

Meg was swirling the green liquid, staring thoughtfully at it, when he returned. "I got it." He held out the glasses, kicking his door shut. If his parents noticed, it wouldn't be for a few minutes, and that was all the time they needed.

"Give it here." She shook her head when she saw the small cup of sugar. "You don't have sugar cubes?"

Sol shook his head. "This is all."

Meg made a disapproving "tsk" noise. "No point in bringing out the spoon, then. I'll just mix it. Should still work."

"It did the other night." Sol curled his tail down as Meg glared at him. She poured the last of the absinthe equally into both glasses and added sugar.

"You're still not off the hook for that," she said, handing him his glass. Light green clouds swirled and played in the ordinary drinking glass, only about a third full. "But this is it. You want more, I'll give you my vampire fox's e-mail address. Just don't mention sparkles."

"Thanks," Sol said. "But I think this'll be it for me."

Meg picked up her own glass of cloudy green liquid. "Now, prepare to receive the gift of the Green Fairy. May she give you the dreams you seek."

All he wanted was one chance to see Niki's side of his last meeting with Jean. Meg dranks hers, but Sol hesitated with the glass at his lips, the anise smell strong in his nose. If he got the dream he expected, it would be bad, probably a nightmare.

"What's the matter?" Meg set down her glass and shoved the empty bottle in her backpack. "You miss the frankincense? Sorry, I would've brought some, only…" She tapped her nose. "Your mom freaked out the last time we lit incense over here."

Sol lowered the glass. "This might be one bad dream."

She reached out as if to take the glass from him, but didn't touch it. "You're going to see him die, aren't you?"

He watched reflections bob on the surface of the liquid. "Probably."

"Don't do this if you think it's dangerous." When he looked up, she was staring steadily at him. "I mean it, Sol. Even if it's just a bad trip, you take drugs in a bad state of mind, and you could end up seriously fucked up or even dead. If you think it's going to be that way—"

He shook his head, pulling the glass toward him. "I don't think so. But it doesn't matter. I have to do this."

"Listen, um." Meg started to say something, then her expression softened. "If I'm right, then they're just dreams. They can't hurt you. If you're right, then…this spirit, whatever it is, it stopped you from getting in the bathtub before. It's not going to kill you now, right?"

"Probably not." He raised the glass to his lips, then lowered it again. "Hey, Meg. There's a file on my computer called 'Niki's story.' If…if something happens to me—"

"Jesus, Sol."

"Just listen. Take a look at it. I'd like someone else to remember it. Even if it was just a crazy dream. And remember who really painted that painting."

She hefted the pack over her shoulder. "Any other last will and testaments?"

"Yeah. Tell my folks it was an accident. And…you're a good friend."

"Great." She patted him on the shoulder. "I'll see myself out. See ya tomorrow on the bus."

"See you, Meg. Thanks again."

She raised a paw and walked out, closing the door behind her.

Sol took a breath. He cast an eye down at the rolled-up painting, and then raised his glass. "To you, Niki," he said softly, and drank.

Chapter 24

He is in Jean's room, the gleam of white marble soiled with the reflection of his russet fur, his dirty clothes. He gestures at the painting. "There was no need to send the gendarmes to find me," he says. "I intended to bring this to you in any case. All you think of me is a work of art, so here, here is your work of art. You may remember me by it."

"You think this captures your spirit? You think this decoration, this wall hanging, is a replacement for you?" The chamois steps closer, barely glancing at the painting. Niki can see himself reflected in the cold brown eyes, can smell Jean's disarmingly sweet breath. "You mean to leave me forever, is that it?"

The lost future tugs at Niki, the life of luxury in silk robes and fruit tarts. The coldness in Jean gnaws at his heart. "Y-yes," he says, but as he is thinking it, he wonders what it is he has to return to. With Henri gone, with Cireil gone, he will be as alone at home as he is while dancing, wherever he is able to find work. Henri would tell him to dance, because that is what he must do, but Niki does not know whether he has the strength. And if he is to sell his body like the shadowy boys by the Seine, then why not simply sell it to Jean?

"Just one more night," Jean says. "One more night, and I will pay you handsomely. You may leave, and you may return at any time."

He should not. But who, he asks himself again, will miss him? And the icy eyes of the chamois bore into him. The only times he has seen them warm, relaxed, happy, have been following their nights of intimacy. He would like to see that again. He would like to feel love, and loved, one more time. "Very well," he says.

The chamois's smile shows little joy. "Undress," he says.

Niki removes his clothes, torn between wanting this to end quickly and wanting to do it nicely for the last time. Jean pushes him down and brings the ropes over, and ties his wrists, but this time he does not stop there. He binds Niki's ankles together as well. And when the fox is on all fours, Jean wraps a rope around his muzzle as well.

"You listen to me," he hisses into the fox's ear. "You steal my money, you run away, and then you come back to taunt me with a miserable piece of street art. Did you pay more than a franc for this? Or did you take it from the refuse lying in the street as you walked down from the hill?"

He wanted the painting to be seen by important people. They would have to recognize its talent. He made certain that Henri's signature was visible. And he wanted Jean to remember him, too, in future days.

Jean loves him in his own twisted way, he knows, otherwise Niki's leaving would not hurt him so much. But even if Niki's muzzle were untied, there would be nothing he could say. It will be one night, he tells himself, and then it will be over.

But Jean is determined to take every minute of the night. "You are nothing more than a painting yourself," he says, talking while he undresses, and then after as well. "You are here at my pleasure and for my pleasure, and I will decide when you come and when you go."

And it is not pleasant, not at all. Jean is rough, and he makes it last as long as he can. And when he has finished, he does not favor Niki with a smile, does not tell him how lovely he is. Jean simply walks out, leaving Niki tied and bent over the chaise. The fox reaches up with his bound paws to undo the rope around his muzzle, but it is secure and knotted around the back of his head, where he cannot easily reach. No mouse comes to free him this time. No other living soul enters the room at all.

Niki knows Jean's sitting-room well, the slick white marble floor, the eggshell-white curtains, the marble bust of some long-dead ancestral chamois staring down at him. The polished wooden arm of the chaise digs into his stomach; his nose rests on the reddish satin upholstery because it is an effort to lift his chest. He turns his head from one side to the other, but cannot escape the smell of Jean's pleasure. Even when he presses his nose into the satin, he smells not the residue of the cleaning, but their previous nights, and Jean's lovers before him, all imprisoned in this couch as surely as Niki is confined there. He could roll onto the floor, but it is cold and hard, and even with the smells and the ache in his stomach, he prefers the soft couch. He turns to look out the two windows in the opposite wall, where the night outside is so featureless that the windows might be painted black. Niki closes his eyes, but soon opens them again, because he cannot give in to sleep, can do nothing but wait.

Time expands and contracts. Some minutes or hours later, Jean returns. The chamois walks stiffly across the room to Niki, a silver candlestick dangling from one hand. He stands between Niki's head and the night-black of the windows and taps the candlestick against his leg. "Ah, little streetwalking whore," he says. "I suppose it is about time I let you go."

Niki twists his neck to look up. Jean's face is relaxed, but shows no pleasure, no emotion at all, in fact, except that Niki fancies that a tear gathers in the corner of one large brown eye. He understands what it is the chamois means to do. "Jean—"

"Quiet!" The word echoes against the marble. "You have shamed me, humiliated me!" The candlestick rises, drops back to his leg. "Do you imagine you are of any significance? Do you think anyone will miss you?"

Niki lowers his head. *Of course no-one will miss him, not any more. And yet he does not want to leave the world, not like this.*

"You are nothing, and still you mean to turn your back on me? No. That is not permitted." *Jean breathes harshly.* "You will go when I say you may go."

He will see Cireil soon, and Henri. He wants to tell them how precious are these moments we have, to warn them how easily we give them up. He keeps his eyes open, he breathes deep breaths, savoring the last few moments of sensation left to him. Even the aches in his muscles, the pain in his lip and his back, these are things to remember and cherish. He drinks in the white of the marble, the red of the satin, the white of Jean's robe and the tan of his fur; the smell of fox and chamois and sex and oil lamps and the houses outside. In the corner, the fox in the painting begins to rise from the bench he will never leave.

Jean reaches down and brushes his fingers under the fox's muzzle. His breath smells strongly of wine. "Now, you may go," *he whispers. His other hand brings the candlestick up. It flashes with reflected lamplight as it descends.*

Niki is slung across the chamois's back, being carried through the cool night air with the smell of river in his nose. He is bounced as the chamois rushes down stairs, and he realizes what is going to happen. He tries to make a noise, but it sticks in his throat. He tries to struggle, but Jean cannot feel it with the bouncing; that is what he tells himself.

There is no ceremony, no poetic farewell. Jean reaches the edge of the Seine and then Niki is falling, and he hits the cold water. He makes a splash, struggling, and twists his head frantically to keep his nose in the air. But the water soaks into his fur quickly, and he sinks, breathing in a gulp of water and then another

and then the pressure of the water in his lungs is gone and Sol knows somehow that he is himself again, in the dream. All around him, the world is light green and hazy, as if he is standing in a fog. A wall rises up on his left, and to his right there is a large pillar of thick stone. He reaches out in slow motion and cannot see his paw before him. With effort, he turns. There, on the ground in front of the green-streaked stone pillar, sits a fox.

His fur flows in the air, his bushy tail rippling in waves. He is not sitting, Sol sees now, so much as propped against the stone, knees bent, head lolling to the side. His body, streaked with black strands, is covered with nothing but ropes: around his muzzle, around his wrists, around his feet. His eyes stare ahead of him, just to Sol's right. They are the dull green of algae.

Niki, *he calls.* Niki!

This time, the fox lifts his paws.

The fox doesn't move. Sol makes his way over there, slowly. When he tries to swim using his invisible paws, he moves more quickly.

Niki!

He reaches the fox and stands for a moment or an hour. Then he is reaching down, trying to undo the ropes around the muzzle. Though he cannot see his paws, he pulls on the ropes with the urgency of dreams. They are cold and tight, but they loosen eventually and come away, float to the ground, and vanish. And now, he thinks, something will happen.

He waits. And something does.

The fox's eyes brighten to a shiny emerald. They shift, they focus on Sol. Niki's head straightens, his muzzle closes, and his lips stretch back into a smile.

Hello, dorogoï.

Sol reaches for Niki's wrists, to unbind them. He feels tears as warmth behind his eyes, down through his muzzle, and wonders, how does one cry underwater? Why did you show me this?

The fox's eyes are bright and tender. In the corner of one, flickers of light play off of what might be a tear. You wanted to see the end.

The ropes around the wrists are tighter, less tractable. Sol works at them without knowing how, just that if he keeps trying, he will undo them. The fox is patient, his eyes gleaming through the water. Why did...how could he do that?

There are more predators than those of us born with claws and teeth. Jean wanted so badly to be one, and in the end, he was, even though his hunger was not for flesh. Your world is gentler, more forgiving, but I think you know some Jeans in your time as well.

Sol works and works at the knots around the wrists, but they are stubborn in the manner of dreams, unyielding and frustrating. Is that why you came to help me? Why me?

Niki smiles. There was love in your heart, and you needed me.

The ropes around Niki's wrists resist a moment longer and then give way, in the unknowable manner of dreams. Come back with me. *The young wolf reaches out a paw, invisible, insubstantial.* You came once to save me. Come and stay.

The fox's head shakes slowly, side to side. We are only allowed one chance at living. I have exhausted mine.

To one side, Sol can see the riverbed stretching on and on, pale green into dark green into formless black. I feel like I'm wasting mine. You have your dance—had your dance. Henri had his art. I have nothing. I have no-one.

Art is not life, *Niki says.* Art enhances life. Love is not life; love enhances life.

Sol bites his lip. It is still tender, the lower lip on that side, even in the dream. What is life, then?

You are young. *Niki's smile is kind.* You will have time to discover that for yourself.

The thought of going on alone is daunting, but Sol is at least not bound and dead at the bottom of a river. I won't forget you. I'll make sure people hear your story. I'll write it down.

The movement of Niki's tail, a contented back-and-forth, might be simply the currents of the Seine. If you wish to honor me, then help others as I helped you.

There is one more thing Sol needs to know. He is aware that this is a dream, but he can see Niki so clearly, can see the rough brick of stone behind the fox. He can smell the water all around him and the fox before him, and so he hesitates before asking his last question. The world and the dream wait, but Sol knows he does not have long here. He looks into Niki's eyes. All this—is it real?

What is real? Is it what you believe?

It's…it's what is true.

Niki reaches out to a point on Sol's chest. This, he says. This is real. You, your heart, your feelings. Believe in them. Follow them.

The touch dulls the pain of the memories, warms him, brightens the water around him. He reaches out again, and this time the fox lifts his paws and Sol feels them around him. They are cold, but Niki's love in them is strong and warm. Sol holds him tightly and says, Thank you, thank you. *And then, half-crying,* I'll never see you again.

Niki's eyes blaze emerald above a gentle smile. Liar, *he says, tenderly.*

Sol's alarm blared in his ear, shocking him awake. He sat up, rubbing tears from his muzzle. The dampness didn't surprise him, nor did the chill across his shoulders where Niki's paws had held them. His sheet had slid down, though, and the fan was blowing across his fur; perhaps that was all.

He reached out to shut off the alarm and sat up in bed, drawing his knees up to his chin and curling his tail around his hip. When he rubbed his eyes dry, there was no flood of tears, but he felt as though he would never smile again. It was not the pain of death, because Niki wasn't dead; rather, he was dead but not gone. It reminded him of what he'd felt when Natty went off to college and Sol had come upstairs to walls echoing with his brother's scent and no brother in the next room.

Niki wouldn't want him to cry, but that didn't stop a few more tears from soaking through his fur. In the silence of the house, it would be easy for him to imagine that he was alone. But his parents were just down the hall, and their scent was all over the house as well. Meg and Alexei were out there waiting for him, and Natty was only a few hours away at college. Still, he was going to miss waking up with creepy shit in his bed from the dreams.

That thought made him laugh, half-nervously, and look around his bed, then the room. His phone was blinking, but he ignored it for the moment. There was no water other than the dampness around his eyes, no rope, no candlestick. He did not feel grief, nor Jean's betrayed fury, nor Niki's tragically misguided love. No smells, no marks in his fur—no trace at all that his dream had been real other than the vivid memory of it.

He picked up the phone and saw a message from Meg: *Hey, dream-boy. You ok?*

Now, Sol felt a little more like smiling. He texted back quickly: *I'm ok.*

He set the phone down, rubbed the back of his paw against his whiskers in a gesture that was becoming habitual, and padded to the bathroom. He almost wished Niki had not shown him the final night with Jean; the images and the cruelty of Jean sat heavy in his memory, and he knew they would not soon disappear. But their warning was clear, and against them shone the light and warmth of Niki's love. Whether it was real or not, Sol believed in it.

At the sink, he looked up, and for a moment could do nothing but stare at the mirror. In his black-furred muzzle, the eyes that stared back at him were no longer a light hazel color, but a bright emerald green.

Chapter 25

It was not the largest birthday party Sol had ever had, but the size was pretty much perfect, he thought. Natty had come back from college for the weekend, Xavy and a couple of the wolves from the baseball team were there, and Alexei and Meg sat together over a bowl of chips. Sol had been sitting with them for a while, until Meg told him to pay attention to the other guests, and he'd found Xavy and Natty happy to welcome him into their group. Ears were up, tails swishing lazily, smiles all around.

"Norston here says you played good off the bench last night," Natty said. He elbowed his little brother. "Getting some playing time, huh? Maybe I'll have to come down and see a game. I was gonna come down for Lakeside, but…"

"I was there," Sol said. "It was a great game. Taric went 4-for-4 and had a home run."

"Taric's that coyote?"

Sol nodded. "Yeah, he's good. We had a college scout at the last game."

Xavy drank from a cup that was supposed to contain only Gatorade, but Sol's dad was giving out Busch from the kitchen, and the malty smell reached Sol's nostrils as the other wolf lowered the cup. "He's still a prick," Xavy said.

"Fit right in on a college team." Natty laughed. "He ain't giving you trouble no more, is he, Sollo?"

Sol shook his head. "Nah. We're…well, I dunno about 'cool,' but…he doesn't give me shit. His sister still does, but not as much. Alexei took her down a peg." He grinned at the fox, deep in conversation with the otter.

"Hey, guys!" Sol's dad came out from the kitchen, a beer in each paw, tail wagging. "I got the charcoal started, so we got half an hour before the burgers start cooking. How about a little five on five down at the park?"

So they walked down to the park, drafting some neighbors along the way, and played five-on-five softball for half an hour. Sol was made to be a captain, and Natty the other; Sol drafted Meg and Alexei and his father, while Natty drafted all the baseball players. Predictably, Sol's team lost, though they wouldn't have known if not for Sol's father keeping score; everyone else kept shouting, "How much do we have?" in between laughing at their errors and absurdly trash-talking each other.

On the way home, Sol walked next to his father, helping him carry the equipment. "Not much time left in the school year," his father said.

Sol turned his head, but his father wasn't looking at him. "Mr. Zerling's pretty happy with the lineup," he said. "Taric's doing really well. I'm helping where I can."

"You're better than that 'yote."

"I told you, dad, I'm not." Sol swung the bag of softballs from his paw. "It's okay. The team needs good players on the bench, too. We have to keep the team together late in the games."

"That's just what he says to keep you happy." His father looked at Sol now, sideways along his grey muzzle.

"Well, it's working," Sol said.

His father snorted loudly, but all he said was, "You did good with that softball team there." And Sol accepted that for the compliment it was.

Back at their house, his mother was just putting some thick, juicy burgers on the grill. Charcoal and meat smell filled the hazy air. It was warm enough that all the canids were panting, and even Meg, who couldn't be bothered to chase balls that weren't hit directly to her, drank a big glass of Gatorade.

Xavy patted Alexei on the back as they ate their burgers. "You got a good swing," he said. "Thought about playing baseball?"

Alexei smiled, showing no self-consciousness at being the only fox at the party. "I am teaching Sol football, and he is teaching me baseball."

"Football?" Natty perked his ears up.

"Soccer." Alexei grinned at Sol. "Sol has good speed. Needs to improve his," he gestured to his feet.

"Footwork," Sol said. "We do footwork drills for baseball, but nothing like what they do for soccer. It's crazy. We didn't even do it for the high school team." It was the closest he'd ever come to dancing.

"Long as you're enjoying it," Natty said. "And you ain't neglectin' baseball."

"Sol's out there every afternoon," Xavy says. "Busts his tail."

Sol saw Alexei's briefly furrowed brow, but he didn't want to embarrass the fox by explaining the phrase in front of him, so he made a mental note to tell him later. "I don't know how much longer I'll get to play. So I'm enjoying it while I can."

"Not stayin' till dark anymore." Xavy tipped his beer to his muzzle and drank.

"Nah. I'm staying as long as it's fun." Sol grinned.

"Fun?" Natty flicked his ears. "Not about fun, Sol. It's about working hard to be the best."

Sol elbowed his brother. "Sheesh, now you sound like Dad."

"Whoa, hey!" Natty held up his paws and grinned. "Sorry. Just want you to be the best you can."

"I'm happy," Sol said. "That's all I want out of it."

"Well," Natty said, "I guess that's okay, too. Just tell Dad you're having the most fun of everyone, or something." But he looked at Xavy with an exaggerated shrug, kind of a "what'cha gonna do?" look.

The other wolf grinned uncomfortably back. "He's a lot looser than he was early this year," he said. "That coyote's just a freak of nature, or Sol'd be starting for sure."

"Yeah, so what happened then?" Natty took another swallow of beer, too. "You were all weird up 'til like a month ago."

"Ah…" Sol couldn't restrain a smile; his brother had noticed his moods. Someday, he thought, he might tell Natty everything. "I told you. Senioritis."

"You're still a senior."

"Yeah, well." He grinned. "A friend of mine told me not to take everything so seriously."

Xavy punched Sol's shoulder lightly. "Don't be so hard on yourself. You did great when Zerling moved you away from second."

Natty raised his eyebrows, turning back to Sol. "You didn't tell me about that."

Sol waved a paw. "Wasn't a big deal. Couch twisted his ankle and we needed someone. Anyone can play left field. It's not permanent."

"And shortstop two weeks ago," Xavy added.

"Backup shortstop. Anyway, that's not too different from second base." Sol shook his head and finished off his Coke in one gulp. "I'm just happy to get to play where I can."

And after the burgers, there was ice cream cake, and then the guests drifted away one by one as the evening wore on. There was talk of going out to a movie, but nobody could agree on a movie, and Sol was comfortable just sitting around with his friends talking, so he didn't push it. Eventually, Sol's father went to the living room with Natty to talk and watch the end of the Typhoons game, and the last of the baseball team headed home, and it was just Sol and Meg and Alexei.

"Your eyes still creep me out," Meg said when they were alone.

"I think they are pretty." Alexei smiled.

"You didn't know him for three years." Meg grimaced. "Still feels like he's an alien."

"Mom and Dad got over it," Sol said.

Meg rolled her eyes in the direction of the living room, "Right. Aren't you going to some specialist in Millenport next week?"

"Vidalia, yeah." Sol had told his parents that he didn't want to go to Millenport, and they hadn't argued too much. Vidalia was not quite as large, but was still a good-sized city. "But they don't talk about it anymore. Anyway, it was your Green Fairy."

"I didn't tell you to get so wigged out your eyes changed. That was all you."

"I was pretty screwed up back then."

Meg snorted, play-slapping at Sol. "It was a month ago."

"Five weeks!"

"Whatever." She sat back and looked at him. "I'm glad you came through it okay. And glad for whatever I did to help. You still haven't written about it."

"It's a long story," Sol said.

Alexei laughed. "I want to read it too. I am very happy there are ghosts in this country like in Siberia."

"There are not ghosts," Meg said. "It's just some weird shit. I asked my vampire fox friend, and—"

"Hey." Sol held up his paws. "It's my birthday. Could we not have this argument?"

Meg sighed. "I'm gonna go outside and take a walk." That meant she was going to light up. At least she'd given up asking if Sol wanted to come. "See you guys later."

"She is sad that she is still here," Alexei said softly when Meg had gone.

"Yeah," Sol said. "But I think she'll come with us this summer."

The fox looked toward the door. "She does not like me very much."

"She likes you," Sol said. "She wouldn't be talking to you at all if she didn't. She's just afraid of being a third wheel."

Alexei laughed softly, his gaze returning to Sol. "'Third wheel'?"

"Yeah, she thinks we're—she thinks she'd be in the way. I keep telling her it's not like that."

The fox nodded. "I found listing for apartment. Nice section of Vidalia, near Riverwalk. Two bedrooms."

Riverwalk was the small gay neighborhood where one of Alexei's Internet friends lived. "Cool," Sol said. "I'll take a look. My parents are okay with it as long as I still go to college in the fall."

"I would like to stay here for college as well." Alexei's ears folded down. "There are many papers to be signed, and I must hope that Siberia allows it. I hope the football—soccer—is enough."

"You love soccer, and you're really good." Sol grinned and reached over to pat the fox's knee. "The guy in that league in Vidalia wrote you an awesome letter. It's gonna work out, I can feel it. And Meg's gonna come with us."

She opened the door just then. "I'm gonna do what now?"

When she came and sat with them, Sol didn't smell any marijuana on her breath. "Where'd you go?"

She shrugged. "I told you. Just took a walk. Leave you two alone for a bit."

"I like talking to you," Alexei said. "Sol is just saying you will come with us to Vidalia. I find two-bedroom apartment."

"One for me, one for you two." She snorted and looked between them.

Alexei shrugged. "If you and Sol want to share room, is all right also."

"Or we all sleep in one room and use the other one for video games." Sol grinned.

Meg shook her head and lowered her voice. "You two make the worst couple I've ever seen."

"Yeah, so? Come with us. Come on, it's my birthday." Sol leaned in to Meg.

She pushed him away. "Yeah, yeah, I'll think about it." But she smiled and her tail thwapped the floor. "Not like there's anything else to do in fuckin' Midland."

"Told you," Sol said to Alexei.

She pointed a finger at both of them. "But I swear, if you wake me up in the middle of the night with any kind of…noises…" She leaned back in the chair. "Lived with that for eighteen fucking years and I really need a good night's sleep for once."

"Cross our hearts," Sol said.

Alexei mimicked Sol's gesture, and Meg said, "You're already starting to act alike."

Sol pushed her back and laughed, and the conversation moved on, but he couldn't keep his tail from wagging for the rest of the evening.

When Alexei and Meg went home, Sol hugged his parents and Natty goodnight. All in all, his birthday had gone as well as it could've without a car in the driveway. And even the loss of the car didn't sting, not now. Sol had his friends, and everything else would work itself out in time.

He closed the door to his room and picked up the main present his parents had given him: the giclée of Niki, mounted under glass with a nice wooden frame and mat. They hadn't asked any questions about why he wanted a picture of a nude male fox, nor where he'd gotten it from. Neither of them had recognized it, but then, he hadn't really expected them to.

He rapped a painting hanger into the wall and slipped the wire on the back of the frame over the hook. It took a small adjustment to straighten, and then it was up on the wall. He had just stepped back to admire it when his mother knocked on his door. "Happy birthday, honey. I saved a birthday present," she said, and handed him a small envelope.

"Oh, Mom. Thanks." Sol ripped it open and pulled out a small plastic card. He turned it over. It was a Visa, with his name on it. "What…?"

"Well, it's not a car. But at college…or if you go live on your own this summer like you've been talking about…it would be useful. You'll be responsible for it, but we'll have access to the account. We can help out if you need it."

Or take it away if he didn't use it well, in addition to being able to see everything he bought. But he smiled, because it was a nice gesture. "Thanks, Mom. This is really cool."

"It was hard to shop for you this year." She leaned against the door frame, right against the stone where Natty used to lean, looking into the room. "I didn't really know what you wanted."

Sol placed the card on his desk, caught his reflection in the mirror. "I've been trying to figure that out myself." Bright green eyes stared back at him. His mother was here alone, and smiling, and it was his birthday. "Mom, can I talk to you for a second?"

She nodded and stepped into the room, and he met her eyes. "What's on your mind, hon?"

Was this the right moment? Sol had no idea. But it was in his heart, he felt it was right, and so he followed that before he could chicken out. "Um, I've been thinking about stuff a lot." His throat was dry, but the words burst out. "I think I'm gay."

For a split-second, Sol had no idea what to expect. Then his mother smiled and walked across the room to hug him. "We still love you, no matter what."

"We?"

She pulled her muzzle back, eyes fixed on his. "Oh, your father loves you. We might not tell him right away. But you know, between you and me, I think he'd be more upset if you went vegetarian again."

Sol laughed. "You don't seem too surprised."

"We-ell. I didn't want to say anything, but I never thought you and Meg were a couple."

"Really?"

"Mother's intuition. But mostly, you were just too good friends." His mother nodded at the framed painting. "And then you find this painting, which is real nice, but…"

"It's from the project me and Meg did. We got an A on it."

"I guess what I'm trying to say is, they painted a lot of ladies back then, too, didn't they?"

Sol rubbed the back of his paw along his whiskers. He couldn't meet his mom's eyes. "This is the one I found in the attic."

"Sweetie." His mother hugged him again. "I'm trying to tell you, it's okay. I'm really glad you decided to tell me."

Sol pressed fingers to his eyes. He felt a twinge of regret for the months spent hiding, afraid, unsure. "Thanks, Mom," he said.

She didn't move, looking hesitant and awkward. Finally, she said, "So did I do that okay, hon?"

He flicked his ears. That seemed like the question he should be asking. "Do what okay?"

"After you almost ran away, you know, I wondered…so I read some websites. In case it was true, in case you decided to tell me."

"You just read some websites. Just like that." Sol tilted his head. It seemed fantastical.

"Well…" His mother looked abashed, tail flicking from side to side, not quite wagging. "I had a nightmare, if you must know. I wanted to make sure you didn't run away again." She lifted her paws. "It wasn't just about being…funny, like that. There were some websites about drugs, too. And one about devil-worship."

He wanted to hug her again, out of love and guilt, so he did. "I never ran away, Mom," he said, which was technically true even if they both knew it was also partly a lie. "I told you about Meg and Alexei and me going to Vidalia."

"And we support that." She held him, then stepped back, her nose an inch from his. "You don't have to tell me, but…is he…I mean, are you and he…"

"No!" Sol's fur bristled. He willed it smooth. "We're just good friends. Like me and Meg."

Her mouth twitched, a half-smile at his attempted joke. "It would be okay." Those words came with an effort, he could tell. Her ears were half-down, but she perked them up when she saw him looking.

"I…really, he's not. But I might have one. One day."

His mother nodded, and held her paws out to him. "I hope you find someone who makes you happy. That's all we ever wanted for you."

Privately, Sol thought that his father wanted a few other things, like for him to be a baseball star. But this wasn't the time to mention it. "You won't tell Dad yet, will you?"

"Not if you don't want me to."

He shook his head. "Sometime, I guess. Not right now."

"You may be surprised. He didn't much care for how Nolan handled things, with…with Percy."

Sol's tail stilled at the reminder of his cousin. "He didn't? He never said anything."

"Well, not to you. But he yelled at him on the phone, oh, he carried on. Said family always comes first…of course, that was before…" She sniffed, and her voice cracked. "I'm glad you didn't run away, that's all."

"Me too." Sol felt a wave of unexpected respect for his father. "I love you guys."

She kissed his nose, and now her tail wagged for real, and the smile and the love shone out of her. Her brown eyes looked into his. "Happy birthday, sweetie. You're eighteen now. You can decide to be whatever you want to be."

Sol grinned. "Maybe that's all the birthday present I wanted."

"If I'd known that, I could've saved us the trouble of the credit card." He laughed with her, and she reached up to brush his whiskers. " You know, I think I might be finally getting used to your eyes. They're so pretty, and the doctors say there's nothing wrong…"

"I like the change."

"It's hard for us to see you change, sometimes," his mother said. "But hazel eyes or green, you'll always be our son."

When she'd left and closed his door, he walked to the window to feel the breeze before going to bed. Below the stately stars, fireflies danced together in the trees, darting, dipping, soaring with no choreography but passion. Sol watched them, remembering the days when he and Natty had run after them, snatching them out of the air to keep in jars until their light faded and they died. Now he just enjoyed watching their yellow-green flashes come and go. You could trace the flight of any individual one if you watched closely enough, its flash calling, *Here I am! Here I am!* out to the world. And if you stepped back and watched them all, you could see that there were multitudes of them calling out to each other, bound together in their search for company, not one of them truly alone. For if you truly believed you were alone in the world, what was the good of casting your light out into it?

He turned back to the painting, sliding a finger down the fine wood of the frame. His parents had chosen just the right wood to complement the bright colors: a dark oak with highlights that called out the fox's lush pelt. Sol's eyes looked back at himself from the glass, and behind them, the fox in the painting with one green eye smiled, mysteriously, still turned away.

He'd thought about Jean's story and his dream a lot in the past weeks. Though he was still trying to understand everything that had happened, the one thing that stood out to him was that Jean had a book and Niki did not. "I'm still working on your story," he whispered to the painting. "And Henri's. I haven't forgotten."

For a moment, just a flash, the bright green reflection of Sol's eye overlapped the fox's. For that moment, the fox was looking back, right at him; the smile was meant for him. Sol leaned closer to look, and the illusion was broken. He stepped back, but the picture remained frozen, the fox forever caught in the act of sitting down.

Joy bubbled up in Sol. He closed his eyes, threw out his arms, and danced, hoping that someone, somewhere, was watching.

About the Author

Kyell Gold is best known for his gay fiction using animal people to represent human archetypes. He has won the Annual Anthropomorphic Literature & Arts (Ursa Major) Award ten times for his novels and short stories, and the Rainbow Award twice (2009, Best Gay Novel and Best Fantasy Novel, for *Out of Position*). He has also been nominated for a WSFA Small Press Award ("Race to the Moon," 2009).

His various online presences are linked from *www.kyellgold.com*. He lives in California with his husband, but can often be found at conventions around the country and internationally.

About the Artist

Rukis is a fantasy artist and comic creator who achieved commercial success with her comic *Cruelty* and went on to create the ambitious *Red Lantern*. Her work can be found at *www.furaffinity.net/user/rukis*.

About Sofawolf Press

Sofawolf Press was founded in 1999 to provide a venue to showcase great writers of anthropomorphic fiction and to promote the genre to a wider audience.

Since the debut of its flagship publication, *Anthrolations*, a literary anthology of short stories, the Press has added to its lineup other magazine-length anthologies, novels, shared-world anthologies, and other novel-length collections, comics and graphic novels, artists' sketchbooks, and calendars. The Press continues to seek out new and creative ways of expanding its offerings of printed creations.

Please visit our website at *www.sofawolf.com/catalog/* for a full list of titles available. Thanks for reading!